Praise for the Series

"Well written, intense, and twisted. This is a book you will remember."
—Karen Fisher, NetGalley Reviewer on *Courting Darkness*

"Questions and secrets come out of the shadows, and I still love this series!"
—Matthew Shank, Librarian and NetGalley Reviewer on *Courting Darkness*

"Great Plot. Lovable characters. Heart-pounding action. Just great."
—Lauren Davis, Reviewer on Saints and Sinners Book Blog on *A Drop of Magic*

"*A Drop of Magic* is a damned fun and original read, with sass, action, hot men, and a whole lot of magic."
—Diana Pharaoh Francis, author of the Diamond City Magic, Magicfall, and Horngate Witches series

Faerie Forged

The Magicsmith
Book 3

by

L.R. Braden

Bell Bridge Books

This is a work of fiction. Names, characters, places and incidents are either the products of the author's imagination or are used fictitiously. Any resemblance to actual persons (living or dead), events or locations is entirely coincidental.

Bell Bridge Books
PO BOX 300921
Memphis, TN 38130
Print ISBN: 978-1-61194-982-7

Bell Bridge Books is an Imprint of BelleBooks, Inc.

Copyright © 2020 by L.R. Braden

Published in the United States of America.

All rights reserved. No part of this book may be reproduced in any form or by any electronic or mechanical means, including information storage and retrieval systems, without permission in writing from the publisher, except by a reviewer, who may quote brief passages in a review.

We at BelleBooks enjoy hearing from readers.
Visit our websites
BelleBooks.com
BellBridgeBooks.com
ImaJinnBooks.com

10 9 8 7 6 5 4 3 2 1

Cover design: Debra Dixon
Interior design: Hank Smith
Photo/Art credits:
Arches (manipulated) © Artshock - Dreamstime.com
Woman (manipulated) © Inara Prusakova - Dreamstime.com

:Lfff:01:

For Connie

Here's to a sharp mind and a generous heart.

Chapter 1

BRONZE DUST AND red buffing compound coated my work surface, my jeans, and my hands. Pulling down my respirator mask so it hung over my collarbone like a necklace, I set the Dremel aside and, fingers clasped, pressed my palms toward the ceiling until my back popped. My stomach growled, and I glanced longingly at the dregs of coffee staining my empty mug. Breakfast had been a long time ago. The air in the studio smelled of warm metal and sulfur patina, and my nose twitched with the warning of an oncoming sneeze.

Sniffing, and brushing the back of my wrist over my upper lip, I snatched up a polishing cloth to wipe out the residual red rouge caked in the corners of the bronze queen chess piece. I was careful to keep my mind clear as I worked, blocking off my emotions so they didn't accidentally spill over into Uncle Sol's Christmas present due to my magical ability.

That would be a fine gift. *Here's a fun game full of anxiety and stress that makes you sick to your stomach when you touch the pieces.*

When the queen shone with a mirror finish, I set her beside her king, ready to lead her army across the cherrywood chess board.

On one side of the battlefield, fractal-pattern pawns guarded a court of frozen snowflakes—all sharp angles and hard lines—their shapes as bright and clear as their finish. Across the no man's land of checkered space, a second army sat, ready for war. These pieces were dark, stained to an oil-slick finish. In contrast to their counterparts, the patinaed court swooped and curled with organic curves.

The set was done. One more item checked off my to-do list, and not a moment too soon. I'd be on my way to the fae Winter Festival in less than a day. My tutors, Kai and Hortense, had been cramming almost every waking moment with fae etiquette lessons to help me survive my debut at the Court of Enchantment. Most of the lessons boiled down to "Don't be yourself."

Standing, I brushed what metal dust I could off my jeans, then scrubbed my hands raw at the sink in the corner.

I had a box all prepared for Sol's gift, kept safe from the studio's mess in a cabinet off to one side of my work space. The chess pieces each slipped into individual pockets in two felt-lined drawers under the board. Once the armies were laid to rest, I set the board on a bed of bubble wrap, covered it, and tucked it in. I secured the box with packing tape and scribbled the address for Uncle Sol's New York apartment—the closest thing he had to a home—across the top. Then I cleaned my Dremel, placed it back on its peg on the wall, and swept up the evidence of my work.

Straightening, I turned a slow circle, making sure everything was tidy. Thanks to the time-dilation between realms, this would be the last time I set foot in my studio for at least a week. Assuming I came back at all.

A colorful sheet hung like a ghost in one corner of the room, suspended on the copper sculpture it was keeping safe from my creation process. All the tools were in their places, the kilns were off, the forge was cold.

Grabbing Sol's present, I turned out the lights and locked the studio door. The mid-morning sky was clear but cold, tightening the skin across my cheeks. Tendrils of mist still huddled in shadows, close to the ground where the sun couldn't find them. I breathed deep, and crossed the clearing to my house.

I set Sol's package on the breakfast bar that separated the kitchen from the living room, and glanced at the clock on the wall.

Crap. I only had thirty minutes until my shift at the bookstore.

I FLEW THROUGH the back door to Magpie Books, purse dangling from one hand, keys clenched in the other. I'd stripped off my dirty clothes, wiped the worst smudges off my face with a damp rag, and pulled on a clean outfit in two minutes flat. I'd also careened down the Boulder Canyon like a maniac, so I was only five minutes late for my shift.

Shoving my belongings into a locker in the back room, I pushed through the employee-only door to the store proper and jogged up an aisle of bookcases toward the front.

Dozens of people were perusing the shelves, arms piled high with popular titles, and the front door jingled constantly with the flow of holiday traffic. The scent of pine and cinnamon mixed with the smell of books and coffee. A row of over-stuffed stockings hung on one wall, each embroidered with an employee's name. Mine was third from the end.

Kayla stood by the register. Her platinum blond hair was pinned back from her face with two tiny silver clips. She wore her usual high-collared, ankle-length dress to hide the gossamer pixie wings she'd once shown me. I licked my lips, recalling the heady sensation caused by the magical dust that came off those wings.

"Hey, Kayla. Sorry I'm—" My apology stalled as my gaze shifted past Kayla to the café area and a knot lodged in my throat.

Standing at the counter was an agent of the Paranatural Task Force—PTF for short. He wore blue jeans, brown boots, and a button-up shirt with a beige plaid pattern, nothing to mark him as a PTF agent, but I'd recognize Benjamin O'Connell anywhere. Hard to forget a man who'd sworn to ruin your life. Especially when he had the means and authority to actually do it.

Clenching my fists, I continued past the register, ignoring Kayla's furrowed brow. I stepped up to O'Connell. "What are you doing here?"

O'Connell raised one eyebrow. "Getting a coffee."

I crossed my arms. "Why here?"

He shrugged. "Why not?"

Emma, the barista, pulled a lever on the copper machine behind the counter and a hiss of steam poured out. She jingled as she worked, her many chains and piercings clicking with each motion, but her usual perkiness was absent. Her shoulders sagged, and when she turned I saw dark circles below her eyes.

Last month, Emma took, and passed, the test to become a practitioner—a rare human who could use magic. She'd also convinced a local healer named Luke to take her on as his apprentice, which would explain her glazed expression. I knew from experience that using magic was exhausting.

I inched closer to O'Connell and pitched my voice lower. "What do you want?"

"I was worried you might get lonely after I saw the list of potentials brought in this morning."

My heart stuttered, and my mouth went dry. Potentials were people reported for exhibiting magical behavior. They were rounded up, dragged to the nearest PTF facility, and tested for paranatural abilities. I'd seen firsthand how brutal PTF tests could be, and the consequences of failing... I was just lucky my ability to handle iron protected me from suspicion, since that was the main way they tested for fae heritage. Not all my friends were so lucky. If he'd gotten his hands on any of them.... I swallowed the sour taste in my mouth.

"Gonna take all day to get them processed." He sighed and rubbed the back of his neck—the picture of an overworked employee just trying to get through the day. "Then there's the testing. Could be days. Weeks maybe, backed up as we are." He leaned toward me like a friend sharing a secret. His nearness made my skin itch. "We've been up to our eyeballs in suspicion reports since the election results came in."

Colorado's governor-to-be, Gary Anderson, had run a Purity campaign, aligning himself with the extremist group that endorsed wholesale slaughter of anyone with a drop of magic in their blood. I'd already noticed several disturbing changes around town, like iron bead curtains hanging in doorways, anti-fae stickers in storefronts, and a recent call for magical-segregation in schools.

News that the number of reports had risen since the election wasn't surprising, but it *was* disturbing. The same thing happened right before the Faerie Wars broke out, when tension between the humans and fae had been at its highest. I shuddered to think how much worse the situation was going to get come January, when Anderson was officially sworn in.

"I guess between the halfer," O'Connell cut his eyes to Kayla, "and the witch," he nodded toward Emma, "you've got all the company you need." He smiled. "For now."

Emma set a to-go cup on the counter and O'Connell stepped away from me to grab it. He lifted the steaming container to his lips, hissing when the hot liquid hit his tongue. Then he raised his drink in salute and walked out the door.

"Hey, Alex." Emma smiled. The steel ring in her lip glinted. "Want your usual?"

I set my hands on the counter, leaving sweaty smudges on the glass. "Was that guy bothering you?"

She frowned. "No. Why?"

I shook my head and walked back the way I'd come. Passing Kayla, I said, "I need to make a phone call," and hustled back through the "employees only" door before either of my coworkers could do more than blink.

Yanking open my locker, I grabbed my cell phone and stood with my finger over the contacts icon. Did O'Connell really have one or more of my friends? Or was he trying to trick me into giving someone away? Could he have bugged my phone?

I frowned. The CSI shows on TV always talked about cloning cell phones, but people had to steal the phones first. And even the PTF needed a warrant for a legal phone tap . . .

I scrolled through entries, wondering who was most exposed.

My first thought when O'Connell hinted a friend had been taken was of Kai. But O'Connell wouldn't have called him a potential. Kai was a fully registered fae, living at my house on a visa granted by the PTF. Plus, O'Connell had already dragged Kai in for *extensive* testing.

I shivered, recalling the way Kai had screamed during those tests.

No. Kai was safe. As safe as a fae could be, considering the growing influence of Purity.

But James—a vampire hiding in plain sight—was definitely not safe. O'Connell knew we were friends, and potentially more. Our complicated relationship status had come under close scrutiny when James was investigated for murder. I'd since slammed the brakes on dating, but the jolt of dopamine and the way my body tightened whenever he was around made it painfully clear that my heart and my head weren't on the same page.

I pressed the call button. As soon as the line connected I asked, "Where are you?"

"The nest." The sound of James's voice loosened some of the ropes of tension squeezing my chest.

I rubbed my forehead, fighting back a headache. James had spent the better part of a week preparing for the arrival of a new master vampire—some woman named Victoria—who'd claimed ownership of the Denver area nearly as soon as we'd put the old master down. How she'd known about the vacancy so fast was anybody's guess, but she'd come to town two nights ago.

"You're all right?" I asked. "No . . . problems?"

"I'm fine." Worry crept into his voice, stretching his syllables. "Has something happened?"

"It's nothing. I'll see you at dinner tonight." I disconnected before he could press me for more information. If he wasn't O'Connell's prisoner I didn't have time to waste chatting with him, and the last thing he needed while dealing with a new, powerful vampire was to be distracted.

I scanned through my remaining contacts. Some names were missing, like Chase and Jynx, the shifter siblings crashing at my house, and Hortense, the tutor sent by my grandfather to fill the gaps in Kai's lessons. They were all full fae, and I had no way to contact them except face-to-face, but Chase had been a snoring ball of gray fur at the end of my bed when I left for work, and Jynx had been watching television. I bit my lip. I couldn't imagine Hortense being careless enough to get caught by the likes of O'Connell.

That left the wolves. I knew several members of the local werewolf pack, thanks to my recent exploits, but I didn't have all their numbers. One number I *did* have was Marc's. As the leader of the pack, he was sure to know if any of his members had been picked up by the PTF.

The line rang . . . and rang. No answer.

I took a deep breath. No reason to panic yet. Maybe he was just in the shower. Scrolling further down the list, I clicked the entry for Oz, a pack member I'd actually known before I discovered, rather violently, that werewolves were real.

The line rang. I bit my lower lip, my heart rate starting to climb. No answer there either.

I didn't have a direct line to Sarah Nazari, a werewolf detective with the Boulder police department. And Sophie—my human friend turned werewolf the night we both learned they were more than just stories—had her phone privileges revoked after sneaking out to go clubbing and nearly shifting in a building packed tight with tasty mortals.

I thumped my cell phone against my forehead. A couple missed calls was hardly conclusive, but my gut told me O'Connell had gotten his hands on some or all of the werewolves. Waves of dread rolled through me. I had to know for sure.

Lifting the phone one more time, I called Maggie. A month ago, talking to Maggie would have been the most natural thing in the world. Now, the prospect made my insides writhe. Maggie was one of my few remaining human friends, and the only one I'd managed to keep completely out of the craziness my life had become. But my secrets had driven a wedge between us, and I wasn't sure how to bridge that gap.

Before I'd walked into the near-certain death of Merak's nest, I'd written a letter to Maggie explaining everything and apologizing for keeping her in the dark, just in case. I hadn't died. I also hadn't given her the letter yet. I'd stuffed it in my nightstand drawer, too afraid to face the fallout of laying my secrets bare, especially as the gulf between us grew larger.

"Alex?" Maggie's voice was sharp. "What's wrong?"

"Nothing, I just—"

"Are you at the store?"

I looked at the employee door, then at the exit. "Yeah, but I need to leave."

"Bloody hell, Alex. Your shift just started, and this is the last shift you've got before the *two weeks* you requested off during *the busiest shopping season of the year*." Her voice rose as she spoke, her London accent becoming more pronounced.

"I know, but something's come up."

A loud sigh came through the phone. "Something always comes up with you these days, and you've told me bugger all about it."

"I know. I—"

"How long?"

"What?"

"How long do I need to cover? The morning? The whole day? Forever?"

I shuffled my feet and looked up at the speckled ceiling tiles. "Better not count on me today."

"I can't ever count on you anymore."

Dead air filled the line as I struggled to find something to say, something to make things right between us, but she was right.

"I can't take this anymore, Alex. Not with . . ." A sharp exhale and a shaky breath. "You're sacked."

The words dropped like a bomb in my head, splintering my thoughts into a million shards of jagged shrapnel. I opened my mouth to argue, to come clean about my heritage, to explain why I'd missed all those shifts, but all that came out was a ringing silence.

"I'm sorry, Alex."

The line went dead.

Pressure built behind my eyes.

I'd thought about quitting the bookstore dozens of times—usually when I was fighting to get out of my nice warm bed before the sun came up—but I'd never *really* considered it. Magpie Books had been Maggie's dream, but we'd built it together. I'd been there from the start, and I'd always assumed I'd be there till the end. Magpie was supposed to be a place I would always belong.

Dropping the phone in my purse, I blinked until my tears were no longer in danger of falling. Somehow, I had to repair my friendship with Maggie. I couldn't afford to burn any more bridges. But first, I needed to find out what, if anything, had happened to the werewolves.

Chapter 2

ROLLING OUT OF the lot, I headed back up the canyon toward Nederland, retracing my morning drive. Boulder Creek was sculpted in ice, patches of running water showing through only where it tumbled against rocks. The path alongside the river was shoveled clear and spread with thick, pink salt crystals, until I reached the edge of town. Then packed snow claimed the sidewalk, marred by tire and boot tread.

Ice sparkled on Barker Reservoir as I came up over a hill and headed down into the valley that held Nederland, but I turned off the main road before reaching the town proper. I passed by the dirt driveway that connected my little piece of nowhere to the rest of the world, and several others just like it. Then I turned up the road to Marc's house. He lived about a mile back from the main road on a mountain estate similar to my own. A large yellow sign proclaiming bodily harm to trespassers greeted me at the edge of his property. The house was two stories above ground, and two below, including a dungeon I hoped never to see again.

My Jeep shuddered to a stop behind a silver pickup truck, a red Jetta, and a black SUV.

I whistled. "*Somebody's* home."

I stepped out of the cab, but hesitated with my hand still on the Jeep's door. That many vehicles meant I was likely to find quite a gathering inside.

I'd met a number of werewolves over the past two months, but usually one at a time. The idea of being surrounded by them was. . . . I rubbed my hand over the jacket sleeve covering my left arm, imagining the scars beneath. There hadn't been much I could do against even one werewolf, and the group inside might not be happy to see me since my last escapade resulted in several of them getting hurt.

My breath formed clouds that hung like fog around my face while I hesitated. Finally, I stepped away from my Jeep and crunched past the line of vehicles leading to Marc's front porch.

I raised my hand to ring the bell, but before my finger connected, the door swung open.

It wasn't Marc who answered.

Standing just inside the door was a fine-boned, middle-aged Asian woman with papery brown skin. She stood straight and tall, except for a slight bow in her shoulders, but still only came up to my chin. A few strands of jet black streaked the loose, steel gray braid that trailed over her shoulder.

The woman pursed her lips. "Alex Blackwood."

I dropped my hand back to my side and raised an eyebrow. "Do I know you?"

Then I remembered. I'd seen her before, in the aftermath of the vampire nest infiltration. She'd made a report to Marc about the wolves who'd been injured during the battle.

"You may call me Yumiko," the woman said. "Why are you here?"

I frowned. "I was looking for Marc."

"He's not here."

My fear ratcheted up a notch. "Did the PTF take him?"

Yumiko's expression stiffened. "What do you know of it?"

"I had a visit from a PTF agent this morning who implied someone I knew had been brought in for testing. When I couldn't get Marc on the phone..." I raised my hands, shrugging. "I came to investigate."

She pursed her lips, then stepped back from the door. "Come inside."

Stomping my boots on the welcome mat, I stepped into the home of the local werewolf alpha. The smell of frying sausage hit me on a surge of warm air when I crossed the threshold. Pushing the door closed behind me, I followed Yumiko's bobbing braid farther into the house.

A lanky black man lounging on a faded blue recliner peeked over the top of last month's *Make* magazine in the living room. I didn't recognize him, but if he was comfortable in Marc's home, chances were he was a werewolf. He watched me pass, then tossed the magazine onto an already cluttered coffee table.

"In here." Yumiko gestured through an alcove to one side, and I followed her through to the kitchen.

A rustic wooden table and chairs filled one side of the room. The middle of the room was taken up by a large marble-topped island surrounded by bar stools. A slender man with reddish-brown hair perched on one of the stools. He wore a checkered shirt and a tweed jacket. A pair of rectangular glasses sat on his nose. Behind those lenses, his eyes were red and puffy.

He lifted a hand in greeting. "Remember me?"

His face was easy enough to place—he'd been my ride home after the vampire infiltration—but I'd been so exhausted after coming back from the dead that the trip home was a blur. I wracked my brain for a name, but came up empty.

He smiled. "Gilbert, but you can call me Gil."

Beyond the island, a large Hispanic man with dark hair and darker eyes was standing by the stove in a plaid, grease-spattered apron.

"What's *she* doing here?" The cook jabbed a pair of metal tongs in my direction.

"Don't mind Jedd." Yumiko motioned me to one of the island stools. "He's just cranky because he hasn't had breakfast yet."

"I'm—" The man, Jedd, pressed his lips together and turned his back on the room. Tongs scraped, and a storm of violent sizzling ensued, punctuated by muttered curses.

"You sure Marc would be okay with this, Auntie Yu?" The man from the living room had followed us. He now leaned against the arch, arms crossed over a baggy gray sweater. "Her being able to ID so many of us?"

"Marc vouches for her," Gilbert said. "And so does Sarah."

Jedd snorted and began lifting seared sausages out of his pan and piling them on a nearby plate. "Sarah wanted to kill her."

Gil shrugged. "She got over it."

"Good to know," I muttered.

"Besides," Yumiko said, pinning me with an unyielding look. "It's not like we don't know her secret, too."

A shudder rippled through me. Somehow, it hadn't occurred to me that the whole werewolf pack, including a bunch of people I'd never met, would know I was a halfer—part human, part fae. Was that how Marc had convinced them not to kill me when I hadn't turned into one of them? Since I'd never registered with the PTF as I was supposed to, my secret was like a looming death sentence. If I was outed, the best I could hope for would be exile to the fae reservation. More likely, I'd be locked up in a testing facility and spend the rest of my life as a PTF guinea pig while scientists tried to discover why I was immune to iron. And if they ever did. . . . My relationship to the fae Lord of Enchantment was a secret even the wolves didn't know.

"So how did the PTF get their hands on Marc? I'd have thought he'd run rather than risk exposing you all."

"Except it wasn't just Marc," Yumiko said. "Sarah and Oz have been taken as well."

I gripped the island, finding comfort in the solid stone. "How could they have found so many of you?"

Yumiko crossed her arms. "The PTF has only ever needed suspicion to pull people in for testing, and with Governor-elect Anderson's victory, they've become more aggressive." She looked away, and her eyes became unfocused. "I hate to think what his policies will mean for the paranatural community once he takes office."

I shook my head, trying to recall the tests administered in schools when the fae first came out. Scraps of iron shavings were mixed with blood samples and tested for reaction. Chances were they'd made some changes since I was in middle school, but when I'd "come out" to my adoptive guardian, Uncle Sol, he'd assured me the standard PTF test wouldn't identify me as fae. And he would know, being a high-ranking official in the organization. If I could pass thanks to my immunity to iron, maybe the werewolves could, too.

"PTF tests are designed for fae. If it's just the basic test, a werewolf should be able to pass."

"Maybe, maybe not." Yumiko sighed. "Either way, it's a moot point."

"What do you mean?"

Ceramic clinked against marble as Jedd set his plate on the island and pulled up a stool. "The moon. Marc might be okay, but Oz . . ." He shook his head. "Considering the stress he's under, I doubt he'll make it to the full moon."

"Sarah won't do much better," Gil added. He paled visibly as he spoke, and his hands fisted on his thighs.

I tapped my fingers against the stone countertop as an idea started to form in my swirling thoughts. "Maybe I can help."

Jedd snorted.

"I owe you for that debacle with the vampires," I said. "Speaking of which, where's Sophie?"

Gil looked away. Yumiko just scowled.

The man still standing in the arch said, "She's around."

I nodded and let it go. She wasn't a prisoner of the PTF—a good thing considering the complete lack of control she'd shown the last time we were together. If O'Connell had gotten hold of her, there'd be confirmation of werewolves by the end of the day.

Sophie's safety was a relief, but I was happy not to have to see her in the flesh. There'd been a time when Sophie and I were friends. Before I'd invited her on the hike that turned her into a werewolf. Before her outburst in Abandon—a vampire-owned dance club—kicked off a cycle of imprisonment and torture that led to the wolves bailing my ass out of the fire when shit went sideways. Before a lot of things.

"And what exactly can you do?" Jedd spoke around a mouthful of sausage. "You can't even—"

"Jedd." Yumiko cut him off without raising her voice, then turned to me. "If you can help . . ."

Uncle Sol was a big enough muckety-muck in the PTF organization that he could probably pull some strings to get a few potentials released. He was also important enough that it would be pretty damn strange for him to do so, and the last thing I needed was to raise red flags for O'Connell to follow.

"I can't promise anything, but I know someone who might be able to get them out before the full moon."

Gil set a hand on my forearm. "Please try. Sarah. . . . She's my mate. If they find out about her—"

"We're *all* done." Jedd stabbed his fork into a sausage. Clear liquid seeped from the wounds. "Once they're sure about even one of us, they'll hunt down the rest. They'll cage us, study us, and kill us."

The smell of cooked meat suddenly made my stomach clench, and I looked away as Jedd bit into his skewered sausage.

I nodded. "I'll make the call."

I pulled my arm out from under Gil's hand, trying to ignore the squishy gnashing sounds of Jedd enjoying his breakfast, and slid off my stool. "I'll let you know what he says."

The man who hadn't introduced himself watched me pass. His arms were still crossed, but the edge of his lip lifted when I met his eyes.

"Good luck," he said. "For all our sakes."

I was halfway across the living room when a familiar voice stopped me in my tracks.

"You think it's a coincidence the only wolves taken were the ones *you* interacted with?"

Pulse thundering in my ears, I turned. Sophie was peeking out from the laundry room that led to the back door. It also led to the basement and, below that, the dungeon. The long cascade of her hair had been cut short. Blond clumps stuck up every which way on her head. Her cheeks and eyes were sunken, her lips thin.

My fingers curled into fists. She might not have meant to leave me to the tender mercies of a sadistic vampire any more than I'd intentionally led her into the jaws of a rampaging werewolf, but that rationale didn't quell the wave of anger that boiled through me when I saw her. From the look in her eyes, she hadn't forgiven me yet, either.

"They didn't take you."

"I've been on lockdown since—"

We both looked away.

"You shouldn't be up here." The man who'd been leaning against the arch stepped between us, eyes locked on Sophie. His voice rumbled like rocks in an avalanche.

"Back off, Dillon. I just wanted to say hello."

Dillon kept glaring until Sophie dropped her gaze to the floor. Then he straightened and looked at me. "Don't you have a call to make?"

With one last look at Sophie, I pushed through the front door and trotted to the Jeep.

I cranked the heat up to chase back the cold that had seeped into the cab, and thought of Marc, Sarah, and Oz in the PTF's basement, a.k.a. torture chamber. Werewolves weren't fae; they were humans who'd been infected, changed. They didn't have the protection of the Faerie Peace Accords, flimsy though those were. If the PTF found out what the werewolves really were, they'd be hunted, trapped, and experimented on.

You think it's a coincidence the only wolves taken were the ones you interacted with? Sophie's words pounded in my mind like a hammer. O'Connell was after *me*, but he'd take down anyone associated with me if it gave him a chance to hurt me. I'd seen as much when he targeted Kai for the murder of a human woman, despite having no evidence against him. I couldn't let the werewolves suffer O'Connell's misplaced wrath.

I pulled out my cell phone.

Uncle Sol spent a good deal of time out of the country. Even if he was willing to help, he might not be in a position to do so. At least, not in time. Pushing the thought away, I pulled up his entry in my contact list and pressed the call button.

His voicemail picked up right away.

Stammering through a greeting, I left a message for him to contact me as soon as possible. I couldn't risk leaving a detailed message, even if I could find a way to explain the situation quickly. Hopefully, by the time he called back, I'd have thought of a way to convince him to break three people out of PTF lockup without telling him they were werewolves.

KAI'S LITTLE BEIGE Toyota was parked in front of my house when I pulled up. The engine was still clicking as its warmth was sapped by the mountain air. He must have just gotten back from his shift at the convenience store. Crunching across my ice-crusted yard, I stomped a few times on the porch and pushed open the front door.

". . . wouldn't make a difference." Hortense, the curmudgeonly old river hag sent to tutor me on fae protocol, was standing, arms crossed, in front of the drooping, four-foot Christmas tree in my living room. Her perpetual frown was in place, crinkling the pale skin of her human glamour. Another knot loosened in my chest at seeing the grumpy old fae. I'd been *pretty* sure O'Connell hadn't gotten his hands on her, but it was nice to have confirmation.

Despite her sour expression and matching attitude regarding my education, Hortense had started to grow on me. At first I'd done my best to shut her out, but after she helped me make a stealth charm for my vampire infiltration, which she wasn't supposed to know anything about, I realized she wasn't so bad. She hadn't mentioned my foolhardy mission either, before or after, for which I was grateful, and she'd done her best to teach me enough fae etiquette that I hopefully wouldn't get myself killed as soon as I set foot in a fae realm.

Turning to face me, she brushed a stray wisp of steel gray hair away from her face, tucking it back into a tightly braided bun. She arched one thin eyebrow and pursed her lips. "Malakai informed me you would not be back for several hours."

I closed the door. "I shouldn't have been."

"What happened?" Kai was still wearing his work outfit, a red smock with a tacky iron-on image of the convenience store's logo displayed on the breast. His eyes swirled with the glamourless galaxies I'd come to expect when we were at home.

"I had an unexpected visitor at work," I said. "O'Connell."

Kai scowled. "What did he want?"

"The usual. To ruin my life. He dropped a hint about someone I know being brought in for testing."

Kai visibly shuddered.

I met and held his gaze. "Are you guys all right?"

Hortense didn't know about the two shifters who'd been staying in my back room. At least, I didn't think she did. We'd done our best to keep them a secret, sending them out of the house when Hortense was scheduled to visit, having them hide when she dropped by unannounced. Since my grandfather was the fae Lord of Enchantment, I doubted he'd approve of my association with Chase, who was a spy for the Shifter Lord. Though in Chase's defense, he'd saved my life, which was more than Gramps had ever done.

"We're fine," Kai said with a glance down the back hall to include our friends.

Hortense crossed her arms. "I trust this O'Connell situation won't impede your departure plans."

Twenty hours. That's all the time I had left before my trip to faerie land. Frowning, I mentally corrected myself. The Realm of Enchantment. Best get used to keeping even my thoughts formal, lest something slip out that shouldn't.

I'd had a little over a month to learn a lifetime of fae facts, like the proper angle of a bow, the hierarchy of titles, the names of the races, the schools of magic, and a million other things that might come up at court, including how to handle a sword in case my education failed and I ended up in a duel over hurt feelings. Of course, that time had also been filled with saving my vampire would-be-boyfriend from a crazed psychopath who kidnapped and tortured me, being interrogated for murder, avoiding PTF scrutiny, and dragging the local werewolves into a paranatural war beneath the streets of Denver.

What I wanted to say was yes, of course O'Connell's machinations would impede my departure to Enchantment. Hell, I hadn't wanted to go in the first place. But what came out was, "I'll leave tomorrow, as planned."

Hortense tipped her chin up, inspecting me down the length of her beak-like nose. "Good. I didn't spend all this time in the mortal realm to have you fail before you even arrive."

I opened my mouth, but Kai cut in, stepping between us. "She'll be there."

Hortense pursed her lips. "Then I shall see you upon your arrival."

Hortense was traveling ahead of us to make preparations and deliver a final report to my grandfather informing him of my progress . . . and shortcomings.

I pulled the door open and stepped out of her way. "See you on the other side."

Hortense crossed my parking area and stepped between a pair of ice-crusted pine trees, then she was gone. I shook my head and closed the door. Despite all my recent fae education, I still hadn't figured out how she did that.

Kai crossed his arms. "O'Connell might have been lying just to get under your skin, make you worry."

I shook my head. "Marc, Oz, and Sarah were taken." The words came out even, but my insides twisted as I spoke.

The skin around Kai's eyes pinched, and the lines around his mouth grew deeper. No doubt he was remembering his own time with O'Connell and the PTF.

"They might be able to pass." He met my gaze. "If they pass the first test, there should be no reason for the more in-depth examination that would reveal them as inhuman."

I was shaking my head before he finished speaking. "O'Connell's going to keep them as long as he can. Even if he doesn't get around to the harsher tests, the wolves won't be able to control their change under that kind of stress."

Kai pursed his lips. "And the full moon is in less than a week."

"I called Uncle Sol to see if he can help, but no luck yet."

He fixed his galactic stare on me. "I'm sorry about the wolves, I really am, but this doesn't change our timetable. We leave for Enchantment tomorrow. No detours for prison breaks."

I hugged myself, trying to ease the pain in my chest. "I know."

There was a muffled thump and crash from the back of the house.

Kai stiffened, then rolled his eyes. "At least she waited till Hortense was gone."

Nodding, I headed for the back bedroom I used for storage, and lately stowaways, to see what the racket was about.

Chapter 3

JYNX WAS MOSTLY hidden behind shelves of junk when I walked in, tucked in the corner as far out of sight as she could get. If I'd been Hortense, it wouldn't have been enough. At least some good came with the arrival of my fae court debut—juggling three unregistered fae, one of which couldn't know about the other two, had been a serious hassle.

Blowing out a sigh of relief, the fourteen-year-old girl straightened and stepped out from her hiding spot. Above her sharply tapered ears, her snowy white, pixie cut hair was tousled, like she'd just rolled out of bed. Or in this case, the nest of blankets tucked in the corner.

I suppressed a smile, thinking of the present I'd ordered Jynx for Christmas. It wouldn't arrive before our gift exchange tonight, but I'd taken care of that.

"Sorry," she mumbled.

"No harm done. Hortense is gone, and she shouldn't be coming back."

The girl hopped up and down like a bobber with a fish on the line. The hem of a teal sundress I recognized as a resident of my closet flapped around her knees. Jynx was quite a bit shorter than I was, but that didn't stop her from raiding my closet like an entitled little sister. I wasn't big on sharing, but I was willing to be flexible if it meant she'd wear clothes when she was in human form ... most of the time at least.

"So I don't have to hide anymore?"

Frowning, I ran a hand through my frizzy, auburn hair. "Not from Hortense."

Her smile melted a little. "But?"

"But you're an unregistered fae. And I'm under scrutiny from the PTF. As long as you're here, you need to stay a secret."

The rest of her smile disappeared.

I hated to dampen the girl's enthusiasm, but I couldn't take any chances. O'Connell would latch onto any excuse to arrest me, and harboring an unregistered fae was more than an excuse, it was a felony.

Then it would only be a matter of time before he learned I was hiding a fae identity myself.

Shaking my head to clear an image of being strapped to a dissection table, I gestured to a broken cardboard box with its contents strewn across the floor—presumably the source of the crash I'd heard. "What's this about?"

She poked the fallen box with the big toe of one bare foot. "I was trying to make a little extra space."

I cocked my head to one side, and she bit her lip.

"I was thinking . . . hoping . . . since you'll be gone . . ."

I crossed my arms. "Just spit it out, Jynx."

"Could my girlfriend come over while you and Kai are away?" she blurted.

My mind groped for examples of how to handle this request, but all I could come up with were ridiculous sit-com references. My own teenage dating life had consisted of a number of first dates followed by moving across the country. I hadn't made it to the home-visit stage until college. Was it normal for a fourteen-year-old to have a significant other over? Did it matter that the fourteen-year-old in question was actually a forty-seven-year old fae who only *looked* like a human teenager?

"What does Chase have to say about it?"

"*Pfft*. My brother doesn't care what I do, so long as I don't get in his way."

"Where is he, anyway?" I glanced around the room as though I might find the gray tabby that was his animal form on one of the shelves.

"Said he had some errands to run. He'll be back in time for our party tonight."

Chase, Jynx, and James had been invited to Kai's early Christmas—his attempt to make it up to me that I'd be missing the real thing because of our trip to Enchantment. Kai and Jynx were especially pumped, since neither had experienced the mortal holiday before.

"I'm not sure I'm comfortable having a stranger in the house while I'm gone," I said.

"She's not a stranger. You met her at Crossroads."

My brow crinkled as I thought back to the handful of times I'd been in the local fae bar. The first time I hadn't met any girls. The second time there'd been—"You're dating Morgan?"

It was Jynx's turn to look confused. "Who's Morgan?"

"She's the only one I—"

She waved her hands. "Doesn't matter. I'm dating Ava, Targe's niece."

Again I cast back, scouring my memory. Then it came to me. "The redhead that can walk through walls."

Jynx nodded. "She said she took you back to your car after you drank too much at the bar."

Heat flooded my cheeks. Yeah, I probably didn't have much right to worry about other people behaving responsibly. Though, in my defense, I'd been distraught that night.

"I guess, if it's okay with Chase, she can visit while I'm away."

Jynx bounded over the fallen box's contents and threw her arms around my neck.

"But first," I said, prying the girl loose, "help me clean up this mess."

"Of course." She dropped to her knees and began stuffing items back into the crumpled box.

Looking around at the nest of blankets and pillows surrounded by shelves of art supplies and old memories, I sighed. I'd need to move some of this stuff to make space for Jynx's gift.

"Shouldn't this be under the tree?" Jynx held up a small package wrapped in green and silver paper.

My heart stuttered and seemed to stall, then it came back with a rush of adrenaline that pounded through my ears and made my vision blur.

I snatched the box out of Jynx's fingers. "This isn't—" I couldn't finish the sentence. I didn't know how it ended.

"Get this place cleaned up." I tried to smile, but my face felt carved of marble. "Wouldn't want your girlfriend thinking you're a slob."

Mentally kicking myself, I retreated from the room and Jynx's confused expression, and locked myself in my bedroom. There I collapsed on the edge of the bed and slowly opened my hands, cradling the little package as if I were holding a moth with broken wings.

I hadn't laid eyes on that present since I was seventeen years old. I'd found it, along with a few gifts that hadn't yet been wrapped, on the top shelf of my mother's closet when I was cleaning out her room. I hadn't had the heart to open it—the one present she'd wrapped before dying. I hadn't had the heart to toss it either, so I stuck it in a box and forgot about it for a decade.

I traced one finger over the shiny paper, turning the box over. One corner had torn, probably in the fall, and an edge of white cardboard peeked through.

Licking my lips, I wiggled my finger into that tear, forcing it wider.

The paper parted easily, snagging only when I came to a piece of yellowed cellophane tape. Beneath the wrapping paper, a folded note was taped to the lid of the little box.

I tugged the note free and set the box aside. I expected the blue lines on the paper to be faded with age, like the tape, but they'd been protected from the bleaching effects of the outside world, tucked safely in the wrapping paper cocoon. Along those lines flowed the tight, slanted script of my mother's handwriting.

The world fuzzed out, and two wet drops splashed against the paper, staining it gray.

Holding the message out of harm's way, I wiped my cheeks with the back of my sleeve, took a deep breath, and reminded myself that I was an adult now. I could handle this.

Gripping the note in both hands, I looked down and read the single, short sentence huddled in the center of the paper: *I think you're ready to have this back.*

I stared at those words for a full minute. Then, hands shaking, I set the letter aside and lifted the lid of the little white box.

Inside, on a bed of tissue paper, was a small, silver locket with a capital *A* engraved on the front.

Reaching out, I set the tip of one finger against the shiny metal. My breath froze in my lungs, and the world fell away.

I was eleven years old, standing on a cold beach. A gust of salty wind hit my face and flipped scraps of trash over the sand. At one end of the beach, waves crashed against the slime-coated supports of an old dock, rushing nearly to the high-tide mark, then sucking away like a giant drawing in a breath. Three kids hunted shells in the sand while the old woman with them huddled in a blanket near a pile of rocks streaked white with seagull droppings.

"Your father made a choice."

I turned, and there was my mother. Tall, and beautiful, and alive. Long strands of dark hair fluttered in front of her face. She pulled them back with a sigh.

"Who are we to say if it was right or wrong?"

"He abandoned us." Cold stung my cheeks and nose. The tips of my ears ached.

"He might come back."

"I don't want him back." I fumbled under my scarf until my numb fingers found the thin silver chain around my neck. "I don't have a father."

I pulled. The chain bit into my neck for a moment, resisting. Then it snapped.

I threw the locket as hard as I could, and it streaked through the air like a silver comet, chain-tail streaming behind it. I didn't wait to see it land. I was already tromping back to the hotel, fists shoved deep in my pockets.

My bedroom became solid around me once more, springs creaking as I shifted on the bed. I took a shuddering breath and blinked away the lingering image of the imbued memory, my own, sealed in the locket by magic I hadn't known I possessed back then.

Dad never came back. Mom had been wrong. But then, so had I. Despite my words, I'd wanted him back. And I'd waited. Waited until Uncle Sol told us there was nothing left to wait for, and nothing left to bury.

I slid my nail between the two halves of the locket and tugged. The latch released.

Inside, my father held my six-year-old self in his arms and smiled for the camera. On the facing surface, in tiny script, were engraved the words: *I'll give you the world.*

He'd given me the locket for my eighth birthday—two years before he left to fight the fae. I never expected to see it again.

Tears welled in my eyes.

Mom must have gone back to the beach after walking me to the hotel. Then stashed the necklace, knowing I'd get over my anger someday. And she was right.

Not about everything. I was still angry at my father for leaving, at the fae for killing him, and at myself for being so self-absorbed. But my anger was tempered now by time and perspective. I had plenty of good memories of my father, memories I'd pushed aside and forgotten in my misery. Now that I was an adult, older than my parents were when they had me, I could see them as people, individuals, doing the best they could with the choices they had.

Sniffing, I wiped my eyes and nose with my sleeve. Then I set the locket back in its box, chain coiled over the tissue paper like a silver snake, and pulled open my nightstand drawer. We all made choices . . . and we had to live with the consequences.

I tucked the box away and pulled out the crumpled piece of paper I'd stashed there weeks ago. The folded paper had ragged edges down one side where I'd torn it from my sketchbook, and a small tear right in the middle along the creased edge where I'd started to rip it in half.

Unfolding the paper, I smoothed out the confession I'd written when I thought I was going to die, and kept because I was too much of a coward to come clean face to face.

I shook my head. The letter was too dangerous to keep with O'Connell sniffing around. It would make his Christmas to get evidence I was a halfer, not to mention revealing that not all fae were allergic to iron despite it being an accepted fact among humans. The letter in my hands would land me a one-way trip to a PTF testing chamber if it fell into the wrong hands. I couldn't risk O'Connell showing up with a search warrant while I was away.

Folding the paper once more, I stared at the loops in Maggie's name scrawled across the front. Then I gripped each side with shaking hands and tore the letter down the middle. I stacked the pieces and tore again, and again, and I kept tearing until I held a pile of white confetti, each piece decorated with no more than a single word.

I couldn't risk leaving the confession around, but Maggie still deserved to know the truth. Given Kai's assertion that half the fae at court would be looking for a way to kill me, there was a chance I wouldn't be coming back from tomorrow's trip. The idea that Maggie would never know why I'd let our friendship fall apart twisted like a knife in my heart.

Pulling out my cell phone, I called the bookstore.

"Magpie Books, how can I help you?" The voice belonged to Jake, the bookstore's newly-appointed assistant manager.

"Jake? It's Alex. I thought Maggie would be covering my shift."

"She had a doctor appointment. Practically begged me to come in."

I drummed my fingers against my thigh. Maggie used home remedies for pretty much everything, and aside from a few colds, she rarely got sick. I could count the times she'd seen a doctor on one hand. "Any idea what it was about?"

"No clue."

"All right. I'll try her cell. Thanks, Jake."

"Have a good trip, Alex. See you when you get back."

A lump lodged in my throat as the line went dead. Jake didn't know I'd been fired. He thought I'd be back at work in two weeks, after the fictional road trip I'd told everyone I was going on.

I dialed Maggie's number and chewed my lower lip.

No answer.

Stuffing the phone back in my pocket, I paced the length of the room several times. How long was a doctor appointment likely to take? Depended on why she'd gone . . .

My fingers continued to drum their incessant beat against my jean-clad leg.

Dropping to one knee beside the bed, I pulled my suitcase out of the space beneath, dropped it on the comforter, and flipped it open. I stared at the empty space inside. What exactly did one bring on a trip to another world?

Kai assured me appropriate clothes would be provided once I arrived, but "appropriate" didn't sound very comfortable, so I grabbed an extra pair of jeans and a couple of shirts and dropped them in the case. I also shoved in enough socks and underwear for two weeks, because who knew if they had laundromats in Enchantment. Then I stepped back and considered the items on top of my dresser.

My sword wouldn't fit inside my bag, but the knife beside it would. Most fae wore hidden weapons, even during social events like the Winter Festival, so it would be totally appropriate for me to bring a knife . . . even this knife.

I slipped it out of its sheath to inspect the faintly glowing metal. The blade was my first attempt at imbuing a magic artifact. What would Gramps think if I showed it to him? I squashed the fluttery nervousness that sprang up inside me, disgusted by the sudden need for approval from a man I'd never even met. Being a relative did *not* make him important to me.

I slammed the blade back in its sheath and placed it in the suitcase.

A pile of leather-bound books sat beside my sword. My suitcase was barely half full, but I wouldn't be able to bring all my reference materials.

I picked up the species encyclopedia Kai had lent me to help with fae identification. I'd spent hours memorizing entries, but my knowledge was far from complete.

Whiskers tickled my ankle. A gray tabby rubbed against my leg, scraping his cheek on my jeans.

I smiled, looking down. "Welcome back."

Luminous green orbs with vertical pupils stared up at me. Chase flicked his tail, then the air around him seemed to bend and melt. Between one breath and the next, a six-foot tall man with long silver hair and not a stitch of clothing stood beside me.

He stretched, reaching his fingertips to the ceiling, and I pulled a blanket off the bed and shoved it at his stomach.

"Ever the prude," he said, but he wrapped the blanket around his waist.

"Where were you?"

"My business is my business." He smiled, eyes twinkling. "Did you miss me?"

"Not as much as you're gonna miss me."

"Touché. Who will I tease when you're gone?"

That made me laugh. Chase could be moody and insufferable, but he was also fun—a trait that had been in short supply lately.

"You sure you don't wanna come with us?"

He snorted. "To Enchantment's Winter Festival? Those stiffs don't know the meaning of the word party. Now *shifters* know how to throw a shindig." He waggled his eyebrows at me. "Maybe *you* should come with *me*."

I stiffened. "You're not staying here?"

"My assignment is to watch you." He shrugged. "Not much to watch if you're gone."

"But . . ." I licked my lips, wondering if Jynx had really cleared her plans with her brother. "What about Jynx?"

Chase's lips tightened and turned down. "She's part of why I'm taking this opportunity to go home."

"You're leaving her here alone?"

He shrugged again. "I'm sure she'll find some way to entertain herself. If all else fails, she's got years of YouTube to catch up on."

"What if she gets . . ." I traced my thumb along the edge of the encyclopedia. "Lonely."

One silvery eyebrow rose. "Is this your incredibly awkward way of asking if I know about Ava? If so, the answer is yes, I know Jynx won't be spending her alone time . . . alone."

Heat lit my cheeks. "Fine. Get out of my room."

I threw a pillow at him, which he caught and tossed on the end of my bed as he headed for the door. He let the blanket fall as he walked out.

Sighing, I dropped the encyclopedia on top of my clothes, added a few more useful titles, and zipped the case shut. Then I pulled my phone out again.

Maggie didn't answer.

Was she still at the doctor? Or was she ignoring my call?

I began pacing again. I didn't want to leave for Enchantment with so much unsaid between us.

Kai rapped lightly on the door frame. "Everything all right?"

I jumped, jerking to a stop.

Kai propped one hip against the wall and crossed his stick-thin arms. "I see you've packed." He nodded to the suitcase. "You thinking about the trip?"

Pressing my lips together, I shook my head. It wasn't just the trip to the fae court that had my thoughts and emotions tied in knots, it was that there was so much to sort out before I left. Sol and the werewolves, James's position with the new master vampire, Maggie. . . . "I need to talk to Maggie before I go, but I'm worried what'll happen when I spill the beans."

Kai's eyebrows came together over his nose, mimicking his frown. "Why would you spill beans? How do you even know beans will be offered? Maybe she'll give you a sandwich."

The corners of my mouth pulled up despite my growing list of concerns. I clapped a hand on his shoulder. "Don't ever change."

He gave me another confused frown and shook his head. "Anyway . . . I'm starting the preparations for dinner. Care to join me?"

"Actually . . . why don't you start without me. I've got an errand to run."

Pushing past him, I snatched Sol's present off the counter, stomped into my boots, and pulled on a coat. If Maggie wouldn't answer her phone, I'd camp out on her front porch. One way or another, I'd have my say. I'd tell her the truth, and burn the last bridge to my normal, human life.

Chapter 4

KAI FOLLOWED ME to the living room but veered off toward the kitchen, where he began reading the instructions on a packaged ham. Jynx was sprawled on the couch, eyes glued to the TV. *Animaniacs* blared from the speakers and danced across the screen in cartoon mayhem.

"Don't watch it all day." I tucked Sol's package under my arm and wrapped a thick, maroon scarf around my neck. "It'll rot your brain."

She didn't even blink. "That's just a human tale used to scare children."

Smiling, I pulled open the front door and took a deep breath of cold mountain air.

Confessing to Maggie was the right thing to do. She'd yell at me, sure, but then she'd forgive me . . . probably.

I was halfway across the porch when a flash of movement brought my attention to a break in the trees at the edge of my property. The whine of spinning tires seeking traction reached me a second before the mud-splattered body of a gray SUV crawled into view.

I took a step back, resting one hand on the doorknob behind me.

The vehicle's windows were tinted, hiding its occupant. It rolled to a stop beside Kai's car and the engine cut out.

I licked my lips and tightened my grip on the doorknob. Was this O'Connell, or some new threat?

The driver's side door opened, and one shiny black shoe stepped onto the packed snow. Above that shoe were the pressed trousers of a steel gray suit, a heavy wool jacket, and the weathered face of Uncle Sol.

"You have ESP now?" he asked, closing his door.

Relaxing, I stepped to the edge of the porch. "What are you doing here?"

"There's a fine howdy-do." He pushed the bridge of his wire-rimmed glasses farther up his nose. "I take it you weren't waiting for me, then."

I stepped off the porch and my boots settled in slush. "I called you earlier. When you didn't answer I figured you were out of the country."

"Your message said you needed to speak with me." He spread his arms. "Here I am."

I frowned. "But—"

"I was already in town. I wanted to surprise you."

I smiled. "You succeeded, but what brings you to Colorado?"

"Is it so strange to want to see family during the holidays?"

Guilt weighed like an anchor on my mood. I'd assumed Sol would be busy through the holidays, as he so often was. I hadn't bothered to tell him I was going out of town.

"What's that?" He pointed to the box in my arms.

"Actually, it's your Christmas present. I was on my way to drop it at the post office."

"Let me save you the trouble." He strolled across the snowy clearing and lifted the box out of my arms, then tipped his chin toward the door. "Shall we go inside?"

I hesitated. I wanted to talk to Maggie before I left, and I was running out of time. But I didn't know exactly where she was or how long it would take to find her. The wolves needed help *now*.

Sol frowned as I failed to retrace my steps to the door. "Is this a bad time?"

"No." I glanced toward the western ridge. The winter sun sat heavy on the horizon, casting long shadows across the mountain. Would there ever come a day when conflicting loyalties weren't tearing me apart? I could only hope. I hugged my arms over my abdomen, trying to squash the wobbly feeling in my guts. Maggie would have to wait. "Come on in."

I trudged back across the porch, but paused with my hand on the doorknob.

Sol knew I was part fae and was helping keep my secret. He also knew about Kai, who was legally registered with the PTF. He did not, however, know about Jynx or Chase. Unregistered fae living in the mortal realm were a big no-no, punishable by banishment or execution. Harboring them wasn't much better.

I opened the door a crack, straining to hear anything over the cries of cartoon mayhem emanating from the TV. Kai was standing behind the kitchen counter, a wooden-handled carving knife raised in one hand. Tufts of Jynx's white hair stuck up above the back of the couch.

I caught Kai's gaze when he looked up. Widening my eyes in a human gesture I hoped he could understand, I glanced at Jynx then twitched my head toward the back of the house.

"Jynx," Kai hissed. "Hide."

Blue eyes peeked over the back of the couch, widened. Then a medium sized snow leopard vaulted the back of the couch and darted down the hall. The *Animaniacs* continued their skit on the screen.

I stepped fully inside, making space for Sol.

Sol closed the door behind him and handed his present back to me so he could take off his coat. His gaze settled on Kai, who now had his human glamour in place. He frowned. "Malakai, wasn't it? I hadn't realized you were still living here."

Sol and Kai had met, briefly, when Sol helped me prove self-defense against the PTF agent I killed back when this whole mess started. That was before I knew I'd be taking a trip to the Court of Enchantment, and before Kai announced he was sticking around as my tutor.

Sol gestured between Kai and me, a twinkle in his eye. "Anything going on here I should know about?"

A burst of laughter erupted before I could stop it. "Me and Kai?" I shook my head. "No."

Kai pursed his lips and stared at the ham in front of him. Had my quick dismissal hurt his feelings?

Sol stepped up to a shelf of knickknacks and traced his fingers over a small glass flower. He'd given it to me the first time he introduced himself, back when Mom was alive and Dad was fighting to destroy magic on the other side of the world. The corners of his mouth lifted, creasing folds into his sagging cheeks. "Got anything to drink?"

"I'll grab you a beer. Make yourself at home." I kicked off my boots and headed for the kitchen, switching the cartoons off along the way.

Sol gestured to the little Christmas tree slouched beside the TV as I walked past it. "Haven't seen you with one of those in a while."

I licked my lips. Christmas trees had been a non-starter in my house since Mom died. Something about seeing her bloody body beside the mangled branches of the tree she'd been bringing home had short-circuited my brain where the classic decoration was concerned. Go figure.

"Kai's idea." I shrugged. "He's never had a Christmas. Wanted to do it right."

"Good to see you're moving on." He gestured to the ham in front of Kai and the assembled ingredients for various other classic holiday dishes. "Is this practice for the real thing?"

"Actually," I said, pulling a beer out of the fridge. "We're having an early Christmas this year." I joined Sol in front of the couch and handed over the bottle. "Kai and I are going out of town."

He raised an eyebrow.

I gave him the cover story I'd fed to Maggie when I requested time off from the bookstore. A trip around the American Southwest—Zion; Arches; the Grand Canyon.

"We're having some friends over tonight as a sort of . . . kickoff." I glanced down the hall, then quickly away. Sol's presence would complicate matters, not to mention ruining any chance I had of catching Maggie before I left. But I was about to ask him for a massive favor. A twenty-to-life if you're caught kind of favor. I bit the inside of my cheek. "Would you like to join us?"

He stared at me for a full minute. Then tipped the beer bottle to his lips. "It'll be nice to relax somewhere other than a hotel lobby for a change." The couch springs squeaked as they took his weight. "Now, what did you need to talk to me about?"

I looked back toward the kitchen. Kai had finished making incisions and was now jamming cloves into the meat, but he'd frozen with his hand raised. His brown-glamoured eyes hid the sparkling galaxies I'd grown used to seeing when he looked at me, but I could imagine those stars swirling with agitation.

"Kai, could you give us a second?"

Kai looked confused, but set aside the cloves he'd been stabbing into the ham and headed for his bedroom. I hated to kick him out, especially when I wasn't going to say anything he didn't already know, but Sol might be uncomfortable discussing clandestine plans in front of an audience.

When the door to Kai's room clicked shut, I sat down across from Uncle Sol. "I need a favor, and it's urgent."

His frown returned. "Were you discovered?"

I shook my head. "But I have some friends."

"Fae friends?" He leaned forward, resting his elbows on his knees.

Yumiko hadn't given me permission to out the wolves, but lying to Sol while asking him for help felt wrong. "They've been taken in for testing. I need you to get them out, fast."

"When were they brought in?"

"This morning, maybe last night."

He stared at the beer bottle dangling from his fingers. "They might already have been tested."

"Could you check?"

He sighed, then slipped a phone out of his pocket. "What are their names?"

"Marcus Howard, Sarah Nazari, and Oscar Patil."

His thumbs flew over the screen in practiced patterns. "They're still in holding, tests pending."

"Can you get them out without raising any red flags?"

He pursed his lips. "Maybe."

"Please." I set my hand on his forearm.

He sighed. "So much for relaxing." Setting his beer on the coffee table, he pushed to his feet. "Let me grab my laptop. I'll see what I can do."

As soon as the front door shut, Kai's head poked out of his bedroom.

"Why did you invite him to dinner?"

"He's family," I said. "And I only see him once or twice a year. I could hardly send him back to a sterile hotel room while I enjoy a holiday dinner without him."

"Have you forgotten there are two unregistered fae hiding in your back room?" He hooked a thumb down the hall.

"We'll sneak them out and pretend they came from . . ." I flapped my hands in exasperation. "Somewhere else."

"But—"

"Shush." I waved him away. "He's coming back."

Kai grumbled, but ducked out of sight before Sol got the front door open.

Sol took another swig of beer before settling in with his computer. His fingers flew across the keys.

"They're scheduled for preliminary testing . . . huh."

"What is it?" I scooted to the edge of my chair and tried to peek around the laptop screen. "What's wrong?"

He shook his head. "They're not scheduled for another six days. That's a longer than usual wait, even with the backlog we've been seeing."

"O'Connell implied he'd hold my friends as long as he could. Can you get them out?"

"If I pull them from the testing roster the morning they're

scheduled, then plant bogus results when the reports are run that day, they should be cleared and released."

Six days. The moon would be full in five. I shook my head. "They won't last that long. We need to get them out now."

His dark eyebrows pulled together above his nose and his mouth turned down. "Why the rush?"

"Can you do it or not?"

"Faking tests is risky business. I could move them up the schedule, but changing the test dates will raise flags, especially if someone has taken a special interest in them. Scrutiny from the wrong people could land us both in a lot of trouble." He closed the laptop. "Are you certain these friends of yours are worth the risk?"

I looked away, studying the rug between my feet. I'd promised Sol I'd keep a low profile, stay out of the PTF's way. This felt like poking a wasp nest with a stick. But Oz had helped me save James, and Marc and Sarah helped me saved Oz, not to mention overthrowing an evil vampire who wanted to keep me as a pet.

"I'm certain."

Sol nodded, slowly, his frown still in place. "The earliest I can get them out is the day after tomorrow."

By then I'd be dancing at the Winter Festival with no way of knowing if Sol had been successful, or if he'd gotten caught. But it was the best chance Marc and the others had. The only chance.

"Do it," I said.

"Then I want something in return."

My eyes snapped up. Sol had never asked me for anything before. Sure, there'd been the platitudes of "be good" or "study hard" when he became my legal guardian, but never an actual request. I clasped my hands in my lap and straightened my shoulders. "What do you want?"

"A promise." He leaned back, stretching his arms along either side of the back of the couch. "Something may be coming, something big. If it does, I'll need your help. So it's a favor for a favor. I get your friends out, and when the time comes, you follow orders. No questions. No arguments. Deal?"

A cord of worry wrapped around my stomach, slithered up my spine, and squeezed my heart. What kind of problem could Sol possibly need *my* help with?

But "something big" might never come, and the wolves were waiting now. Sol was my only option if I wanted to get them out.

"Deal."

Sol nodded, and the snake wriggling around my insides settled into place. I got the sense that slithery feeling would be keeping me company until my debt was cleared.

"THIS ISN'T FAIR." Jynx crossed her arms over the rhinestone-studded waist of her lime-green dress. Her lower lip jutted out so far I almost laughed, but the last thing I wanted was to make her tantrum worse.

"It's just a quick walk through the woods. What's so bad about that?"

She kicked at a pile of magazines, the many turned down corners evidence of her time in seclusion. "First you keep us stashed in here for *hours*, now you want us to run two miles through the snow. You're treating us like animals."

I raised my arms in exasperation. "You're a *snow leopard*."

The pout deepened.

Chase was lounging against the only wall not blocked by shelves, his arms and ankles crossed. "While I share your annoyance at bending to Alex's whims, in this case, her proposal makes sense. Whatever else he may be, her uncle is a PTF agent. We don't want to make him suspicious."

"And people suddenly stepping out of my back room would definitely be suspicious," I added.

She gestured to me. "He's keeping her secret."

"That doesn't mean we can trust him to keep ours." Chase pushed off the wall. "If you intend to celebrate this mortal holiday tonight, you'll need to make a mortal entrance."

"Besides," I said, "you're providing a service. Picking you up is the perfect cover so I can slip over to Marc's and let the wolves know what's happening."

Her muscles sang in taut rebellion for a moment, fists and jaw clenched. Then her whole frame seemed to sag as the tension left her.

"Fine. But my dress better not get ruined. I borrowed it from Ava." Sliding open a zipper on her side, she slipped the single, silver-studded strap off her shoulder and let the fabric pool around her feet.

Turning my back, I shoved Chase's shoulder to turn him as well.

"You really are a prude," he whispered.

"You really are an ass," I replied.

A paw batted my pant leg, claws snagging the denim despite being retracted. I turned to the mid-sized snow leopard glaring up at me.

"You'll also need to wear the jacket I put in the bag."

Her nose wrinkled.

"I know you don't need it, but a human would. It's cold outside, remember?"

She swished her tail, which I took as sullen agreement.

"Your turn," I said to Chase.

He immediately started stripping, and I busied myself with collecting Jynx's dress and stuffing it into a backpack. Layer upon layer of gauzy green went in—more fabric than seemed to match the slinky, form-fitting dress Jynx had removed. When the last tendrils of cloth were tucked away, I scooped up the strappy sandals Jynx had borrowed to match the dress and dropped them in on top.

Chase's dark jeans and gray sweater were in a pile on the floor when I turned back around. There didn't seem to be any underwear.

"Shoes?" I looked at the gray tabby, who looked back with a green-eyed stare.

"Sol's going to notice if you walk in barefoot." I sighed. "You'll have to borrow some of mine."

Chase hissed.

"You'll survive a few minutes of crunched toes."

If a snow leopard expression was anything like its human counterpart, Jynx was definitely gloating as she strutted past her brother, tail swishing.

I pushed open the window. A gust of frozen air rushed into my face. The screen was already out, tucked safely behind the shelves thanks to Chase's frequent forays and apparent aversion to the front door.

Jynx cleared the window in a single bound. Chase lighted on the sill.

"I'll meet you at the bottom of my road, just before the mailbox."

Chase's whiskers twitched. Then he dropped to the ground outside and darted into the trees.

I chucked the backpack out after him. I'd grab it on my way to the car. Closing the window, I headed back to the living room.

"Everything okay? You were back there for a while." Sol twisted to look at me over the back of the couch. *Magnificent Seven* was playing on the TV. I could just picture Sol as one of the old cowboys making his last stand in some hopeless gesture of heroism.

I lifted the two frozen pies I'd pulled out of my chest freezer and tipped them like I was balancing a scale. "I couldn't decide between cherry or apple. Any opinion?"

"Make 'em both," he said, and turned back to his movie.

"Can't argue with that," Kai piped from the kitchen. He held a potato masher in one hand and a carton of milk in the other.

I took the pies to the kitchen and set them beside the oven, breathing in the warm smell of baking ham. I moved to wipe my hands on my thighs, but stopped short of the dark red fabric of the dress I'd changed into and grabbed a hand towel instead. "I'm gonna go pick up our friends now. You guys okay?"

Gunshots blared on the TV as another cowboy was riddled with bullets. Sol lifted his beer in affirmation.

Kai pounded potatoes into creamy white pulp, his glamoured eyes narrowed. I guess walking on eggshells all night wasn't exactly the holiday celebration he'd been hoping for.

Grabbing the milk off the counter, I returned it to the fridge and eyed the bottle of wine I'd picked up for dinner. A PTF officer at the table with two unregistered fae and a vampire. I couldn't afford to relax tonight either.

I closed the fridge with a sigh and headed out to tell Yumiko and the wolves my plan. Hopefully I could convince them not to do anything crazy until they knew if my gambit with Sol had paid off. I grabbed a pair of worn sneakers on my way out. Sol's eyes were glued to the TV. The cowboy was bleeding out in a woman's arms.

Chapter 5

THE SMELL OF honey-glazed ham mingled with green beans, sweet potatoes, and fresh rolls as I pushed through my front door. Kai was placing covered dishes on trivets on the table. Savory steam escaped the lids in curling wisps that made my mouth water.

I stomped my boots, knocking off a layer of snow, and stepped to the side so Chase and Jynx could file in behind me. I'd delivered my message to Yumiko while the two of them were changing back into their party clothes. The rest was out of my hands.

Sol pointed a remote at the TV and the screen went dark. Then he pushed to his feet and rounded the couch to meet my guests.

I turned to make introductions, and frowned. Chase's face looked subtly wrong, like someone I recognized but couldn't quite place.

Then it struck me. I'd never seen Chase wear a glamour before.

The differences were small, but the overall effect was unsettling, like he'd suddenly become a stranger. The contours of his face were smoother, the tips of his ears blunted. The long silver braid of his hair was duller than usual, lacking the metallic quality I'd grown accustomed to. It hung in stark contrast against the fabric of his dark gray shirt, creating the impression of a black-and-white picture. Only the bright green of his eyes escaped the desaturation. He'd already kicked off the shoes I'd lent him and was wiggling his sockless toes in accusation.

"Sol, this is Chase. Chase, Sol."

The two men clasped hands and gave one stiff downward jerk, then broke contact.

"Alex has told me so much about you." Chase's smile was sweet enough to turn my stomach.

"Wish I could say the same." Sol's expression matched Chase's. "But I don't get to catch up with Alex as often as I'd like." He tipped his head in my direction. "Are you two—"

"No." I chopped my hand through the air between them like I could cut them off from each other and glared at Chase, daring him to make some smart-ass remark. When I was relatively certain he wasn't going to say anything I'd regret, I transferred my glare to Sol. "Please stop asking that."

Sol shrugged. "I'm curious about the people in your life."

"Chase and his sister are friends. That's all."

Sol raised his hands in surrender.

"I'm Jynx." Hanging my borrowed jacket on a hook by the door, she bobbed up beside Chase like a nervous prom date greeting her chaperone, and again I was struck by the unsettling feeling of meeting a strange not-stranger. The differences of her human glamour were even less noticeable than Chase's, but I still found myself staring.

"Pleasure to meet you, my dear." Sol shook Jynx's hand, but lighter than he had Chase's, as though his grip might hurt her.

I smiled. Jynx could probably crush the bones in Sol's hand if she tried.

"Anything left to do?" I called to Kai, who'd remained in the kitchen.

He shook his head. "Places are set, pies are in the oven."

Sol clapped his hands and rubbed them together. "Then let's dig in. I've been smelling this meal for hours, and I can't wait to taste it."

We all turned toward the table. Six chairs sat around the feast. Four that matched the table, the black office chair from my computer desk, and one folding metal seat with a worn, blue cushion. In front of each chair was a place setting, complete with matching plates, glasses, and a set of cloth napkins I received years ago from someone who obviously didn't know me very well. There was also a full set of polished, fine silver utensils I'd inherited from my mother.

Sol frowned. "I count an extra chair."

"I'm expecting one more," I said.

Sol squinched his eyes, as though trying to dig some clue out of his brain. "David?"

I shook my head. "He was busy." The lie left a sour flavor in my mouth. David hadn't been invited. He and Maggie were human, and this had been a strictly paranatural gathering—until Uncle Sol showed up and threw a wrench in the works.

Sol snapped his fingers and pointed. "That lass from the bookstore. Maggie."

Hearing her name brought a rush of memories and misery. I hated that I'd failed to reach her, failed to set things right between us before my trip. But I'd made my choice. I'd just have to do my best to get back in one piece and hope the wreck of my life could still be repaired.

I shook my head again.

Sol frowned. "I hadn't realized your social circle had grown so much."

"James," I said. "I've mentioned him before. He runs the gallery where I show my work."

"Ah, yes." Sol nodded. "I remember now. Heard he was caught up in some unpleasantness a few weeks back involving that new drug, Fantasia."

"As the victim," I clarified. "He didn't have anything to do with the drugs."

Other than planting them on the vampire he framed and pretended to execute. I frowned. I'd been too rattled to wonder at the time, but where had he gotten those drugs? Did he know who was making them?

"You okay?" Sol leaned in, studying my face.

I nodded and glanced at the clock. "Just wondering what's taking him so long."

Kai pulled a lighter from a kitchen drawer and lit the two, tall candles on the table. "He knew the time, and the food's getting cold. I vote we start without him."

GLASS PLATES WITH crumbs, fruit smears, and in one case, a rejected pie crust littered the coffee table. I eyed the mess, willing myself to get up and clear it away, but the warmth in my body and the weight in my gut kept me pinned on the couch, feet propped beside Chase's on the table.

Sol patted his stomach and reclined deeper in the chair opposite me. "So," he drawled with a satisfied stretch, and pointed between Chase, Jynx, and me. "How do you three know each other?"

The pleasant weight in my stomach constricted and became hard, pulling the warmth out of my limbs. This was exactly the kind of conversation I'd worked so hard to steer Sol away from during dinner. It had been easy enough when there was food and drink to offer and eat, but my tools of deflection were gone, turned to crumbs and dirty dishes.

"The bookstore," I piped before anyone else could open their mouth.

Before I could elaborate, Chase added, "I'm an artist as well."

I struggled to keep my face neutral. If Chase said it, it had to be true—fae couldn't lie. But I'd had no idea he was an artist. He'd certainly never mentioned it before.

Sol gestured between us. "Is your work in the same gallery?"

Chase lifted his palms. "Nowhere so grand for me, I'm afraid. But Alex has been a source of great inspiration and . . . insight."

Sol nodded and shifted his gaze. "And what about you, Kai? I never got the whole story of how you came to be living with Alex back in October. I was a little distracted the last time we spoke."

I snorted. Aside from helping clear me of a murder charge, Sol's hands had been full cleaning up the mess left by the PTF agent I'd killed.

"We were acquainted through Aiden," Kai said. The room fell silent for a moment as a ripple of loss washed through it. "I would have stayed with him, but after what happened, Alex was kind enough to take me in."

Not a lie. Not exactly the truth either. I was beginning to see why James warned me about the fae having slippery tongues. I cringed. Not that he was any better.

"You're here on a work visa, right?" Sol continued. "How long do you plan on sticking around?"

"I'd like to stay for the full term of my visa." Kai lifted his shoulders. "But who knows what the future will bring?"

My mouth went dry.

Despite Kai's repeated assurances that he intended to come back with me after the Winter Festival, even if only to say goodbye, there was more than just my impending court appearance and meeting my grandfather for the first time that made me dread our upcoming trip to Enchantment. I'd gotten used to having Kai around. Against all my mother's advice and some grade-A abandonment issues, I'd gotten attached, and a small, terrified part of me kept insisting it was time to pay the price.

Pushing the thought aside, I clapped my hands. "Who wants to open presents?"

Jynx shot to her feet fast enough to blow her human cover, but Chase wrapped a hand around her wrist and brought her up short before Sol could do more than glance in her direction.

"Perhaps Alex should distribute the gifts," Chase said.

Jynx dropped back into her seat, but she perched at the edge like a bird about to take flight . . . or a cat about to pounce.

I crossed to the little Christmas tree with its drooping, dried-out limbs. Blue and silver plastic balls dangled from the branches. Glitter shed from the tinsel to mix with a layer of pine needles that coated the presents, the blanket they rested on, and the surrounding floor.

I brushed dead needles off the first present.

"This one's for Jynx." I handed her a little package wrapped in shiny blue paper with silver snowflakes.

She tore into it like a rabid dog.

"It's a . . ." Her nose wrinkled. "Picture of a bed?"

I smiled at her confusion. "A real bed, actually. Just hasn't arrived yet."

Chase's smile faltered.

Jynx stopped bouncing, stopped fidgeting. She didn't even blink. It was probably the first time I'd seen the girl entirely still.

"You're giving me a bed?"

I looked from Jynx to Chase, then glanced at Sol. I couldn't ask what the problem was in front of him.

I'd thought it was a perfect gift. I'd move my storage shelves into the laundry room to make space, then set up the little wood-frame daybed so Jynx didn't have to sleep on the floor anymore.

Kai cleared his throat.

"Kind of an odd gift for a friend," Sol commented.

Cheeks warming, I stared at my hands. "She'd mentioned her current sleeping conditions weren't all that comfortable. I thought this might help."

I glanced at Jynx, who remained unsettlingly still.

"That was very thoughtful of you," she said. Each word was carefully chosen, deliberate. A diplomatic answer.

Again, I was reminded of the years she didn't show.

"Do I get a bed, too?" Chase asked.

His question broke the tension that had been building in the room.

I smiled, relieved, and shrugged. "Wait and see."

Setting the controversial slip of paper aside, Jynx resumed bouncing in place. "Now do the one I got you."

Sol's forehead crinkled, creating deep creases. "You didn't come in with presents."

"We dropped them off ahead of time," Chase said smoothly. "Less to worry about before the party."

I found a gold-wrapped box with my name written on it in big curly letters and held it aloft, shaking it to draw everyone's attention. "Is this it?"

Jynx bounced again, her whole body nodding. "Yup."

I shredded the paper and tore open the cardboard box to find my own little slip of paper.

"It's a Netflix subscription," Jynx blurted. "So you aren't stuck watching the same shows all the time."

More like so *she* wasn't stuck. I almost never watched TV. Still, I plastered on a gracious smile and said, "That's great, Jynx. I love it."

Yay for mostly mortals being able to lie.

I tucked the slip of paper with my apparent Netflix username and password back in its box and set it to one side.

Next, I lifted the unwrapped cardboard box I'd been planning to ship Uncle Sol's gift in and delivered it to his hands. "Merry Christmas, Uncle Sol."

The corners of his mouth lifted. Wrinkles multiplied on his cheeks until his face looked like the surface of a pond after a stone's been thrown in. "Thank you, my dear. I—"

A knock cut him off, and we all turned toward the front door.

"Looks like James finally decided to show up," Kai said.

I crossed the room in three long strides. Even before I reached the door, I could feel a press of thoughts and emotions that weren't my own. They were dim—shadows dancing on the invisible wall James kept in place to shield us both. This telepathic connection was a side effect of the tiny chunk of demon soul James had shared to save my life. He assured me our bond would fade as my fae blood overwhelmed the residual demon material. In the meantime, it was hard to tell which feelings were mine and which were just bleed-through from James.

When I opened the door, James was there, huddled in a thick, knee-length coat with his collar turned up against the cold. He stood at the edge of a half-circle of warm, yellow light cast by the bulb beside my door. Beyond that arc, pale blue moonlight glinted off a fresh layer of snow.

He met my gaze with eyes the color of glacial ice, and a warm wave of emotion slammed into me—desire and frustration surging through our link, pounding at the barrier.

I braced a hand against the door frame for balance. This was one reason I'd insisted we take a break from any attempt at romance for the time being. I was in no condition to make decisions on something so complicated when I couldn't even be sure the emotions I was sorting through were my own.

Taking a deep breath, I straightened and pushed away from the doorway. "You're late."

"I was caught up with Victoria." A flicker of guilt pattered against the invisible wall when he said her name.

I glanced over my shoulder, then stepped farther onto the porch, pulling the door partly closed behind me. Pitching my voice low, I asked, "Is everything okay?"

He frowned and glanced at the gap of light shining out from the living room.

"Uncle Sol stopped by," I explained. "He's inside."

"Ah." He tucked a loose strand of ebony hair behind his ear. "Things are moving . . . smoothly."

"Good." The last thing I needed the night before I was set to leave for the fae reservation was to find out we had another homicidal vampire master to put down. "Then come inside. We just started opening presents."

I reached for his arm, intending to pull him into the house, but he jerked away the second my fingers made contact.

Another wash of guilt hit me, this one stronger than the first.

"I'm sorry, Alex, but I can't stay. I just wanted to see you before you left, to wish you luck . . . and to give you this." He reached inside his coat and pulled out a long, thin box.

I hooked a thumb toward the door behind me. "Your gift is inside. Can't you come in just for a minute?"

He shook his head. "Things are . . . delicate right now. I need to get back before Bryce does something we'll *all* regret."

Bryce's name was enough to chase away any lingering contentment from dinner. I shivered, clammy and nauseated as though from a sudden onset of flu. Bryce had been Merak's lieutenant, a grade-A asshole, and my personal bogeyman. Our last encounter left him short one eye. In my opinion, he got off easy. We never should have let that bastard live.

"Best get back then."

"Here." He held his box out toward me.

Careful not to brush against his fingers, I took the box. It was heavy. The sides and bottom were stained a rich chestnut brown. A small brass latch hooked a matching ring on the front. The top was inlaid with perfectly fitted swirls of dark and light wood that created a mosaic in the pattern of blooming flowers with tiny mother-of-pearl centers.

"It's lovely."

He smiled. "The gift is *inside* the box."

The latch was tight but not stiff, just enough to hold the lid secure. Inside, on a bed of red velvet was . . .

"A hammer?"

"Not just any hammer."

I studied the gift. The steel of the head was dull and dinged, the wood of the hammer was dry, splinters showing around the bottom. One solid hit and the tool would probably fall to pieces.

"An old hammer," I amended.

James smiled. "A hammer used by Hester Bateman." He leaned in close. "Her favorite."

"Seriously?" I looked down with renewed interest. Hester Bateman had been one of the most successful silversmiths of the Georgian era. "How did you—"

"You aren't the first metalsmith I've befriended."

I wracked my brain for dates. Hester Bateman worked during the 1700s. Even if most of her work came from the later part of that century, the hammer had to be nearly three hundred years old.

As a vampire, James could theoretically live forever. He'd certainly been around longer than his appearance suggested, but he refused to tell me his actual age. I filed Bateman's friendship away with other snippets and comments he'd dropped containing clues to his earlier life.

I closed the box on the antique hammer. "I can't accept this."

He frowned. "You don't like it?"

"I love it. But Bateman was a historical figure. This belongs in a museum."

"So it can gather dust behind a glass case?" He shook his head. "The museums have plenty of examples of her work. This," he gestured to the box, "she would have preferred go to someone who can truly appreciate it. Trust me, she would have liked you."

Cradling the box against my chest, I smiled and gave a little nod.

"Now, I really must be going," he said.

"At least let me run in and grab your present."

"Give it to me when you get back." He smiled, and brushed my cheek with the back of his knuckles. The contact was fleeting, but warmth spread through me as though I'd tipped my face toward the sun. "I could use something to look forward to in the week ahead."

"Seeing me again isn't enough?"

"Always." He leaned in as he spoke, his breath warm across my skin.

I responded in kind, hating the distance I'd forced between us, wanting to erase it. But even as I considered crossing those last few inches I couldn't be sure if the desire I felt was mine . . . or his. The closer he got, the more the invisible wall between us wavered. Stray thoughts began to leak through. Bryce, dark and brooding. Worry. Doubt. Hope. Lust. Then the face of a woman I'd never met, with fine features and blond hair.

Victoria. Her name flashed across my mind with a jolt like I'd stuck my finger in a light socket.

I pulled away, and James did likewise. The cold night air rushed in to take his place.

"The link should be gone by the time you get back," he said.

The link wasn't our only problem. Even without the complication of our over-sharing bond, he was a vampire and I was a halfer. A relationship between us would never be simple.

"You should go," I said.

He shifted like he wanted to reach for me, but clasped his hands together instead. "Be careful, Alex. Come back safe."

"Assuming I can even enter Enchantment with this piece of you still in me." I set a hand against my chest, feeling the beat of my heart. "Vampires can't cross fae portals. Maybe I'll bounce off and be back in a day."

"I doubt the Lord of Enchantment would let you off so easy. There are always ways around rules."

"So much for wishful thinking."

He smiled, and stepped off the porch. "I'll be waiting for my gift."

Chapter 6

RUBBING BLEARY EYES, I shuffled up the hall in my slippers. It was hard to imagine I would be waking up somewhere different tomorrow. Harder still since I had no idea what to expect. Waking up in a hospital after killing a man had been different. Waking up in the dungeon under Marc's house had been different. Tomorrow, I'd be waking up in another world.

Tomorrow would be more than *different*. I shuddered and rubbed my arms, trying to flatten the goosebumps there.

The Christmas lights on the little tree were unplugged, the bulbs dark. In the shadows at its base, nestled in a bed of dry needles, sat a single lonely present. A metallic silver bow clung to the red paper. Inside was the scarf I'd knitted with blue yarn that would perfectly match James's eyes. I'd poured my feelings for him into each and every stitch, literally. When James wore that scarf, he'd be carrying me with him.

I sighed. *I should have made him take it last night.*

Shaking my head, I continued to the kitchen to pour myself a cup of coffee. I was going to need all the energy I could get to make it through the day.

Kai opened his door a moment later, probably drawn by the French roast.

"Big day ahead of us," he said as he stepped around me to grab his own mug.

"Yeah," I mumbled. "Big day."

He patted me on the arm. "You'll be fine. I'll be there to help. Hortense too."

Frowning, I stared into the brown depths of my drink. "What was wrong with Jynx's present?"

Sol had insisted on a game of chess after opening his gift, so it had been late by the time he left. Then we'd had to convince him Chase and Jynx didn't need a ride down the mountain. At least, not from him. By the time the house was quiet again, we were all done in and I'd forgotten about the strange reaction my gift had evoked until I saw the picture of the promised bed sitting on the coffee table as I walked past.

"I'm sure she'll love having a bed."

"That's not what I mean. You guys got all . . . weird when she opened it."

Kai sighed. "Gift-giving is complicated among the fae."

"Is that why you and Chase didn't get each other anything?"

He nodded. "It wouldn't have been appropriate."

"So much for experiencing a mortal Christmas," I grumbled. "What was the point if you were going to drag your overly-complicated fae rules into it?"

Kai pressed his lips tight and sighed. "We can't change who we are. But I still enjoyed the experience."

"So what was it about the bed? No one flinched when I gave you your present." I gestured to the silver chain dangling around Kai's neck. I'd asked Hortense to help me with a simple protection charm.

"Giving Jynx a bed implies you intend her to stay. That, in turn, denotes a certain amount of . . . responsibility for her."

"But she was already staying here. This will just make it more comfortable."

"And more permanent. You've offered her a place in your home."

I downed the last of my coffee and set the empty mug next to the sink. "You've got a bed."

"A bed that was already in place. I'm only borrowing it."

Again I was struck by the thought that once we crossed into Enchantment, Kai might not be coming back.

"You really think Gramps will let you keep training me?"

He hesitated, shrugged. "Unless something goes terribly wrong."

"Comforting."

He set his empty cup next to mine and patted me on the shoulder again. "Time to get moving."

I showered, dressed, and checked the contents of my suitcase. I'd added a few more books I thought might come in handy and a bag of candy Kai asked me to smuggle into Enchantment for him. I'd also added the stealth charm I made with Hortense. The fused pendant of sticks and snow would clash hideously with a party dress, but best to have it just in case.

I traced my fingers along the sheath of my knife, then glanced at the nightstand drawer and bit my lower lip. Guns weren't considered courtly weapons. Most fae couldn't even hold them. But I wasn't most fae, and if things went sideways at court I'd want every advantage I could get.

Pulling open the drawer, I grabbed the Ruger LC9 my friend David had given me to protect myself. The thick leather of the holster was stiff and smelled of oil. I turned the gun over in my hands, thinking of my human friends. I hadn't treated David much better than Maggie—missing or canceling dates, calling only when I needed something... keeping secrets. I'd had my hands full preparing for this trip, but that was no excuse for being such a shitty friend. I'd pushed them away, telling myself it was for their protection. But I'd only been protecting myself.

I owed them both an apology... and an explanation.

I wedged the holstered, unloaded gun and a box of bullets along the edge of the case and zipped it shut.

When I got back, I'd make things right. I'd find a way to fix the mess I'd made of my relationships.

Please let me make it back here in one piece.

I hefted my suitcase off the bed, slung my sheathed sword on my shoulder, and took one last look around the room.

My gaze fell on the drawer to my nightstand. I hesitated for a moment, then pulled it open and grabbed the black box I'd tucked inside. Slipping the little silver locket with its engraved *A* into a pocket, I headed for the door.

Kai was waiting in the living room when I stepped out. Chase and Jynx were beside him.

Setting my bag down, I stopped in front of the sleep-matted teenager. "Listen, Jynx, about your present—"

"Sorry about my reaction. I was—"

I shook my head, raising a hand to forestall her explanation. "I shouldn't have gotten you something so... permanent without checking with you first. I've canceled the order for now. We can talk about it when I get back. In the meantime, feel free to use Kai's bed. As I understand it, there are no strings attached."

Jynx smiled. "I'll do that. And I'll think about your offer... if it still stands."

I wanted to say yes, but I couldn't promise something I didn't fully understand, so I set my hand on the girl's shoulder and said, "We'll talk when I get back."

Nodding, she closed the space between us and wrapped her arms around me. "Be careful in Enchantment. Those guys don't have a sense of humor."

"Hey!" Kai piped.

I squeezed her back, then stepped away. "Try not to burn the place down while I'm away."

Chase gestured to the front door. "Shall we?"

I frowned. "Are you bumming a ride to the reservation?"

He shrugged. "Saves on gas."

I opened my mouth, but the words I'd been about to speak abandoned me as all three fae turned in unison toward the front door.

"Someone's here," Kai said.

I rushed to the window.

Big, fluffy flakes of snow were falling from the sky. There was already at least an inch of new powder on the ground.

The whine of a motor heralded an approaching vehicle. A moment later Emma's yellow VW Bug rolled up the icy driveway and skidded to a stop behind my Jeep.

"Chase, Jynx, you need to hide," I called over my shoulder.

Chase rolled his eyes and Jynx grumbled, but the two of them headed for the back room.

Kai stepped up next to my elbow. "Get rid of her quickly. We need to go."

Nodding, I shoved my sword into his hands, tugged on my coat and boots, and stepped out the front door to meet Emma on the porch.

Emma slipped getting out of her car, gripping the open door to keep from falling. Her knee-high black boots with three-inch heels were not handling the icy, uneven ground well. Above the impractical boots, Emma's jeans were full of dozens of holes that looked like they'd been put there on purpose. Slamming the door, she shrugged her thick, red coat tighter, and cinched her hood until she was peering out a narrow tunnel.

Catching sight of me, she lifted one hand in greeting and made her way across the clearing, one arm out for balance like a tightrope walker. When she stepped into the relative shelter of the porch, she flipped back her hood. Her skin seemed pale, and more yellowish than usual. Aside from two loose, pink spirals that bobbed on either side of her face, her hair was an explosion of short, tufted pigtails, dyed black with fuchsia tips, that left the hoops and chains dangling from her ears exposed.

I frowned. "Shouldn't you be at the bakery?"

Emma's mother, Loni, owned the bakery that supplied pastries to Magpie's café, and Emma often complained about having to help there before opening up at the bookstore.

Emma tried to smile, but her chin quivered and the corners of her mouth fell like an anchor dropped at sea. Tears glinted, casting a glassy sheen over her soft, brown eyes. "I can't go back."

I grimaced, guessing the source of Emma's misery. "You had another fight with your mom?"

Loni Yamada was as conservative as they came, so Emma's becoming a practitioner had caused more than a little friction between them. Loni lost her husband to the Faerie Wars, so she had good reason to mistrust magic. Still . . . Emma was her daughter.

Emma gripped the front of her coat with shaking hands. "I'm not giving up being a practitioner. The damage is done. I'm registered as a magic-user whether I study or not."

I nodded.

"This morning—" She sniffed and wiped her sleeve under her nose, leaving a dark streak. "I said some things, and . . . and . . ."

"She's your mom," I said, setting one hand on her shoulder. "I'm sure she'll forgive you."

"Like she forgave me for taking the test?" she asked bitterly. She turned big, teary eyes on me. "Can I stay here?"

I jerked away as though her shoulder had become hot. "What?"

"Please, I can't go home."

I shook my head. "I'm on my way out of town. I was about to leave when you—"

"I can house-sit while you're away. You know, water the plants and stuff."

"I . . . already have someone to watch the house."

Her face fell, but the determination didn't leave her eyes. "Please, Alex. You have to let me stay here. I have nowhere else to go."

"So you're just going to hide from your mother for the rest of your life?"

"No." She lifted her chin. "Just for a week or two."

I sighed, casting a glance back at the window. Kai wasn't visible, but I knew he'd be tapping his foot, staring at the clock. I needed to wrap this up.

"Like I said, I've already got someone staying here while I'm away, so—"

"I can share. I won't get in the way, I swear." She lifted one hand and placed the other over her heart. "At least ask if they'd be willing." She pressed her hands together as though praying. "Pleeeeease?"

This time my sigh came out more as a groan. "Wait here."

I slipped back inside and closed the door on Emma's pleading gaze.

"She's not leaving," Kai observed.

I waved his comment away and tromped down the hall to Jynx's hiding place. Chase was lounging against the wall again. Jynx was slouched in her nest, arms crossed.

"Is she gone?" Chase pushed off the wall and took a step toward the door.

"Not yet." I turned to Jynx. "How would you feel about a roommate while I'm away?"

She narrowed her eyes. "You mean a chaperone?"

I shook my head. Of course Jynx wouldn't like the idea of a third wheel when she was looking forward to time with her girlfriend, but Emma's situation wasn't all that different from the reason Jynx ended up in my storage room a month ago—hiding from the judgment of overbearing parents. "My friend, Emma, made a decision her mom didn't approve of. They got in a big fight, and she ran away from home. She needs a place to stay."

Jynx's scowl softened, her mouth puckered. "Is she nice?"

"Very."

She lifted one shoulder. "I guess we could share the space. As long as she understands I'm in charge."

"You'd need to stay glamoured," I warned. "I doubt she'd turn you in, but it isn't worth the risk."

Chase crossed his arms. "I don't like this."

"Even better," Jynx teased. "Don't worry. I can keep a mortal in the dark, no problem."

"And don't say anything about where I'm going," I added. "Or why Kai's been staying here. In fact, don't talk about anything fae-related at all."

My stomach squirmed unpleasantly. This was a bad idea. There were too many things that could go wrong. Seeing Emma so upset. . . . I hadn't thought the consequences through properly.

"It'll be fine." Jynx sprang to her feet like gravity had no hold on her. "You guys better get moving if you don't want to be late."

She grabbed my arm and towed me into the hall. "Let's go meet my roommate."

"Better shift," I called over my shoulder.

Chase was already undressing.

Kai raised an eyebrow when Jynx and I reemerged. "What's going on?"

Blocking the question with a raised hand, I pulled open the front door.

Emma practically flew through, stomping and shaking like she was having a convulsive seizure. "Damn it's *cold* out there!"

"Helps if your pants don't have holes in them," I said. "Emma, this is Jynx, the girl who's house-sitting for me. Jynx, this is Emma, a friend from the bookstore."

My voice stuttered on the last word as my brain registered the implications of yesterday's conversation with Maggie. Emma, Jake, Kayla. They were all fixtures of my life at Magpie. Take that away, and . . .

I rubbed a hand over my forehead, smoothing the worry-wrinkles there. "Kai and I need to get going. There are two bedrooms and two bathrooms. You can work it out, right?"

Jynx and Emma glanced at each other, then back to me.

"We got this," Emma said. "Have a good trip."

"Try not to die," Jynx added.

That earned a funny look from Emma, and my stomach sank even further. This was such a bad idea.

Kai grabbed my suitcase and headed out the door, my sheathed sword still dangling from his other hand. Had Emma noticed the weapon? A streak of gray raced up the hall and impacted my chest. I wrapped my arms around Chase as I staggered for balance.

"I didn't know you had a kitty." Emma reached out to pet Chase, who hissed. Emma pulled her hand back. "Not very friendly, is he?"

Jynx snickered, and I glared at the cat in my arms. "You won't have to worry about him. He's coming with me."

"You're taking your cat on vacation with you?" Emma gave me another confused look.

"I'm dropping him at a kennel. You two play nice." I bolted out the door and slammed it before there could be any more delays.

Chapter 7

KAI PAUSED NEXT to a battered stop sign at an unnamed junction, looked along the empty stretch of intersecting road, and turned toward the golden hills of the Great Sand Dunes where they nestled at the base of the snow-tipped Sangre de Cristo mountains.

After fifteen minutes skirting the northern edge of the national park, I caught sight of a dark line that cut through the foothills, too straight and solid to be anything natural.

I pointed through the windshield. "Is that . . . ?"

"The edge of the reservation," Kai confirmed.

Despite living only a few hours away, I'd never actually seen the fae reservation.

As we neared the town of Crestone, the last human settlement before entering fae-controlled land, the dark line resolved into a row of sixteen-foot iron bars embedded in cement and topped with razor wire.

It had taken two years and several billion dollars to erect the wall, and plenty of people had seen it as a waste. What good was a wall when the fae had magic? Case in point: I wouldn't be going in through the front gate. But some politician made it his mission to build the damn thing, more a monument to his ego than a practical deterrent. What kept the fae on their own land, for the most part, was the threat of execution if they were caught breaking the rules.

Humans were technically allowed to enter the reservation, but they did so at their own risk. Some had tried, back when the wall was new. Mostly ex-soldiers thinking to end the fight on their own terms. None of them ever came out.

A weathered wooden sign with the words "Welcome to Crestone" came into view.

Like many Colorado cities, Crestone started out as a mining town, and it nearly joined its neighbors in becoming a ghost town until a movement to celebrate world spiritual organizations breathed life back into it. Driving through town was like taking a tour of international religions. A hodgepodge of architectural styles lined the road—buildings ranging from yoga studios and boutique shops to Buddhist temples, monasteries, and even a ziggurat. People claimed the area had a unique spiritual quality, and there'd been plenty of reports over the years concerning strange, inexplicable experiences.

Of course, that was before we knew about the fae. The fact that a number of faerie-realm portals could be found in the mountains just to the east of town explained a lot of those mysteries.

A fortified complex sat at the edge of town. The buildings had no labels, but the iron-laced uniforms of the guards patrolling its fence marked it as a PTF base. I shuddered. I'd put a few hundred miles between me and O'Connell. That didn't mean I was safe. The Crestone compound made the testing facility in Denver look like a day spa.

The base dwarfed a large temple with a One Earth symbol carved in stone above its door, and an office building with a Purity emblem painted in its front window. Even with all those converging organizations, the town's population topped out around 200, and it took less than ten minutes to put it in our rear view.

The wall loomed—iron bars as thick as my waist, spaced so not even a child could slip through. From this distance, it looked solid.

Kai turned off the main road, taking a little dirt path on the left.

We passed through a gap in a split-rail fence, and my arm started to itch like a thousand ants had bitten me all at once. I scratched, pulling up my sleeve to reach tattooed skin.

The sensation passed as quickly as it had come.

I twisted in my seat to look at the unassuming fence encircling the property. "What was that?"

Chase was curled up on the back seat, tail wrapped neatly around his body. He looked at me with sleepy eyes, and yawned.

Kai cut his gaze to me. "You felt it?"

I nodded.

"Warding spell," he said. "To dissuade uninvited guests."

I rubbed a thumb over my tattoo. "Guess that makes me uninvited."

"What makes you say that?"

"My tattoo . . . charm . . . whatever. It acts up sometimes."

"Acts up?"

"Gets itchy. Sometimes it stings. Only when magic is involved. But it didn't react when we forged the light-knife or when you Jedi-wiped people's memories, so I figure it's like a warning system for magic that's directed *at* me."

His brow creased, but he kept his eyes on the pitted dirt road. "A sound judgment. Why didn't you mention this before?"

I shrugged. "You said yourself you weren't sure what the charm could do, and it didn't seem like that big a deal, all things considered."

The car lurched over one last wash-out, and we pulled into a little parking space in front of a small brick house nestled in a copse of trees.

Kai twisted to face me. "You should ask the lord for a complete accounting of what the charm does."

"I'll put that on the list."

Chase hopped over the center console and dropped in my lap like a sack of potatoes. He meowed and pawed the door.

"You could have fingers if you wanted," I said, but I pulled the lever and opened the door.

Chase dropped to the ground and bounded toward the house, disappearing through a small hole to one side of the front door. *Damage in need of repair, or a special entrance for furry fae?*

"What is this place?" I asked. "I thought we'd be going all the way to the wall."

"A way station, to make the transitions easier. There may be other fae here, but rest assured, this place is protected. All will keep the peace."

I unfolded from my seat and stretched like I was trying to pull down the sky. A dusting of snow coated the ground and drifted in the shadows of the trees. The air was thin and crisp, and reminded me of home.

To the side of the building, six cars huddled in a loose grid, snow piled up around their tires.

"What's with the salvage yard?"

"A selection of vehicles fit for fae use." He gestured to the car I'd just stepped out of. "Like this one."

Like Kai's, all the cars seemed to have plastic or carbon fiber panels, and I was willing to bet they used a minimum of interior steel.

"Shall we?" He lifted my suitcase from the trunk, along with both our swords, and carried it all up to the porch like a gentleman.

"I can get my own bag, you know."

He shrugged. "Best I hang on to it. You're not used to portal travel, and who knows where it might end up if you drop it."

I couldn't argue with that, so I trotted up the steps to hold the door for him.

A string of silver bells tied along a length of red ribbon jingled when we entered, just like the bell on Magpie's front door. A cramp tightened my chest, but I forced myself to breathe through it. There was nothing I could do about Maggie right now.

The interior of the building was split into a sitting area with an unmanned reception desk, a small kitchen, and a wooden picnic table with two benches. The far wall held three identical doors. To one side of the front entrance, near the little hole where Chase had come through, was a box of clothes. The faded fabric of a purple sweater draped the edge as though it were trying to climb free.

Chase lounged on a plaid fabric couch that looked like a reject from a rained-out garage sale. Loose gray sweats covered his legs, but his chest and feet were bare. His long silver hair fell in an unbound waterfall around his face and shoulders.

A little old lady—or someone who looked like a little old lady—with tight, steel gray curls clinging to her head and a blue and white checkered apron tied around her waist, straightened from where she'd been peering into the oven. The smell of fresh bread and cinnamon filled the cozy space.

"Make yourselves at home," she said. "Rolls'll be out in a minute and I'll get you checked in."

"We're not staying," Kai corrected. He set my bag to the side of the door. "Just need a lift home."

The woman nodded, slipping on a pair of singed oven mitts. "Otis will be around shortly."

Kai walked behind the reception desk to a pegboard with a number of keys hanging from it. Each peg had a white label stuck above it, and every key had a uniquely patterned rubber guard covering its top, probably so the fae wouldn't burn their fingers. He added the blue-capped key from his Toyota to the collection.

I dropped into one of the unoccupied seats, draped my arms over the sides, tipped my head back, and settled in to wait.

"Finally," said a deep voice behind me.

The three of us turned as one toward the back of the room, where one of the doors now stood open. In the doorway, leaning against the frame, was a short, Asian man with tattoos that covered one side of his face, looped his neck, and trailed down his arms. His black hair was mussed and stood on end like he'd just stuck his finger in a light socket.

I'd met Enzo only once before, when I'd retreated to Crossroads—

the fae bar near my home—to forget my troubles. That had been my first mistake. Accepting a drink from a strange, ashy-faced woman with spider leg pigtails had been my second. Still, the evening hadn't turned weird until Enzo showed up.

He crossed his arms and frowned at me, lightning flashing in his dark eyes. "I've been waiting three days."

Kai's gaze shifted between us, the crease on his forehead growing deeper. "Alex?"

I shook my head, as confused as he was.

Kai stepped around the desk. "What's your business here, raiju?"

Enzo lifted a finger in my direction. "Her."

I stiffened.

Kai shifted to stand between us, blocking my view of Enzo. Chase continued to lounge, his eyes half-lidded like our little skit was putting him to sleep.

I pushed to my feet and stepped even with Kai, who frowned, but didn't move to block me again.

"Why are you waiting for me?" I asked.

He pushed away from the door and reached behind him. "To give you this."

Kai's hand dropped to where his sword would hang, but groped only air. The way station was supposed to be a peaceful place. No weapons. No fighting. His sword was balanced beside mine on top of my suitcase just inside the door.

Enzo's gaze flashed to Kai, and one side of his mouth quirked up, wrinkling his tattoo. Then he brought his hand back around and held it out to me. A thin, shimmering ribbon of black fabric draped his palm.

"A token," he said. "From Galen."

Kai frowned. "You're Enzo?"

He nodded.

Kai relaxed. He even took a step back, leaving me to take the lead.

I frowned and tipped my head toward Enzo. "You know this guy?"

"You remember Galen?"

I rolled my eyes. Galen was a shadow walker we'd stumbled across while rescuing James from Denver's previous master vampire, Merak. "Hard to forget a guy we sprang from a vampire's dungeon."

"*You* sprang," Kai corrected. "Galen is known to keep the company of a certain raiju . . . named Enzo."

I raised an eyebrow at Enzo. "So you're like, his boyfriend?"

He stiffened. "I am his companion, his confidant, and his lover, yes. He asked me to deliver this token to you."

"Why wait here? Why not just bring it to me?"

Enzo took a deep breath, probably trying to hold his temper. "It was Morgan's idea."

Morgan was the girl who'd bought me the ill-advised drinks in Crossroads. She was also Galen's sister.

"A visit to your home might have been seen as a threat, so she proposed I meet you on neutral ground. My first thought had been to find you at Crossroads, but I understand you've had your privileges revoked."

Kai raised an eyebrow, and I did my best to keep my expression neutral as I continued to stare at Enzo. Kai did *not* need to know about my drunken blunder in the fae bar. Especially when we were on our way to a party that might literally be the death of me if I were to freak out like that a second time. Besides, I had a much higher tolerance for weird these days.

"It's known that you are attending the Winter Festival in Enchantment," Enzo continued. "And it was likely you'd pass this way to get there. Now please." He thrust the ribbon closer. "Take this. My arm is getting tired."

I shook my head. "Fae gifts are a big no-no."

"It's not a gift." Enzo cast a glance to Kai, as though asking for help.

"Take it, Alex," Kai said.

"But—"

"He can't lie. It's not a gift. It's a debt marker."

I wrinkled my nose but lifted the ribbon off his palm. It was cold against my skin and weighed almost nothing. The cloth slid like smoke between my fingers.

Enzo let his arm fall. "Should you find yourself in need of help, tie three knots in the ribbon and Galen will come."

"If he feels like it," I added, remembering the way the shadow walker had abandoned us after I'd freed him from his prison.

Enzo quirked an eyebrow.

"The last time I asked for his help, he left us to die."

"You're still breathing."

I narrowed my eyes and shivered at the memory of Merak's sword piercing my abdomen. "But I *did* die."

That seemed to catch him off-guard.

"Just three knots?" Kai asked. "Nothing else?"

Enzo did that little half-smile again. "Three knots, and call his name." He fixed me with an electric gaze. "He will come."

Then he collapsed into a ball of light that arced toward the ceiling and disappeared.

Kai tipped his chin toward the ribbon. "Keep that safe."

He moved toward a chair, but before he could sit down, my ears popped, and a man who could have been a twin of the woman in the kitchen—except that his skin hung loose on his bones while hers bore the evidence of too many sweet rolls—was suddenly standing in the middle of the room.

"Pleasant trip, dear?" The woman dropped her mitts on the counter and wiped her hands on her apron.

"Uneventful," the man said. His voice grated like gravel in a tumbler.

"These nice folks are looking for a lift." She gestured to us.

"Hmph." The man shuffled over to the picnic table and slid onto one of the benches. "After lunch."

The old woman brought a plate of freshly-glazed rolls to the picnic table and set the whole stack in front of the man I assumed was the "Otis" we'd been waiting for, who promptly dug in.

I settled back in my seat and examined the silky black ribbon, chewing the inside of my lip. I definitely wouldn't stake my life on Galen's assistance, but in the right circumstance.... I shrugged. "Don't look a gift horse in the mouth."

Kai looked over at me. "What?"

I shook my head. "Just something my mom used to say."

"Did she do a lot of horse trading?"

I laughed and wrapped the ribbon around my wrist. "Help me tie this off."

By the time I was satisfied my new bracelet was secure but would pull free with a single well-placed tug, the rolls in front of Otis were nothing more than a sticky plate of sweet memory.

"Five minutes." The man wiped his mouth and shuffled toward the middle of the three doors. I caught a glimpse of bathroom fixtures before it slammed behind him.

Chase continued to pretend to sleep as our hostess bustled about the kitchen. She added Otis's empty plate to a stack by the sink, retrieved a ball of dough from the fridge, and started kneading. It seemed another batch of rolls was on the way.

A toilet flushed, and Otis reemerged from the center door wiping his hands on faded jeans that sagged around his hips. "Ready to go?"

Chase finally opened his eyes, rolling to his feet with smooth grace. Kai grabbed my bag and our swords from their place by the front door.

Otis held out his hands, palms up. "Hold tight."

Chase twined his fingers with Otis's on one side, and I mimicked his motion on the other. Kai wrapped his hand around the older man's wrist, his fingers closing a full circle around the narrow limb.

Chase winked at me. "Deep breath now."

The cozy kitchen blinked away in a flash of white. Every cell in my body screamed, and my right arm became a glove of napalm. Then the contents of my stomach heaved onto a bed of slush and soggy leaves, stomach acid mixing with the smell of mildew and rotting wood.

Otis's steady grip kept me on my feet while the world came back into focus. The trees around me were pine and fir, dormant aspen and birch. I could have been standing in my own front yard.

Releasing Otis's hand, I spit again and wiped my mouth with the back of my sleeve. "Sorry."

Otis didn't say anything. He simply blinked out of existence in another flash of light.

"Chatty guy," I grumbled. I placed a hand over my churning stomach. "I thought teleporting was supposed to be easier the second time."

Kai raised an eyebrow. "You've done that before?"

I frowned. "It was different. She . . . the fae . . . sort of opened a hole in the world, and we stepped through."

He nodded. "Portal travel. That's more like what you'll experience when you cross into Enchantment."

"Speaking of which," Chase said. "This is where I leave you. I'd ask for a kiss, but well. . . ." He glanced at the yellow splatter on the ground and patted me on the arm.

"We'll meet you back at the way station after the festival," I said.

He shook his head. "I'll make my own way back. Take care of yourself, Alex. Try not to get too bored without me."

He gave Kai a mock salute, then melted into his cat form and darted into the trees. The soiled gray sweats he'd borrowed lay abandoned on the ground.

I pointed at the fabric. "Should we—"

"They'll be reclaimed eventually." Kai hefted my bag, and headed in the opposite direction. "Come on."

I cast one last look toward the trees where Chase had disappeared, then followed Kai.

We tromped over sticks, and leaves, and plants waiting for spring to return. There were no paths. The trees I'd found comfortingly familiar on my arrival grew thicker, and within a dozen steps I was faced with a wall of twisting branches and unnaturally dense shadows.

I stopped in the last patch of visible sunlight and shivered.

Kai glanced back over his shoulder, meeting my gaze. "Don't wander. You shouldn't be in these woods alone."

I rubbed the back of my neck, trying to wipe away the prickly feeling of being watched. A wisp of frosty air lifted a strand of my hair, and invisible fingers seemed to trail over my cheek.

I hurried to close the distance between me and Kai, staying only a step behind. "What's out there?"

"Guards."

There were stories from the war about fae who couldn't be seen. Fae who could make air cut, blood boil, and the earth swallow people whole. Thanks to my studies with Kai, I now knew what to call such fae. Elementals. Having a name didn't make them any less terrifying.

"Can't they tell I'm part fae?"

"That's why you're still alive." Kai's eyes darted from side to side, tracking every creak and snap, every shift in the wind as he blazed a trail through the forest.

"I thought the reservations were neutral ground for the fae."

"Which means anyone might be present." He pressed through a clump of juniper that snapped back and snagged at my clothes. "Not far now."

Beyond the junipers, we stepped into a little clearing blanketed in snow.

I blinked. Not snow. The forest floor was covered with tiny white flowers. "How can there be flowers here in winter?"

Kai gave me a long-suffering look and I raised my hands in surrender. "Right, magic. Sorry."

At the far edge of the field of flowers was a tall oak tree, its bare branches stretching far above the green tops of its pine tree neighbors. Beside the oak was an ash tree that had grown so close its limbs became tangled with the oak's a dozen feet up. Kai headed straight for the space between the two trees.

"Is that the portal?" Each Realm gateway required certain criteria to be met, usually the presence of certain plants or other naturally occurring things, but Kai hadn't said what exactly constituted Enchantment's portal. I tilted my head from side to side, trying to catch a glimpse of distortion or heat shimmers like those I'd seen when looking through Ava's portal.

Kai stopped in front of the oak and turned to face me. "Walk straight between these two trees. Don't stop. You'll come out in another clearing . . . in the Realm of Enchantment. Hortense should be there to meet you." He shifted his weight from foot to foot. "Be on your guard. Remember there are many at court with hidden agendas, and plenty who'd like to see the lord fall. They'll use you if they can."

I wiped suddenly sweaty hands on my jeans. At least I didn't have anything left to throw up.

Taking a deep breath, I clenched my fists and stepped into the space between the trees.

Chapter 8

AS WHEN I'D STEPPED—or fallen—into Ava's portal, there was a moment of feeling like my whole body was being turned inside out. Unlike last time, the sensation didn't flare, then stop. It dug deeper. I was undone down to my very consciousness.

Ribbons of magic burrowed into me, setting my nerves off like firecrackers. I turned my focus inward, following those questing tendrils. The magic arced toward a dark shape, a tiny cluster of foreign matter nestled beside my heart. I recognized that sliver of darkness, though it was a pale shadow compared to what I'd glimpsed through my connection to James. Within that darkness lay a portion of the silver-eyed demon that had saved my life.

My blood started to burn.

I screamed, or tried to. My body seemed to be frozen in a state of limbo—some sort of magical quarantine. Vampires couldn't pass through the portals to fae realms. Apparently, neither could those contaminated by them.

I tried to turn back, to retreat the way I'd come, but I couldn't move, I didn't even seem to have a body anymore. I couldn't see anything outside myself besides a screen of hazy opalescence that seemed to drift in front of my vision no matter which way I looked. I was trapped.

The portal's magic continued to bombard the darkness within me, and every attack sent a shock wave through my system. The magic was burning out the last of James's gift—the portion of soul he'd offered, tainted though it was, to keep me alive.

Another hit came, and I instinctively curled around the dark shape, shielding it. The magic slammed against me, but the darkness remained.

I pulled that darkness closer, hiding it deeper, not sure what I was doing or how I was doing it. The magic struck again, and another ripple of pain tore through me. In that incorporeal space somewhere between thinking and feeling, I clung to the sliver of James nestled inside me.

The magic smashed through me. The world became a curtain of white hot pain. Then I toppled to my knees in a field of snow. The air froze my lungs with each gulped breath, numbing me from the inside out. Billows of fog formed around my face as I exhaled.

I tried to look inside myself, to find the darkness I'd seen in that space between realms where I hadn't been bound by the rules of a physical existence. But grope as I might, all I found was a lingering ache that pulsed with each beat of my racing heart and a spreading sense of loss. Eager though I'd been to regain the privacy of my mind, the abrupt severance of my connection to James doubled me over like a physical blow.

I bunched my unguarded fingers in the snow, focusing on the tiny pricks of ice against my skin until my breathing returned to normal. Then I tipped my chin up to take my first look at another realm.

Snowflakes hung in the air, suspended like time itself had frozen around me. The space I'd fallen into was an unbroken field of snow, except for where I'd crashed through its frozen perfection. The clearing was a near-perfect replica of the one I'd just left, save for the snow and the fae staring at me from the surrounding trees.

My gaze slid over the group, not really processing, and came to rest on the glinting tip of an arrow that was pointed directly at me.

"Stand down." Hortense's tight command was music to my ears.

The arrow tip lowered, and the bow string went slack. In one smooth motion, the arrow was plucked from the bow and tucked into a shoulder quiver. The fae who'd been aiming at me didn't apologize. He stared at me with yellowish eyes that contrasted sharply with the bruised purple color of his skin. His features were long and sharp, like Kai's, and his ears tapered to sharp points on either side of his tightly bound black hair. Strips of leather covered his forearms and wrapped his hands like boxing tape. The olive green fabric of his clothes made it hard to see him clearly against the backdrop of the forest, and did nothing for his complexion.

Leather creaked, and I jerked my attention to a woman at the other end of the group. She wore the same green and leather outfit, had the same purplish skin, and watched me with the same blank expression. She held a bow loose at her side, but her arm was up, as though she'd also just returned an arrow to its quiver.

I shivered.

Kai stepped out of thin air beside me, glanced at the assembled group, set down my suitcase, and offered me his hand. "You managed not to throw up."

"Nothing left in my stomach."

Ignoring his hand, I levered myself to standing and brushed the snow off my knees. It drifted down to dust the ice like powdered sugar. The ice... and Kai's shoes. I frowned, looked up at Kai's face—which was a good three inches higher than it should have been—and back down at his shoes—which were standing on the snow like the ice protecting it was a foot thick.

"Ahem."

I swung my gaze to Hortense, and had to stop myself from taking a step back. I'd only seen the leathery green skin and red-rimmed eyes of her true appearance once before, and her long, seaweed-black hair was swept back in a braid that left her features unsettlingly exposed. Her appearance was no less disturbing in the forest than it had been in my dining room.

I stiffened my shoulders and lifted my chin. Fae didn't wear glamours in their own realms. That would have been like sleeping in a prom dress and makeup. It wasn't just because of politics that Kai and Hortense had insisted I familiarize myself with the fae who frequented Enchantment. I took a deep breath and reminded myself not to react as I took in the remaining fae standing behind Hortense.

"Rhoana will see to your luggage and transportation." Hortense lifted one taloned hand to indicate a tall woman with broad shoulders but the same high cheekbones and tapered chin as Kai. Her eyes were deep indigo flecked with silver that spun in a lazy whirlpool. Bright red hair pulled tight over her scalp and coiled in intricate braids that trailed over the deep green cape draping her shoulders.

Rhoana stepped forward, the soles of her tall leather boots resting on the ice as though she weighed nothing at all. When she was an arm's length away, she slammed a fist to her leather bodice and bowed, tipping her head so the back of her neck was exposed.

"My lady," she said. "I am Rhoana, Captain of the Court Guard, Knight of the Realm, and loyal servant to the Lord of Enchantment. I have been asked to escort you to the palace."

Suppressing a sigh and reminding myself I'd trained for this kind of awkward formality, I inclined my chin in the way Hortense had taught me and said, "Rise, Rhoana. I accept your service."

She straightened, tossing the edge of her cape over her shoulder, and turned to Kai. "Well met, Malakai."

Kai folded nearly in half. He looked like he was trying to kiss his shins. "Captain Rhoana."

Rhoana placed two fingers in her mouth and blew, piercing the clearing with a shrill whistle.

I looked around, and noticed for the first time that the lighting had changed. It had been early afternoon beneath a clear blue sky when I stepped through the mortal side of the portal, but long streaks of sunset pink were now stretched across a ceiling of clouds. The shadows of the forest were both deeper and flatter, creating an impenetrable wall just beyond the tree line as darkness claimed the land.

Time moves differently here, I reminded myself.

Shapes moved among the trees. Then three fae emerged, detaching from the shadows. Two were sidhe, like Kai and Rhoana, and had the typical elven features of that race. They also wore the green and leather uniforms of Enchantment knights. The third was only three feet tall, green, and had what looked like leaves sprouting from his head, back and arms. He wore leather pants, and dangling from his waist were a dagger and a dented brass bell. Unlike his sidhe companions, the eloko's feet sank into the snow. At least I wasn't the only person present who had to answer to gravity.

The three fae clutched thick, leather reins in each hand, and behind them, six beasts emerged from the deep shadows of the forest. At first I thought they were deer, because racks of antlers decorated each of their heads, but their faces were too long, and thick manes of hair cascaded over their necks. Coarse brown fur coated their bodies, trailing down each of their six legs.

I blinked, and counted again. Then glanced at Kai.

"These are gaala," he said, walking up to stroke the nose of the nearest beast. "Fast and sure-footed." He motioned for me to come over.

I tromped through the snow, plowing a path as I approached. The gaala was roughly the size of a large horse, made taller by the fact that its cloven hooves rested on the surface of the snow rather than sinking in.

I lifted my hand, and the gaala snorted a puff of warm, moist air into my palm. Then it nuzzled its nose against my fingers. The fur was velvety soft.

While Kai introduced me to my ride, Rhoana strapped my suitcase onto the back of one of the other gaala. Hortense was already atop hers, sitting side-saddle and straight-backed in her brocade dress like a proper lady in some medieval painting—the image was somewhat ruined by her marshy complexion and the yellow claws that tipped her long, thin fingers.

"Up you get." Kai knelt on the snow and laced his fingers together to make a step.

I raised an eyebrow and pursed my lips at the tall, furry back. "Shouldn't there be some kind of saddle?"

Kai opened his mouth, but Hortense beat him to the punch. "These are not pets or slaves, Alex. We do not bind them."

I wanted to point out that they all had reins strapped to their faces, but the eyes of every fae in the clearing were on me, the weight of their judgment suffocating me.

Pressing my lips closed, I fit my snow-covered boot in Kai's hand and hoisted myself onto the gaala's back. I'd like to say I mounted like a pro, but horses were not a part of my upbringing. My stomach slammed into the gaala's spine, and I rested there a moment to catch my breath before swinging one leg over and pushing myself upright. Smoothing my clothes, I ignored my audience and took the reins from Kai, trying to look like I had some idea how to use them.

Hortense sniffed like she'd caught a whiff of something foul, a common sound during our lessons, and I bit back my defense of riding astride versus side-saddle. A Lady of the Court need not explain herself to those of lesser rank. That much she'd drilled into me.

I relaxed a little when Rhoana mounted astride, albeit considerably more gracefully than I had.

Rhoana nodded to the eloko guard and the two fae who'd trained arrows on me when I first arrived. "Back to your posts."

In unison, they each slammed a fist to their chest and faded back into the forest. I squinted, but they were lost in the shadows, invisible guards over the portal to the mortal realm.

Kai sidled his gaala up beside mine. "Leave the reins loose, the gaala knows where to go. Hold on with your knees." He frowned. "If you need to, you can grip his mane."

I nodded, and tried to relax my grip on the leather straps. My fingers were numb from their plunge in the snow, and didn't respond right away.

"Ha!" yelled Rhoana, and her gaala took off at a dead run.

My gaala charged after them, and I rocked back with the sudden motion. My stomach lurched. The reins tore free from my stiff fingers.

I clenched my thighs, pressing them tight to the gaala's ribs, and threw myself onto its neck. Strands of billowing, black mane whipped my face, and I twisted my hands into them as we galloped toward the fast approaching line of trees on the far side of the clearing.

Rhoana's cape flared behind her, snapping in the wind.

No way could a creature as large as the gaala dodge such tightly packed trees at this speed. We were going to hit.

I scrunched my eyes closed and huddled lower on the undulating back of my gaala. Its neck pumped back and forth with each surge forward, its six legs gobbling up the distance to the forest.

Then the bottom dropped out of my stomach like an express elevator.

There was no impact, no scream, no mangled wreck of trees, beasts, and fae like a multi-car pileup on the highway.

I cracked one eye and found the world falling away beneath me.

My gaala continued to run, all six legs pumping like pistons in an engine, but they connected with nothing but air. Far below, the snow of the clearing twinkled, then disappeared under a carpet of trees that stretched in every direction. We strode on currents of wind just beneath a ceiling of clouds.

Kai was on my right, a wide smile on his face. He rocked with the motion of his gaala with the ease of relaxing on a porch swing.

I glared. He could have warned me.

Far beyond Kai, the peaks of a distant mountain range reached up to scrape the bellies of low-hanging clouds streaked orange and red by the setting sun. The range looped around the edge of the forest to form glittering, white peaks in front of us, then tapered down to dark, rolling hills on either side.

Twisting just enough to look behind me, I spotted Hortense and our other two escorts striding through the twilight sky like it was the most natural thing in the world. Hortense caught my eye and lifted her palm in the "straighten up" gesture she used when I was slouching in my seat.

I pulled in a deep breath that made my lungs ache with cold, and blew it out in an even stream. Then I rolled my hips forward and straightened my back, careful to keep my grip on the wild mane. Puffs of warm air that smelled of fresh mulch billowed from the gaala's flared nostrils like the smoke of an old steam engine. The six undulating legs rocked me like waves under a boat, but if I relaxed into the motion rather than trying to fight it, keeping my balance was relatively easy. I rolled my neck, forcing my shoulders down from where they'd bunched around my ears. The tips of my nose and ears stung, and the wind made my eyes water, but I couldn't help smiling.

I was flying!

I laughed, resisting the urge to throw my arms wide like Rose on the rails of the Titanic, but the sound was stolen by the wind whipping past. My clothes billowed and snapped, sails left loose in a storm, and my hair snarled around itself in a crazed frenzy that would probably take days to unknot . . . or a pair of scissors.

Clamping my knees tight and ensuring my right hand was twisted securely into the gaala's mane, I relaxed my left hand and leaned back until I was sitting straight and tall. Then I stretched my free hand up to trail in the underbelly of a low-hanging cloud. My fingertips collected rain that hadn't yet had a chance to fall and freeze.

At the far edge of the horizon, the sun hunkered below the gray dome of clouds that blocked out the unfamiliar stars and the two moons Kai had told me graced Enchantment's sky. Streaks of red and gold poured between the distant peaks, casting burning shadows over the forest like a wildfire. Then the sun bled away, and night licked up the remnants of its light.

I blinked and squinted. My companions had become silhouettes against a dark sky, barely discernible even with my better-than-human vision. Chances were the rest of our flying caravan could still see just fine, so I tried to relax, but the sensation of traveling through a void set my nerves on edge. Somehow, being unable to see the distant ground made it seem farther away, more of a threat. Seeing the trees wouldn't stop my body being dashed apart if I fell, but their absence was . . . unsettling.

Far ahead, near where the sun had disappeared, a light still burned— a beacon in the night. I locked my eyes on that light like a drowning man heading for a boat on the horizon and leaned forward to share the warmth radiating off my gaala's back. It was like snuggling up to a furnace.

The light we rode toward split, then split again, dividing as we got closer until a city of sparkling lanterns twinkled in the darkness. The yellowish glow illuminated the top of a white cliff, and the tightly-packed buildings that covered it. The cliff face was split in two by a river that poured over its edge in a sparkling ribbon and plunged into the darkness below. I couldn't see the splash at the bottom, but I could hear the roar even over the rushing wind.

As we crossed the boundary of the city proper, I took in as many details as I could in the dim blur below, swinging my head like a pendulum from one lantern-lit facade to the next. Every building I passed was large and intricate. Thin strands of flowing stone twisted together to form columns that stretched into canopies of woven support and draped balconies like marble spiderwebs gluing them to the walls. Everything had an organic quality, like the buildings had simply grown from the mountain itself.

A few fae scampered below, there and gone before I could get a good look. As we neared the center of the city, the lights became more frequent, closer together. So did the people. The scattering of fae I'd seen in the side streets became a densely packed crowd as we passed into the solid glow of hundreds of multi-colored lanterns strung along store fronts and draped on sagging strings from upper stories. The lights reflected off polished white stone to create a tie-dyed disco splashed across the streets below.

Wooden stalls lined the plazas and streets, set on the porches and steps of more permanent buildings. A din of voices rose into the air, too faint or too numerous to make out. A whiff of hot grease and spices drifted on the wind and I spotted several open fires lined with skewers of sizzling meat. Farther along, a massive man with dark green skin and a brown leather tunic ducked under the hanging lights. He stood at least fifteen feet tall. Smaller fae swirled around his leather-clad legs like eddies in a river as he made his way through the night market.

Within the space of a few breaths, the market was behind us. The colored lights became simple lanterns again, few and far between. I blinked in the darkness, wishing I'd had the chance to walk the streets rather than glide above them. But the white walls of the keep were looming before us, and all thought of sightseeing fled as my muscles grew tight in anticipation.

My gaala followed Rhoana's over the outer wall of the keep. We gained some altitude, then banked into a tight spiral toward a well-lit courtyard at the top of one of several towers. I braced for the impact of connecting with a solid surface, but the gaala's hooves brushed the frosted marble with the same weightlessness it displayed when walking over the snowy field without so much as cracking the surface.

Kai swung off his gaala and stepped up beside mine to grab the dangling reins. "I said hold the reins loosely, not drop them."

Sliding gracelessly down the side of my gaala, I turned and

slugged Kai in the shoulder. "You should have warned me."

Kai rubbed his arm. "And ruin the surprise?" He grinned. "What did you think?"

I patted my gaala's neck, smiling, and traced my palm over the velvety fur of its nose. Its sides heaved, and clouds of hot breath formed around its head. "It was amazing."

The courtyard we'd landed in was ringed by arches, the columns between them each holding a glass lantern that revealed smoky gray streaks of impurity in the stone. For a moment, my imagination replaced the warm yellow glow with watery blue, and I thought I saw faces peering from the deep shadows of those arches.

I shuddered and rubbed my arms until the memory faded and the arches were just arches, not portals of darkness to hide the monsters waiting to eat me.

One of the guards who'd accompanied us from the clearing took my gaala's reins from Kai and led the beast toward the far end of the courtyard, where a trough of water and a basket of what looked like dandelions waited. I gave the gaala one last parting pat. "Enjoy your meal. You earned it."

Rhoana said something to the remaining guard, who led her mount away with his own, then she came to stand with Kai and me. "The Lord of Enchantment is currently in session and will not be free until morning. He has instructed I take you straight to your room and see that you are settled. He will meet with you tomorrow, before the festival commences."

Hortense stepped up near my elbow. "This is where I take my leave. I shall collect you for your audience with the lord tomorrow. See that you are well rested and properly attired. And . . . try to stay out of trouble until then."

Swishing the heavy blue cloak that draped her shoulders and trailed the ground, she sauntered through the largest arch and rounded a corner.

"G'night then," I called, strangely bereft. Hortense and I weren't friends, but she'd been teaching me for nearly a month. She was familiar; even her scowls and sniffs had a level of comfort to them, and I could use all the comfort I could get in this strange place.

Two small fae shuffled out of the shadows. Each had white hair, a wrinkled face, and long, drooping ears. Hobs. One took the reins of Kai's gaala, the other headed toward the gaala bearing my luggage.

I moved to retrieve my bag so the gaala could be led away with the others, but Kai gripped my wrist.

"You're a Lady of the Court now. Let the servant get it."

"Seriously?" I whispered, gesturing to the little hob struggling with my case. "He can barely reach it."

"He'll manage."

I gritted my teeth, but didn't comment further. This was another formality I'd been warned about. My one consolation was that the situation had nothing to do with gender, it was all about rank. A female servant would have to carry the bag of a big, burly man if that man happened to be a member of the court. The rule still made me queasy. In fact, the pretentiousness of this whole society made me want to hit something.

I took a deep breath, counted to three, and exhaled slowly. One party. Just a few days. I could do this.

Rhoana stood to one side, back straight, hand draped loosely over the hilt of her sword. I'd thought Hortense was unusually uptight, but I was starting to reconsider. Perhaps Kai was the odd man out with his easy smile and nearly mortal sense of humor.

Once my bag was detached and the last gaala led to its meal, Rhoana spun and started walking toward the arch Hortense had vanished through. The hob who'd unloaded my suitcase tipped the bag onto its little rubber wheels and trundled after Rhoana, my sword gripped in his hand. I glanced at Kai, who offered a strained smile and gestured for me to follow.

The lantern-lined arch Rhoana led us to opened onto a large balcony. Smaller lamps dotted a guardrail that circled the edge of the open space, marking where the floor dropped away.

Kai stepped up to the rail and spread his arms wide. "Welcome to the great city of Abonaille Malmür, Court of the Iron Throne."

Chapter 9

THE ROADS WE'D flown over on the way here were ribbons of light winding through the night like iridescent veins. The market cast a shining dome over a four-block area—a pulsing heart at the center of the city. The reach of those lights cut off abruptly at the castle wall.

On the near side, a sea of night stretched below me, punctuated by a few scattered lanterns like stars cast down from the cloud-covered sky. The shadows between those lights seemed darker, denser than they should have been. Like they were hiding something.

I rubbed my arms, suddenly wishing I had a wall at my back. This balcony was clearly designed to offer visitors a grand overlook of the city, but all I saw was an alien darkness into which I was about to descend.

"It's . . . um . . ."

"It will be more impressive in the daylight." Kai let his arms fall.

Rhoana was waiting at the top of a set of stairs that wrapped the face of the cliff the balcony capped. The steps were carved of the same smooth stone as the floor and walls.

"Was this castle carved right out of the mountain?"

"As was the city," Rhoana said, and started down.

The stairs led to a second balcony, one with an intricately sculpted fountain at its center. Water poured over five tiers of carved basins before trickling into a pool set flush with the floor. I stepped to the edge to admire the graceful curves of the marble, the arcs of the water as it dropped from different heights to create a symphony of harmonious splashes. The skill required to carve something so detailed would take a lifetime to master . . . for a human.

Magic broke all the rules.

"This way." Rhoana moved toward a door on my left and I trotted to catch up, my footsteps resounding like hammer falls against the marble.

I slipped through the door and found myself in what appeared to be a guard station. There were two wooden tables with benches. One held a smattering of food on wood trays—rolls, fruit, cured meat. Two guards in livery were seated at the second table. They seemed to be playing a game with thin, stone tiles.

The guard facing us, a purple-skinned sidhe, snapped to attention, dropping his tiles on the table so he could press a fist to his chest. The second fae was slower and a little less crisp, but then, he had a lot more mass to move. The troll guard made the bouncer at Crossroads look like a child's toy. When he straightened, his head brushed the twelve-foot ceiling.

Rhoana nodded. "As you were."

She headed straight for the door on the far side of the room. Both guards watched me as I passed, following only with their eyes as they settled back to their game.

Beyond the guard room, Rhoana led us down a short corridor, down three flights of stairs, along another, longer corridor, and finally through a hall so narrow my shoulders brushed both sides. I stumbled out of the claustrophobic passage into a hall that was wide enough to drive a car through. The *clack, clack* of my footsteps suddenly muffled.

I looked down. My boots rested on thick, red carpet.

Rhoana turned to the right and stopped in front of a light-colored door with carvings of roses covering its surface. "These are your rooms."

I reached for the equally ornate, carved wooden handle, but she raised one hand to stop me. Fingers coiled around the hilt of her sword, she opened the door herself, stepped inside, and scanned the room. Nodding, she beckoned me to enter, then headed toward the open doorway of a connecting room.

I stepped into what looked like a Victorian sitting room. Plush lavender carpet covered every inch of the marble floor and beautifully woven tapestries draped the walls. A couch and matching chairs were arranged in a loose circle in the center of the room, each carved from dark wood with royal purple cushions. Between them was a round table carved from the same dark wood. It was polished to a mirror finish and its feet were carved to look like scaled and taloned toes gripping the carpet.

Kai and I followed Rhoana through the second door, which led to a bedroom. The little hob who'd been lugging my suitcase through the castle set my bag beside an oversized, four-poster bed, bowed deeply, then scurried out. The purple theme continued, with a deep violet bedspread and gossamer lavender drapes tied at each post. Similar curtains fluttered in front of twin patches of night framed by tall arches on the far wall.

"Somebody really likes purple," I muttered as I moved toward the arches.

Pulling back one of the curtains, I found a small semicircle of marble jutting off the side of my room. Unlike the balcony near the landing courtyard, there were no lights lining the guardrail. The world was awash in darkness beyond the dim glow of a lamp set to one side of my bed.

"I'd advise you not to use the balcony when you are alone." Rhoana was peeking into corners, checking behind doors. I pictured her as a cop in a TV show moving from room to room, shouting, "clear."

"You really think someone would attack me *here*?" I spread my arms to indicate the room around us. "In my grandpa's palace?"

"Only if you are foolish enough to give them the opportunity," she replied.

A soft knock sounded at the door, and Rhoana went to answer it.

I turned to Kai. "Not much for small talk, is she?"

"She's on duty." Kai pitched his voice lower. "But no, she isn't."

"You were awfully quiet on the way here, too."

He shrugged. "We're not in your world anymore, Alex. The rules are different here. For you . . . and for me." His expression tightened, deepening the creases around his eyes and mouth. "It's imperative you remember that."

"Hard to forget when everything about this place screams, 'You're not in Kansas anymore.'"

He raised an eyebrow. "Don't you mean Colorado?"

"Seriously? You've never seen *The Wizard of Oz*?"

"Isn't that what you call your werewolf friend?"

Laughing, I shook my head.

My laughter did not, however, seem to relax Kai in the least. "Just . . . tread lightly, Alex. Try not to be—"

"Myself?"

He pressed his lips together, though whether he was fighting a smile or a frown, I couldn't tell.

Rhoana poked her head through the doorway and beckoned us back to the sitting room. "Your dinner is served."

A woman who couldn't have been more than three feet tall bustled around the table in the center of the main room, arranging a tray stacked high with fruits, cheeses, and steaming rolls. My mouth began to water.

The woman set out a single wooden plate with matching utensils and a blown glass goblet. A carafe sat to one side of the food, filled with purple liquid that smelled of alcohol. She wore a loose dress the same green color as the guards' clothes, with a thick leather apron that seemed to consist of hundreds of pockets tied around her waist. A green fabric cap covered her head, and turfs of straw-colored hair stuck out around the edges where they'd escaped from the braid that trailed down her back.

I glanced at Rhoana's still perfectly styled hair, and reached a hand up to my own snarled locks. Spending time on my hair was rarely a priority for me, but I was starting to appreciate the practicality of a good braid.

The little woman straightened the last fork, then stepped away from the table. She clasped her hands loosely in front of her apron and kept her eyes on the floor.

I looked at the place setting and cleared my throat. How was a lady supposed to talk to a servant again? I lifted my chin and tried to channel my inner Hortense. "We'll need more place settings."

Her eyes shifted up to meet mine, and I adjusted "woman" to "girl" before I remembered that a fae's age couldn't be judged by her appearance. The girl's deep, brown eyes were set wide apart and seemed to fill half her face, crowding out a button nose and small, pouty lips. Her gaze darted from me to Rhoana and back again.

"This meal is for you alone," Rhoana said. "I have other duties I must attend to, and Malakai will return to the barracks as befits a knight."

I frowned. "Surely he can share a meal with me first."

Rhoana opened her mouth, but Kai held up a hand to forestall her. "That would be inappropriate, Alex."

Rhoana opened the door to the hallway. "Do not leave these rooms without an escort. There are plenty at court who would use your ... unique position ... to further their own agendas."

The girl who'd set out my dinner bobbed a deep curtsy to get my attention and pointed to a small brass bell with a wooden handle. "If you should need anything, simply ring and I shall come." She performed another curtsy, then shuffled past where Rhoana was waiting in the hall with her arms crossed.

I turned to Kai. "This is stupid."

"This is etiquette. It's what Hortense and I have been preparing you for." He gripped my shoulder. "Eat your dinner, take a bath, and get some sleep. I'll see you tomorrow."

The warmth of his hand lingered on my shoulder until the door clicked shut behind him. Then even the smell of fresh-baked bread couldn't hold back the lonesome chill that filled the room.

Retreating to the bedroom, I pulled out my cell phone and sat at the edge of the bed. The screen lit, but the words "no service" were displayed across the top. I hadn't really expected to be able to call between realms, but the isolation was still a heavy weight that settled over me and made my shoulders slump. I wanted to ask James if he'd felt the moment our connection was severed as I crossed into Enchantment. I wanted to find out if Sol had succeeded in getting the werewolves out of PTF custody.

I turned the phone over in my hands, then opened one of the smaller pockets on my suitcase and shoved the useless device out of sight.

As I was pulling my hand back, my fingers brushed against cold metal. Grabbing the silver chain, I dangled my locket at eye level. The stylized *A* reflected the light of the lamps as it spun slowly one way, then the other. I couldn't reach James, or Marc, or Sol. I couldn't even count on Kai's company. I was alone in a strange place . . . again.

I unlatched the clasp and draped the locket around my neck. Its weight settled against my collar bone, and I felt a little less adrift. I took a deep breath. I'd get through the festival, learn what I could about imbuing from Gramps, then hightail it home so I could get my life in order.

HAZY LIGHT FILTERED through the lavender curtains that blocked the balcony, tinting the walls and ceiling. I twitched the curtains aside, conscious of Rhoana's warning not to stand exposed on the balcony, but curious about the view. My room was low enough that I couldn't see more than a few spires of the city beyond the wall. Between that wall and the castle proper, where I'd found only darkness the night before, walls of living greenery alternated with dark spaces to create a giant garden maze that grew to nearly the height of the surrounding wall.

The maze ended abruptly at a green field several stories below me, which in turn cut off at the sheer cliffs against which the keep nestled. Off to the right of my balcony was a thin line cut into the face of the cliff—a path perhaps? A hundred feet or so above that line, snow coated the mountain.

I looked back at the lush greenery of the garden maze and burrowed deeper into the plush, purple robe I'd found hanging from one of the marble hooks carved into the bathroom wall. The meadow Kai and I arrived in had been covered in snow, and we'd gained elevation to reach this mountain fortress. Judging by the white peaks above, the garden—the whole city—should have been under ice. Yet there I was, in a room with an open-air balcony that somehow managed to be comfortably warm in the dead of winter. The whole city must have been wrapped in an amazingly strong temperature-control spell.

I rubbed my arms, trying to shake the feeling of being coated with magic.

Turning away from the disturbing juxtaposition of tropical plants and arctic cliffs, I headed for the room's closet, which could have doubled as a tailor shop. Hundreds of dresses dangled on wooden hangers hooked to marble bars. They all appeared to be my size, but that was the only similarity between them. Trailing my fingertips along the skirts, I tried to guess the types of fabrics, but I didn't find any cotton or polyester. None were as soft as my borrowed bathrobe.

What would be appropriate for meeting my grandfather, the Lord of Enchantment, for the first time?

I lifted a train of green fabric that shimmered yellow when it moved. It seemed to be made of millions of tiny scales. The dress had long sleeves, no back, a cut-out section that would stretch from my bra to my belly button, and was basically a tube from the hips down. I doubted anyone could move faster than a penguin waddle in such an outfit.

I let the dress fall back into place and glanced longingly at my suitcase, which sat at the end of the unmade bed. My spare jeans and a selection of shirts taunted me from the open case.

Sighing, I glanced once more at the rainbow of fabric surrounding me. I could suck it up and pretend to be a lady for a couple of days.

Toward the back of the closet I found an ankle-length green dress with long sleeves. The fabric was soft, warm, and smelled like cloves.

Pulling my selection off its hanger, I slipped the dress on in place of my comfy bathrobe and stepped to attention in front of the full-length mirror in the bedroom. The dress was simple compared to its closet companions, accented only by a subtle pattern in shades of deeper green. Other than ties that cinched the fabric at my waist, the dress hung loose. My hair—which had taken half a bottle of conditioner and an hour under a comb to untangle—draped my shoulders. Judging by the artistic braids I'd seen on everyone from guards to servants the night before, the simple ponytail that was my usual style was unlikely to impress.

I glanced at the rows of shoes under the dresses and wiggled my toes, thinking of Chase in my borrowed sneakers. Then I considered my boots, discarded next to the pile of yesterday's clothes beside my suitcase, and sighed. Court ladies did *not* wear hiking boots.

I studied the woman in the mirror, trying to convince myself it was still me. Was it my imagination, or were her cheekbones a little more pronounced? The tips of her ears a little sharper?

Shaking my head, I returned to my suitcase and lifted the sheathed knife off my rejected clothes. The solid weight made me feel a little better as I strapped it to my thigh. It would be impossible to retrieve without flashing half the room, but I breathed a little easier once it was in place. Lastly, I replaced the silver locket I'd taken off for my bath. The pendant settled against my sternum, and I rested my fingers over it, taking comfort in the solid reminder of my human origins.

I'd been curious about the fae realms, curious about this unknown branch of my family tree, but the more time I spent in Enchantment, the more I missed my simple house on the mountainside.

The corners of my lips twitched. I'd moved enough as a kid to wonder if I'd ever have a place I could miss. Was this ache in my chest homesickness . . . or just a natural reaction to being somewhere so entirely alien?

A knock broke into my contemplations.

I passed through the main room and the aromas of yeast and jam drifted to me, making my mouth water. My stomach growled. The tray from last night had been replaced. The new offering looked almost identical to the first, except the grape stems and cheese crumbs I'd left on my plate had been cleared away and a new place setting, gleaming and empty, was in its place.

Had a servant come in while I slept? Or while I was taking my bath? Either way, the thought sent shivers down my spine. The door to my apartment didn't have a lock. No deadbolts or chains. Not even a "do not disturb" sign. I'd been up half the night jumping at shadows until I slipped the Ruger under my pillow.

Hortense's glamourless appearance was like a splash of cold water when I opened my door. As uncomfortable as the unnatural climate and ridiculous wardrobe had made me, the visual reminder that I was surrounded by fae was a solid one-two punch. Even Hortense's relative familiarity didn't lessen my sense of disconnect. It didn't help that she was wearing a different face than the one I'd gotten used to.

"Good day, Lady Blackwood. You've been summoned to the presence of the lord."

I stiffened at the formality of her speech. "What happened to Alex?"

"We are at court." She scanned me up and down and pursed her lips.

Frowning, I looked down at the dress I'd chosen. "You don't like it?"

"It is . . . tolerable. In any case, you don't have time to change." She stepped back from the doorway. "Come along."

I clenched my jaw, wishing I'd stuck with my jeans. If I was going to be a disappointment anyway, at least I could have been comfortable.

Hortense led me down the red-carpeted hallway to a set of wide stone stairs that spiraled down several stories, each with landings opening onto similar hallways. Eventually, the stairs led to a large room with a matching staircase snaking up the far wall. Arches of thin marble strands spun together like yarn supported the stairs and allowed access to rooms that opened off either side of the main space. Through those arches, I caught glimpses of vaulted ceilings, fine furniture, and bustling fae in green and leather livery.

Thick, forest green carpet muted my footfalls and dampened the voices trickling from the adjoining rooms. As I hustled after Hortense, my slippered foot came down on something small and white. I crouched to pluck a crushed flower off the floor, then brushed my fingers over what I'd assumed was carpet. The carpet was *alive*—soft moss growing over the keep's stone floor, dotted with tiny white flowers.

Hortense passed beneath a narrow arch under the staircase we'd descended, and I jumped to my feet. If I lost sight of her, I'd never hear the end of it. I jogged along the mossy path, cringing each time my foot came down on one of the little flowers, but there were too many to avoid. At least, for someone like me. I reached the arch and looked back the way I'd come. A trail of compressed moss and bent petals clearly marked my passage. Mine were the only footprints visible.

I pressed my lips tight, feeling more and more out of place, and ducked after Hortense.

She was waiting in front of a wide, white door with a golden handle. The Lord of Enchantment's coat of arms—a sword and hammer crossed over a flame—was carved in the pale wood.

When I stepped up, she brushed a hand over my shoulders, smoothed my hair, and tugged the seams of my dress straight like a mother prepping her kid for a family photo. "Remember what Malakai and I taught you. Think before you speak. And above all," she caught my gaze and narrowed her eyes, "keep your temper."

My hands started to shake and I flattened them against my thighs to keep them steady. The Lord of Enchantment was a big deal; intimidating; one of the strongest fae alive. But that wasn't why I was afraid. I was about to meet my grandpa, however many generations removed. For the first time in years . . . I had a living relative.

I took a deep breath and pushed the door open.

At the far end of the room—which was about the length of a football field—Kai stood to one side of a raised dais. He wore dark green boots, tan pants, and a loose green shirt covered with a leather vest and pinched at the wrists by leather bracers. His katana hung at his hip, and a knife sheath was belted to one thigh.

On the other side of the dais, Rhoana stood with her chin up and her hands clasped behind her back. Her outfit matched Kai's except for the dark green cape trailing from silver pins at her shoulders.

Between them, sitting on a throne, was the man I'd come to see.

Chapter 10

I SWALLOWED. THE sound was deafening.

Hortense gave me a little nudge between the shoulder blades.

The mossy carpet ended at the door, turning the floor into a lake of polished marble. My footsteps echoed, marking off each step like a gunshot, as I crossed the open space between me and the man waiting on his throne.

As I passed through the center of the room, I craned my neck to watch blue fae the size of my splayed hand buzzing around on hummingbird wings high above me. They were setting candles into the hundreds of holders in a massive chandelier overhead. Similar, though smaller, fixtures hung in the corners of the room. None of the candles were lit.

Two stories up, a gallery ran around three-quarters of the room, jutting out from the walls and suspended by columns that dropped from the vaulted ceiling like the cords of a suspension bridge. Trailing from the lower edge were rows of icicles, each as long as my forearm. Interspersed with the icicles were dangling glass lanterns that glowed with purplish light. The cold illumination made my skin crawl, reminding me of the watery torches lining Merak's throne room in the vampire nest.

By the time I crossed the vast space, my mouth was a desert. All the missing moisture seemed to be seeping from my sweaty palms. I stopped ten paces from the dais, as Hortense had taught me was proper, and bowed until my back was parallel to the floor. My reflection stared back from the polished marble with wide eyes.

"My lord," Hortense dropped to a knee beside me, curling until her forehead nearly touched the floor. "Lady Alyssandra Blackwood, as requested."

"Rise, both of you." The lord's voice was a high tenor.

I straightened and forced myself to focus on the man draped on the throne in front of me. He wasn't what I expected.

His body matched his voice—thin, smooth, and young. I'd been calling him Gramps since I learned of his existence, but I couldn't reconcile that title with the boy before me. He appeared to be in his early twenties, maybe even late teens. One leather-clad leg crossed the other, his foot bobbing from the ankle. He wore a shirt of deep burgundy that shimmered red and purple when he leaned forward, light rippling over the surface like a cold fire.

While I assessed him, he assessed me. Lips pursed, he scanned me up and down. When his gaze reached my face, I leaned onto the balls of my feet as though drawn in by the swirling embers of black and gold that sparkled in his blazing red eyes.

Swallowing, I shifted my weight back on my heels and let my vision refocus to take in his whole face. He could have been Kai's younger brother by the shape of his features. Long, purplish-black hair crowned his head, twisted and braided with golden beads that jingled like bells when he moved.

He set both feet on the floor and leaned over his knees, hands dangling between his thighs. "You're not quite what I expected."

I shifted my gaze to Kai and back. "Neither are you."

His thin lips turned up at the corners.

"Come." He stood and stepped to the side of his throne, lifting a hand, offering the seat to me. "Sit."

I looked to Kai, Hortense, even Rhoana, but all their faces were cast down. The only eyes I connected with were the fiery ones staring right at me. I wiped my palm on the soft fabric of my borrowed dress, and moved forward until I was within reach of the throne. It was large and black, made of sharp edges and hard surfaces. There were no cushions to soften the seat.

Was this some sort of etiquette test? No one had mentioned what to do if the lord offered me his chair—his *throne*.

I glanced back at Hortense, but she was studying her slippered feet.

Biting my lower lip, I sat in the throne. The metal was cold. It leached heat from my thighs and back like a thirsty man who'd just found an oasis. Shivering, I wrapped my hands around the armrests and tried to pretend I didn't feel like my life was being sucked away.

A loud clap snapped my attention back to the man at my side. His smile was wide, showing straight, white teeth. The echo of the clap faded.

"Excellent," he said. "Follow me." He strode off the dais and headed toward a red door set in the back wall.

I practically jumped out of the throne to join him. Side-by-side, he was an inch shorter than I was, but I had to trot to keep up with his quick pace.

Kai and the others remained where they were. They never even looked up.

I waved one hand back toward the throne as I walked. "What was that about?"

"Just a little test. I had to be sure after all."

We stopped in front of the red door. Carved flames covered its surface.

"Sure of what?"

He glanced back at the throne, but I got the impression he was staring at something in the distance. "That you belong."

Belong, huh? I wrapped my arms around my middle. I didn't feel like I belonged there. But then, I didn't seem to belong in the mortal realm anymore either. Was there anywhere I belonged?

"Come," he said again.

The Lord of Enchantment held the door for me like a polite prom date. It was hard to believe someone who looked like he should be worrying about acne and how to talk to girls was actually the ruler of one of the largest fae courts.

Beyond the door was a workshop. Huge windows lined one wall, filling the space with natural light and offering a view of steep cliffs and clear sky. The bare marble floor was scuffed and dusty. Wooden tables dotted the room, and tools were strewn over their surfaces. Hammers, saws, files. It was bigger than my studio, and not nearly so well organized, but my tense muscles eased a little. The space was different, but somehow familiar, and I clung to the comfort that familiarity offered.

One wall was lined with shelves piled high with partially finished projects, much like the cabinet I had at home for in-progress pieces. Nestled amongst them, I spotted a familiar object. Half-buried beneath a chunk of carved wood and a piece of black cloth was an engraved silver box... the same box I'd helped Kai retrieve from the mortal realm... the box that held a magic-devouring artifact used to destroy an entire world.

The door closed behind me, and I jumped at the sound, running my hands over goosebump arms.

"This place is warded," the lord said. "We can speak freely here."

I bit my lip, glancing once more at the innocuous looking weapon of mass destruction tucked away on his shelf.

He moved to the middle of the room and spread his arms wide. "This is where I do most of my imbuing. What do you think?"

I moved among the tables, trailing my fingers along the edges and inspecting dozens of partially completed projects. I smiled. "It reminds me of home."

He nodded. "That's good. I want you to be comfortable here since this is where we'll be conducting your imbuing training. I had hoped to test your abilities *before* the festival, but . . . well, you've cut your arrival rather close."

The lord had wanted me to visit nearly as soon as I found out he existed. It had been Kai who convinced him I needed time to adjust to finding out I was part fae. In truth, I needed more time than I'd gotten.

"I appreciate you taking the time to instruct me personally . . . my lord." The title stuck in my throat, a foreign shape as uncomfortable as the concept.

He wrinkled his nose and waved a hand. "When we are alone, you may call me Bael."

I nodded. "And please, call me Alex."

"Yes, both Malakai and Hortense mentioned that." He leaned back against a table and crossed his arms. "Tell me, how did you find their tutelage?"

"Fine." I shrugged. "Hortense was pretty intense at first, but we sorted it out."

"Malakai seems quite taken with you."

I matched his posture, leaning against another table. Ten feet of open space separated us. "We went through a lot together."

"So I've heard." He arched one dark eyebrow. "I trust he remained professional?"

The words jolted me back to Sol crashing Christmas dinner, and the way Kai seemed to sulk when I said there was nothing between us. "Of course. We're just friends."

He nodded. "Good. Your status here is . . . complicated."

"Kai mentioned there were people here who might try to hurt me."

He waved the comment away. "You are a means. I am their target. But the fact that you are of mixed blood has raised some concern among my retainers."

I scowled. Means or target, if someone decided to kill me I wouldn't be any less dead.

"I understand the . . . purists, I believe you call them . . . are gaining strength in your world. Well, there is a similar faction here. Fae who believe anyone with mortal blood has no place in our courts. They wish to restrict those without a pure lineage, much like your human laws deny fae from holding positions of power or influence."

I curled my fingers around the edge of the table I was leaning against. *Your* human laws. So much for belonging. And it seemed like the fae were about as friendly toward halfers as humans were.

"Maybe I should leave," I blurted. "Or at least skip the festival. You can teach me some imbuing, here, out of the way. Then I can go home. That way we can avoid any . . . complications."

He pushed away from the table, straightening his shoulders. "I never retreat." He lifted his chin. "There are many, both in my realm and out, who constantly scheme against me. Your presence changes nothing."

"And if these schemers have a plan for my big court reveal?"

Lines crinkled around the edges of Bael's eyes. The fires swirling inside them seemed to flare. Those were not the eyes of a young man. "Let them try."

I swallowed and looked away. This was a man who'd decimated an entire realm and kept the evidence on his shelf like a souvenir. He was not a man to back down from a threat, but he was gambling my life as much as his own.

"I have something for you." He brushed past me and pulled a polished, black box with silver hinges down from one of the shelves that lined the walls. "Perhaps this will help put your mind at ease."

I clasped my hands behind my back, remembering the last time I touched a box from this man. I didn't need any more tattoos burning away my humanity.

He opened the lid and tipped the box toward me. Inside, a metal necklace crouched against the wood. The surface was polished to a glossy finish, but the metal was dark, like hematite. The thick curve of metal coiled around a deep ruby, then looped in a thinning ribbon to wrap around itself like a snake's tail.

I stepped back, rubbing a thumb over my forearm. "I . . . You've given me enough."

The corners of his mouth rose in the barest of smiles. "You've learned to be suspicious of gifts. That's good. You're starting to think like a fae."

I frowned, not liking that he considered suspicion a praiseworthy trait.

"I understand you were taken off-guard by my previous gift. This is different. It is not imbued, merely an ornament to display your status."

I peeked in the box again. "It's iron."

"It is." He closed the lid and thrust the box toward me. "Wear it tonight."

I wrapped my hands around the smooth, black wood, taking its weight. "You promise it won't do anything weird?"

He smiled. "It will adorn your neck. Nothing more."

"And I'll be able to take it off?"

"Of course."

I shuffled my feet, holding the box against my stomach. "About your other gift. I know it made my fae blood stronger—I can see through fae glamours, read imbued memories, move faster, see better in the dark—but did it do anything else?"

Bael pursed his lips. "It will give you some measure of protection against magic of malicious intent."

I nodded. "It tingles. Sometimes it burns."

He shrugged. "I suppose it could feel that way."

"You don't know?"

"I have no need for such a trinket." He waved the comment away. "The charm is designed to warn you of unseen danger, and counter it when possible."

I recalled the way my arm burned when Merak had me enthralled, the pain helping to clear my mind. And when I'd first met Enzo at Crossroads, he'd grabbed my arm, then released me as though he received a shock. The charm had been reacting to magic, just as I thought.

I crossed my arms over the box with the necklace. "You should have sent an instruction manual. A list of features, at least."

He spread his arms, palms up. "There was no way to know how strong an effect it would have, or what abilities would manifest in you."

I shuddered. He'd had no idea what the charm would do to me, but he'd sent it anyway, booby trapped it to burn itself into my flesh on contact without warning or consent. I set the polished box on the nearest table.

"After the festival, we can talk more about how the charm worked out. I'll even show you how I made it." He clasped his hands and smiled. "I'm eager to see what you can do."

I pressed my lips tight over the first two responses that presented themselves. Part of me was jumping up and down at the opportunity to learn real imbuing. With Bael's help, I'd finally be able to really control my power. No more magic leaking in where it wasn't wanted, ruining my projects, or failing to activate when I needed it most. Learning to use my magic reliably was the first step to getting my life back on track.

On the other hand, the idea of letting more magic into my life made my stomach cramp. I didn't trust Bael, relative or no. He'd used me as a guinea pig. He'd skewed the balance in my blood, stealing some of my mortality. He'd dragged me into a political war I didn't fully understand, without explanation or apology.

"What can you tell me about our family," I blurted.

He frowned.

"When did you . . ." I waved a hand. "How are we related?"

"Your line started in Ireland, at the turn of the seventeenth century." He leaned back against a table and tipped his head to look at the ceiling. "I spent a lot of time in the mortal realm back then, and I met a pretty little thing named Dana. She had bright red hair and skin like cream."

I shook my head. "That was four hundred years ago. How can I still have the same last name?"

He shrugged. "A minor enchantment. Though not one hundred percent effective, members of my line are predisposed to keep the surname Blackwood. It makes tracking you down easier, should the need arise."

I'd always thought it odd my mother fought my father on giving me his last name. The consolation was that he got to saddle me with Alyssandra, handed down from a dead great-aunt. Again I felt the weight of my name, like chains bearing me down.

"Am I the first to have magic?" I asked.

He shook his head. "Most of my early progeny showed at least some talent. Many were burned as witches."

I choked on the spit I was swallowing, pounded my chest, and coughed. "I'm sorry, that must have been—" I snapped my mouth closed, frowning.

His expression hadn't changed. His eyes carried the same wistful reflection when he spoke of his children burning at the stake as when he'd described red-haired Dana.

Four hundred years, I reminded myself. And who knew how long before that. Of course he'd be used to mortals dying. But still... his children? Didn't he care at all? Then again, this was a man who decimated an entire world and pushed the dragons to the brink of extinction.

"You'd best go prepare for the festival." Bael pushed off the table and strolled across the room, pulling open the fire-carved door. "We'll talk more after, when we begin your training."

I GASPED, STRAINING against the laces constricting my ribs.

"Just a little more." The tiny woman who delivered my dinner tray the night before gave another mighty tug and tied off my fabric prison. Then she wiped her forearm over her brow with a sigh like she'd just diffused a bomb.

"Why do I have to wear this one?" I gestured to the closet. "There are plenty of dresses that wouldn't cut off my circulation."

Hortense sniffed and rounded the end of the bed to stand in front of me. Her own dress looked nearly as tight as mine, but she didn't seem to have any trouble breathing. "This dress will best match the lord's attire, marking you as his personal guest."

I snorted. As if there could be any doubt. Everyone at the party was going to know exactly who I was as soon as I walked in, if only because I'd be the only mostly human person there. The purist fae might not have cleared all the halfers out of the courts yet, but according to Hortense, they made sure anyone with less than pure blood knew they weren't welcome.

If only Bael had agreed to let me skip the festival. I would have been happier steering clear of the whole lot of them. Better yet, the whole realm. If only I had some alternative to Bael when it came to learning to use my magic—but the rarity of imbuers made that impossible. Still, it was tempting to run back to the portal, magic lessons or no. Not only was I dreading my debut at the festival, worries about the mess I'd left behind continued to plague me. What if Sol's meddling had been noticed? Would he be arrested? Would Marc's pack make a suicidal run on the testing facility rather than wait for the sure exposure of the full moon? And what about the new vampire in town? Was she really better than Merak? And why had James felt so guilty when he talked about her? Then there was Maggie... I'd put off telling her the truth too long and broken our friendship as a result. Now that I'd finally decided to come clean, being forced to wait was like sitting under a dentist's drill without Novocaine.

"Next layer." The servant, who had introduced herself as Tess when she arrived with my lunch, held up a gauzy piece of maroon cloth. She was a nisse, one of the husvaettir who kept things running smoothly in the keep, so Hortense had no trouble enlisting her to help shoehorn me into my dress.

Sagging in defeat, I lifted my arms so Tess could slip the weightless robe over my shoulders. She had to stand on the edge of the bed to reach. The fabric draped my sides in long folds that hung to the floor but split along the outer seams so my arms could move freely. Straightening the robe, Tess tied ribbons that pulled the trailing fabric back under my arms, then forward at my hips to create a layered waterfall of gossamer cloth, the colors growing deeper where they overlapped.

I looked down and set my jaw. The dress made it look like my lower body was encased in deep, red flames. The fabric swished when I walked, shimmering in a burning ripple.

Kai whistled when I opened the door to the main chamber. He was sprawled on a chaise lounge chair popping grapes into his mouth from the replenished silver tray. He still wore the green and leather livery he'd had on in the throne room. Apparently knights didn't have to dress up for the party.

"You clean up nice," he said, the galactic swirl of his eyes spinning lazily.

I rubbed a hand over the short hairs exposed at the back of my neck. Hortense and Tess had taken nearly two hours pulling my hair into the dozens of tight braids that wove together in an intricate pattern atop my aching scalp. If I were to ride a gaala now, not a hair would be out of place when I landed.

"You don't look too shabby yourself." I smiled. In his uniform, with a sword on his belt and a knife on his thigh, Kai finally looked like the knight he'd claimed to be when he'd bowed to me in jeans and a t-shirt in the alley behind Magpie Books.

Kai rose, tugged his tunic straight, and repeated the bow he'd offered at our first meeting. "You honor me, my lady." The solemn display was shattered when he lifted his laughing eyes and grinned, still doubled over.

"Aren't you forgetting something?" Hortense stepped into the room, carrying the polished black box I'd brought back from my audience with Bael.

I shivered, and reached up to wrap my fingers around the silver locket hanging around my neck. "I'd rather just wear this."

"To do so would be an insult to the lord." Hortense held the box at arm's length and pulled back the lid. The three fae tensed, as though the simple act of exposing the iron had hurt them. I imagined every person at the festival cringing when they met me, when I walked by. Even the sight of me would make them uncomfortable. Was it Bael's intention to alienate me more than my human heritage already did?

"It will help keep you safe," Hortense said.

I gestured to Kai. "That's what he's for."

"Malakai and I will do our best to run interference for you, but we cannot account for every situation."

Kai set his hand on my bare shoulder. His fingers were cold. Or maybe I was too warm. "There's no use fighting it. The lord wishes you to wear his necklace. In the end, he always gets what he wants."

I clenched my fists. Kai's words just made me want to fight harder. Then I took a deep breath and forced my hands to relax. Kai wasn't the enemy. Neither was Bael. There was no point offending one of the few fae who would be on my side tonight.

Teeth locked so tight my jaw ached, I reached behind my neck and unclasped the silver chain. The locket pooled in my palm, and I rubbed my thumb over the etched metal, staring at the tiny, smudged mirror. The Court of Enchantment was no place for my father's memory. He'd probably fought fae like Rhoana during the war. . . . And one of them had killed him.

I swallowed past a lump in my throat and closed my fingers over the locket, fighting a wave of guilt. I was betraying his memory just standing there, in the keep of a fae lord. But then, what did I owe him? He'd abandoned me. Abandoned Mom.

The rationale didn't lessen my guilt any.

Crossing to the bedroom, I tucked the locket in a small pocket on the inside of my suitcase. Tess watched with wide eyes from the corner she'd claimed. I forced a smile to my lips—might as well get in practice for the party—and zipped the case shut.

Hortense was still waiting with the open box extended, like she was another statue carved from the mountain. My arms ached just looking at her.

My palms began to sweat as I approached the box. Despite Bael's assurance that this was just a plain necklace, I couldn't quash the nervous tremor rolling through me.

The metal was cool under my touch, cold even, sucking the heat from my fingertips as the throne had from my legs. The coiling tail of metal had just enough spring to be unwound from its thicker end and parted to slide around my neck. The iron settled on my shoulders, cold and heavy. Then I re-wrapped the clasp, sealing the circle like a noose around my neck. The ruby gleamed just below the hollow of my collarbone, deep as blood, proclaiming my owner as much as any dog tag. It was a beautiful collar, but a collar nonetheless.

Chapter 11

I WAS BACK IN front of the throne room, where the festival would take place, but this time I stood in front of two massive, carved-stone panels that depicted a fae with a shining halo atop a dark throne. Beneath the figure stretched a mountain covered with bowing fae. The juxtaposition made it seem as if the mountain upon which the throne rested was made of people.

I shifted my feet, the soft, satin soles of my slippers squashing the springy moss beneath me. Bael, the shining king depicted on those doors, stood beside me. He'd given me a cursory once over, his eyes pausing briefly on the ruby at my throat, nodded, then turned to face the entrance.

"Head high. Match my pace. Don't stop. When we get to the throne, stand to the right with your hand on the back." The command in his voice was at odds with the fact that I had to look down into his baby-face features, but his bearing left no doubt that he was a force of authority. Power seemed to radiate off his small frame, and I reminded myself that, like their age, a fae's strength could not be judged by appearance.

He lifted one hand, palm down, and I rested my fingers on his forearm as Hortense had shown me. Rhoana flanked us on the left, Kai on the right, honored above his station thanks to his unofficial position as my personal chaperone.

A voice boomed on the far side of the closed doors. Then the din I'd been hearing dropped off. The carving split down the middle, and the doors swung open.

I licked my lips and took as deep a breath as I could with the dress's laces digging into my ribs.

The room seemed even larger than it had when it was empty. The candles in the chandeliers had been lit, but the flames that cast flickering light to the farthest corners of the room were cool and white rather than the warm glow of fire. I shivered. At least they weren't blue.

Hundreds of faces turned in my direction, and only the steady presence under my hand kept me from bolting. I tightened my grip and flicked my gaze to the side.

Bael stood with his back straight, his chin raised. He wore the same dark leather pants and flame-colored shirt as before. Now, however, the shirt was draped by a burgundy vest that created a rippling effect similar to the layers of my dress, and dark, tooled bracers wrapped his arms. Golden clasps pinned a long fall of midnight fabric to his shoulders that billowed like smoke behind him despite the stillness in the room.

Fae of every size and description waited like the figures in a sculpture garden. Some towered like trees, while others hovered like insects. The galleries above were packed as well, and faces leaned over the railings, pressing in from the back. The waiting guests were wrapped in rich fabrics—some thick, some sheer, some barely present. Most wore hues of green or cream, some wore blue or purple. There was not a hint of red in the room until we stepped inside.

The crowd parted at our approach, moving like a choreographed dance, and we swept along the corridor of bodies like fire searing a path through the forest. We stepped onto the dais in unison, and I silently congratulated myself for not tripping on the ludicrously long fabric of my dress.

Bael turned and sat, his arms draping the throne's armrests. I continued past him, taking my position to the side and slightly behind. My hand hovered just above the backrest, shaking. I didn't want to touch the throne again.

Hundreds of eyes bore into me. Waiting.

I settled my hand on the cool iron.

Bael lifted his chin. "Let the Winter Festival begin."

The hush over the room broke like a wave. Sound rushed back to my ears, carrying whispers about half-breeds, and fairness, and speculations of intent. Bael didn't seem to be paying them any mind, so I tried to tune them out as well. I focused on keeping my watery knees straight and breathing deep enough to clear the dizzy anxiousness of being surrounded by so many strangers, any of whom might wish me harm.

The gap Bael and I passed through was gone, filled in with milling bodies. An army of husvaettir—nisse like Tess, as well as hobs and brownies—swerved through the crowds, sagging under trays piled high with fruits, cheeses, pastries, and meats. Fae lifted glasses to their lips, sipping bubbling, bright pink liquid I recognized from my last trip to Crossroads. The phantom taste of blackberries and cream filled my mouth, and I licked my lips. Then I shook my head. Ambrosia and I hadn't gotten along so well the last time I tried it, and I needed to keep a clear head.

Above, what looked like a circus troop in matching purple and green outfits began a series of aerial stunts on gossamer threads that stretched across the room from one gallery to the other. Two of the performers were sidhe, one with dark skin, one with light. There was also a white-furred pooka with large yellow eyes and bat-like ears who danced along the threads as if he didn't realize he was two stories up. A sylph with purple ribbons streaming from each hand wove through the aerial pattern on iridescent wings.

Despite the crowding in the room, the space around the dais remained clear. Other than Kai and Rhoana, who had taken up positions on either side of the raised area, no one stood within ten feet of the throne.

I gripped the metal under my hand. The dais wasn't just a status symbol, a way to elevate the lord. It was a warning—the minimum safe distance. I'd expected to feel isolated among the fae. I hadn't imagined that isolation would be so literal.

Bael lifted one hand off its armrest, curling his fingers in a "come" motion. A lithe, dark-skinned woman detached from the crowd. Vines snaked through her long, yellow hair, punctuated by tiny purple and white flowers. The vines also crept over her shoulders and down her arms and sides, twisting and twining even as I watched. Other than the questing green and occasional bursts of floral color, the woman was naked.

I cut my eyes to Bael, then back to the crowd from which the woman had emerged. No one seemed to give her state of undress any notice. Maybe Chase was right. Maybe I was too much of a prude.

The woman stared ahead with huge, dark eyes until her feet rested on the raised dais. Then she dropped, curling over her knees as if she was trying to protect herself more than show fealty.

My palm was now the same temperature as the metal beneath it. Either the iron had warmed under my hand, or it had stolen as much heat as I had to give. The shiver that prickled my scalp made me suspect the latter.

"Aurelea," Bael said. "How fares the forest?"

Her wide eyes raised. Sweat beaded her forehead. Long, dark ears poked through the fall of her hair like driftwood parting a current, but rather that perking up as they had when she first approached, they now sagged at the tips, wilting like cut flowers.

My stomach clenched. Kai had managed to stand in my studio for over an hour once, to cast an enchantment, but sidhe had one of the strongest resistances to iron of any fae. Hortense, on the other hand, could barely peek inside my studio without feeling sick, and the throne beneath my hand held more cold iron than all my tools put together.

I frowned at Bael's profile. He wanted to make those who approached him uncomfortable. Even the ones he invited.

The woman cleared her throat and braced one shaky hand against the floor. She remained curled over her knee. "Many of your subjects sleep now the cold has set in, but the frost sprites are enjoying themselves."

"Any trouble from the jotun?"

She shook her head. "They have not yet come down from the far north."

Bael pursed his lips, then flicked his hand.

The woman was on her feet and off the dais like a shot. She didn't slow until she hit the wall of bodies that marked safety. Even then, she didn't stop moving.

"Being this close to your throne made her sick." I didn't mean to speak my thoughts, but the woman had looked ready to throw up.

"It happens."

I turned toward him. "Then why force them to speak with you here when you could easily go to them?"

Bael's back stiffened. "I do not bend to accommodate the weak."

My thoughts echoed with words Kai had spoken long ago, back when we first met. *You'll not find many weak or poor among the fae.* Kai had since tried to drill it into me that, for a fae, to show weakness was to invite attack. I'd done my fair share of putting on a brave face through the hardships of life, but the fae took shows of strength to a whole other level.

The next fae to approach stepped onto the dais with four huge furry feet and sat like a cat at the edge of the raised area. He wore no clothes over his gray, spotted fur, but a teal scarf with swirls of yellowish-green draped his neck. His eyes were small, red orbs set deep beneath a prominent brow. Tufts of yellow mane lined the sides of his face and traced down his chest. From the center of his face, a nose like a miniature elephant's trunk drooped over a wide mouth framed by two ivory tusks.

Baku, I thought. A creature said to be made up of leftover animal parts. According to Hortense, the baku ate bad dreams. They also ate hopes and desires, leaving mortals hollow.

The baku sniffed and turned slightly in my direction, like he could smell the dreams that kept me up at night. A black tongue slid along his lower lip. Then his ruby eyes settled back on Bael. He bowed, lowering his head until his tusks brushed the floor. If the throne made him nervous, I couldn't tell. "Festive greetings, Lord Bael."

"Zhang." Bael tipped his chin up. "I'm pleased to see you made the trip. News has reached me of stirrings in the east."

Zhang's eyes flicked to me as he raised his head, but returned to Bael when he spoke. "There have been some disappearances."

Bael's frown stretched thin. "But the wards hold."

Zhang nodded. "She has not broken through."

Bael stroked a hand over his chin, then waved the baku away. "Double the watch, and keep me informed."

Zhang bowed again, keeping his head down until he'd backed all four feet off the dais.

Above, the acrobats invited guests into their gossamer web. Fae with wings darted through threads, sometimes brushing close enough to make the lines thrum. Those without wings stepped off the surrounding balcony, stepping along the thin ropes like tightrope walkers—or like beings who believed they'd live forever.

"Problems?" I asked.

Bael twisted slightly to look at me. "An old one." The corners of his lips lifted. "She gives me trouble from time to time."

He faced front again and raised his hand to the next waiting fae, a pair of light-skinned sidhe. They approached the throne in perfect synchronization, their slippered feet stepping onto the dais at the same moment. The shift in their weight matched so perfectly they looked like two pieces of the same person moving toward me. They dropped into perfect bows, the depth marking them as higher nobles of the court.

Bael smiled. "Lady Circe, Sir Kane."

The nobles straightened. Then turned in unison to look at me. Lady Circe's eyes swirled with green and teal that matched her form-fitting dress. Sir Kane wore a baggy shirt in matching colors and tight, tan pants. His eyes were deep purple with spiraling flecks of red, gold, and black.

"This must be the Lady Alyssandra." Lady Circe beamed, showing her sharp, white teeth.

"I prefer Alex."

Her smile dimmed.

Sir Kane set a hand on his companion's shoulder. "I understand this is your first visit to our realm. Do you find it to your liking?"

Threads of eerie music began to play, and I glanced toward its source. A high, rich voice filtered over the din of the party.

"I haven't seen much besides the keep." I shifted my gaze between Kane, Circe, and Bael's expectant expressions. "Riding the gaala was fun."

The silence stretched between us for a moment, amplified by the noise surrounding the dais. Then Kane stepped sideways. "Lady . . . Alex, may we present our son, Mica."

Circe rested her hand against her son's back. "Perhaps, if you are looking to explore more of Abonaille Malmür, Mica could escort you." Her eyes shifted to Bael. "He grew up in this city after all."

"A generous offer," Bael said before I could form a response. "We shall consider it. For now," he turned to look me squarely in the face, "why don't you let Mica show you around the party?"

I stepped back, finally pulling my hand away from the throne. My arm ached. "But I thought . . ." I scanned the fae who filled the room, dancing, drinking, talking. It was like Crossroads, but multiplied by a few hundred. *Most of the fae at court would like nothing better than to cut your heart out.*

"Malakai will keep watch." Bael glanced to Kai, who bowed. "Go. I'll be greeting guests for hours yet."

Bobbing a small curtsy, I stepped up to Mica. His parents each took a step back, creating a bubble of awkward space around us. Their faces shone with eager approval that made my skin crawl. This was worse than Maggie trying to set me up with Charlie's friends.

Mica bowed, then offered his arm. "My lady." His voice was a quiet baritone.

I set my hand on the slick, blue fabric of his shirt, glanced at Kai to make sure he was following, and stepped off the dais with my escort.

People glanced in our direction as we wove through the crowd. Some smiled, some glared. They all moved away, repulsed like bearings from a magnet by the collar around my neck. Beside me, Mica stood as far from me as our joined arms would allow. Kai kept pace behind us, far enough away to give the illusion of privacy.

Mica kept us moving away from the dais until the crowd filled in enough to hide the faces of his watching parents. We circled to the outer edge of the room, stopping beside a group of fae who swayed with their eyes closed in time to the strange melody played by the band. The singer's voice sent shivers down my spine and filled my head with images and a desire to dance. Definitely a siren.

I took my hand off Mica's arm. He turned to face me.

"You don't have to stand so close if this makes you uncomfortable." I reached up to touch the ruby hanging at my throat.

"It isn't that." He cast a look over his shoulder, back toward the dais.

"They can't see us."

He shook his head, glanced at Kai, then focused on the floor between us.

"If you want to go, go." I crossed my arms. "I won't tell. And neither will Kai."

"An empty assurance," he said. "Knights serve their lords . . . always."

I sighed. Bad enough to be blind-sided by an arranged date, but it seemed Mica was even less happy with my company than I was with his. I turned away from him and took a few steps toward the source of the music. A hand wrapped around my wrist.

"Wait." Mica's eyes were marbled blue and green with tiny silver flecks. "Can we start over?"

I looked at his hand until he released me, then folded my arms over my abdomen. "Kai can be my escort if you don't want to."

Again, his eyes flicked to Kai. "I *do* want to be your escort." He offered me his hand. "Please?"

I set my fingers against his palm and let him pull me forward until we were less than an arm's length apart.

"It isn't the iron." He gave me a sheepish smile, then reached toward my collarbone.

I stiffened, but didn't pull back.

He tapped the necklace, the impact resonating through the heavy metal, then lifted his pointer finger in front of my face. His fingertip was shiny pink, but not burned.

"High tolerance," he said. "They actually thought I might be an imbuer when I was born, but . . ." He shrugged and dropped his hand to his side.

I frowned. Kai had said imbuing only ran in one family. "Are you related to Bael?"

He glanced back in the direction of the dais. "The Lord of Enchantment is my great-uncle."

The knots in my shoulders and stomach relaxed a little. Maybe this wasn't a blind date after all. Then another thought struck me. Kai had said there were three known imbuers—Bael, his niece, and me. I looked back toward the dais as well. "Does that mean your mom is the other imbuer?"

Mica shook his head, frowning. "That's my aunt, Marron. My mother's never gotten over the inequity."

Sighing, Mica dropped my hand and reached into his shirt to pull out a small silver box, like a classic cigarette case. He didn't seem to be paying attention to what he was doing. His eyes focused on nothing as he flipped open the lid. Inside, a layer of shimmering glitter coated the case. Pixie dust.

He licked his seared pointer finger and dragged it through the glitter, then popped it into his mouth. The tension around his eyes eased. His frown relaxed. Then he refocused, and found me staring.

He held the open box out, offering. "Want some?"

The last, and only, time I'd had pixie dust, was the same night I tried ambrosia. Kayla had wiped the glittery substance off her wings in the back room at Magpie, promising it would help me relax. Before I'd had the drink, I hadn't noticed much effect. Still, I shook my head. "I'd better not."

"It's only pixie dust," he said. "Calms the nerves." He pushed the box a little closer. "Something we could both use."

Kai cleared his throat next to my shoulder, making me jump. Mica snapped the lid closed on his drug supply.

"Everything all right?" Kai asked.

"Fine," Mica and I replied in unison.

Kai glanced at the silver box in Mica's hand. "Alex is only part fae. Probably best not to experiment tonight."

Mica tucked his stash back inside his shirt.

"Have you ever . . . ?" I tipped my head toward the silver case as it disappeared into Mica's pocket.

A hint of pink crept into Kai's cheeks. "That's not important."

The music changed, shifting to a livelier beat, and several fae paired off and headed for a space clearing in the middle of the room.

Mica offered me his hand. "Care to dance?"

The nervousness that had been clinging to him was gone. His smile was now relaxed, inviting, and I found myself smiling in response as I set my hand in his. We headed for the center of the room with the other dancers.

Kai stayed where he was at the edge of the crowd, standing at easy attention.

Fae spun and swayed, alone and with partners. Some were practically naked, some wore enough fabric to bury them. Some glided across the polished stone floor, some skipped overhead on fluttering wings. Most of the dancers moved in prearranged steps, and Mica pulled me along to the unknown choreography. I focused on the motion of his body like it was an Aikido exercise, trying to anticipate his moves. Eventually, I found the rhythm and relaxed enough to grow curious about my dance partner.

"Are you and Bael close?"

"He raised me." Mica spun me out and back. My dress flared in rippling flames, a sharp contrast to the cool blues and greens flowing around me. "But once it became clear I wasn't an imbuer..." He shrugged.

I frowned. "What do you mean he raised you? What about your parents?"

"They have an estate on the western edge of the forest."

"So you grew up without them?"

"They visited."

He spun me out again, and I concentrated on not tripping as my thoughts spiraled around the idea of absentee parents. At least his were still alive.

"What about now?" I asked. "Did you move back home once you knew you weren't an imbuer?"

A bitter smile tightened his lips. "Lord Bael prefers to keep me close, disappointment though I am."

I could tell by the strain in his voice and the lines around his eyes that Mica would rather have left Bael's keep. Staying had to be a constant reminder of his inadequacy. No wonder he dulled his senses with pixie dust.

I glanced at the dais as Mica spun me out once more. *Why would Bael hold Mica against his will after it became clear he wasn't an imbuer? What did he have to gain?*

I shook my head. *Why would he brand his granddaughter without consent and build a weapon to decimate a whole world.* The more I learned about Bael, the less I liked him.

"May I?"

Mica stopped short at the request, and I bumped into his chest.

Long pale fingers rested on Mica's shoulder. Above them, I found the pale face of a man in his mid-twenties. His features were sharp, with a straight nose and pointed chin, and his wide-set eyes shone like the crystal waters of the Mediterranean Sea. Furry, red-tipped, triangular ears sprung from a mop of snowy white hair.

Mica stepped back, releasing me, and turned toward the interloper. "Haru? I thought you weren't attending."

Loose white robes with long sleeves and pearl embroidery draped the man's lean frame. His feet were bare. I counted seven fluffy white tails with crimson tips waving like reeds in a breeze behind him.

Kitsune. I thought. *Fox-shifters who grow a new tail every hundred years.*

The last notes of the current dance trailed off, and another, slower tune took its place. Haru stepped in to fill Mica's vacated position. "I changed my mind."

"This dance is taken," I said, backing up.

Haru waved Mica away like he was shooing a fly. "He won't mind sitting this one out."

Mica glanced between us, frowning. "I'll wait by your knight." He bowed, and left the dance floor.

I glared at his retreating back, then transferred my glare to Haru as he took hold of my hands and pulled me back into the swirl of dancers.

Haru leaned in, his lips brushing my cheek as the rhythm of the dance brought our bodies close together. "I believe you know a shifter named Chase."

I stiffened. How would a kitsune from Enchantment know about a shifter spy? "Doesn't ring a bell."

He chuckled. "I envy the mortal ability to lie. Though . . ." He drifted back to a more comfortable distance. "You're not very good at it. Chase and I grew up together," he continued. "I haven't seen him in years. If you do happen to meet him, would you deliver a message for me?"

I bit my lower lip. "If I come across someone matching that description."

His smile grew, stretching his lips so I caught a glimpse of pointed teeth. "Tell him Haru says hello."

"Is that why you wanted to dance with me? To give me your message?"

He gave a noncommittal shrug. "That, and I thought you could use saving from the prince who wasn't."

I glanced to the side. Mica had his little silver box out again and was offering it to Kai, who shook his head. My guardian knight was frowning, but made no move to extricate me from my dance partner. On Kai's other side, Hortense stood with her arms crossed. Her heavily embroidered dress managed to compliment the greenish hue of her skin, and her hair was tied back in a fine net of intricate braids. If not for the deep scowl on her face, she might actually have looked pretty.

Haru turned, blocking my view, and moved us toward the other side of the room.

My heart beat faster with every step and spin that took me farther from my allies. Surely Kai would have intervened if he suspected Haru meant me harm?

"What do you think of Bael's stud?" Haru asked, reeling me in from another spin.

"What?"

"Is he your type? Or are you looking for someone a little more . . ." He slid his hands down to encircle my hips.

I pressed my palms against his chest and shoved.

He spun away, chuckling, and bowed with a flourish. "It was a pleasure meeting you . . . Alex." Then he sauntered off into the crowd.

"Temper, temper," said a melodic voice behind me.

Chapter 12

TIME SEEMED TO slow as I turned.

My gaze fell upon a woman with diamond-white eyes swirling with silver glitter. She was tall and slender, and wore a trailing white dress that barely covered her naughty bits but dragged behind her in a long train. Her hand rested on the arm of a man in a blue suit with gold embroidery that looked like it belonged in a military procession. His chest was crossed with a green sash.

Both fae had the high cheekbones and sharp features of the sidhe, but the man didn't share the pale complexion of his companion. Neither did he have the dark, purplish skin of the sidhe I'd seen in the forest. Rather, he looked a sickly green color.

The man sniffed and tipped his chin up like he'd caught a whiff of something rancid and said in a deep, rich voice, "It seems even the best court tutor couldn't teach the half-breed manners."

The woman smiled, laying one silver-painted, talon-like nail against her cheek. "From what I've heard, half is a bit generous. She's a mongrel, through and through."

I clenched my fists.

The two split apart, circling to either side. I turned my head, trying to keep them both in view. These fae were obviously antagonistic. Would they attack me, thinking me a weak link? I shifted, wishing there wasn't so much fabric between my hand and the knife strapped to my thigh.

I glanced across the dance floor. Kai was moving toward me, Hortense and Mica close behind, but their progress was slowed by dancers and spectators.

"Whatever could the lord have been thinking, bringing her here?" My attention whipped back to the man, who'd circled around to my other side, trading places with his partner.

"Perhaps it was pity," the woman replied. "Rumor has it, even her own parents didn't want her."

"That's not true!" I spun to face the horrible woman, frustration and anger burning in my chest.

A smile curved her lips.

The fae around us had all gone still, their eyes shifting between me, vibrating with rage, and the smiling woman.

"For my honor." Her words were quiet, but passed through the crowd like a plague, drawing more attention to our little tableau.

Kai stepped up beside me, his face ashen. "What happened?"

I shook my head. What *had* happened?

"She insulted my blood," the woman said. "For that, I demand satisfaction."

She held her hand out to one side, and her companion set the hilt of a long, silver sword against her palm.

My stomach dropped. She wanted a duel. I turned to Kai, shaking my head in denial. "I didn't. She's the one throwing insults."

The man gestured to me. "Again she seeks to besmirch us."

Grumbles spread through the crowd.

I opened my mouth, but Kai set his hand on my arm. "Alex, the fae can't lie."

"But—"

"To claim she did is to call the purity of her blood into question."

All the heat and anger I'd felt a moment before boiled off, leaving me cold and hollow. I'd walked right into their trap. Shame ripped through me, followed by a wash of fear. Even after all the hours I'd spent training with Kai, I was still a beginner with a sword—no match for a court fae who'd grown up with a blade in her hand.

Kai tugged my arm, pulling me back so he could step between me and the diamond-eyed fae. He straightened his shoulders. "I claim the right of substitution."

The woman's eyes narrowed. "By what right do you make such a claim?"

"I was tasked with Lady Alyssandra's education. Her slight is a result of my failing." He set his palm against the hilt of his own sword. "Therefore, I will meet the challenge."

A space was beginning to clear around us as the nearest fae pushed back against those straining to see.

I looked around. No one was dancing now. The music had stopped.

The man in the blue suit gestured to Hortense. "The tutor was sent to oversee the girl's instruction."

Hortense shook her head. "I was sent in support. Lady Alyssandra was primarily Malakai's responsibility."

"Why have the festivities stopped?" Bael's voice boomed through the room, echoing off the walls. All the fae turned to face the dais, pulling back to create a path between my little group and the iron throne. Bael lifted one hand. "Come here."

Kai and Hortense led the way. Mica walked beside me—a show of support for which I was grateful—until his mother grabbed his arm and pulled him back in line with the other spectators. The fae conspirators brought up the rear.

"What is this about?" Bael asked when we were arranged in a line in front of him. None of us had stepped up onto the dais.

The woman who'd called for the duel tossed her head so the long fall of her golden hair rippled down her back. She pointed at me. "Your charge has slandered the purity of my blood. I demand restitution."

"And I have claimed Alex's place in the duel by right of substitution."

Bael waved a hand and settled back in his chair, looking more like a bored teenager than a powerful ruler. "Then duel."

The woman bowed. "Due respect, lord, but that will not sate me."

Bael frowned. "You wish to withdraw from your own challenge, Lady Pimm?"

"I merely point out that killing a Knight of the Realm gains me nothing, and deprives the court of a true and loyal fae."

I bunched my fingers into the soft fabric on my thighs. She didn't believe Kai could win. *Kai*, on whom I'd never landed a solid hit in all our hours of practice.

"My issue is with the lady." Pimm's nose wrinkled on the last word. "I shall not accept a substitute."

"As the one responsible for her behavior, it is his right and duty." Bael tapped a finger against his iron armrest. "Duel, or withdraw the challenge."

Responsible for her behavior. I ground my teeth. This whole stupid mess was Bael's fault for dragging me to court in the first place.

I crossed my arms, trying to ignore the little, chiding voice in my head that said I was shifting blame, but it wouldn't go away. I should never have let them goad me into losing my temper. It was *my* fault. *My* responsibility. I couldn't let Kai die for my stupidity.

I took a deep breath and opened my mouth, but strong fingers clamped around my upper arm before any sound came out. Hortense gave a minuscule shake of her head.

"Very well." Pimm folded her arms over the patch of creamy, bare skin where her dress dipped to her navel. "If they wish to substitute the defendant, I change the terms of restitution."

Bael lifted an eyebrow. Kai went stiff beside me.

The cruel smile was back on Pimm's lips. "I demand a sentencing of no less than fifty years."

Mutterings broke out around the room. Bael straightened and swept his glare over the crowd. Silence fell.

"Fifty years is a long time for such a slight," he said.

Pimm shrugged. "I estimate that to be the length of time Lady Alyssandra gains by his intervention. An even exchange."

My heart thundered in my chest. Surely Bael wasn't actually considering imprisoning Kai over something I said? But then, the alternative was a fight to the death. And for the fae, fifty years was hardly anything. I cast a sidelong glance at Kai. Would he rather serve the sentence than fight?

It had been my fault, not his. A knot twisted my stomach. Fifty years was a mortal lifetime.

Bael pursed his lips, then slapped his palm on the arm of the throne. "So be it."

Rhoana raised one hand, and two guards in green and leather livery detached from their stations along the outer wall. The crowd parted to let them through.

Kai stood rock steady, but his face was ashen. My blunder had cost him fifty years.

Shaking off Hortense's hand, I stepped in front of Kai. "The fault was mine. I will serve the sentence."

Another wave of muttering swept through the crowd, louder than before. The distraction gave me time to realize what I'd just done. Fifty years. My whole life. A cell in the faerie Realm of Enchantment. No more David. No more Maggie. No more Sol. My hands started to shake.

No chance to explore what there was between me and James.

The pounding in my ears drowned out the sounds of Bael calling for order.

Would James try to find me when I didn't return? *No.* Vampires couldn't enter fae realms. He'd move on. He'd have to. Just as he'd moved on after each of his previous mortal lovers.

Pressure built in my chest, suffocating me. We hadn't even gotten

Faerie Forged

the chance to *be* lovers. Now we never would.

"The sentence has been passed." Bael's voice was hard, cold as the throne he now stood in front of.

I took a step forward. "But—" My voice cracked.

"Stop," Kai whispered urgently. His eyes were wide and scared. A guard now stood on either side of him, holding his arms.

Hortense, tugged me back, her fingers digging into my shoulders. "You'll only make it worse."

Every face in the room seemed to be turned toward me, eyes focused, waiting to see what the mortal in their midst would do next.

The guards led Kai away. He didn't struggle, didn't resist. He didn't even look back.

A black hole opened up inside me. Only Hortense's solid grip kept me from running after him.

Pimm's companion snickered. "Perhaps the half-breed should have been kept on a shorter leash."

Voices erupted around the room. No longer quiet mutterings now that the show was over, but forceful comments of agreement and dissent. Bael frowned, but didn't call for silence. He settled in his throne and motioned to the band. Music filled the hall once more, but it couldn't compete with the heated debates that had taken over the dance floor.

I stared at Pimm and her co-conspirator, and mentally kicked myself. This was what they'd wanted. Sure, they'd been hoping for my death, but that would have been icing on the cake. What they'd needed was to undermine my position. Cast doubt on my competence. And I'd granted their wish like an eager genie. My failure would call into question the status of all the halfers allowed at court, as well as the soundness of Bael's judgment.

Pimm had been right to come after me. I was the weak link.

I CLAWED AT the ribbons holding the many layers of my dress in place, tearing them free. Tess paced along one side of the room, wringing her hands. Her eyes were wide, frightened. Just like Kai's had been.

Growling like a cornered animal, I ripped the gossamer fabric off my shoulders. I crumpled it into a wad and threw it at the wall. It fluttered as it fell, negating the impact.

"Calm down, Alex." Hortense stood just inside the door, scowl still firmly in place. She'd stayed glued to my side for the rest of the festival. All thirteen hours that I'd been forced to remain while the guests around me pointed and whispered.

Where had that dogged oversight been when I needed it? Had her absence at the beginning of the party been accidental? Or arranged? Had someone told Pimm about my quick temper? Haru could easily have led me to Pimm on purpose, abandoning me far from help. And what about Mica? It was his idea to dance in the first place.

I shook my head. Kai was the only person at court I was sure was on my side. And now he was gone . . . because of me.

I yanked loose the delicate coil holding closed the collar around my neck. The heavy metal lifted free, and I threw it across the room.

Unlike the gauzy fabric of my overdress, the metal flew true. It struck the marble wall with a resounding *clang*, then dropped to the floor with a clatter. A chip of white stone landed beside it, and white dust sifted down to speckle the iron like snow.

Tess squeaked and ran out of the room.

Hortense stared at the circle of dark metal lying on the floor. She pursed her lips. "Feel better?"

"I'm leaving." I stomped into the bedroom, making a beeline for the suitcase at the foot of my bed.

"You can't." Hortense trailed after me like an annoying shadow. "You are training with Lord Bael tomorrow."

"Screw Bael, and screw training. I don't want to be a part of any of this."

"And yet you are." She crossed her arms. "To wish otherwise is unreasonable."

I slammed my palm down on the bed, making my suitcase jump. "What's unreasonable is sentencing Kai to fifty years in prison because I was stupid enough to let a couple of assholes goad me into yelling at them. How is that fair?"

"Fair has nothing to do with it. You made a mistake. Accept that and move on. Use your position to negotiate for the future."

I crossed my arms. "He didn't listen before. Why should tomorrow be any different?"

"Because tomorrow, you will not have the entire court hanging on your every word."

I gritted my teeth, but there was nothing more to say. She was right. I owed it to Kai to face Bael one more time, beg him if necessary. And as much as I wanted to distance myself from all things fae at the moment, the fact remained that learning to understand my imbuing was an important step in reestablishing some semblance of control over my life.

"I'll collect you in the morning. Try to get some rest."

A soft rustling noise marked Hortense's passage. The door to the apartment clicked softly behind me.

I stripped off the rest of the dress, leaving the red fabric on the floor like a pile of smoldering embers. Then I pulled a baggy Green Day concert t-shirt over my head. The hem fell to my thighs, not quite covering the knife still strapped there. Bunching the fabric in my hands, I buried my face in it. The shirt was soft, and familiar, and carried the memory of simpler times—late, care-free nights with my friends.

I let the fabric fall.

Aiden was dead. Maggie was so fed up with me she'd cut me off from the bookstore. James was a looming question mark. And Kai. . . . Twisting vines of emotion strangled my chest and slithered up my throat.

At least I still had David. Though he'd been acting strange since I killed that serial killer PTF agent. I shook my head. Maybe that was just my imagination, the stress of so much loss poisoning my thoughts.

Yearning for some connection to my old, human life, I ran a hand along the inside pocket of my suitcase, where I'd stashed my locket when I took it off for the festival. At least, I thought that's where I'd put it. . . . The pocket was empty.

Frowning, I turned the pocket inside out, then did the same with the others. I found the silence charm I'd made with Hortense, but my locket wasn't in any of them.

I pulled the clothes out of my bag one by one, shaking them out before tossing them on the floor. My books and the bag of contraband candy I smuggled in for Kai landed on top. When nothing remained in my suitcase, I turned it upside down and shook the whole thing.

Nothing.

Dropping the suitcase, I sat back on my heels and rubbed the mounting pressure in my temples. Was I remembering wrong? Had I put the necklace somewhere else?

I searched all the tabletops in the room, dug through the drawers. My gun lay, undisturbed, under my pillow. The box of bullets sat on a table beside the bed. I stepped into the bathroom. My toothbrush and other toiletries were beside the giant basin carved into the marble counter. Warm water steamed from the bowl, filling the room with an aroma of thyme and rosemary. Similarly scented water filled a clawfoot tub, fresh and clean despite my having washed in it. Neither fixture had drain or faucet, and there were no visible pipes.

Panic crept through me as I continued to search for, and failed to find, my locket. I'd only just gotten it back—a connection to my past, my parents, my life before magic.

When I'd turned the whole apartment upside down and inside out, I settled heavily on the edge of the bed. The pillows and covers were on the floor with my clothes. I gripped the mattress until my fingers ached.

My locket was gone. Someone had stolen it.

I turned my eyes toward the loose curtains covering the balcony, and the black expanse beyond.

Chapter 13

THERE WAS A CRACKING sound, then a muffled *thump*.

"I'm up," I mumbled with a start, and raised one heavy hand. The Ruger wavered in my cramped fingers, wobbling from side to side as I tried to focus on the room around me. Hortense stood just inside the front door to my apartment in a dark purple gown that brought out the yellow in her skin in a rather unpleasant way. The chair I'd used to wedge the door shut lay on its side next to her. Its back legs were cracked.

"Did you spend the night there?" Her hands were pressed to her hips. Her scowl was deeper than usual.

"Mmm." I set the gun gently on the floor to one side of the nest of pillows and blankets I'd arranged in one corner of the sitting room. Sandy grit scraped my eyes every time I blinked, my mouth tasted like roadkill, and sharp pain shot through my neck and back when I tried to turn my head to the left. I pushed to my feet, groaning with every pop of my stiff joints. I hadn't gotten much actual sleep, but the little bit I'd managed had ruined me.

"Why choose the floor over a perfectly good bed?"

I glanced at the bedroom door. The chair I'd jammed under its handle was still in place. Then I walked over to the silver tray on the table in the middle of the room. It was piled high with picked-over fruit and day-old rolls. I smiled and popped a grape into my mouth. No one had managed to sneak in last night.

Picking up a roll, I dropped onto the couch. "Someone broke into my room."

Hortense stiffened. "What makes you think that?"

"My necklace was stolen."

Her gaze shifted to Bael's iron collar, still on the floor in its little pile of white dust.

"Not that one," I said. "Mine. The locket I brought with me."

"Are you sure you didn't just misplace it?"

I glared, shoving a chunk of stale bread into my mouth.

She sighed. "I shall report the theft to Rhoana. She'll get to the bottom of it."

A flicker of hope sprang to life. I snuffed it. Best not to hold my breath for a fae's help. I finished off my roll.

"Mortals require a good amount of sleep to function well, do they not?"

I shrugged.

"Perhaps we should postpone your training. I'm sure Lord Bael could be persuaded to—"

"No." I leaned forward, elbows propped on my knees. "Every second I spend here burns time back home. I'll meet with Bael, convince him to let Kai go, and hopefully get a handle on my powers. Then I'm gone. I need to get back to my real life before it unravels any further."

She pursed her lips. "Then we'd best make you presentable."

Shifting the impeding chair to one side, she crossed into the bedroom and headed straight for the closet. I trailed after.

"Any advice on how I can convince Bael to let Kai go?"

"*Lord* Bael has informed me he wishes your company for dinner tonight. My advice is to wait until then. In the meantime, focus on your lessons. Show him you are capable of restraint."

"But—"

"You must gain the lord's respect if you wish him to consider your plea. Dwelling on the past shows weakness of character, and no fae, least of all the Lord of Enchantment, will respect you if you are weak."

I stopped on the threshold to the closet. "Do you respect me?"

She turned, the fabric of a deep blue gown trailing from one hand. "You are rash and ignorant . . . but you are not weak."

I shook my head, the hint of a smile pulling at my lips. "Can't you ever give a straight answer?"

She pushed the dress against my chest. "This will be suitable for today."

THE BLUE DRESS Hortense forced me into was about as far from my festival dress as possible. The cloth was thick and dark, but not nearly as restrictive as last night's dress had been. It had wide straps, no sleeves, and a loosely fitted torso. The skirt hung in panels split up to my thigh, allowing easy access to my knife should I need it. The slippers I wore matched my dress perfectly. Silly though I would have looked, I couldn't help missing the solid comfort of my boots as I set out through the hostile halls once more. It was hard to feel like myself when I was walking around in borrowed shoes.

Fae glanced in my direction when we passed, but no one made eye contact. Whispers sprang up in our wake like dolphins playing in the turbulence of a passing ship.

I tugged at the iron collar once more settled around my neck. Hortense insisted wearing it would improve Bael's disposition toward me, and I'd take all the help I could get in softening him up for my request.

Hortense led me down the winding staircase we used before, then doubled back when we reached the mossy, flower-dotted carpet of the entrance hall. We stopped once more in front of the wide, white door that bore Bael's coat of arms—a crossed sword and hammer on a field of flames.

I smoothed the slick fabric of my dress and patted my fraying braids, still up from the night before. Hortense had deftly tucked back the unruly strands that pulled free while I'd dozed. I took a deep breath, and nodded.

Hortense opened the door.

The throne room felt vast and empty after the crowd of the festival. Even more so than my first look at it, because only one person stood inside. Rhoana waited in front of the fire-engraved door at the back of the room, hands clasped loosely in front of her. Walking toward her was like crossing a desert of painful memories, each step draining a little more of my resolve.

I'd had one job—don't insult anybody—and I'd screwed it up. I'd failed Kai and Hortense, embarrassed Bael, undermined the position of halfers allowed in fae courts. Probably the only people who were happy I came to the party were Pimm and her friends. They'd danced and laughed for the rest of the night as I stood off to one side of the dais, no longer touching the throne but once more isolated by its toxic force.

Icicles still hung from the underside of the gallery, and gossamer strings crisscrossed above, but they glinted strangely. The candles in the chandeliers were out, and only a dim glow came from a row of narrow windows near the ceiling, casting long, dark shadows around the room.

By the time I stopped in front of Rhoana, my mood was as black as the deepest corner and as heavy as the collar around my neck.

Rhoana nodded to me, her expression neutral, then tipped her head toward the door behind her. "He's waiting in the workshop."

I swallowed what felt like a marble, glanced at Hortense, and headed for the door. The hairs on the back of my neck tingled when I passed Rhoana. If I turned, would I find her glaring at me . . . or poised with a knife, about to plunge it into my back?

I knocked against wood flames. The sound echoed dully.

"Enter." Bael's voice was strong and steady, even muffled by the door.

I set my shoulders. *Show no weakness.*

Bael was sitting at one of the tables, sanding a piece of light red wood. He blew a cloud of dust off his project, then set it aside and brushed off his hands. "Close the door behind you."

I pulled the door closed, sealing us in.

"How are you doing this morning?" He stepped around the table, dusting off his clothes.

I forced my jaw to relax. "I'm fine. How are you?"

"I was up half the morning taking audiences." He frowned. "Too many people wanting to voice their opinions."

Opinions about me, I thought. It was nice of him not to throw it in my face.

I balled my fists and sealed my lips over the words pressing to get out. I couldn't stop picturing Kai chained up in a dungeon, but I had to wait . . . for Kai. If I could show Bael I was composed, capable of moving past the events of last night, I could broach the subject of Kai's release without coming across as an emotionally volatile mortal.

Shoving my regrets and worries aside, I slammed a door on my feelings and gestured to the lump of wood Bael had been working with when I came in. "You're working awfully early for someone who was up all night."

"Working—this type of working," he gestured around the room, "relaxes me."

I smiled, thinking of all the late nights and early mornings I'd spent in my studio over the years. It seemed Gramps and I had something in common besides our last name. "Me too."

He matched my smile and moved toward a row of small black pillows set along the middle of another long table. "I've prepared a challenge for you. Something to hone your imbuing skills."

Each of the pillows held a little ball, but every ball was different. He waved a hand over the line. "These were all carved from the same piece of white marble."

I frowned, looking more closely at the balls. One was red. One was transparent. One looked furry.

"Malakai told me he used clay and light to test your ability."

My chest clenched at the mention of Kai's name, and I had to mentally brace against the door keeping my emotions in check.

"Imbuing attributes while forming is the simplest way to express our ability. It comes naturally. That's why imbuers tend to be tinkers, artisans, and the like." He lifted the first marble. It was plain, smooth, white stone. He held it out to me. "It's time for you to move beyond that."

I held out my hand, and he dropped the marble over my palm. It fell like a bubble drifting on a breeze. I could barely tell when it came to rest against my skin. My mouth dropped open.

"Do you know the inherent difference between imbuing and enchanting?" he asked.

I frowned. "Enchantments can be broken."

He tipped his head to one side, as though assessing my answer. "Enchantments are a veneer placed over an object. They can trick people into reacting a certain way to it, but the object remembers what it is."

He pointed to the sheath strapped to my thigh. "Malakai also mentioned your experiment with the knife. May I?"

I pulled the blade free and handed it over.

He turned it, lips pursed. He tested the weight, the edge, the balance. Then he flipped the knife and handed it back. "A decent attempt for the untrained, but what you have there is an enchantment pinned to a knife. It doesn't go deep enough. Imbuing is a form of transmutation. We change the core of an object. We don't just change how it looks or what it does. We change what it *is*."

"That's a pretty fine distinction," I said, sliding the knife back in its sheath.

"It's the difference between a lie and reality," he said. "If that stone you hold were enchanted, a strong enough will could know it for the simple rock it is. But imbued, there is no deeper truth for them to find. It is what it appears to be, implausible though it may seem."

I pinched the marble between my thumb and finger and lifted it to the light. It looked solid. Even the thinnest stone shell should weigh more than what I held.

Change the core, huh?

I set the feather-light stone back on its pillow, and with a glance at Bael for approval, lifted the next one. My fingers sank into a surface like Jello. The coloring was the same as the first, smooth white with thin veins of gray streaking the stone.

The third ball was completely transparent. Only the glint of light on its surface gave away its shape. It looked like the bubble the first ball had been imbued to be, but when I picked it up, it felt like a bowling ball.

I continued down the line, awed by the variety of textures, colors, and weights. The last ball was plain white. It felt like a stone, looked like a stone. I rolled it around in my hand, searching for something special. Finally, I cast a questioning glance at Bael.

He smiled. "That one's for you."

"But it's already formed."

"Imbuing is easiest, and strongest, when you are creating. But you won't always have time to build what you need." He plucked the marble from my fingers and held it between us. The surface began to swirl. Blue clouds rolled like a storm across a tiny world. Then fractal patterns spider-webbed over the stone. He handed it to me.

The marble was cold. So cold it stung my skin. Hissing, I dropped it on its pillow and rubbed the red surface of my palm to warm it.

Bael lifted the frozen sphere. "Stone, to ice..." The cracks cleared. The blue bled to white. "And back to stone."

He held the marble out to me. "You try."

I cleared my mind. That part was getting easier. Then I tried to open myself up to my magic, but the guilt and anger I'd hidden behind the door in my mind hammered for release. If I let myself feel those emotions, I wouldn't be able to concentrate. But if I didn't, I couldn't access my magic. I frowned at the little stone ball.

"Connect with the object," Bael said. "Follow your magic to its core. Find the truth inside."

I pictured the way I'd been able to feel James through our strange link, how I could sometimes see his thoughts and feelings. Once, when it was fresh, I'd followed those threads deeper and found the cold, dark knot of the demon lurking in his soul.

I shivered. Was that James's *truth*?

Pushing that thought away, I wrapped my fingers around the marble and gripped it tight. How was I supposed to connect with a rock? It didn't think. It didn't feel. It just... *was*.

Scrunching my eyes shut, I focused on the weight in my hand. It was solid, and slightly cool. I latched onto that coolness. What made the stone cool? I followed the thought to deep, lightless caves. The stone had come from the mountain beneath me, carved from the surface like the rest of the city. Even the sun couldn't warm more than the skin of the mountain, and the vast depths drew that heat out like a poison.

Focusing on that image, I tried to convince the tiny stone in my hand that it rested at the heart of a great mountain. A place the sun never reached.

I opened my eyes. Then my hand.

The stone lay against my palm, white and warm from my body heat.

I sighed.

Bael folded his arms. "Again."

IT TOOK HALF a day for me to give the white stone a bluish tinge and make it cold to the touch. Not the subarctic surface Bael had achieved, but a few degrees below its natural state. I'd wasted over an hour on the marble before I realized I was just reinforcing its nature by picturing the mountain. Then I'd had to come up with another image. I'd settled on an ice cave, to represent the attribute I wanted. Little by little, I'd managed to coax the stone toward the ice I wanted it to become.

Wiping a sheen of sweat off my brow, I set my moderate success back on its black pillow and flopped into a chair. My stomach growled.

Bael looked up from the piece of wood he'd gone back to carving while I worked. More details had taken shape, turning it into a mini gaala with six spindle legs and adolescent antlers. "Lunch should arrive any minute. We'll replenish your energy, then move on to the second lesson."

I suppressed a groan.

As if on cue, a soft knock rattled the door.

"Come," Bael commanded.

The door opened, and Rhoana stepped through carrying a large silver tray. Guess the kitchen staff wasn't allowed in Bael's sanctuary.

Rhoana eyed the line of marbles, then glanced at me. Did she think I'd changed them? Shifting her focus to Bael, she set her tray on the nearest table, bowed deeply, then backed out of the room.

Lunch was a salad of grains and vegetables drenched in pungent sauce. It wouldn't have been my first choice—what I was really craving was a juicy hamburger—but I grabbed a bowl and dug in with relish. After plowing through half the meal, I finally slowed down enough to taste the food.

"Magic sure makes me hungry," I said between bites.

"Naturally." Bael had barely made a dent in his salad. "Magic, like most endeavors, requires energy and focus. You can't climb a mountain or run a race and expect not to be hungry at the end."

I nodded toward his mostly full bowl. "So why aren't you?"

"I have a much larger reserve of energy than you." He grinned, the expression making him look even younger.

I scraped up the last grains clinging to my bowl, licked my spoon clean, and set the dishes back on the tray.

Bael set his own bowl, still half-full, beside mine and clapped his hands. "This is where things get really interesting."

I raised an eyebrow. "Ice balls and bubble stones not cutting it for you?"

I snapped my mouth closed. My salad turned sour in my stomach. For all that he looked like a boy, I was still talking to the Lord of Enchantment. I'd relaxed in the hours of comfortable silence in the workroom. Bael had left me to my studies, working at a separate table like a classmate sharing studio space.

Bael gave me a strange look, then laughed.

My stomach unclenched.

Leaning forward, Bael lifted the spoon out of his bowl. He held it vertically between us. "Can a spoon cut a table?"

I stared at the slender curve of the spoon, then looked at the table. Was this a trick question?

"What is it that changes the objects we imbue?"

I shrugged. "Magic."

He nodded. "We infuse objects with magic, and that magic becomes a part of it, shaping it. So why limit the changes to things like color or temperature?"

He lowered the spoon to the table's edge. The spoon connected, then sank in. When he lifted the utensil away, a narrow gash marred the tabletop. "If you can use magic to make a sharp tool sharper, why not a dull one?"

I frowned, eying the spoon like it might suddenly lunge at me. "But sharp isn't some abstract concept. It's determined by shape. The shape didn't change."

"Didn't it?" He held the spoon out to me.

Reluctantly, I took it.

"Find the spoon's truth. How does it see itself?"

In my head I kept replaying a scene from *The Matrix*. "There is no spoon."

Bael frowned.

I shook my head. "Never mind."

As I stared at the wooden spoon, the outline seemed to blur. I let my eyes unfocus further, like I was trying to find the image in one of those optical illusion pictures. A faint reddish glow appeared around the bowl of the spoon.

I turned the spoon from side to side. The glow tapered from the edges of the wood to a sharply beveled line. Reaching out with my free hand, I traced a finger along that line. My skin split apart.

I blinked, and the spoon was just a spoon. A thin line of blood welled along the cut in my fingertip.

"You can shape magic the same way you shape a piece of wood or metal." Bael leaned forward and plucked the spoon from my grip. "And if you're an imbuer, you can make it permanent."

Chapter 14

TURNING MY GAZE inward, I focused on directing my magic toward the spoon. I pooled power in my hand and wrapped it around the wood. The coverage was spotty, incomplete, but I forced the magic into shape, molding it as best I could into a straight edge. Then I pressed the spoon against the table for the umpteenth time, and like every time before, the magical edge wavered and collapsed. The spoon slid harmlessly over the wood.

"This is impossible." I tossed the spoon onto the silver tray.

Bael shook his head. "You'll get there. I didn't expect you to master imbuing in a day. Especially considering your current... condition."

"What condition?"

He lifted one shoulder. "One cannot change the order of the world when conflicted about oneself."

I crossed my arms. "I'm not conflicted."

"Aren't you, daughter of two worlds?"

I frowned.

He pushed his chair back from the table and stood. "That's enough for now. You need to get ready for dinner."

Orange light filtered through the windows, and long shadows cut across the room. The stiffness I'd woken up with had been compounded by hours hunched over marbles and spoons. Every vertebra in my spine felt welded in place.

Bael went to stand in front of the windows, looking out over his domain, and clasped his hands behind his back. "About last night..."

My breath caught. I'd been waiting to broach the subject of Kai's release. Now Bael had beaten me to it. My throat constricted, but I forced a swallow. Time to take responsibility.

"It was my fault for letting Pimm goad me." I straightened my aching shoulders and lifted my chin. "Kai should not be punished for it."

"Hmm?" Bael glanced over his shoulder at me, his eyebrows

drawn together. "Oh, Malakai." He waved a hand as though dismissing the thought. "That's not what I want to talk about."

"But—"

"You made a mistake. Malakai fixed it. End of story."

I clenched my fists. "That's *not* the end of the story. Malakai is facing fifty years of imprisonment!"

He pursed his lips. "Pimm and Elliot were hoping to corner me into stepping in on your behalf. They had not counted on Malakai superseding the court tutor's authority, nor his caring enough to intercede on your behalf. Their miscalculation left an opening, which Malakai exploited to save us both. There's nothing more to be done."

"You're the Lord of Enchantment. You could pardon him."

"And void his sacrifice?" He set a hand on my shoulder. "It's not ideal, but it really is the best solution given the circumstances."

"But Kai didn't do anything wrong!"

"No. You did, and Malakai is paying the price."

The words slammed into me like a head-on collision.

He turned back to the window. "Learn from your mistake and move on."

I staggered back. "How can you be so cold?"

He tipped his face up to the dying light. "Practice."

Grinding my teeth to keep from saying something I'd regret, I stomped toward the exit.

"What did you think of Mica?"

I froze with my hand on the door knob. "What?"

"Mica. You danced with him before the unfortunate events that landed Malakai in the dungeon. What did you think of him?"

I shook my head. "Goodbye, Bael."

Hortense and Rhoana were still standing by the dais as though neither had moved since I left them that morning. I stalked past without looking up.

Hortense fell into step behind me.

I pushed through the double doors by which Bael and I had entered the party the night before, stomped across the fragile flowers of the moss carpet in the entryway, and shoved past one of the tall doors that led out of the keep. I didn't stop moving until I had clear sky above me. Clouds streaked the twilight, their bellies glowing with warm light already denied the world below. Tiny gaala galloped far above, their details lost to distance. They danced on an evening breeze that chilled my nose and cheeks, and stung the tips of my ears.

The impenetrable plants of the garden maze loomed in front of me, dark and dense, walling me in. I paced back and forth across the clear area between maze and keep, fists balled and teeth bared.

Hortense crossed her arms with a sigh. "I take it your lesson didn't go well."

"The lesson went fine." I spun on her. "But he won't release Kai."

She pursed her lips. "I thought you were going to wait to broach that subject."

"I did. I . . . tried." I dug my fingers into the braids on my scalp. "He's supposed to be in charge—some all-powerful lord. Why can't he just let Kai go?"

"It's not that simple."

"It should be!" I tore at the iron collar that suddenly felt like it was choking me, struggling with the delicate spiral of the clasp. Cold wind shivered against my skin when the metal lifted free. I threw the ornament down, where it clattered against marble like a hammer hitting a bell.

I made another circuit of the clearing. Pressure squeezed my heart and lungs. My head felt like it was going to explode. The muscles in my arms shook. Dropping to the ground like a discarded puppet, I bunched my fingers against the cold, unyielding stone. "I want to go home."

Hortense knelt on the grass beside me. "You must attend dinner with the lord tonight."

"Why should I? He's given his answer. There's nothing to be gained by staying."

"Such a narrow perspective." She shook her head. "And tell me, how will you get back to the portal without the lord's leave?"

I looked up sharply, meeting her gaze. "You—"

"Will do as the lord bids me. As do all sworn to his service."

A cold knot twisted in my chest as I realized the depth of my foolishness in coming to Enchantment. Mica said he hadn't moved home because Bael preferred to keep him close even though he was a disappointment. I was an imbuer. Would Bael really let me go?

"Come." Hortense rose and extended a hand. "We must get you ready, before Rhoana comes to collect you."

TESS WAS PINNING the last of my freshly woven braids with a clip of gold-set pearls when Rhoana knocked at the door.

Hortense fluffed the ruffled folds of my spider-silk dress, making the iridescent fabric shift from silvery-white to pale purple like liquid moonlight. "Remember, there will be no one to intercede this time. Hold your temper, and your tongue."

I wiped sweaty palms against the smooth fabric covering my hips and nodded. The pearls dangling in my hair clinked together like muted chimes.

Tess opened the door. Rhoana strode through and cast an appraising look over the room, severe as ever. "I've made some inquiries about your missing property."

I rubbed a hand over my bare neck, seeking the small comfort my locket would have provided. A tiny piece of home in this hostile, alien world. At least the iron and ruby necklace Bael had given me clashed with my dress. It was resting back in its dark wood case, slightly dented from its repeated, forceful meetings with the ground.

"What did you find out?"

"No one was seen entering or leaving your room, either by the door or the balcony. Of the keep residents who did not attend the festival, I've received alibis for most." She clasped her wrist behind her back and lifted her chin. "I will continue to investigate, but it seems unlikely we will get to the bottom of this quickly."

My shoulders slumped under the weight of another loss.

"The lord is waiting." Rhoana nodded to Hortense, and backed out of the room.

Hortense gave me a pat on the arm. "Just one more night. Then you can go home."

Right, I thought. *Unless Bael changes his mind.*

Rhoana didn't lead me down to the throne room this time, or even to the fancy dining hall I'd seen off to the side of the keep's entrance. This time, she took me up.

"Where are we going?" I asked.

"You'll be dining in the lord's private garden tonight."

At least a private dinner should mean Pimm wouldn't be there. My steps took on a little more bounce.

"I'll be leaving tomorrow," I said without preamble.

Rhoana glanced at me. "I'm aware."

"I'd like to say goodbye to Kai." *And thank him for everything he did for me . . . and apologize.*

She turned a corner. "If you wish to see Malakai, you will have to take it up with the lord."

"Aren't you the Captain of the Guard? Surely you have access to the dungeons."

"Of course I do." She raised her chin. "That changes nothing. I will not take you without the lord's assent."

Assent he seemed unlikely to give for such a sentimental venture.

We climbed a set of wide stairs, stone echoes punctuating our steps—or mine, anyway—warning of our approach. At the top, a single guard stood in front of a heavy, wooden door. The guard was a panotti, with long, leathery ears that draped down his back like a cape. He snapped a salute when Rhoana stopped in front of him, making a ring of silver keys hanging from his leather belt jingle.

"The lord is expecting you," he said, and stepped aside.

Lush, green carpet muted my steps as I continued along the hallway on the far side of the door, and the marble walls were lined with paintings in ornate, gilt frames. Most were fanciful landscapes—a lake reflecting the light of three moons; a blue desert with fine powder blowing from the tops of towering dunes; a dark jungle of purple trees and crimson vines with bright eyes looking out from its shadows. I shivered. Were these real places in the fae realms, or just an artist's imaginings? There was no way to be sure.

There were a few portraits too. One was of Bael standing beside another boy. They had the same ember eyes and purplish hair, the same sharp-toothed smile. The next portrait showed Bael standing alone. He wasn't smiling in that one. Since he looked the same age in both pictures—the same age he still looked—it was impossible to tell which came first.

Between sets of pictures, the walls were broken by wooden doors. These were each carved with the same pattern of flames as the workroom door attached to the throne room. If these were Bael's personal rooms, perhaps the pattern had something to do with the wards he claimed to have set on his workspace.

That thought should have made me feel safer. . . . It didn't.

Rhoana pushed open a door about halfway down the long corridor, and the sound of splashing water rushed into the silence of the hall. A soft melody strummed on harp strings blended with the natural noise of water trickling over rock as though playing a duet. Rhoana stepped to one side and gestured for me to enter, then retreated, closing the door behind me.

Guess she wasn't invited to dinner.

Bael lounged on a stone bench popping grapes into his mouth, looking exactly like the carefree teenager he wasn't. When the door clicked closed behind me, he tossed one last grape into the air and caught it in his mouth, then swiveled to face me. A wide, welcoming smile curved his lips.

I tried not to imagine myself as the grape being torn apart behind that smile as he chewed.

He swallowed and swung his arm in a wide arc. "Welcome to my garden."

Bael's garden sat on a balcony that was filled wall to rail with dirt. I stood on a path of gray stones half-sunk in moss. Trees and bushes created privacy screens between small clearings, each with a unique theme and floral arrangement. Paper lanterns hung above the garden, providing a soft glow and wavering shadows, and groups of sharp, bright lights flickered through the foliage like fireflies. To one side, water cascaded down a bed of gold-flecked granite. I couldn't find where the harp music was coming from, though it continued to play.

Bael led me along the stone path to the farthest edge of the garden. A grassy clearing butted up against the marble railing, and in the center sat a six-foot table piled with silver-capped trays. Enough for a feast.

Only two chairs waited, one at either end of the table.

I swallowed. Apparently this was to be a *very* private dinner.

"What do you think?"

I turned away from the intimate setting, focusing instead on a cluster of bright blue flowers that drooped from thin reeds at the edge of the pond where the musical water pooled. "It's beautiful."

"As are you." He trailed the back of his fingers down my bare back where the dress dipped low. "The maid outdid herself."

I shivered. I'd chosen the dress because I liked the fabric. Now I wished I'd thought to pick something that didn't show so much soft, vulnerable, mortal skin.

"You never did answer my question. What do you think of Mica?"

I frowned. "I was a little preoccupied when we met."

He nodded. Then, gripping my elbow, led me back toward the dinner table. "Hence this less crowded setting."

I froze, my arm tugging Bael to a stop beside me. "The second chair is for . . . Mica?"

Chapter 15

"YOU TWO NEED to get better acquainted." Bael tapped the silver dome of one of the serving dishes as he spoke. The lid evaporated in a puff of steam, revealing strips of dark, juicy meat soaking in a thick sauce that smelled of cherries.

I licked my lips. "Why?"

"Because I need an heir." He touched another lid. A tray of root vegetables cut paper-thin and arranged like a mosaic sunset lay beneath. "Neither of you is fit on your own, but perhaps together you could produce one who is."

The savory aromas that had been making my mouth water now turned my stomach. I took a step back, crushing the thick, waxy leaves of a groundcover plant.

"I realize arranged unions are out of favor in your world." He said it like "unions" were a type of hat that had gone out of style but would surely be making a comeback soon. He tapped another lid. The tray beneath held a pile of fluffy white rolls with butter-glazed tops.

I shook my head, taking another step back. I was fully off the path now, standing in the bushes with a tree at my back. He couldn't possibly be asking what he seemed to be asking. And yet, as he tapped more silver covers and more flavors mixed and mingled in the evening air, I caught no hint of joking, no smile or wink.

"No." The word caught in my throat, coming out garbled. I coughed, and said more forcefully, "No."

He revealed the last tray, a decadent trifle in a crystal bowl, and stepped away from the table.

"What do you mean, 'no?'" The burning embers in his eyes glinted like the fire behind them had flared in a sudden gust of wind. His mouth set in a firm line and all of his hundreds of years suddenly showed. How could I ever have thought this ancient being looked like a carefree teenager?

I swallowed, bunching my hands in the soft fabric of my gown. "If you're asking me to marry Mica, the answer is no."

Just like that, the shadow that had fallen over Bael's face lifted. He smiled his teenager smile and waved a hand as though clearing smoke from the air. "I'm not asking you to marry him."

I exhaled. My muscles sagged in relief.

Bael plucked a strawberry off the top of the trifle and dipped it in cream. "You just need to produce a baby." He popped the cream-covered berry in his mouth.

The world hazed out, growing dim around the edges. All I could see was the red juice on Bael's lips as he chewed. My chest ached. I took a shuddering breath and gripped the tree behind me. "You can't just ask something like that."

"I'm not." Berry juice stained his teeth. "I'm negotiating. You want Kai released from his imprisonment. I want an heir. Produce one for me, and Kai will be free."

I dug my nails into the trunk. "So you *can* pardon him."

"If I have a reason."

"Like blackmail."

"A bargaining chip." He shrugged. "Think about it."

There was a knock at the door to the garden.

"Ah," Bael said. "It seems our other guest has arrived."

He moved toward the entrance, but I couldn't make myself follow. The bark of the tree was a rough comfort against my exposed back.

A baby. Who asks for a baby? And who would ever consider trading one like a commodity?

Thoughts clustered like a gathering storm inside my head. Kai, Bael, James, Mica, guilt, duty, and the possibility of an unborn child. That last settled like an anchor around my heart. I'd never really pictured myself having kids. Hell, I hadn't imagined I'd have a relationship that lasted more than a month before James, and even that was questionable.

Bael reappeared, and he wasn't alone.

Mica stood sandwiched between his parents. He wore dark leather pants and a billowy teal shirt that was a perfect balance between his mother's sky-blue dress and his father's green tunic. His eyes were locked on the ground just in front of his feet.

"Lady Alyssandra," said Mica's mother. The three fae bowed in unison, Circe and Kane slightly lower than their son.

I was too stunned to respond.

Bael clapped his hands. "Lady Circe, Sir Kane, shall we retire to my chambers to let the young ones get better acquainted?"

Kane and Circe cast side-long glances at Mica, and I thought I saw Circe jab him in the ribs before she stepped away.

Bael glanced at Mica, then settled his gaze on me. "Enjoy yourselves."

The co-conspirators departed, leaving only the soft burble of water and the melodic harp music to contend with the silence that settled over the garden.

Mica recovered first. Clearing his throat, he finally raised his gaze to meet mine. Silver specks jumped like shimmering fish in the lazy whirlpool of his eyes. Those eyes were beautiful and deep—eyes a mortal could drown in.

I looked away.

Was Mica in on it too? He hadn't seemed bad when we talked before the dance, but the fae were nothing if not ambitious. What had Bael offered him in exchange for bedding me? Circe and Kane clearly wanted something to come of this, and producing an heir for Bael would make Mica . . . what exactly? What would it make me? A queen? A brood mare?

But it was my fault Kai was stuck in a dungeon. I owed it to him to get him out. How much was that debt worth? Nine months stacked against fifty years. *Could I give up a child to Bael?*

I shook my head. Was I really considering Bael's offer?

I pushed away from the security of the tree. The wind prickled against my back.

Mica stood like a statue as I walked past him. I couldn't bring myself to speak.

I went all the way to the farthest edge of the garden and braced my hands against the cold stone rail. The city of Abonaille Malmür spread out beneath me, trickling down the side of the mountain like a river of light. But the lanterns, the market stalls, the gaala stables—they were a shallow carpet of civilization clinging to the surface. The city, like the fae, only looked warm and alive. In truth, they were hard, and cold, and unchanging as the mountain itself.

I shivered.

A glint like reflected starlight caught my eye. To my left was a bush with thick, heart-shaped leaves and fruit that looked like apples cast in gold. Each heavy fruit weighed down its branch, nestling deep in the cushion of its leaves. They seemed to shine with a light of their own rather than reflecting the paltry light of the garden lanterns.

I stepped closer to the bush, breathing in the sweet scent of honey and citrus. Saliva filled my mouth. I reached out to touch the nearest fruit.

Mica's fingers wrapped around my wrist. "Don't."

I blinked, and the rest of the world came back into focus.

"Goblin fruit is terribly addictive for mortals."

Sweat broke out between my shoulder blades, making me shiver. Kai had warned me about goblin fruit. A golden orb that made mortals wild with craving. Humans who tasted it even once were said to go mad with desire, willing to do anything for another bite.

Mica frowned. "I'm surprised the lord would let you near it without warning."

Unless he intended me to taste it.

The thought sent ice through my veins. Would Bael poison me to make me compliant? Hook me on a drug he could easily provide, knowing I'd have no access to it in the mortal realm? How much did he want me to agree to this union?

I looked at the table, crossing my arms over my growling stomach. Could I trust the food? What if Bael slipped goblin fruit into the salad? Or dripped some juice in the wine?

Mica pulled one chair out from the table and gestured to it. "Shall we dine?"

I glared at the chair, then at him, then moved to the far end of the table and pulled out the second chair. I sat down, back stiff.

Mica slouched in the chair he'd pulled out for me, then seemed to remember himself and sat up a little straighter. We both stared at the feast on the table. Neither of us moved to eat.

With a sigh, Mica pulled the same silver box he'd had at the festival from the inside pocket of his jacket and flipped it open.

"You seem to use that a lot," I said.

He glanced up. "It helps me relax." He dipped a finger in the sparkling dust. "Besides, I need *something* to dull the passage of time." He licked off the pixie dust and waved a hand loosely at the view beyond the balcony. "I've been stuck here for seventy-three years. Staring at the same view, talking to the same people." He sighed. "It was all well and good when everyone thought I'd be the lord's heir, but now..." He took another hit. "This is the first time the lord has spoken to me in over twenty years."

I looked out over the glittering city. "Why won't he let you leave?"

He shook his head. "I may not have lived up to Bael's expectations, but he still owns me, and disappointment or no, I'm a valuable commodity."

My stomach twisted. "What do you mean, he owns you?"

"Contract with my parents." He shrugged and popped his finger in his mouth, sucking off the last of the glittering drug.

"Your parents sold you?"

"More like bartered." He snapped the silver box closed and tucked it back in his pocket. "And now that you're here, everyone's thinking I might be useful again."

"You know what he wants?"

The corners of his mouth pulled up in a tight, bitter smile. "Of course."

"Did you agree?"

He raised an eyebrow. "Did you?"

I pressed my lips tight. "Why does Bael's heir need to be an imbuer?"

Mica shrugged. "It's what he wants. And what the lord wants . . ."

"He gets." I frowned. "What about your aunt? She's an imbuer."

His smile fell and creases formed at the corners of his eyes. "Auntie Marron went insane . . . a long time ago. And she's barren to boot, so he can't even use her for breeding."

"I'm sorry."

He waved the comment away and filled his goblet from a carafe of bright green liquid. He tipped it toward me. "Would you like some?"

I shook my head. "Why not make an heir himself? Surely he'd have the best chance of producing an imbuer."

Mica snorted. "He would have, if he hadn't been cursed."

A knot swelled in my throat, making it hard to swallow. "Cursed?"

"By a jilted lover, or so the story goes." He sipped from his glass, the liquor shimmering green on his lips before he licked it away. "No one's confirmed it—no one would dare—but he's bedded practically every female in the realm. So far, you're the first offspring he's produced with the ability to imbue, but you're far too mortal to take the throne."

A muscle under my eye twitched at the word "offspring."

"All that effort, and it was a random dalliance with a mortal that got results." Mica chuckled and drained the rest of his glass. "If that isn't a curse, I don't know what is."

I frowned. Mica wasn't at all like the other fae at court. He reminded me of Chase, relaxed and irreverent. "I get why you're bitter about being passed over, but I'd think you'd be jumping up and down at the prospect of getting back in Bael's good graces. Your parents certainly seem to be."

His brows drew together. "I can't remember the last time I saw my parents jump. I doubt my mother ever has."

Guess Kai wasn't the only fae mortal colloquialisms were lost on.

"It means excited. Why aren't you doing everything you can to please Bael? He is your lord after all."

He tipped his cup back, draining the liquid, and slouched in his chair. "I'm used to being a disappointment. Nothing much will change for me if I don't manage to bed you."

My cheeks grew warm.

"Besides," silver flashed in his eyes, "I'm not my parents."

His words sounded in my heart like a bell, his emotion echoing a familiar bitterness I felt whenever I recalled my father, and the way he'd abandoned me. Sure he'd had his reasons, his justification, but that didn't make the pain any less, or the sense of rejection I'd carried my whole life.

"No," I said, shaking my head. "Neither am I. Bael can go fuck himself. I won't bring a child into this world only to abandon it."

Mica's forehead wrinkled. "I'm not sure what you've heard about fae anatomy, but we don't really work that way."

I blinked. We stared at each other. Then he laughed, rich and wild like waves crashing against a rocky shore.

He refilled his cup and lifted it high in salute. "To being our own people."

Decision made, I grinned and leaned back in my chair. My muscles turned to liquid with the release of tension, and I tipped my head back to study the star-studded sky. One swollen moon hung just above the snowy peak that jutted up behind the keep. The purple orb looked like an overripe fruit atop an ice cream sundae. A second, smaller moon glowed on the distant horizon, pale and orange.

My relief was short-lived. Refusing Bael was the right decision, but the Lord of Enchantment was not a man accustomed to the word no. Plus, there was still the issue of Kai's imprisonment and my guilt for putting him there. I drummed my fingers against the table.

"He said it was a negotiation," I muttered.

Mica narrowed his eyes. "What was?"

"This." I gestured between us. "Maybe I can find something else he'd accept."

Mica leaned forward until his elbows rested on the table. "Out of curiosity. What did the lord offer you?"

"Kai's freedom."

He cut his eyes side to side as though searching for spies. Then he whispered, "I might be able to help with that."

THE GAUZY PURPLE curtains guarding my balcony fluttered lazily in a breeze, and I shifted the aim of my gun to track the shadow that fell across them. Tired though I was when Rhoana delivered me back to my room, I hadn't crawled into the nest of pillows and blankets I'd made the night before. Instead, I'd shucked the revealing dinner dress, donned my stealth charm, and slipped into jeans and a t-shirt. Then I crawled under the bed, where I laid for over an hour, gun drawn, arms extended, watching the breach in my defenses.

The shadow solidified, taking on the shape of a man, and stepped into the room, still silhouetted by the purplish glow of the moon.

I exhaled, steadying my aim. Fae had amazing night vision—even my halfer abilities let me see better than a full mortal—but the only light was coming from behind my intruder. I couldn't make out any identifying details.

The figure moved closer, leather boots silent on the dark carpet. The boots paused, turned, searching.

"Alex?" Mica's whisper rang in my straining ears like I'd fired a shot.

Exhaling, I relaxed my grip and lowered my face to the carpet.

Mica moved toward the living room.

I shimmied out from under the bed while his back was turned. Now that the moon was at my back, I could pick out the shape of his profile. "I wasn't sure you'd come."

He whirled, eyes wide.

His surprise made me smile. Nice to know the stealth charm under my shirt was still working. Especially considering what we had planned.

Then his gaze dropped to the gun in my hand, and the corners of his mouth turned down. "You planning to use that?"

I rolled my shoulders, stretching out some of the stiffness. I was really looking forward to spending a night in my own bed. Or anywhere other than a floor. "Not on you."

"You should leave it here. It'll only get in the way."

I tucked the gun back in its holster and set it on the nightstand. "I was planning to."

"Are you sure you want to do this?"

"Are you sure you can get us there?"

Mica had whispered in my ear under the pretense of dancing after dinner—which I'd agreed to sample only after his assertion that the food wasn't laced with anything. Mixed with the dulcet tones of the harp and the burble of the brook, he'd made me a promise. He could take me to Kai.

"I grew up in these halls. I know passages even the guards have never seen."

I sat at the edge of the bed. "And what do you want in return?"

"Who says I want anything?"

I thumbed the black ribbon around my wrist. "The fae don't grant favors for free."

Mica nodded, leaning back against the wall. "True."

"So what do you want?"

He sighed and wiped a hand over his face. "There's someone I care about, but he.... Let's just say there are complications to having a future with him."

Him? Guess Mica wouldn't be producing any heirs on his own. I tapped my index finger against the mattress. "What do you think I can do to help?"

"You have certain . . . connections."

"I doubt Bael will listen to anything I have to say if I succeed in breaking Kai out of his dungeon."

Mica shrugged. "Perhaps. Regardless, I don't need anything from you right now. Just your promise that when the time comes, you will grant me your help."

My instincts recoiled, and one of Kai's endless warnings echoed through my head like the blare of a fire alarm. *Never grant an open-ended request.*

What if he wanted me to help him kill somebody, or steal something, or start a war? I shook my head. "You'll have to be more specific."

He pursed his lips. "Very well. I shall send my friend to the mortal realm. When I do, I ask that you grant him the hospitality of your home for the duration of his stay."

I pictured Chase curled at the end of my bed, Jynx and her girlfriend tucked away in the back room, Emma hiding from her mother . . . and Kai. Once I got him back to the mortal realm, he'd have about two months left on his visa. I'd have to smooth things over with Bael before it expired. I rubbed away the crease between my eyebrows. One worry at a time.

"My house isn't exactly roomy."

"He can sleep on a floor if necessary."

"Room and board in exchange for your help getting Kai out." I stuck out my hand.

Something flickered across his expression. "Just to be clear, I promise to do my best to get you to your friend, and get you out. I can't guarantee nothing will go wrong. I expect you to hold up your end of the bargain regardless of our success."

I pursed my lips. While a guarantee would be nice, I could hardly hold Mica responsible for every possible obstacle, and he'd be risking as much as I was, breaking into the dungeon. "Assuming I'm still in a position to offer lodging after this, your friend will be welcome whether or not we get Kai out."

Pushing off the wall, he clasped my hand and shook it once. "Agreed."

"Then let's get moving."

My suitcase was already packed. I dropped my gun on top of the neatly folded clothes and zipped it shut. The bag was too bulky for a stealth mission. We'd need to swing by and grab it on our way out of the keep. Worst case, I could leave it behind. There was nothing in it I couldn't replace. Not anymore. I reached up to touch the charm around my neck, wishing my silver locket hung beside it.

Sighing, I checked the cinches belting my knife to my thigh, and the sword hanging at my hip. Then I headed for the front door.

Mica caught my wrist. "Not that way." He tipped his head back toward the balcony.

My heart stuttered. It was a good seventy feet from my room to the ground. I pulled my arm free. "Mostly mortal, remember? There's no way I can survive a fall from this height."

He smiled. "Trust me."

I shuddered. The last thing I wanted to do was trust my life to a fae I barely knew.

Grinding my teeth, I let him tug me out onto the balcony, praying I wouldn't regret it.

He wrapped one arm around my waist, then scooped behind my knees with the other so I was cradled against his chest. "Hang on."

I wrapped my arms around his neck. This close, the scent of nutmeg wafted off his skin.

My stomach lurched as he hopped up onto the balcony rail. Empty space yawned beneath me, all the way to the ragged white marble of the cliffs below. I buried my face against Mica's neck, gripping tighter.

His voice drifted over me, a whisper on the wind, in a language I couldn't decipher. Then he launched off the side of the balcony.

Chapter 16

A BLAST OF COLD air swirled around me. I squeezed my eyes shut against it, clinging to the solid warmth of Mica's body as we both plummeted toward the ground. Except, we didn't.

The howling whistle of the wind eased. The rush of air pulled back like a drawn breath.

I cracked open one eye in time to see Mica's feet come to rest on polished stone like a feather drifting to the ground. He set me on my feet, but I kept one hand on his shoulder to steady myself as I looked around.

We hadn't gone down so much as sideways. My balcony jutted from the keep wall a little above and thirty feet to the right, outlined dimly by the warm glow of the city lights beyond. The path we were on was thin, with a sheer drop below and a towering wall above. A door at one end led to the keep. In the other direction, the path hugged the cliff face, fading into darkness.

I'd left my hair in the intricate braids Tess had arranged for dinner, so despite the mini tornado we'd traveled through, only a few windblown wisps of hair tickled my face. I tucked them back, finally releasing my hold on Mica. "Impressive."

He shrugged and turned toward the keep door. "It's not for nothing that I was thought to be Bael's heir. I might not be an imbuer, but my enchantments are first-rate."

Mica led us through the door and down narrow, darkened corridors, dusty from disuse. We didn't pass any courtiers, or even any servants. Wherever we were, these tunnels seemed long forgotten, and we drifted along them like specters in the silent night.

Eventually, light bloomed ahead. Mica pulled to a stop just shy of the lit intersection, staying out of the lantern's glow. Turning to me, he pressed a finger to his lips.

I glared. I hadn't spoken a word since reentering the keep. Did he think I was about to start singing now that we'd reached the dangerous part?

Crouching low, he pressed his fingertips to the white stone and mumbled another unintelligible phrase in that haunting whisper. The light seemed to dim slightly for a moment, but other than that there was no change.

He motioned me forward and stepped into the intersection.

When I passed the safety of the corner, I froze. A little way down the side corridor was a heavy set of wood panels with silver bars crossing its surface. Sidhe guards stood to either side. I assumed this was the entrance to the dungeon... until Mica passed it by with barely a glance.

He continued straight. I trotted after, glancing back once before rounding the next corner to ensure neither of the guards had followed. The hallway remained empty behind us.

First-rate enchantments indeed.

Mica wound through a labyrinth of uniform stone hallways. Smokeless lanterns cast even illumination over the halls since we'd passed out of the unused section. Occasionally, plain wood doors would break the monotony. Sometimes voices drifted through the stagnant air, but we didn't see any more guards.

The wall Mica eventually stopped in front of was smooth marble, just like all the others.

"What are we—"

Mica placed his palm against the wall, and the stone beneath disappeared.

"This is the path to the dungeon," he said, and stepped through.

I hopped over the threshold like a child afraid the elevator doors might suddenly close and crush her. As soon as I was through, the stone returned, sealing off the well-lit hallway behind me. Torches lined this section too, but they seemed dimmer, farther apart. The ceiling and walls were closer, and a feeling of being crushed beneath the weight of the mountain crept over me. My palms began to sweat. I licked dry lips.

Mica was already moving, and my adrenaline spiked as he rounded a corner and passed out of sight.

I raced to catch up.

Two turns later, he led me down a winding staircase that corkscrewed into the belly of the mountain. Each step I took added to the pressure bearing down on me.

"How far does this go?" My words bounced around the tight space, ricocheting back up the stairs as though racing for the exit.

He kept his eyes forward. "Past the dungeons. Deep into the mountain."

Three landings splintered off the staircase, each a momentary reprieve to the endless spiral, before Mica finally stepped through a stone arch set in the wall. A silver gate blocked our path. No torches shone beyond the gate. The light from the hall petered out about three feet past the bars.

Mica approached the gate, but didn't reach for the silver bars. Instead, he called to the empty hall beyond. "We've come to see the prisoner Malakai."

I'd mentally prepared myself for what Kai's incarceration might look like, but I'd hoped he'd been granted some kind of leniency, afforded some comfort. After all, he hadn't done anything wrong. If anything, his sacrifice had allowed Bael to save face, not to mention saving my life. But here we were, deep in the bowels of the cold, hard mountain to see a *prisoner*.

I glanced around the empty hall, fingering the ribbon wrapped around my wrist. Had Mica set me up? I thought we were going to sneak into the dungeons, not walk right up to the front door and say hello.

A shadow detached from the wall, stepping into existence. He solidified as his foot touched the stone, the details of his features filling in like a time-lapse drawing. He wore the same green and leather uniform as the other guards, but the colors seemed duller, less saturated. His skin was ashen gray, lacking highlights or shadows. I'd seen skin like that twice before, on Galen and Morgan—shadow walkers.

The man squared his feet in front of the gate, watching us between the bars. His gaze settled on me, dark and inscrutable.

Mica lifted his chin. "Val."

The shadow walker gave a small nod, reached out, and pulled open the gate. It swung on silent hinges. There didn't seem to be any latch.

Mica passed the ashen-faced man who still held the gate.

I hesitated, but whatever was happening here, it was too late to turn back. I'd made my choice when I jumped off the balcony with Mica. I'd have to face the consequences.

I stepped over the threshold, and the gate closed. I was trapped.

The gatekeeper moved around us to take the lead. Then he held out his hand.

Mica gripped it and offered his free hand to me.

Frowning, I twined my fingers with Mica's.

Our guide stepped forward . . . and disappeared into the wall of inky black shadows that hid the rest of the room. Mica followed, pulling me after.

I was in a place without light, without sound. I couldn't even feel the ground beneath my feet or the stale air against my skin. The only anchor I had was Mica's hand, and I clung to it like a lifeline. Without it, would I be lost in the darkness forever?

I forced my feet to keep moving despite an overwhelming desire to curl up on the spot. I was too exposed, too vulnerable. Anything could be out there in the darkness. It could be right next to me, and I wouldn't even know it.

Sweat prickled over my skin, making me itch.

I took another step, and stumbled into the light.

Tears streamed from the corners of my eyes as I blinked, trying to adjust to the sudden, blinding sun of the torch on the wall. I looked behind me. Shadows rippled like an oily curtain pulled across the path. In front of us was another gate, identical to the first. The shadow walker held it open.

I released Mica's hand, but followed close on his heels until I was past the gray-skinned man and the silver bars. When I turned, the gate was closed. The man was already fading back into the shadows.

"What was that?" My voice wavered.

"Shadow road," Mica said. "It's the only way through. Luckily, Val owed me a favor." He nodded toward the empty hallway leading away from the gate. "Not far now."

Straightening my shoulders, I set my jaw and followed him along the passage.

Mica stopped in front of a door three turns past the gate. He reached into a pouch tied to his belt and pulled out a slip of paper. Muttering, he set the paper against his palm, where it stuck, then pressed it against the dark wood. The door swung open.

"And thus your friend is freed." Mica stepped back. "I'll give you a moment."

Kai was lying on a mattress on the floor, a book held open above him, just as I'd seen him dozens of times in his room in my house. My chest constricted. Off to one side was a toilet seat, and a pedestal sink full of grayish water, both carved from the marble floor as though they'd grown in place. A single shelf spanned half the back wall, holding a collection of books, a wooden puzzle cube, a stack of papers, and a quill pen. A sealed lantern glowed on either side of the shelf.

Kai was on his feet by the time I crossed the room, and I threw my arms around his neck.

The door clicked closed behind me.

"I'm so sorry," I said at the same time as he asked, "What are you doing here?"

We pushed to arm's length, each shaking our heads.

"It's not your fault," he said.

"It is," I insisted. "And I told Bael so, but he didn't care."

Kai's lips lifted, but the smile was sad. "Of course not."

"But—"

"You shouldn't have come." He tipped his head to the side, looking past me to the closed door. "Who brought you?"

"The guy from the party. Mica."

Kai's gaze swung back to me. "The failed prince? Why?"

I shrugged one shoulder, not wanting to go into the whole story about babies, blind dates, and favors. "We're getting you out of here."

Kai backed away from me, crossing his arms. "What are you talking about, Alex? Unless the lord decrees it, I can't leave."

"But you didn't do anything wrong!"

He shook his head. "It doesn't matter. I am a Knight of the Realm. This is my duty. What kind of knight would I prove myself to be if I ran away?"

"Screw being a knight. You can come back to the mortal realm with me."

"And what happens when my visa runs out in two months? Where would I go then?"

"It's fifty years." I sank down on the edge of his mattress, knees pressed to my chest. "How can you be okay with that?"

"Honestly, this is not the worst outcome I had pictured for your debut. At least we're both alive."

He sighed and settled down beside me. "When I was dispatched to the mortal realm, it was not because I was respected or trusted... it's because I was convenient. After this, I will have earned my place among the knights, proven my dedication. Besides, fifty years isn't such a long time for the fae."

"It's a lifetime for a mortal." I hugged my knees tighter. "If I hadn't lost my temper—"

"Don't." His expression softened. "It does no good to dwell on the past. Substituting in the duel, accepting this," he gestured to the walls of his cell, "was *my* choice. I will fulfill this task as I would any other knightly mission—for honor, for fealty," he set a hand on my knee, "and for friendship. Do not try to undermine my sacrifice."

"Coming here was a mistake," I whispered.

Kai frowned. "Yes. But I'm glad you did. It's nice to get to say goodbye."

"Not *here*, here." I waved at the walls. "Enchantment. I should have refused to come to court."

He shook his head. "What's that saying you have about spilling milk? Or was it beans?"

I smiled despite myself. "You're hopeless."

He smiled too.

"Thank you," I said. "For saving me."

He looked me up and down, a serious expression on his face. "I don't suppose you have any candy stashed in your pockets?"

I snorted. "It's all in my suitcase, waiting for our triumphant return."

He sighed, pushing his toe against an empty wooden tray at the end of his bed. Pale crumbs and a smear of something brown dirtied its surface. "Pity. The food here is somewhat lacking in the sweets department."

I clenched my jaw. Kai might have resigned himself to his fate, but I couldn't. It was my mistake. He didn't deserve to suffer for it. "I can't just leave you here."

"There's nothing else you *can* do."

My throat closed up. That wasn't exactly true. I could agree to Bael's deal. Kai would be released, his stupid knightly honor intact.

Sitting there in Kai's prison, knowing I'd never see him again, it was hard to care about a child who didn't exist, might never exist. Bael would only want the kid if it was an imbuer, and what were the odds?

I shook my head. I couldn't do it. I couldn't trade one life for another. "I'm sorry."

Kai draped his arm over my shoulder, giving me a squeeze. "I was able to both serve my lord and save my charge. There is no higher honor for a knight."

The door cracked open and Mica stuck his head inside. "Time to go."

Kai stood, pulling me to my feet as Mica retreated into the hall. "Be careful with Mica," he whispered. "I heard he's been hanging around Haru a lot lately."

I froze. "The kitsune from the festival?"

He nodded. "I don't know much about Haru except that he came here from the Shifter Court broken and bitter. Best to avoid him if you can."

I thought about the way Mica had stepped away from me when Haru cut into our dance. He'd moved *toward* Haru. . . . Could Haru be the friend Mica wanted a future with? The friend I'd agreed to house?

"Get going." Kai gave me one last hug and pushed me toward the door.

I paused on the threshold. "I'm not giving up on you."

"Don't do anything stupid."

I forced a smile onto my face, and pulled the door closed on his prison.

Mica was a little way up the hall, peeking around the corner. He turned when the door shut, though it made barely a sound. He looked from me to the closed door and the empty hall behind me. Then he said, "He's not coming."

"You don't seem surprised."

He looked away. "I thought this might happen. Knights are loyal to a fault."

I stepped away from the door, nodding. Loyal enough to get himself thrown in prison for fifty years to save a stupid mortal with a big mouth. "That's why you reworded the deal so it didn't depend on Kai's release."

"Do you still want to take him with us?"

I frowned. "It doesn't matter. He's made up his mind."

Mica pulled a small pouch off his belt. "My favor is to you, not him, and I said I'd give you my best. If you want him out, we can still do it."

My foot came down at an odd angle as his words hit me, and I reached out to steady myself against the rough stone wall. "You mean take him against his will?"

"You could both be in the mortal realm before he woke up."

My mouth went dry. I glanced back at the wood door leading to his cold, stone prison with its flat mattress and bad food. I could still save him from that fate.

But . . . he wouldn't forgive me.

I shook my head. "He's made his choice. I may not like it, but I have to respect it."

Mica shrugged and tied the little pouch back to his belt. He didn't seem to care one way or the other about Kai's freedom, so long as our deal was intact. "Then let's get you back to your room."

We didn't speak as we made our way to the silver cage that guarded the only exit. Val emerged from the shadows as soon as Mica called, and once more he opened the gate for us. Once more he took us into those shadows that weren't shadows, to that emptiness between. When I stumbled free of that cloying darkness on the tether of Mica's hand, I bumped into his stiff back.

"Ouch," I said. "Why'd you stop?"

Mica turned cold eyes on Val, who raised his palms to the ceiling. "You were not the only one to call in a favor this night."

The shadow walker melted back into the black.

"I'm disappointed." Rhoana's voice bounced flatly against the stones, filling the hall.

Holding my breath, I peeked around Mica's rigid shoulder.

The Captain of the Guard stood just past the open silver gate, flanked by two liveried guards holding spears. She shook her head. "But I am not surprised."

Chapter 17

"WHAT HAVE YOU to say for yourself?" Bael's back was to me. He looked out over the glowing city of Abonaille Malmür from the garden balcony where Mica and I had had dinner, where we'd made our alliance. The first blush of dawn lit the distant horizon like a swirl of blood in the indigo sky.

"What have you done with Mica?"

Bael glanced over his shoulder, one eyebrow raised. "I will deal with him later. First, I would like the story from you. Why were you in the dungeon?"

"I didn't get to say goodbye to Kai when you had him dragged out of the festival."

"So you went merely to say goodbye?"

I raised my arms to either side, indicating the empty garden around us. "He isn't here, is he?"

I was getting good at this whole lying while telling the truth thing. I just hoped Mica would be as careful.

The corners of Bael's mouth turned up. "Malakai is ever the faithful knight."

I frowned. It seemed Bael understood Kai better than I did.

"Very well," Bael turned fully to face me and leaned back against the stone railing, arms crossed. "You foolishly went behind my back to bid your friend and savior goodbye before leaving for the mortal realm. Since you could not get there on your own, you negotiated for Mica to escort you."

His smile widened. "I'm glad to see the two of you getting along so well. Rhoana said you seemed displeased when she escorted you back from dinner."

I rubbed a sweaty palm over my hip. I'd been happy enough not to have to face Bael right after the meal, not to have to answer the question I could see burning behind his eyes as we spoke now. I cut my gaze to the goblin fruit bush near Bael's elbow. "Did you mean for me to eat the fruit?"

"Why would I want that?"

"Why didn't you warn me about it?"

"It should have been covered in your training. That *is* why I left Malakai with you, and even sent you one of the finest Court tutors."

I shook my head. Bael could bandy words all day and never give a straight answer. He'd had centuries to practice.

Bael plucked a golden fruit from the bush and polished it against his shirt. "You needn't say goodbye to Malakai today."

I took a step back, putting more distance between us as he took a bite of fruit. Juice dribbled over the ruptured skin, filling the damp morning air with a sweet aroma that made me lightheaded. "I can't give you what you want."

"We won't know until we try." He pushed off the rail, walking toward me with the dripping fruit in his hand.

I balled my fists. "I *won't*."

"That's disappointing." He set the partially-eaten goblin fruit on the table that had held my dinner, now clear of silver trays and wiped clean of every last crumb. "A different deal then. Stay, let me teach you more about your abilities. You've barely scratched the surface. I'll give you leave to visit the dungeons as often as you like. Perhaps I'll even have Malakai transferred to more . . . accessible accommodations."

His words sent prickles across my skin.

Lord Bael prefers to keep me close, disappointment though I am.

Was Bael really interested in training me, or did he intend to keep me close, like Mica, so he could wear away my resolve? I got the feeling if I caved to Bael's wishes, even a little, I might never climb free.

"I have to get back."

"To what? As I understand it, you've lost your employment. You have few mortal friends, none of whom you trust to keep your secret. And there's a PTF agent with a personal vendetta against you. Not a life I'd miss if I were you."

"But it's *my* life. And you're not me."

He pursed his lips. "Very well, but know that my offer stands. After all, mortals can be so very . . . changeable."

RHOANA STOOD against my bedroom wall with her arms crossed, as still as the marble that supported her. She hadn't taken her eyes off me since relieving the guard who'd escorted me back to my room. She also hadn't spoken. Not about catching me in the dungeon, not about my conversation with Bael, and not about what had become of Mica after she hauled him away.

Sighing, I sank onto the edge of my bed. "Can't you at least tell me if he's being punished?"

She continued to stare at me with tight lips and flinty, indigo eyes, just as she had the last dozen times I'd asked after Mica's fate.

A soft rap sounded at the front door, and I gave Rhoana a good glare as I passed into the living room to answer it. Hortense stood on the red carpet of the hall in a lavender dress embroidered with butterflies. She pushed past me without greeting or permission, a breach of etiquette that would have made me smile if my insides weren't twisted in knots over Mica's fate.

"That was reckless," she said as I closed the door behind her.

"Good morning to you too."

"What were you thinking?"

I bunched my fists and squared my shoulders. "That no one else was willing to help me. That Kai was being punished for my mistake. That I don't just abandon my friends, no matter what some pompous ass on an iron throne may say."

Hortense and Rhoana, who'd followed me from the bedroom, both jerked as though slapped. Insulting their lord and master was an insult to their honor as much as his, but I didn't care. They'd both stood by while Kai was imprisoned. Then again, so had Kai. Twice.

I ran a hand over the tight braids holding my hair in place. "I was trying to help."

Hortense crossed her arms. "The next time you want to help . . . don't. Your antics nearly landed Mica in the dungeons right beside Malakai, and you're lucky to have avoided that fate as well. If you'd been discovered inside his cell, rather than leaving without him . . ." She cut her eyes to Rhoana.

I turned away. If Kai hadn't been such a stubborn, honor-bound knight we'd all be roommates in the dungeon right now. He'd saved me again. At least Hortense had given me a clue about Mica. *Nearly* meant he hadn't been thrown in prison for his part in our ill-fated outing. I exhaled, releasing some of the tension I'd been nursing since we were separated.

"I trust you at least got some closure?" She sank into a chair beside the picked-over fruit platter.

"I'm still not happy leaving him there."

"Nor should you be." She lifted an apple and rolled it between her palms, not looking at me. "I understand the lord has given you an option for buying Malakai's release."

I snorted. "Did he send you to change my mind?"

She shook her head. "I'm here to caution you. Deals with the fae are a dangerous business. Whatever you decide, be careful."

"Hold your tongue, Tutor." Rhoana had uncrossed her arms and taken a step toward Hortense.

Hortense raised an eyebrow. "You disagree?"

The tutor and knight glared at each other. Rhoana looked away first, which made me smile.

"You should show more loyalty to the lord," she said.

"It is my duty to educate Alex in our ways. I am merely following orders."

Rhoana snorted, then shifted her glare to me. "It's time to go."

"One sec." I lifted a finger to Hortense. "Wait here. I have a favor to ask you."

I trotted back into the bedroom, leaving the two women to ignore one another. My packed suitcase rested on the purple covers of the bed, right where I'd left it, but I pulled up short when it came into view. Sitting atop the case was a tiny, carved wooden gaala.

I stared at the figure for a moment, then took the last couple steps and lifted it off my bag. I glanced around the room. Empty. The curtains to my balcony shifted on a light breeze. I shoved them aside and stepped onto the balcony, scanning side to side.

Far to the right was the path Mica had jumped us to the night before, clinging to the mountain's face and winding away like a white ribbon. To the left, far below, was the edge of the garden maze. And beyond that, the city of Abonaille Malmür, its white walls ablaze under the glow of the morning sun.

A chill wind trickled down from the mountain's peak like the last breath of the night. It tugged my braid and tickled my exposed neck, making me shiver.

I looked down at the little gaala in my hands. Its antlers were as thin and sharp as toothpicks. The front left and middle right of its six legs were slightly raised, as though it could spring into motion at any moment. Its hide was textured such that I almost expected the fur to be soft against my fingertips. Dark stain colored the gaala's body, while the nose and antlers were pale brown. Its eyes were tiny dark stones set on either side of its head. The creature was so detailed it looked alive.

I closed shaking fingers over Bael's creation. Was this meant to be a peace offering? A consolation prize since he refused to give me what we both knew I wanted? And why sneak it into my room rather than just knock on my door? What game was he playing?

"I've had enough of faerie games and unwanted gifts." Drawing back my arm, I threw the carving as hard as I could toward the jagged rock of the uncut mountain.

The little gaala fell like a comet for about three feet. Then it curved, and circled back toward my balcony.

I stumbled away from the edge as the gaala flew over the railing. It hovered at eye level, less than an arm's length away. Its tiny wooden legs pawed the air, just as its living counterpart's had.

"You've got to be kidding me," I muttered, edging away from the little creature.

When I backed through the curtains, it followed me into the bedroom, coming to rest once more on top of my suitcase. Guess Bael hadn't snuck into my room after all. He hadn't needed to.

Licking my lips, I lifted the carving again. It was still once more, though frozen in a slightly different position. Perhaps it was my imagination, but the slightest heat seemed to come off the tiny body.

I clenched my jaw. The novelty of the gift didn't change the fact that Bael was trying to buy me—tempt me into taking his offer by showing me what my magic might be capable of. I set the gaala on top of the dressing table and crossed my arms.

Taking a deep breath, I forced my muscles to relax as I exhaled and unfocused my eyes like I was looking into a 3D picture. The gaala glowed a faint red. I followed the threads of magic binding it the way Bael had me practice, and found the shape of its center, the imbued soul of the thing. It was a bright, tangled, knot—far more complicated than the sharpened spoon or altered marbles of my practice session. Bael had woven intricate commands into the creature's existence. Commands it would take me years to understand, let alone alter.

I could leave his gift in the room, but it would probably just follow me. If I wanted to be rid of it, the best bet was to break it.

I reached for the little creature and lifted it on the palm of my hand. The magic inside it flared, the red ribbons pulsing and coursing like blood through its veins. It pawed my palm with tiny, sharp, hooves and shook its head with a snort.

I smiled.

I couldn't do it. Angry as I was with Bael, I couldn't destroy something so . . . amazing.

Crossing back to my bag, I lifted the top and tucked the little gaala into one of my shirts. Then I pulled out the bag of candy I'd come in for.

Hortense and Rhoana were where I'd left them—the tutor in her chair, studying the fruit, and the knight against the wall, studying the carpet. I dropped Kai's bag of candy on the table. The thick, plastic package crinkled, reminding me of the sound of wrappers that so often accompanied Kai's presence. "Will you give these to Kai?"

Hortense wrinkled her nose at the bag of Snickers bars, Jolly Ranchers, caramels, and Smarties. "He brought these from the mortal realm?"

"He said you didn't have food like this here. And apparently, the dungeon food is even worse."

She sniffed. "Of course we don't eat anything like that here. I'd hardly call it food." She reached out and lifted the package. "But I will deliver it to Malakai."

I pressed my lips shut over the "thank you" that tried to slip out, and nodded.

"If you're quite finished . . ." Rhoana pushed away from the wall.

I set my hand on Hortense's arm. "Will you come with us to the portal?"

She shook her head. "This is where I shall say goodbye." She gave a deep, formal bow. "Lady Alyssandra, Alex, it has been my pleasure."

I shifted my feet, uncomfortable. Hortense and I hadn't always gotten along. In fact, we barely got along at all, but she'd become a part of my everyday life. Her lectures were dry and boring, but I'd learned a lot. And while she liked to complain and point out my faults, she'd also helped me. I touched the stealth charm still tucked under my shirt. I owed her a lot. She was stuffy and stuck up, but I would miss her. "Will I see you again?"

She lifted her hands to either side. "Who can say? But I would not be surprised."

A small smile curved my lips. "Take care of yourself."

She nodded, then left. When the door closed behind her, the room felt colder, empty.

I grabbed my suitcase from the bedroom and took one last look around my temporary home in Bael's keep. Then I nodded to Rhoana. I was ready to leave Enchantment.

THE CROWDED streets and shining stones of Abonaille Malmür fell away beneath the heaving body of my gaala. It wasn't the same one as before. This one was smaller, its hide lighter and faintly spotted. Its hooves pawed the air just as my little carving's had, raising us into the sky in a series of expanding circles.

Ahead, Rhoana's green cloak snapped in the wind.

Unlike the entourage that accompanied my arrival, my departure from Bael's domain was limited to the two of us and our steeds. No guards, no Hortense, no Kai. At least the wind made it impossible to talk, so Rhoana's steely silence was a little less uncomfortable.

I let myself relax into the motion of the gaala as its muscles stretched and contracted beneath me, gobbling up the sky, and pretended I was alone.

Unlike my nighttime ride, this time I could see the city clearly. The colorful tapestries that softened the hard, uniform edges of the buildings, the market vendors with both physical and magical signs advertising wares that ranged from fresh produce and used books to poached fetuses and deadly poisons. Fae in the lower sections of the city ran errands, hung out laundry, and stopped to gossip in the street. With my growing distance blurring the details, it looked just like a human city.

My gaala banked to the right, following Rhoana's out over the side of the cliff where the river that split the city plummeted to the forest below in a cloud of mist and spray. The trees that had been uniform silhouettes on my last ride now showed their colors, peeking out from the snow not only in shades of green, but an occasional blue, red, and purple as well.

The sun had cleared the horizon and was warm on my skin, chasing back the chill of the whipping wind. I held the reins loosely this time—not having been surprised into dropping them—and sat straight rather than hugging the gaala's neck. When Rhoana started her descent, I glanced back. The mountain was a white peak jutting into the sky, but there was no sign of the distant city nestled in its folds. Then I dropped below the tree line, and even the mountain disappeared.

My feet sank into the snow when I dismounted, crunching through the thin crust of ice my light-footed gaala managed not to crack. Rhoana unstrapped my suitcase from her gaala and plopped it in the snow in front of me, then motioned me to follow her.

I gave the amazing creature one last stroke down the side of its long neck, then tromped through the unbroken snow after Rhoana. As soon as I stepped away, an eloko in green and leather livery, possibly the same one as before, stepped out of the woods as though he materialized out of thin air, and took the gaala's reins. He gathered up Rhoana's as well, and led both beasts back into the forest.

The portal was just as I remembered it, an unassuming space between two trees marked only by a slight shimmer in the air, like heat rising off asphalt. Rhoana stood to one side, her hands clasped loosely behind her back.

I stood, frozen, in front of the portal for a moment, remembering the intense pain of my last passage. Then, hefting my bag, I took a shuddering breath, set my jaw, and stepped through the invisible wall between realms.

A wave of cold followed by tingling heat washed over me, but it didn't escalate to burning. There was no pain. I stumbled across damp dirt and dry pine needles as my momentum carried me another few steps and came to a stop in the middle of a sparse forest with beetle-kill trees infecting the view and patchy snow less than a quarter as deep as what I'd waded through to get there.

I set my bag down and stared at my shaking hands. My link to James was really gone. I'd expected it, but that didn't lessen my sense of loss.

"Come on." Rhoana stepped around me—I hadn't even noticed her come through the portal—and headed off through the woods. Clearly, this wasn't her first trip to the mortal realm.

Lifting my bag once more, I followed to the clearing where Kai, Chase, and I had first arrived on the reservation. I scanned the trees, hoping against hope to see a familiar face. Chase said he'd make his own way back to my house when his visit was over. That didn't mean he *couldn't* come back with me if we bumped into each other. But the forest remained still except for a small brown bird hopping over a mound of thawed earth in search of food and the rustle of the wind through the creaking trees.

Rhoana examined our surroundings too, but more like a general looking for weaknesses in a battle plan. Her hand rested lightly on the hilt of her sword.

I cleared my throat. "You don't have to wait with me."

"It is my duty to ensure your safety until you leave the reservation. Then you're on your own."

I lifted one shoulder and turned away from her. If she wanted to wait, let her wait.

The mortal forest seemed strangely dull compared to its fae

counterpart. I licked my lips. Would the towns seem that way too, filled as they were with a single, unimaginative species? I'd grown somewhat accustomed to people who were unusual colors, or walked on four legs, or flew, and I was a little sad to see them go. Not that there weren't fae among the humans, but still.

A small *pop* rang in my ears, and I turned to find Otis, the old man with sagging skin and tired eyes from my previous trip, standing in the middle of the clearing.

"Come on, come on, I don't have all day." He waved a hand at me, and another at Rhoana.

"Just one for this trip," she said, taking a step away from the teleporter. Then she turned to me. "I'm sure I'll be seeing you again. In the meantime, be careful."

I nodded, and grasped Otis's offered hand.

Rhoana frowned, a curious expression in her eyes as she studied me. "Malakai is lucky to have a friend like you."

I opened my mouth, but before any words came out, the forest around me blurred to white and was replaced by the four walls of the way station cabin.

Otis dropped my hand and shuffled over to the picnic table, where he sank onto a bench in front of a plate piled high with sausages. The smells of pine and soil were replaced with hot grease and maple syrup. Grainy music played through a small speaker set on a knickknack-covered curio cabinet. A wooden stand of postcards sat on the check-in desk beside a tear-away calendar that showed I'd lost a week and a half since the last time I stood in that room. The old woman from before was up to her elbows in soapy water at the kitchen sink.

I was back in the mortal realm. Alone.

Chapter 18

"WILL YOU BE RESTING a bit, luv? Or pushing off right away?" The curly, gray hairs on the woman's head bounced as she shook her hands over the sink, sending water droplets flying. She grabbed a checkered hand towel. "We've got plenty of beds available."

I shook my head. I was tired of being surrounded by strangers. Now that I was back on planet Earth, I just wanted to get home as quickly as possible. "I'm leaving."

I shifted my feet and studied the wall behind the reception desk. Kai's blue-capped key hung on the peg board beside a dozen others. Kai had promised to escort me home even if he was recalled from the mortal realm—a quick day trip to see me back safe and say goodbye. We hadn't imagined he'd be unable to leave Enchantment.

I could call a cab, or maybe catch a bus in the nearby town, but either option would leave a trail tying my absence to the reservation. Something we'd been trying to avoid.

I studied the hob wiping her hands. Would she give Kai's key to a mostly mortal? Would she wonder why he hadn't come back with me?

"My friend left his car here . . ."

The woman nodded, then tossed the damp towel on the counter and waddled over to the rack of keys behind her desk. She reached up and grabbed the one with the blue cap, the one that had come off Kai's keyring.

She held the key out to me. "We moved the car around back."

The key's solid weight settled on my palm like a heavy truth. Kai wasn't coming home. Pressure prickled behind my eyes. I sniffed and closed my fingers around the rubber-capped key.

"You sure you don't want to rest first?" Her eyebrows pulled together. "You look done in."

I shook my head and coughed to clear the lump in my throat. "Do I need to sign anything?"

"For what?"

I lifted the hand with the key. "The car."

A wide smile split her face. "Why? Are you planning to steal it?"

I took a step back, caught off-guard by the question. "Of course not."

"Just bring it back when you're done." She patted me on the arm and shuffled back to the kitchen, where she started kneading a large blob of dough.

"Right, well . . ." I raised one hand in a little wave. The woman didn't look up from her dough. The man didn't look up from his sausages. I grabbed the handle of my suitcase, adjusted my sword, and headed out the door.

Kai's car was parked behind the way station, wedged between a dented white van and a green Dodge Neon. I pulled my cell phone and wallet out of my suitcase and stashed the bag in the trunk, tucking my sword safely along one side. Then I settled behind the steering wheel.

I lifted the key toward the ignition, but hesitated. It felt wrong to drive Kai's car home. But life wasn't going to stop just because I'd screwed up. I didn't have time to wallow.

I turned over the engine and cranked up the heat. Then I pulled out my cell phone and plugged the adapter into the car. Once I had power, I called Marc and crossed my fingers he'd answer.

"You're back." Marc's voice was deep and rich, and I relaxed a little when I heard it. At least *something* had gone right.

"Just," I said. "Is everyone okay?"

"All good. Released with clean records."

I blew out a noisy sigh of relief. Sol had come through.

But what would he want in return?

When Mica offered his help in exchange for a favor, I'd forced him to be specific, afraid to make the kind of open-ended promise I'd made to Sol. But Sol was one of the few people I could actually trust. Whatever he asked, it would be worth it.

"Thanks for looking out for us," Marc said.

"Glad it worked out. Do your best to steer clear of O'Connell in the future."

"You too."

Hanging up the phone, I threw the car in gear and turned it toward the dusty road.

KAI'S CAR STRUGGLED up my driveway, tires skidding, turning the snow to slush and mud. It had been a long, lonely drive back from the reservation. The sun set while I ate a burger and fries at a McDonald's off the highway two hours from home. I would have driven straight through, but I hadn't eaten since breakfast and my hands had started to shake.

Now, with home just around the next bend, it looked like the poor little Toyota might not finish the trip. Perhaps it was as reluctant to admit we'd abandoned Kai as I was.

The engine gave a high-pitched whine as I forced it around a thickly drifted bend that rarely saw the winter sun. The rear end swung to the side. The car lurched, slipping into the gully of a washout ditch. Gripping the wheel to keep from punching the dash, I threw the car in reverse and tried to back onto the higher section of road, but again the tires refused to find purchase. The car rocked back and forth, grudgingly shifting mere inches each time I switched directions. My energy waned with each attempt until I sat slumped in the still car.

Sighing, I cut the engine. The Toyota was far enough over to allow another, more capable vehicle to pass. That would have to do.

I tucked Kai's key safely in my pocket, popped the trunk, and stepped into half a foot of snow. The bend in my driveway where I'd gotten stuck was shaded by conifers, so that particular section froze early and didn't thaw until late spring. It was sometimes a struggle even for my Jeep. I'd been a fool to think the little Toyota could make it through.

I trudged to the back of the car and pulled out my suitcase. Then I slammed the trunk and started the cold, wet trek up the last stretch of driveway to my house. I walked mostly where tire tracks had compressed the snow, but the packed ice was slick, and the awkward weight of my bag brought me down to a knee several times.

Cold and numb, I finally crested the last hill, bringing me in sight of home. The deep tracks I'd been following led to my Jeep, parked right where I'd left it. Off to one side, a VW Bug huddled under a dome of snow, yellow peeking out where sections of the white stuff had sloughed off.

Right . . . Emma.

I tightened my grip on the suitcase. I'd imagined having to explain Kai's absence to Chase and Jynx as soon as I got in, but with Emma there we wouldn't be able to speak freely. A wash of relief flooded me, making me feel like a traitor for my cowardice.

It would all come out soon enough. The fact that Kai was stuck in a dungeon for the next fifty years . . . and the fact that it was my fault. I'd failed him. Now I'd come home without him. My fingers started to ache on the handle of my bag, so I forced them to relax.

Following the grooves left by my Jeep, I headed toward the house, but when I came within a dozen paces of the front porch a wave of pain washed over me like I'd passed through a curtain of acid. I gasped, dropped my bag in the snow, and stumbled backward. The pain passed almost as fast as it had come, but a sensation like a sunburn lingered on my skin, making me want to scratch my arms and face.

I leaned over and planted my hands firmly against my thighs, digging my fingers in to keep them still. My lungs pumped in double time, racing my heart. What the hell had happened?

The front door of my house opened and Emma burst out, along with a rectangle of warm orange light that glinted across the snow and the smell of fresh-baked cookies.

"Alex?" She trotted across the yard and leaned down so her eyes were even with mine. Jaw-length hair framed her face, deep red near the roots fading to bleach-blond yellow at the tips. Her eyebrows drew together, metal rings glinting above her shadowed eyes. "Are you okay?"

I glanced at my suitcase, half-buried in the snow three feet away. My sword had tumbled free in the fall, its dark sheath a streak of black over the snow. Prying my fingers off my thighs, I straightened up and shook my head. The tingle in my skin was fading. "I'm not sure. I got some sort of . . . jolt just now."

Her frown deepened. "A jolt?"

"Like I hit a wall that tried to sear the flesh off my bones." I wrapped my arms around myself, squeezing.

Emma crossed her arms and turned toward the house, staring into the distance. "That's weird. You shouldn't have been able to feel it, even if you are a—" She snapped her mouth shut and swung her gaze back to me, eyes wide.

My lungs froze in place, the air knocked out of me as though I'd taken a punch to the gut. "A what," I whispered.

"I . . ." She shook her head so hard it looked like it would pop off her neck. "Ugh. Me and my big mouth. Don't be mad, okay?"

Coils of dread wound through my abdomen, squeezing my organs. "Mad about what exactly?"

"I know you're a fae."

I stumbled back. Emma's voice faded to a muted mumble as a ringing filled my ears like the shock of a bomb blast.

My secret was out.

Who had she told? Could Sol cover it up? Did she know about my imbuing? My connection to Bael? My thoughts skittered in all directions like roaches running from a light, scurrying away from the awful exposure that would surely bring their death.

I swallowed and took a shaky breath. "How?"

She frowned. "I'm not stupid, Alex. And I'm a practitioner's apprentice."

"Luke told you?"

"No," she said. "He would never. But I overheard things. All the weird stuff going on around you lately, plus your involvement with Luke and the werewolves? You had to be some kind of paranatural. Then I walked in on Jynx the other day and . . . well, let's just say your nervousness about having me stay here makes a lot more sense now. I admit the whole being-able-to-handle-iron thing threw me for a loop, but once I convinced Jynx she could trust me she filled in some of the gaps." She raised both hands. "Not that she blabbed your secrets or anything. She just confirmed what I'd already figured out."

My fists were shaking at my sides. The threads of my carefully maintained lies were unraveling. I'd come home to clean up my messes, to put my life back together. Now it seemed I was too late.

"I'm sorry." Emma was wringing her hands so hard it looked like she was trying to tear her fingers loose. "But it's okay, really. I didn't tell anyone. Honest. I think it's great."

That snapped me out of my spiral. Of course Emma would think it was great that I was a faerie. Emma, who defied her mother to pursue a life of magic. I shook my head, but smiled. "It's not as great as you might think."

"Are you kidding?" Emma's natural enthusiasm was back, chasing away her worry like a summer breeze clearing clouds from the sky. "It's awesome! I thought passing the practitioner test was cool, but to be fae? What I wouldn't give to have that kind of magic."

I snorted. When Emma told me she'd passed the practitioner test, she'd talked about waving a magic wand and having all her troubles disappear. Since my own magical awakening, I could safely say that magic created more problems than it solved. Especially for those of us still trying to live a human life. "Not all fae are powerful. Besides, I think your mother might explode if you turned out to be fae."

Her smile fell, and I instantly regretted my words.

"Sorry, Em. I wasn't thinking." I rubbed a hand over my hair, still tied back in Tess's tight braids. "It's been a long day."

"Yeah," she said. "I get it."

"How are things . . . with your mom?"

She shrugged. "She's still not talking to me. Sometimes I meet up with May at a park near our house to get the inside scoop, but . . ." She shook her head. "Mom's stubborn, but I honestly thought she'd be over it by now."

"And how about your training with Luke? Still worth it?"

She grinned, and her teeth glinted in the light from the porch. "Oh yeah. I'm learning things I never dreamed of. Speaking of which . . ."

Grabbing my upper arm, she tugged me toward the house. The hairs all over my body prickled like I was about to be struck by lightning.

"Um." I dug my heels into the snow, stopping our progress.

"I just want to test something."

I narrowed my eyes. "What did you do?"

Pride and guilt warred on her face. "Luke taught me how to make a protection field, and, well . . ."

"You put one around my house." I crossed my arms. I was annoyed, but also impressed. Wards were no small magic. "That's what lit my skin on fire."

She grimaced. "It might not be set up quite right."

"What did Luke say?"

Her expression grew even more sour and she started plucking at a loose thread on her white knit sweater.

I frowned. "You didn't tell him."

"I'm not . . . strictly speaking . . . supposed to do magic without his supervision."

I opened my mouth, but she waved her hands to cut me off.

"But I can fix it."

I raised an eyebrow.

"Probably." She scuffed the toe of one of my galoshes into the snow. She must have pulled them on to run outside. "At least let me try. Okay?"

I sighed, but waved a hand at the invisible curtain that had scalded me. "If you can get it to let me pass and still keep out any big bads coming for a visit, I'll owe you one."

Grinning, Emma rubbed her hands together like an eager child in anticipation of a trip to a candy store. "You won't regret this."

"I better not." I crossed my arms again and took a step back to give her room to work. That, and to lessen the tingle still crawling across my skin.

"Although . . ." She tipped her head to one side. "We might have to do this again for your roommate." She looked around the clearing, then glanced at the empty driveway I'd walked up. "Where's your car?"

I hooked a thumb behind me. "The car's back there. Couldn't make the climb."

"Let me guess, Kai didn't want to admit defeat."

It took all my strength to keep my expression neutral. "Kai extended his trip. He won't be back anytime soon."

She frowned, but when it became clear I wasn't going to explain any more about why Kai was a no-show she shrugged and turned away. Planting her feet, she stood still for a long moment, her arms slack at her sides, her eyes unfocused.

I chewed a loose cuticle, waiting. "Anytime now."

"Please don't talk." Her voice shook with strain, and I realized she must already be doing whatever it was she was going to do.

Curious, I shifted my own focus the way I had during my training with Bael. It took a minute, but eventually the invisible barrier became a shimmering, opalescent dome. The wall shifted in constant ripples that pressed against each other, magnifying in some places, canceling out in others.

Swirls of bluish energy wrapped around Emma, twisting like smoke snakes. The energy was concentrated around her hands, but her eyes also glowed faintly with the same bluish color. The world around us seemed washed out, a monochrome of dull amber like an old sepia photo. Except Emma. She shone like a flashlight on a moonless night.

Something moved near the shimmer of the barrier. I strained to see through the gloom. It was as though a dark, gray mist had settled around us, obscuring our surroundings. The stars were gone. Shadows flitted through the densest sections of the smoky haze as though something was hiding there.

"I need you to touch the barrier so it can recognize you." Emma's voice made me jump, highlighting the eerie quiet that had rolled in with the strange murk.

I licked my lips. I'd taken another couple steps away from the barrier without realizing it. A coil of the unnatural vapor passed through the simmering wall. The barrier continued to ripple and glow. Did that mean whatever was in the darkness wasn't hostile? Or was the fog just fog, and I was imagining everything else?

Gritting my teeth, I moved within arm's reach of the barrier and stretched out my hand. Some of the blue coils twisting around Emma changed directions. They slithered toward me, coiling up my arm and coalescing near my fingertips. I shivered, but repressed the urge to shake the creepy ribbons off.

My middle finger connected with the barrier and started to burn. A tsunami cascaded out from the point of contact, rippling across the dome's surface.

The mist shifted, pulling together in darker clumps in some places while gaps where the world was once again clear appeared in others. From those coalescing masses, shapes began to emerge. Long, multi-jointed arms unfolded, slick and smooth as oil. Leathery wings unfurled behind a thin, muscular chest covered in armor plates that shone like beetle shells. From one, a gaping mouth showed row after row of jagged teeth lining a black void. And just to my right, two bright red eyes blinked open. They rolled for a moment while the rest of the creature's face formed. Then its gaze met mine, and we both screamed.

The creature lunged toward me, its thin, leathery fingers reaching. Its eyes were twin infernos in the night.

I stumbled back, breaking contact with the wall and tripping over my own feet to land ass-first in the snow. Slush squelched around me as I scrambled back, groping for the knife no longer strapped to my thigh.

The creature followed my fall, closing in.

I kicked away, scooting back, and my hand brushed something hard in the snow. I glanced to the side to find the scabbard of my sword. Blinking, I grabbed the hilt and pulled the blade free, praying I'd be fast enough.

I swung, and sliced through . . . nothing.

The creature and all its companions had vanished, along with the gray clouds they'd first appeared to be.

I lay panting on the ground, clutching my sword. The cold seeped into me, making me shiver. Adrenaline pumped through my body, impotent, looking for an outlet. The stars were back, glinting like tiny diamonds in a velvet sky.

Emma stood four feet away, mouth open, eyes wide. "I've never seen one behave like that before."

Chapter 19

I STRUGGLED TO my feet, trying to control the shakes that surged through me. "You've seen that before?"

"Of course." She was staring at me as though I was more frightening than the monster who'd just attacked us. "Demons are attracted to practitioners when we use magic. That's why Luke doesn't like me doing it on my own."

I stopped trying to wipe the slush off my pants. "Demons?" I looked around.

She nodded. "The barrier's done. You should be able to cross now."

"Then let's get inside before that thing comes back."

Emma gave me a strange look. "It's still here."

"What?" I whirled, raising my sword to the ready. "Where?"

"We can't see it anymore. They can't manifest in our world unless someone's using magic."

I frowned. I'd worked magic a number of times now, but I'd never seen anything like the creature that attacked me. "Those things show up whenever a practitioner does magic?"

She nodded. "Pretty much, but I've never heard of a non-practitioner being able to see them. Not that I know all that much about magic yet. And I know next to nothing about how fae magic works. Do you think that's why you could see it? Can all fae?"

I cringed at the way she just blabbed my deepest darkest secret like it was the most benign topic in the world, like it wasn't a truth that could tear my life apart if the wrong person found out.

"I don't know." A sharp pain lanced through my chest. Kai would have known. "I'm pretty new to all this too."

She nodded. "I can ask Luke about it at our next lesson." I startled, and she held up her hands. "With your permission, of course."

I slid my sword back in its sheath. "I'm not worried about Luke, but I'd prefer you didn't talk about me in general. You never know who might be listening."

I was pretty sure my teeth were chattering from cold rather than fear, so I picked up my bag and headed for the promising warmth of home. As soon as I stepped through the door though, I stopped. Emma bumped into my back, then slipped around me so she could close the door.

Relief washed over me, rooting me in place. I was home, surrounded by the knickknacks I'd collected with my mom and the paintings and drawings given to me by fellow artists, each with a memory attached. Those things helped ground me, reminding me who I was. Then came annoyance, because none of it was quite right. Objects that weren't mine dotted the room—a fashion magazine, a pair of shoes, someone's long, red coat.

Then my gaze settled on the space where Kai's Christmas tree should have been. I hadn't had time to take it down before I left, but it was gone. An empty space in the room to mirror the one in my heart. My eyes started to itch.

Emma kicked off my galoshes and passed me by, oblivious to my inner turmoil. She dropped onto the couch with a sigh, then turned to look at me. "So how was your trip? Did you get to see the Grand Canyon?"

Shoving my pain down deep, I set my suitcase and sword down and pulled off my boots, using the excuse to look away. "I don't really wanna talk about it, Em. It's been a long day."

Her expression sagged a little. "Jynx and Ava have been staying in your room, but they went out a little while ago so you're good to go if you want to turn in."

Nodding, I grabbed my bag again and shuffled toward my room.

The bed was a mess of crumpled covers and sheets. The floor was a sea of discarded clothing. My bathroom door stood open and through it I could see towels on the floor and two foreign toothbrushes where mine should have been.

Sighing, I pulled open a drawer, grabbed a pair of flannel pajama pants, and stripped off my soggy clothes. When I was dry and dressed, I sat down on the edge of my bed—carefully not thinking about what Jynx and her girlfriend might have gotten up to in it.

"You should tell Maggie the truth."

I jumped, twisting to face the doorway.

Emma was leaning against the frame, her arms crossed. "I know it's none of my business, but you should. She's worried about you a lot lately. Especially since . . . well, you took off right after she . . ."

"Fired me." The words came out flat, matching the numbness I felt.

Emma nodded. "She called you a bunch of times, but you never answered your phone, and no one knew how to get in touch with Kai."

"I told you all I was going on a trip. I took the time off even before she. . . . It had nothing to do with that."

"Then why didn't you answer your phone?"

I frowned. How could I explain that basic roaming didn't cover trips to the fae Realm of Enchantment? "I couldn't."

"Yeah, that's what Jynx said. But Maggie's been moping around the shop like someone ran over her dog. And then with Kayla disappearing—"

"Wait, what?" I pictured Kayla's pale, porcelain doll face and the long, plain dresses she wore to cover the amazing wings she kept furled beneath. She'd told me once that pixies were sometimes kidnapped because of the dust produced by their wings. The same kind of dust Mica carried around in a little silver tin stuffed in his coat pocket.

Emma shrugged. "One day she just—" She snapped her fingers. "No one's seen her since."

"Did you report her missing?"

"Of course. And the PTF looked into it. They said they didn't find any signs of foul play, so she probably went AWOL on her visa, but I don't think Kayla would do that. Not when it could mean permanent exile."

Coils of fear twisted through my gut. "Do you remember who investigated? The name of the agent?"

"No, but it was that same guy you were talking to before you ran out on your last shift at Magpie."

The coils tightened. O'Connell.

It could have been a coincidence—there weren't all that many field agents in the Boulder PTF office—but that didn't sit right. If O'Connell was poking around at Magpie, it was because of me. I clenched my jaw. O'Connell's reason for taking the case didn't change the fact that Kayla was missing. If she'd been taken by some faerie drug addict, how could the PTF hope to find her? How could anyone?

I'd thought leaving Enchantment would untwist the constant, anxious worry tying me in knots, but if anything, my anxiety was getting worse. The inadequacy I'd felt at court had followed me home, whispering like a ghost in my mind, promising I would only mess things up.

Emma gestured to the bed. "Want help cleaning up?"

I eyed the disheveled covers. The last thing I needed was a couple of horny teenagers falling in bed without checking to see if it was occupied. "I'll take the couch tonight."

She followed me back to the living room and helped me stretch a sheet over the couch cushions, all the while biting her lower lip like she was physically holding her words back by pinning her mouth closed. When the sheets and blankets were in place and I'd dropped my pillow at one end of the couch, I turned to her and placed my hands on my hips. "What?"

Her eyebrows rose. "Huh?"

"Spit it out. What are you trying not to say?"

She shook her head. "Nothing, I just. . . . I was thinking about that demon."

I sank into one of the living room chairs. "And?"

She took one of the other chairs. "Have you ever seen one before?"

"Nope."

"Demons don't usually interact with normal people. If I were to cast a spell in the middle of a crowd, the demons wouldn't see anyone but me. This demon . . . it ignored me completely. It went after *you*."

Goosebumps sprang out on my arms, and I rubbed them, trying to chase back the chill. "Maybe because you were channeling your magic through me with those bluish tendril thingies?"

"You could see those too?"

"I take it that's not normal either?"

"Not for humans. Like I said, I don't understand much about fae magic."

I slouched in my seat. "Neither do I."

"Luke says demons are attracted to concentrated energy, so I suppose they could have followed the magic over to you since that's where I was focusing. It doesn't explain why you could see it though."

I propped my cheek against my hand and tapped one finger against my temple. I'd done plenty of imbuing, but I'd never seen a demon before. This time, I hadn't done any magic, but I had done the weird focus shift that let me *see* magic. I'd thought that trick just let me see what was happening on the magical plane, but a window could be looked through from either side. What if my trick also let things on that magical plane see me?

Emma bit her lip. "If you trust Luke, maybe you should come talk to him with me. He might know what's going on."

I got the feeling Emma wanted me there more to run interference when she told Luke about her unsanctioned spell casting.

"Maybe," I said. "But not tonight."

Tomorrow would be soon enough to deal with demons and Emma's misguided magic. Soon enough to find out what price Sol might demand for his assistance in freeing the wolves. Soon enough to face James and the loss of our connection. Soon enough to call Maggie, and David, and try to salvage whatever was left of my old life.

Tonight I would bathe in my own shower, and eat in my own kitchen, and sleep, if not in my own bed at least in my own house. Tonight I would rest. Tomorrow would come soon enough.

SOMETHING THUDDED in the dark, and a titter of giggles filled the silence. I jerked awake, groping for context. Where was I? What was happening? I rolled off the side of the couch and smacked my funny bone against the coffee table. Cursing, I cradled my elbow against my chest.

"Alex?" Light flared through the room, making my eyes water. Jynx stood just inside the front door, her eyes wide. Behind her, a young woman with flame-red pigtails was halfway through pulling off her second boot. She balanced with one hand braced against the wall.

I struggled to clear the cobwebs from my sleep-deprived thoughts as I regained my seat on the couch. The world outside the windows was still dark, turning the glass to mirrors in the sudden light of the living room. I couldn't have been asleep for more than a couple hours.

"It's so good to see you." Jynx bounded over the edge of the couch and tackled me, sending us both back into the cushions. She pulled back, frowning. "But what are you doing on the couch?"

"My bed looked otherwise engaged."

The other girl, Ava, finally managed to yank off her boot. She dropped it with a thud and walked over to join us, bending down until her face was even with mine. "It's nice to see you again. Do you remember me?"

I pushed Jynx off my chest so I could sit up. "Ava. The teleporter who helped me out at Crossroads."

She shook her head. "Not a teleporter. I just open portals."

"How's that not teleportation? You still get instantly from one place to another."

Jynx flopped back, folding her arms behind her head. "You traveled with Otis to the reservation, yeah? *He's* a teleporter. Ava's an ellyllon, one of the tylwyth teg."

I racked my brain. Tylwyth teg was a category of fae found mostly around Ireland and Great Britain.

"In more modern terms," Jynx said, "I guess you'd call her a leprechaun."

Ava wrinkled her nose. "Not my favorite term."

Jynx looked around, craning to see the whole room. "Where's Kai? Or did he kick Emma out already?"

"Shame," Ava said. "I liked her."

I stiffened. "Emma's still here."

"So," Jynx prompted. "Where is he?"

"Where's Chase," I countered, buying time to get my thoughts in order.

"Hasn't come back yet. Don't tell me Kai decided to stay."

My mouth went dry. I cut my eyes to Ava, then Jynx, then focused on my lap, unable to meet either's gaze.

Ava took a step toward the door. "I should get going. Let you two catch up."

"What?" Jynx sprang to her feet. "But—"

Ava set her hand on Jynx's arm, gentle and intimate. "I'll see you tonight." She smiled and tipped her head to look at me. "You should come too. My band's playing at the Caribou Room. We're opening for the Sweet Lillies."

"Oz'll be there too," Jynx added. "He's Ava's guitarist."

"Technically, I think I'm *his* drummer since he started the band."

Jynx waved the comment off. "Anyway, I'm sure he'd love to see you."

"I'll think about it," I said.

Ava pressed her lips to Jynx's, who leaned in like her life depended on it.

I smiled. Jynx's enthusiasm was exhausting even to watch, but it was also endearing. She reminded me of the old saying, "Dance like nobody's watching, and love like you'll never get hurt . . ." I wished I could do that.

My thoughts drifted to James. I should call him, let him know I was back in town.

I rubbed my chest, remembering the ache of passing through the portal to Enchantment. I'd killed a part of him when I went through, let the fae magic burn it out of me. Had he felt the pain of its passing as acutely as I had?

Jynx and Ava finally came up for air, grinning like fools who could never be hurt.

"See you tonight." Ava lifted her boots with one hand, and drew a circle in the air with her other. The air seemed to shimmer slightly. Then she stepped through the faded paint of my living room wall and disappeared.

"So." Jynx turned back to me, hands on hips. "What happened to Kai?"

Chapter 20

MY HANDS SHOOK around an empty coffee mug. The warm drink had cleared my head, allowing me to tell Jynx the story of how Kai had sacrificed himself for my mistake. But by waking me up enough to think, it also laid me bare to the reality of the situation and again I was awash in guilt and regret. I couldn't help feeling I'd abandoned him, for all that it had been his choice to stay in the end. Tears threatened, and I held my breath to keep them from falling. The pressure twisting in my chest was unbearable, and yet I felt hollow.

Jynx patted me on the knee. "I'm sorry."

I stared at her thin, pale fingers, turning the useless words over in my head. We were all sorry. It didn't change a damn thing.

Sniffing, I set my coffee-stained cup on the table. "Who's Haru?"

Jynx pulled her hand back as though my knee had become a red-hot iron. "Where'd you hear that name?"

"Enchantment. I met him at court."

She shook her head, then stood and started pacing like that motion had been too contained. "He's an old . . . acquaintance . . . of my brother's."

"A friend?" I frowned. "Or an enemy?"

She stopped pacing and focused her gaze on me. Her hands were clasped so tight her knuckles turned white. "Both. Neither." She licked her lips. "I thought he died."

"White kitsune with red-tipped tails and bright blue eyes?"

She sank into one of the chairs. "Chase is gonna . . ." She brought both hands up to cover her mouth.

"What?" I sat forward. "He's gonna what?"

She shook her head, eyes wide. "I don't know."

I went cold. If Haru was Mica's friend, and he came here . . .

"What happened between them? I need to know."

Jynx shrugged. "I just know they were close once. Very close. Then something drove them apart. If you want to know more than that you'll have to ask Chase. It all happened before I was born."

"Then how do you know about Haru at all?"

"Chase mentioned him a few times over the years, mostly by accident I think. And I once overheard Chase and my parents arguing about Haru and a girl named Nia. They stopped when they found me listening, and none of them would explain." She bit her lower lip, worrying it between her teeth. "That was right before he left for the mortal realm. Nearly thirty years ago now."

"Do you think he knows Haru is still alive?"

"I couldn't say. All the times he mentioned him, Chase always talked like Haru was dead."

"Maybe just dead to him, if they had a falling out."

Jynx hugged herself, rubbing her arms as though she was cold. "Maybe. Either way, it's gonna be a shock when you tell him."

"Me?" I pulled back. "Why don't you tell him?"

"Nuh-uh." She pushed her palms out. "You met him. You tell him."

Crossing my arms, I slouched back against the cushions, imagining Haru's sly smile. *Tell him Haru says hello.*

"Kitsune get a tail for every hundred years they're alive, right?" I asked.

She raised an eyebrow. "Yeah."

"How old is Chase?"

She pursed her lips. "He wouldn't like me telling you." Then her face split into a smile. "He's seven-hundred-eighty-two."

I stared at her for a moment. Then we both burst out laughing. I don't know why it was so funny. Maybe it wasn't, maybe I just needed the release, but I laughed and laughed until my eyes watered and my ribs hurt, until I could barely breathe.

"What's got you two howling like hyenas so early in the morning?"

Jynx and I both twisted to look over the back of the couch. Emma was standing, hands on hips in the hallway. She wore loose pajamas covered with My Little Pony characters, and her hair stuck up at odd angles.

Frowning, I looked out the window. A silhouette of treetops was visible along the eastern horizon, and the stars had faded from that section of the sky.

"Sorry to wake you," I said.

Emma waved her hand. "You didn't. This is when I always get up."

I wrinkled my nose. "The sun isn't even up yet."

"I told you about the hours at the bakery." She smiled. "At least now I only have to pick the goods up. I don't have to help make them."

Her smile turned brittle and crumbled. She turned away. "I'm gonna hop in the shower." She paused. "I guess you'll be wanting your Jeep back."

Right, Emma's car was buried in snow. As was Kai's. "Tell you what, I'll be your chauffeur for the day. I've got some errands to run anyway. I can drop you off, take care of business, then pick you up after your shift. Sound good?"

"Can you be ready to go in twenty minutes?"

"Sure." I forced a smile. "Who needs sleep?"

Emma went back into Kai's bedroom and closed the door. Chains of emotion squeezed my heart. Would I ever be able to see that room as anything but Kai's absence? Another hole in my life where I'd let someone in and paid the price?

Pushing the thought away, I headed for my bedroom.

Jynx followed me. "I'll clean up while you're gone. Get it all ship-shape." She leaned against the dresser while I rummaged for clothes. The little gaala stood on the dresser top with two of its six legs lifted like it was about to prance across the dull wood, which was unsettling since I'd left the gaala packed away in my bag last night. Jynx eyed the carving.

I cleared my throat and glanced at the bed she'd been sleeping in while I was away. "Are you planning to stay here?"

"Here in your room, or here in your house?"

I snorted. "This room's taken."

Jynx pricked her index finger lightly against one of the gaala's tapered antlers, testing the sharpness, her expression neutral. "Is this about my Christmas present?"

I nodded.

"I know Kai talked to you about what an offer like that means to the fae. Have you changed your mind?"

Kai claimed giving Jynx a bed, offering her a permanent place in my home, would make me responsible for her, but mortal emotions didn't follow fae rules. I already felt responsible for Jynx, bed or no. She'd wriggled her way into my heart when my defenses were down, and now she was a part of my life. Another vulnerable spot that might become a wound if I wasn't careful.

I shook my head. "Here's what I'm thinking. Between you, Chase,

Emma, Kai, and even Hortense I've had an awful lot of people crash here over the past few months, and that doesn't seem likely to change anytime soon." I pictured Mica and Haru showing up at my door, but quickly shoved the thought aside. "So I'm going to buy *myself* a new bed and store it in the back room. It'll be there for anyone who needs it."

Jynx's grin stretched so wide I could count her teeth.

"I'll start making space." She bounced into the hall and down to the storage room.

I closed the door behind her. The little gaala pawed the dresser top as I pulled on a fresh t-shirt, its tiny hooves clicking against the wood. Beside the gaala were my knife, my stealth charm, and the smoky black cloth I'd received from Enzo. I was getting quite the collection of magical knickknacks. There was also a shiny red package with a bright silver bow. The gift I'd failed to give James before I left. I grabbed the present, gave the gaala a careful pat on the nose, and headed out. It was going to be another long day.

EMMA AND I WERE out the door and buckled into the Jeep before my twenty minutes were up. The eastern sky was robin egg blue, but the sun hadn't made an appearance yet. I threw the car in gear and started down the frozen slush slide that was my driveway.

There wasn't much clearance when I went around the bend where Kai's tan Toyota had entombed itself the night before, but I managed to squeeze by. I'd have to figure out how to return the car to the way station, assuming I could get it out of the ditch before spring. Maybe Ava could open a portal for me. How far could her portals reach? Could she make one big enough to drive a car through?

"Thanks for letting me borrow this beauty." Emma ran her hand affectionately over the dashboard.

"No problem." As Kai's car faded in the rear view, my mind drifted across the pine forest to my left, to a house not two miles away.

"Are you worried about Marc?"

I jerked, swinging my gaze back to the road. "What?"

"Those werewolves got nabbed by the PTF just before you left."

"How did—" I shook my head. "Luke must really trust you a lot."

Luke was the werewolves' on-call doctor when they needed to be patched up, not that they needed a doctor all that often thanks to their rapid healing. It made sense he would have told his apprentice about them, but I was surprised she knew any individual identities. Werewolves were insanely protective of their secret. Homicidally so.

"He made introductions last week. He also mentioned you already knew about them, but he didn't say how. When I recognized Sophie from all those times she met you for lunch at the bookstore, I figured she's how come you knew. Does she know you're a halfer?"

I gritted my teeth. "Please stop saying that out loud."

"Sorry."

"You shouldn't talk about the werewolves either." If she knew what Marc and the others could do, *would* do, if she let their secret slip. . . . I tightened my grip on the wheel.

She shrugged. "Well, you don't need to worry about the wolves. They were all released before the full moon, though I have no idea how they managed to pass the PTF's tests."

She didn't know about Sol's involvement. That was one secret I didn't have to worry about her blabbing, at least.

I chewed my lower lip. Emma's energetic innocence was one of the things I loved most about her, but. . . . "Now that you're part of the paranatural community, you need to get better at lying."

She frowned. "But you already knew about the werewolves."

"That's not the point." I shook my head. How could she not see how dangerous it was to talk about people's secrets like they were no big deal? Didn't she understand what was at stake for us? But then, she was a legally registered practitioner. Maybe she really didn't understand. Maybe she couldn't. "Just . . . be careful. None of us wants any more scrutiny from the PTF."

Nodding, she traced one finger along the inside of her window, making patterns in the mist of her breath. "It's getting worse."

"What is?"

"The PTF, the world, everything." Her smile was gone, and lines I'd rarely seen on her face creased around her mouth and eyes. "Ever since Anderson was elected. He hasn't even taken office yet, but already things are changing."

I frowned, cold dread seeping through me as I recalled O'Connell's glee when he told me about the increasing number of paranaturals getting reported to the PTF.

"Last week, Anderson announced his intent to approve the bill to segregate paranaturals in public schools. Kids have already started turning on each other. One registered halfer was hospitalized because a classmate put iron shavings in his lunch." She shook her head. "He was only eight years old."

I'd been about to turn onto Highway 119, the road that would take us to Boulder along the long, winding canyon. There was almost no traffic that early, so I kept my foot on the brake, letting her words sink in.

"Once the bill passes, May will have to transfer."

I twisted in my seat. "But she's not—"

"I am. Any first degree relative is considered *tainted*. Anderson's word." She clenched her fists in her lap. "Mom was right. I messed up."

I reached over and set my hand on top of hers. I knew all too well what it was like to have someone else pay for my actions. There was nothing I could do to lessen her guilt, any more than I could lessen my own, but at least I could help her bear it. Neither of us was alone.

EMMA'S MOTHER, LONI, ran a bakery across town from the bookstore. She'd signed a contract with Maggie, promising to provide baked goods for the coffee shop in exchange for keeping most of the proceeds. The fact that Emma and her mother were no longer on speaking terms didn't change that deal, and the fact that Emma opened the coffee shop every morning meant she was the one responsible for picking up said goods. It had been a simple arrangement when Emma was living with Loni and helping out at the bakery anyway. Now, it was like watching two silverback gorillas circle, testing each other's strength before declaring all-out war over disputed territory.

"Good morning, Mrs. Yamada." I offered a little wave from behind Emma's back, not daring to step between them.

Loni snorted, but finally shifted her gaze off her daughter. She pointed to a stack of aluminum trays, each holding a different type of pastry and mummified in plastic wrap. "Take them."

Sidling around the edge of the room, I lifted two trays. The one on top held big, fat cinnamon rolls, dripping with icing. My mouth began to water.

"Mom, have you seen my English book?" Emma's eleven-year-old sister, May, appeared at the bottom of the stairs that led to the apartment above the shop. She froze, her eyes shifting between her mother and sister. Then she saw me and seemed to breathe again. "Hi, Alex."

"Morning." I tipped my chin toward the corner of a blue-covered text book peeking out from under the pile of trays. "This what you're looking for?"

"Thanks!"

Emma lifted the remaining trays so May could retrieve her book. The cover was smeared with flour.

"Get going," Loni said, crossing her arms. "You're going to be late for school."

I shifted the trays in my arms. Who knew cinnamon rolls were so heavy? "We could give her a ride."

Loni stiffened, shifting her scowl to me. "We're fine."

"It's really no trouble. We're headed that way any—"

"I said we're fine. We don't need you"—her eyes shifted to Emma—"or any of the trouble you bring."

Color crept into Emma's cheeks. "Leave her alone, Mom. She was just trying to be nice. Or have you forgotten what that is?"

Loni's arms uncrossed. She took a step forward, her face going scarlet.

"Stop it!" May stepped between them, her fingers white against the spine of her book. "Both of you, just stop it!"

Everyone froze for a moment. Flour drifted through the air, tickling my nose. The hum of an electric mixer whirred in the back room. The trays in my arms were growing heavier by the second.

Finally, Loni turned away. "Don't be late for school." She marched through the open door beside the stairs and disappeared into the huge kitchen where she worked.

"Thanks for the offer, Alex, but I'll walk. It's not far." May brushed the flour off her English book, dropped it in her bag, and slung the strap over her shoulder. Then she grabbed the violin case she seemed to carry everywhere, gave Emma a quick hug, and raced out the door.

Emma and I managed to get all the trays in a single load. We didn't want to risk a second trip into Loni's domain. Not when May wasn't there to referee.

"Is it always like that?" I asked as I put the Jeep in gear.

Emma was slouched low in her seat. "Pretty much."

"Maybe you could flip shifts with Akshata, have her do the openings? Then you wouldn't have to come here."

Emma sucked her lower lip, then said, "It's weird. It super sucks coming here every morning just to get ignored or chewed out by my mom, but at the same time I'm kinda glad of the excuse. Sometimes I think if we weren't forced to interact like that, we'd just never see each other again. She's too stubborn to come to me, and well, I guess that's a trait we share. At least, seeing each other every day, even if it's awful and awkward. . . . It gives me hope."

I stared out the window at the passing scenery—bare tree limbs and cold buildings waiting for the sun to warm the world. "You'll find your way back to each other, or to some middle ground. You're family."

Family. The word echoed in my head. What did I know about families or forgiveness? My ideas were based on fuzzy-feeling TV shows and a desire for things I never experienced in real life. My mom and dad were gone, and I'd stayed mad at them way past any hope of forgiveness. The closest thing I had to a blood relative was a centuries-old mass murderer in the body of a teenage boy who wanted me to produce a sacrificial baby with a drug addict. I was the last person in the world who should speculate on what it means to be a family.

I pulled to a stop in the alley behind Magpie Books. The same alley I'd parked in for years when arriving for a shift. The familiarity of the place, and the feeling that I no longer belonged there, coiled into a lump of emotion that lodged in my chest, suffocating me. Maggie would be inside already, as evidenced by the white, if mud-splattered, Forester I'd parked beside. Maggie was never late for shifts. She was the first one there when she opened, and the last one out when she closed. She was solid, dependable; she followed through. She was nothing like me.

"Help me carry these inside." Emma stood by the open back of the Jeep, waving me over.

I got out to join her, then stopped, my hand still on the driver's side door. I chewed at my lower lip, eyeing the entrance to the bookstore. I really wanted to talk to Maggie, but at the same time . . . I really didn't.

Emma closed the distance between us and shoved my shoulder. "Don't be a wuss."

"I don't know what to say to her."

"How about hello? That one works pretty well for me." She grinned, lifting a tray of sugar-crusted rolls. "Come on, if you're coming."

She crossed the alley, but paused in front of the door. "You'll find your way back to each other." She glanced over her shoulder and winked. "You're family."

Then she pulled open the door while balancing her tray one-handed, and went inside.

Chapter 21

THE BACK ROOM of Magpie Books was just as I remembered it—a mess. Boxes waiting to be unpacked were stacked in the middle of the room like a cardboard mountain. Shelves of stock waiting to go out lined the walls. New releases waited under dated signs for their turn in the displays. Maggie's desk hunkered in one corner, straining under a mound of paperwork. A half-full box of paperbacks with their covers stripped off was tucked beneath it, so there was nowhere for a person's legs to go.

Maggie was busy at the register when Emma and I made our way to the front of the store.

"Morning, Maggie," Emma called.

Maggie looked up with a smile. "Good mo—" Her gaze fell on me, trailing behind Emma with my tray, and her mouth stopped mid-word.

I stopped as well, and for a moment we just stared mutely at each other.

"As you can see," Emma said, "Alex got home last night."

Maggie finally managed to close her mouth. She braced her hands on the counter, one on either side of the register, and shifted her weight from foot to foot. Now that she was no longer staring at me, she seemed unable to make eye contact. "How was your trip?"

I shifted the trays in my arms to relieve the burn spreading through my muscles. I opened my mouth once, twice; on the third time, I finally came back with, "Fine."

She nodded, pressing her lips together.

I looked around the shop, taking in the new displays, the hold items, the packed shelves, the lingering holiday decorations. Everything was the same, yet different from the last time I'd been there. But it wasn't just the books that had changed.

Emma bustled behind her counter, humming as she set pastries in the glass case. Her smile was in place. Her red and yellow spiked hair bobbed while she worked. Her piercing glinted. She looked happy, but there was a tightness around her eyes and mouth I didn't remember. A stiffness to her movements.

Maggie wasn't smiling. Her fingers curled where she pressed them to the counter. Dark circles drooped beneath her eyes, and her smooth, dark skin seemed dull and pale.

Then there was me. What was I even doing there? I wasn't an employee anymore, but there I was, standing in Magpie for the opening shift. Was I there to beg for my job back? To show Maggie I could be dependable? But I couldn't. Not when so much of my life was out of control. I wasn't dependable. I wasn't an employee. I wasn't even human. Time I accepted that.

I took a deep breath, trying to get my thoughts in order. The bookstore aside, I needed to fix things with Maggie. She and David were my oldest friends. And with everything that had happened in Enchantment, I really needed a friend I could trust. But every time I opened my mouth, the words caught in my throat. I found myself looking around the shop, squinting out the big front windows, studying the people and cars in the parking lot. I'd gotten so used to keeping secrets, I didn't even know where to start. And how could I be sure O'Connell wasn't listening in, watching, waiting for me to slip up?

As Maggie and I drowned in the awkward silence that had never existed between us before, Emma stepped up and lifted the trays out of my aching arms. "Alex and I are going to see a friend's band tonight," she said, waggling her eyebrows at me. "They're playing at the Caribou Room up in Ned. You should come."

Maggie jolted, like she was waking up from a dream, and glanced between us.

I tried not to let my surprise show. Jynx had mentioned the concert, but I hadn't actually agreed to go. After the debacle at the Winter Festival, I wasn't eager to subject myself to another party, even a mortal one. And this was the first I'd heard of Emma attending, though I shouldn't have been surprised since Emma was hardly one to pass up a concert.

"Sure." Maggie jerked her head in one stiff affirmative nod. "I'd love to. That is," she turned to me, "if you don't mind."

"What? No. Of course not. I'd love for you to come." And just like that I'd agreed to go. Damn.

"Great." Maggie let out a breath, her shoulders settling slightly. She looked as unsteady as I felt.

"Great," I echoed. A noisy club packed with concert-goers. What better place to reveal my darkest secret to a friend I wasn't sure was a friend anymore? I sighed. "I should get going. Unless . . ." I looked over Maggie's drooping posture, her glazed expression. "Emma told me about Kayla. Do you want me to stay?"

Her eyes widened. "I—"

"Just to help out." I raised my palms as though her response might manifest as a physical threat. "Just for today."

"I appreciate the offer, Alex. Really. But I've got this." Her gaze slid to the side on the last line, marking it as a lie. Mags never was much of a poker player.

"Right, well, I'll be off then." I waved to Emma. "See you at the end of your shift."

She nodded. Neither woman said anything as I made my way back through the empty store, walked through the "employees only" door I no longer had any business opening, and exited through the back alley. When I returned to pick Emma up after work, I'd use the public lot out front.

JAMES'S NEIGHBORHOOD was quiet. A few cars dotted driveways obscured by old-growth trees. Couples walked along the sidewalks, taking children, or dogs, or both out for a little exercise in the space between storms. The sun shone like a white ball in a clear blue sky, having burned away the lingering clouds of morning. Snow clumped under bushes and coated yards, but ended in sharp lines where the shadows failed to protect it. Gutters ran with gray slush, icebergs caught in a current.

I passed a black SUV parked on the street one block over from James's. It was parked in front of a stylish white house. Nothing suspicious about that. Except the windows were tinted to near black, and the silhouette of a man sat inside. The hairs on my arms started to tingle, like Spiderman's spidey-sense right before someone jumped out to attack him.

I watched the SUV in my rearview until I turned the corner. The man inside didn't start the car. He also didn't get out. He seemed to be talking to someone, though he was the only person I could see through the windshield.

I pulled into James's driveway and idled, watching the corner where the SUV would appear if it followed me. I counted to fifty. The street remained empty.

Cursing my paranoia, I cut the engine and grabbed the shiny red package off the back seat.

James's house was a single story made of flat, stacked stones. Skeletal ivy clung to the front wall and wrapped around one side, its vines twisted and brown through the winter. The windows were dark, the curtains drawn. That was to be expected on a Saturday morning. Chances were James had only just gone to bed. While the fae charm he wore protected him from sunlight, he still kept hours more in line with his fellow vampires and stayed indoors during the day.

I hesitated, my fingers crumpling the paper of James's gift.

The last time I'd seen him, I'd been fighting to separate our emotions. The emptiness I'd carried in my chest since passing through the portal to Enchantment was a cold reminder of that lost connection.

I'd wanted to be free of it. Now we could move forward, sure of our own emotions. Except I wasn't sure. Severing our bond hadn't made my choices any clearer. I still cared for James, still thought I might love him . . . but I couldn't see any certain path to a future with him, no road to "happily ever after" for a vampire and a halfer both buried in paranatural politics.

I sighed. Maybe he'd agree to move to Wyoming. We could build a ranch off the grid, cut off from outside influence. Let the Baels and Victorias and O'Connells of the world find somebody else to bother.

I lifted one fist and knocked on the door.

There was no answer.

I bit my lip, foolishly wishing I could see into his thoughts as I had before. But James could have been standing on the other side of the door looking through the peep hole and I'd be none the wiser.

I knocked again.

When a full minute passed with no response, I sat down with my back to the door and pulled out my cell phone.

I stared at James's number for another minute, wondering if I'd hear the chime inside the house. Then I pressed the call button. No noise came from behind the door. James wasn't home.

He answered on the fourth ring with a groggy, "Alex?"

I frowned. If James was sleeping, why wasn't he at home? "Are you at the apartment?"

James kept an apartment above the gallery for late nights, visiting guests, and the occasional artist in need of a place to crash.

"No, I'm—" There was a muffled noise.

"James? Where are you?"

"I'm at the nest."

"During the day? Shouldn't everyone there be asleep? And what are you even doing still hanging around there? I thought you were going to hand over the reins to the new master and step away from the whole mess."

"Victoria requested I stick around . . . in an advisory capacity."

I let that statement sink in for a moment. "So you've been . . . sleeping there?"

When I'd asked for space to get my life in order, James had agreed to wait, at least until I returned from my trip to Enchantment. But here I was, on his doorstep, and he was nowhere to be found. Had I missed my chance? Had James moved on in my absence? Just how close could he and Victoria have become in the time I was gone? My mind spiraled down ever-darker paths of "what ifs."

"We had a late night discussing policies. I didn't see the point in returning home just to come back in a few hours."

"You and Victoria must have grown awfully close for her to have brought you on as her advisor in such a short time." My voice ratcheted up as I spoke, and I took a deep breath to get myself under control. Coming across as a jealous nag wouldn't help anything.

James's sigh rolled across the line. "Victoria and I didn't just meet, Alex. We've known each other for . . . a long time."

I stared up into the frozen branches of an ash tree and tried to process his words. James once told me the world wasn't a very big place for those crowded into its shadows. Any vampire who'd been around more than a century or two probably knew the other players, and a person didn't gain the title of "master" overnight. How could I have been so stupid? "That's how she moved in on the vacancy so fast. You told her Merak was dead. You invited her to come here."

"I believed she would be the best choice for a new neighbor. I still do."

"Were you and she . . ."

Another sigh. "It was a long time ago, Alex."

I shut my eyes and tipped my head back against his closed door. Victoria was an old girlfriend. An old girlfriend James had been spending every waking . . . and apparently sleeping . . . moment with for the past week and a half while I was bumbling around in Enchantment. But then, I'm the one who'd pushed him away. Did I have any right to be jealous?

"Why didn't you tell me all this before?"

"You were about to leave for Enchantment, a place where you would need to keep your wits about you. I didn't want to add to your worries lest they distract you from the task at hand. Speaking of which, I'm glad to see you made it home safely. How did your court debut go?"

I rolled my head back and forth against the hard wood of the door. "Terrible."

"What do you mean? What happened?"

I took a deep, ragged breath that caught in my throat on the way out. "Kai's gone."

"He was recalled?"

"No. He—" I swallowed and wiped a hand over my face. "Look, I don't want to talk about this over the phone. Can you meet me at your house?"

There was a long pause. "Victoria and I are attending to an . . . issue this afternoon. I was only taking a brief rest when you called. We should be done shortly after sunset."

"Can't she handle it on her own?"

"I'm afraid not."

I tried to imagine what kind of issue vampires would need to attend to during the day while most of their kind slept. In the end, it didn't matter. James had made his choice. He was otherwise occupied. I clenched my jaw, making my voice come out tight and strained. "I've got plans with Emma and Maggie tonight."

"Perhaps—"

"Another time." I cut him off and hit the disconnect button for punctuation. It was childish, but I was tired, and the deserted street brought back too many memories of sitting on the front stoop of the last house my dad ever lived in with me. I'd spent way too many days there, waiting for someone who never came.

My phone rang, vibrating in my palm. James's face smiled at me from the screen.

I let my hand drop to the stoop. My knuckles scraped rough concrete just to the side of the welcome mat I was sitting on. I watched a lone, brown leaf flutter on the ash tree, refusing to succumb to winter, and waited for the melody to stop. It looped once, then cut off with a chime telling me I'd missed a call.

If hanging up had been childish, ignoring his call was infantile. Another reason for James—who was already infinitely more mature than I was—to move on. I scrunched my eyes closed and shook my head. I was sabotaging my relationship. Pushing him away like I'd done to every guy I'd ever really liked. I could see it happening like a slow motion car wreck, but I didn't know how to stop it.

Pressure built in my chest and settled, tingling, in my limbs. My breath rattled. In. Out. In.

It seemed, no matter how much I tried to change, I kept falling into the same isolationist patterns, cutting myself off from any chance at love for fear of losing it. But the cost of those choices was becoming painfully clear. Nothing would ever change . . . until I did.

Tucking the phone away, I pushed to my feet. I wouldn't pine away on a guy's front stoop like some love-sick idiot.

I froze, recognizing the urge to move for what it really was—retreat.

I frowned. I wasn't ready to reopen the conversation with James, but that didn't mean I couldn't break out of my self-defeating pattern.

I pulled my phone back out and sent James a text. I apologized for acting like an asshat and asked if he was free to talk tomorrow.

His reply was immediate. He would be there first thing in the morning. He also offered to drop what he was doing and come straight away if that's what I needed.

No. I wrote back, feeling even more ridiculous for my behavior but pleased by his offer nonetheless. *Tomorrow is fine. Sorry for the drama. I love you.*

I stared at those three simple words printed on my screen, dark pixels on a gray background. They hung like an incomplete bridge stretching over a chasm, waiting for a connection to lend it strength.

I licked my lips. I wasn't sixteen anymore, or even twenty. I wasn't going to move again if I could help it. And while my life wasn't exactly stable, if there was anyone who could put up with my crazy it was James. He was a freaking vampire after all. He'd been around. He'd seen it all.

I took a deep breath and typed, *I lov*—my hand started to shake.

Erasing the aborted phrase, I wrote instead, *See you tomorrow,* tacked on a little heart emoji, and hit send. Then I shoved the phone in my pocket.

Baby steps.

I had some errands to run before heading back to the house, but I didn't feel like being alone. With Kai gone, James busy, and Emma and Maggie at work, that left David. I'd promised to check in as soon as I got home from my trip—which he thought was a driving tour of the

Southwest to show Kai the sights. No time like the present.

It was still mid-morning, and David liked to sleep in on Saturdays, so I decided to swing by Einstein's for coffee and bagels before knocking on his door.

My Jeep coughed to life like a cat with a hairball, and I backtracked through the neighborhood. When I passed the house with the black SUV parked out front, the car was gone. I smiled. I was just being paranoid after all.

Highway 93 rolled through the sagebrush foothills that stretched between Golden and Boulder. Cars streamed along the road in both directions, but they were matched equally by bicycles. Men and women with thick calves and spandex outfits pumped up hills and coasted around curves. Even the pockets of snow that lined the gravel shoulders couldn't deter the outdoor spirit of Boulder's devoted cyclists.

I glanced in my rear view. A red Subaru drove behind me, a little too close for comfort. Behind them, a silver pickup carried a tarped load of branches in its bed. And several car lengths behind that truck was a black SUV.

I shifted my gaze back to the road in front of me, but my hands tightened on the wheel. Lots of people owned SUVs, and black was a very popular color.

I entered the southern end of Boulder and pulled into the Einstein's parking lot, snagging a space in the front row when a white Tesla backed out. I stayed in the idling Jeep for a moment, biting my lip. The black SUV passed by the entrance to the parking lot and continued up the street. It didn't even slow.

I released my breath in a loud puff. If I kept jumping at every little thing, my nerves were going to be shot. There was no reason for anyone to be following me. Even if someone was, there was nothing incriminating about bringing breakfast to a friend.

DAVID LIVED ON the third floor of his apartment complex in a two bedroom unit.

Shifting the bag of bagels into the same hand as the carrying case of coffees, I rapped my knuckles against the door just under the brass numbers three-oh-one. There was a moment of silence, then a soft thump and the shuffle of feet over carpet. A chain rattled, and the door swung open to reveal David in navy blue sweats and a Led Zeppelin t-shirt. His hair stuck up like he'd just shoved a fork in an electrical outlet, and the beginning of a beard covered his jaw.

"You're back!" He leaned through the doorway and grabbed me in a one-armed hug. Then he inhaled and shifted his groggy stare to the bag and cups in my hand. "And you brought food."

He stepped away from the door, waving me inside.

"How've you been?" I crossed the threshold and wrinkled my nose. Old takeout cartons and pizza boxes were stacked on the kitchen counters, the island, and the coffee table. The curtains were drawn over the one window that lit the living room, casting the whole apartment into a dim gloom broken only by the light under the microwave and a stripe of sunlight on the ceiling that refused to be denied. I turned to David and did a slower assessment of his disheveled state, no longer willing to attribute it to waking up. "What's going on?"

He took the coffee carrier and bag out of my hand and moved toward the kitchen. "It's good to see you."

"Why is your apartment such a mess?"

"You got plans for New Year's yet?"

"Stop changing the subject." I grabbed his forearm to forestall him from pulling bagels out of the bag. "What happened?"

His muscles tensed under my palm. "Steven broke up with me."

I moved my hand up to his shoulder and gave it a squeeze. "I'm sorry."

"Day after Christmas. Said he didn't want to ruin the holiday." He shook his head. "He even kept the Rolex I gave him."

I whistled. "Don't those cost a few grand?"

He nodded.

"You must really have liked him."

"I loved him. And I thought he loved me. But," he shrugged, "I guess you can't ever know for sure."

I thought of the way James and I had connected after he brought me back from the dead. The open honesty of it. I'd seen into his heart, into his soul. No matter what happened since then, in that moment, I'd been sure. James loved me.

So why hadn't I been able to say it back?

"Are *you* okay?" David's eyebrows drew together over the bridge of his nose. "I heard you got laid off from Magpie. That can't have been easy."

"I'm fine." I grabbed one of the coffees and headed for the couch. "Mind if I hang here for a bit? I could use some company, and it seems like you could too."

"Course. Lemme just go freshen up a bit." He took his coffee into his bedroom and closed the door.

I moved over to the curtain and pulled it aside, letting the light spill into the room. It didn't improve the smell of stale food and unwashed clothes, or the impression that everything I touched was covered in toxic mold, but at least I didn't have to squint.

"She's here." The words came from behind the still-closed bedroom door, a whisper I never would have caught before Bael's charm boosted the magic in my blood.

Curious, I stepped closer and pressed my ear against the wood.

"I don't know. She just turned up." A pause. "Yes." Another pause. "I'll call you again when she leaves."

Coffee and bile rolled in my stomach. David was reporting to someone about me. My mind flashed to O'Connell, and the mess in my stomach surged. I couldn't think. I couldn't even breathe. David had been my friend since college. He wouldn't rat me out to the PTF. He couldn't. He didn't even know my secret.

The door opened, and David stopped just short of colliding with me.

I hadn't moved away from the door. From the way David's smile evaporated, he realized what that meant.

"Alex, I—"

"Who was it?"

"I—"

"Who!"

"Let me explain." He reached out, but I backed away from his hand like it was a poisonous snake.

"How could you?"

"It was for your own good."

A choked laugh burst from my mouth. "*My* good? You expect me to believe that having my friend—one of the only people in the world that I trusted—*spy* on me, was for *my* good?" My voice grew louder until I was practically screaming.

"You weren't supposed to know."

"Oh, well . . ." I spread my arms. "That makes everything better."

"He just wanted to make sure you were safe."

That brought me up short. O'Connell wanted a lot of things for me. Pain, imprisonment, death . . . safety wasn't one of them.

"Who?" I repeated.

David looked away, shaking his head.

There was a rectangular bulge in David's right pocket. His cell phone. Darting forward, I pinned David against the door frame with my forearm and dug in his pocket with my other hand. I'd released my paper coffee cup as I moved, and it hit the floor as my fingers closed around the phone. David's cup hit a moment later as his hands came up to the arm across his throat.

I danced back before he could get a good grip.

He staggered, coughing, rubbing his throat. I hadn't meant to press so hard.

"What the hell, Alex!"

Still backing away, I turned on his phone. The screen was locked, but I'd seen him enter the code plenty of times.

"Give that back."

The last call made was to a number I didn't recognize, and it wasn't listed as a contact.

"Alex, don't." He lifted his hand, and even though he couldn't reach me from across the room, I moved to put the couch between us.

I pressed the call button.

"That was quick." Uncle Sol's voice was like a steel spike in my ear, shattering my mind.

Why would Uncle Sol need to spy on me? He could have just called if he wanted to know if I was home. Besides, he spent most of his time gallivanting around the world, often out of contact. Since when did he care about my whereabouts? But of course, I knew the answer to that.

Since I'd confessed my fae heritage. Since he'd started intervening with the PTF on my behalf. Since O'Connell had made it his mission to destroy me.

But why David?

"Nolan? You there?" A note of suspicion had crept into Sol's voice.

"How long?" I asked. I kept the phone to my ear, my eyes on David.

"Alex?" Sol's voice had gone very calm, his business voice.

"How long has this been going on?"

Sol sighed. "Please put Mr. Nolan on the line."

"As if." I hung up on Uncle Sol. If he didn't want to tell me the truth, he'd never crack. Especially not over the phone. But David, he had to look me in the eye. Him I could break.

I turned off the phone. After a lifetime of isolation, I'd gained three friends in college. Aiden, Maggie, and David. Aiden was dead. Maggie was . . . well, I wasn't sure what Maggie was anymore. I leveled my glare at David. "Why?"

Chapter 22

DAVID RAN BOTH hands through his sleep-matted hair, pulling it back. Then he emptied his lungs in a long, loud sigh and collapsed onto a stool near his kitchen island. "I'm sorry, Alex. The last thing either of us wanted was to hurt you."

I clenched my jaw. "Then answer my questions."

He sighed again. "I've been keeping Sol apprised of your situation, letting him know when you're in trouble."

"So that's why he's been showing up so much lately? Why he happened to be in town when that shit went down in October? Why he visited for Christmas for the first time in years?"

He nodded. "I told him you were going on a trip with your fae roommate, but I didn't know where. Neither of us really believed you were taking him sightseeing around the Southwest." He rubbed a hand over the back of his neck. "How'd that trip go, by the way?"

"Nuh uh." I crossed my arms. "I'm asking the questions here."

He lifted his palms in surrender. "Sol was worried about you, but he was too busy to keep an eye on you himself."

"So he had you do it." I squeezed my arms tighter, suddenly cold. "What did he offer to get you to betray me?"

David shook his head. "I didn't *betray* you."

"Bullshit. You were my friend, and you used that trust to spy on me."

He cringed.

"Unless . . ." I trailed off, unable to finish the sentence, afraid even of the thought that had formed. I shivered. "When did you start working for Sol?"

"Talking to Sol doesn't change how I feel about you, Alex. You're my friend. You always will be."

"When?" The word was shrill, my voice an octave too high.

He looked away. "Since the beginning."

I staggered back, reaching out to steady myself on the wall behind me. David had been spying on me since college. Ever since. . . . "Is that why you were so persistent in talking to me? Why you sat next to me in class and babbled away until I started talking back? Were you just following orders?"

He didn't respond, but the curl of his shoulders—as though he was trying to hide—told me I'd hit the mark. He'd been sent to befriend me. The thought hit me like a sledgehammer. He hadn't betrayed me . . . because he'd never been my friend in the first place. He was just following orders. Sol's orders.

The knot in my stomach twisted tighter. Sol had been spying on me. Why? That was before the mess with the PTF. Before I'd even learned I was a fae. I pictured the way Sol had accepted my confession about being a halfer without batting an eye. The way he'd told me to hide the truth. He must have known. Known for years. But how?

The room felt like it was spinning. I shifted my attention back to David. An ignorant spy wouldn't be much good. "What did he tell you," I whispered, "about me?"

His shoulders hunched even farther. "At first, nothing. He just said he wanted someone to keep an eye on you while he was away. I figured, pretty girl, easy cash, why not? We became friends." He paused and met my eyes. "Really. I never lied about that. Sol's the reason we met, but that doesn't make our friendship a lie."

I looked away.

"I never had all that much to report. You kept to yourself. Didn't get in much trouble."

"Did he tell you why?"

"No. I figured Sol was just an overprotective guardian." He smiled. "I actually thought he was your father until you told me what happened to your parents."

His smile faded. "Then Aiden died, and everything changed. Suddenly you were in the middle of a mess I couldn't even understand. I told Sol what I knew, but it wasn't enough to keep you safe." He pinned me with his dark eyes. "Why did you keep me in the dark? If you'd told me everything, I could have helped you."

"What about Aiden?"

His brow crinkled. "What about him?"

"You introduced us. Was he a spy too? Did he know what you were doing? Or were you spying on him as well?"

He shook his head. "No. Nothing like that. Aiden was just my roommate. Your friendship with him had nothing to do with my deal with Sol."

I wanted to believe him, but a worm of doubt wriggled through my thoughts and I couldn't seem to squash it. "So you told Sol I was looking into the murder, that I had a fae helping me. And what did he tell you?"

My heart was racing in my chest. I'd thought about telling David the truth, back when I first discovered what I was, but I'd thought better of it. Now, it seemed, he might have known all along.

"He didn't tell me what you are. I figured that out on my own." He rubbed his temples like he was fighting off a headache. "I don't know how you can be, considering your occupation, but there's no other explanation. You're some sort of faerie."

I staggered when the word left his lips, then glanced at the door like O'Connell might come storming through with a platoon of PTF agents in riot gear to bring me down.

"I haven't told anyone," David continued. "I haven't even shared my suspicions with Sol, though I assume he already knows. That's got to be why he had me watching you all this time, right?"

He pushed off the stool and took a step toward me, reaching out. "I never meant to hurt you. Everything I told Sol, it was to keep you safe."

I backed away from his hand, sidling around the edge of the room so the couch stayed between us. I shook my head. Tears blurred my vision. Even if he meant what he said, how could I ever trust him again? How could I trust anyone? Who else had Sol hired to befriend me? Or bought off to keep tabs on me? Maggie? Emma?

I turned and bolted for the door.

David called out my name, but I was running as fast as I could. David couldn't keep up. He was only human. I left him behind.

I was halfway across the street, wiping tears from my cheeks, when I noticed the man leaning against my Jeep. I froze, mid-step, in the middle of the road. A car blared its horn as it swerved around me. The noise jolted me back into motion, but I kept my eyes on the man. He wore a rumpled brown suit with a crooked tie pulled loose around his collar. As I approached, he pushed a pair of mirrored glasses into his hair to reveal dark, hungry eyes.

I stopped six feet away, feeling physically ill. "Agent O'Connell."

"Ms. Blackwood." His voice was deep and gravelly, like a distant roll of thunder signaling a coming storm.

We stood like statues, frozen in time while the world moved around us.

A muscle at one corner of his mouth twitched. "Rough day?"

"None of your business."

"You've been out of town for a while."

"You keeping tabs on me?"

"You're surprised?"

We lapsed into silence, studying each other.

He scratched the side of his jaw. "Where's your roommate?"

I'd known the PTF would come looking for Kai eventually. I hadn't imagined it would be this soon. There was no way I could tell them he'd returned to the reservation. If the PTF knew fae were bypassing the checkpoint, it would void the peace treaty. We'd be at war. And I wasn't sure which side I belonged on anymore . . . if either side would accept me.

I crossed my arms and stared, tight lipped.

"He hasn't been at work," O'Connell prompted.

"Fae are allowed to take time off, same as anybody."

"From their jobs maybe, not from the PTF. He hasn't been at your house either."

I narrowed my eyes. "How would you know?"

The corners of his lips rose. "It's my job to know." He tipped his head back, as though inspecting the clouds passing overhead. "First a faerie, now a practitioner. What are you running up there, a halfway house for paranaturals?"

"Who I let crash at my place is none of your business."

He dropped his chin, leveling his stare at me. "Everything about you is my business."

I shifted my feet.

"Being unreachable is a violation of your faerie friend's visa. If he doesn't present himself within the next twenty-four hours, I'll declare him AWOL and issue a warrant for his arrest and exile." His smile grew wider. "He'll be a fugitive, and anyone harboring him will be treated accordingly."

Good luck with that, I thought. With Kai locked away in Enchantment, the PTF would be left chasing their tails. Of course, that wouldn't stop O'Connell from harassing me every chance he got. Not that he needed an excuse. Clenching my jaw to keep my voice from shaking, I waved a hand at my Jeep. "If that's all, I've got places to be."

He pushed off the faded blue metal and stalked toward me.

Every nerve in my body was on high alert. Every instinct told me to run, or fight, anything but stand there. But stand there I did, bracing under the wave of adrenaline that slammed through me. I couldn't give this bastard a reason to arrest me.

He stopped just before he would have run into me.

I didn't move.

He leaned forward, his breath hissing in my ear. "Don't think I didn't notice Solomon's initials on the test results for your friends." He leaned even closer. His cheek brushed mine, scratchy with stubble. "He can't protect you forever."

O'Connell shifted, flowing past me like a current, and continued along the line of cars behind me. I stayed in place, watching O'Connell in the side mirror of the car beside me until he climbed into a black SUV parked three cars back. It hadn't been there when I'd walked into David's building. I was sure of it.

I remained frozen until the SUV pulled out. The breeze of its passing sent shivers down my back and through my limbs. My legs gave out.

Stumbling, I lurched to the Jeep, yanked the driver's door open, and tumbled inside. I drove around the corner and up one street, then tried to change lanes. A car horn blared. I jerked back into my own lane as the angry driver of a white Honda that seemed to have come out of nowhere flipped me off.

Grinding my teeth, I pulled into the first parking lot I saw—one that serviced the faded gray shops of a strip mall. Saturday morning shoppers crowded the sidewalk, and their cars filled the lot. I scouted the first aisle for spaces, and finding none, pulled to the curb in a loading zone. My knuckles were white on the wheel. My breath was coming in short, sharp bursts. Panic flickered through my thoughts as a series of worst-case scenarios played out in my mind, but that wasn't why I had to pull over.

I was getting pretty used to threats and fear as a part of my everyday life. The sense of betrayal and isolation that washed through me when I thought about David and Sol's arrangement was worse. But what tipped me over the edge was the seething lake of rage boiling at my core. I was angry at Kai for taking my place in the duel and at Bael for dangling Kai's freedom like a prize; angry at David and Sol for lying to me and manipulating my trust; angry at James for being too busy to see me and Victoria for being everything I knew I could never be for him; angry at O'Connell for stalking me and my friends like a dog with a scent. I was angry at the world. But most of all, I was angry at myself.

I'd thought I could juggle the two sides of my identity without letting them connect, maintaining the mortal life I'd built for myself while learning more about the fae I was becoming. But a person couldn't have two lives. I thought I could belong to both worlds. Instead, I belonged to neither. My indecision had hurt everyone around me and left me alone.

I slammed my palm into the steering wheel.

I couldn't afford to walk the middle path any more. I either had to cut myself off from the fae entirely, or embrace them and give up the pretense of a mortal life. But the fae were part of a larger paranatural community. Distancing myself from magic would mean more than just giving up on Kai. It would mean ending my relationship with James, evicting Chase and Jynx, severing ties with Marc and the werewolves. . . . Shit! I had to warn the werewolves O'Connell was still after them. I pulled out my phone and dialed Marc.

"Alex, what's—"

"I ran into O'Connell this morning," I blurted, cutting him off.

A low growl rolled over the line. "Are you all right?"

"He knows something was off about your release. I can't guarantee he won't come after you again." I bit my lip, hating what I had to say next. "You can't count on me if he does. I don't have any sway with the PTF." *Not anymore.*

"But your—"

"We're on our own." The words came out harsher than I intended. I pressed my palm against an ache in my chest.

"Understood. Thanks for the warning."

"Stay safe, Marc." I disconnected the call and rested my head against my seat. I couldn't do it. I couldn't cut those connections. Besides, mortals didn't have the power to fight monsters, and the monsters would keep coming no matter what I decided.

I took a deep breath and slowly blew it out. I couldn't go back to the way things were. I could never go back. I had to move forward. I had to let my humanity go.

Releasing the parking brake, I rolled out of the lot and merged with the congested Boulder traffic. The first step was to stop lying to the people I cared about. I wouldn't be like David, like Sol. Tonight, I'd tell Maggie the truth, no matter what. If it ended our friendship, if she turned me over to the PTF, so be it. I was done hiding.

Chapter 23

I STEPPED INTO the hall in my new dress boots, black skirt and leggings, and a red sweater. My hair was clean and combed, but I hadn't had time to put it up.

Emma was leaning against the back of the couch wearing a white t-shirt crossed with rainbow suspenders that were clipped to a school girl miniskirt straight out of a shonen manga. Her black, platform boots reached her knees and each had six sparkling buckles down the side. Her red and yellow hair was up in a number of pigtails that sprung off her head like birthday candles on a cake.

"Ready to go?" I asked.

She pushed off the couch. "Just waiting on you."

"What about Jynx?"

Emma tipped her head toward the kitchen.

Jynx leaned out over the bar so I could see her. She balanced on her stomach, giving a view straight down her sparkly halter top while her jean-clad legs curled off the ground. "Ready and waiting." She popped a Cheeto into her mouth and sucked the orange residue off her fingers. "What took you so long?"

I grabbed my purse and jacket off the hooks by the door, then I jingled my car keys. "I'm waiting on you now."

Emma smiled, and Jynx scrambled off the counter.

The Caribou Room was a renovated warehouse right off the Peak to Peak Highway just north of Nederland, so it didn't take us long to get there. I turned off the road and followed the directions of a parking attendant through the crowded lot to find a vacant space.

It was half an hour till showtime and the place was packed. The bar off to one side was piled three deep. Beyond that was a section of tables, each filled to capacity. People stood elbow to elbow in the large open area in front of the stage, lit strangely by the blue and pink lights that streaked the room. As I stepped farther inside, I craned my neck to see shadowed faces in the gallery above. The layout and lighting reminded me of Bael's throne room, and I found myself cringing away from the press of bodies.

But this wasn't a fae festival. This was a human concert in the mortal realm. Men and women mingled in groups, some in flannel shirts and hiking boots, others in party dresses and high heels. People in their twenties and thirties chatted with snowy-haired seniors. There were no pixies flitting through the rafters or baku stalking the perimeter, sniffing for dreams to devour. No lords and ladies in gossamer robes plotting a coup. No one here was trying to kill me. Probably.

The stage was empty. "Where's Ava?" I asked, shouting to be heard over the din. "Should we wish her luck?"

Jynx shook her head. "She'll be getting ready in the green room by now. We can talk to her after their set."

Emma started wedging her way forward, and Jynx motioned for me to follow.

"You go ahead," I said. "I'm gonna look for Mags."

Nodding, she pressed through the crowd on Emma's trail.

I shot off a text asking Maggie where she was.

A moment later, her reply lit the screen. *Just parked.*

I hung out by the entrance till I spotted her, then waved an arm above my head. She came over, a tight smile on her face.

"I'm glad you came," I said. Part of me had feared she'd stand me up. It would have been no less than I deserved, but that had never been Maggie's style.

"Thanks for inviting me. I was afraid that... you know... after Magpie..." She shifted her weight between soft, brown boots and worried a pendant shaped like two stylized women holding a crystal between them along the little silver chain around her neck.

The ropes around my heart loosened. If Maggie was wearing the necklace I'd made for her—imbued with memories of all the good times we'd spent together—maybe I could fix things after all.

"I was hoping we could talk." I glanced at the people packed in around us. "Not here. After. Maybe you could come to my house?"

I chewed the inside of my cheek and held my breath. If she said no, that would mean our friendship was beyond repair. The last of my college friends would be gone. If she said yes, I'd finally have my chance to come clean, and that would open a whole other can of worms. More emotions, more vulnerability, more danger.

"Sure. I was actually hoping to talk to you, too." She met my eyes, then glanced away.

The lights dimmed.

"Ladies and gentleman." A man in jeans and a pinstripe shirt stood on the stage. He had long gray hair with a matching mustache and beard. Wire-rimmed glasses sat at the end of his nose. "Thank you all for coming this evening. Please put your hands together for tonight's opening act. Toxic Tantrum." He swung one arm to the side, where the band members were filing on stage.

Ava was the first one out, and I could hear Jynx screaming above the applause from her position near the front. Ava waved to the crowd, a wide grin on her face. Her cherry-red hair was up in two anime-style buns with trailing white ribbons that glowed in the purple light. She sashayed across the stage in a short, black dress that swished when she moved and probably gave the folks in the front row a free show. As she settled on her stool behind the drums, the next band member stepped on stage.

The person had an Asian look, but that's all I could tell. Straight, black hair framed a face that could be either male or female, and a straight-line suit hid any curves on the rail-thin figure. Another wave of clapping washed through the room as the androgynous artist took position beside a double bass.

Next up was a large woman who moved toward the keyboard set up on one side of the stage. She had to be at least six feet tall, with a Rubenesque figure. A sparkly purple dress hung to just above her knees, shimmering as she walked. My eyes shifted to the next band member, a middle-aged man in a red flannel shirt and thick tan boots that made him look like he'd stepped out of a lumberjack skit. He tucked a fiddle under his chin.

The last musician to climb the steps was Oz. He wore a rumpled blue suit with the sleeves cuffed to his elbows and a wide, iridescent purple tie that dangled in the middle of his chest. I grinned and cheered, pleased beyond words to see him free and healthy after his time with the PTF. Angry as I was with Sol for spying on me, I couldn't deny he'd come through when it counted.

Oz strode to the center of the stage, guitar slung on a strap from his shoulder, and grabbed the microphone. "Thanks for the warm welcome," he said into the applause. "We are Toxic Tantrum!"

Ava laid out a beat, and Oz and the others slammed into the opening notes of their first song.

All around me, people danced. One old man flailed and jolted like he'd just been zapped by an electric current, his long ponytail swinging wildly. A young woman swayed with her eyes closed like she was bending to the will of some breeze she alone could feel. A group near the front started jumping up and down in time to the rhythm of the music and I saw Jynx's white hair flash in and out of sight as she leapt higher than someone pretending to be human had any right to.

"Which one's your friend?" Maggie was mere inches from my ear when she spoke, but she still had to yell to be heard.

Ava had been the one to invite me, but I pointed to Oz, who strummed his guitar strings so fast his hand was a blur. For the year or so that I'd known him, Oz had been an acquaintance at best—the guy I called when I needed tech support—but defying his alpha to help me infiltrate a vampire nest and rescue my boyfriend bumped him solidly into the "friend" category. He'd nearly died because of me.

The first song rolled over into a second, slower song, and the tall woman playing the keyboard leaned forward to sing into her mic. The lilting lyrics fell from the speakers like a spell, and the tempo of the crowd shifted to match. The popcorn people in the front row settled down, though many still swayed. The man with the ponytail took a break from being electrocuted.

I gripped Maggie's elbow and pointed toward the bar. "Want a drink?"

She seemed to consider, then shook her head. "You go ahead."

Shrugging, I wove toward the bar. I was looking at a long, emotional night, and a little liquid courage could go a long way.

The third song picked up the pace again as the bartender traded out my cash for a Long Island. The beat tripled in tempo, whipping the dancers into a frenzy. Elbows, shoulders, and hips jostled me as I made my way back to Maggie. I took a gulp, cringing at the slight burn that scalded my throat.

On and on the band played. I deposited my empty glass in a bin by the bar, a nice buzz dulling my senses, and pulled Maggie closer to the stage. Jynx and Emma were still dancing, drenched with sweat and grinning ear to ear. I joined in, letting my thoughts fade as my muscles took over. It had been a long time since I just let go. Then a memory cut through my calm—the last time I'd danced at a club.

Aching shivers ricocheted through my bones as I recalled being carried into the darkness below the dance club, draped over Bryce's shoulder. I stumbled, catching a wayward smack on my arm as the dance continued around me.

Maggie squeezed my shoulder and leaned close. "Are you okay? You've gone pale."

I shook my head, though whether to deflect her comment or answer her question I wasn't sure. Perhaps I was just trying to wipe away the images playing in my mind. After the debacle at Abandon, I hadn't danced again until the Winter Festival in Enchantment. And that's when everything went sideways once again.

A heavy weight settled in my gut. A terrible dread.

It was silly to equate dancing with trouble. A foolish correlation. And yet, I couldn't shake the feeling that something bad was going to happen.

An hour had passed since the band started playing, and as the last, sustained notes died out on the current song, Oz grabbed the microphone. He was breathing hard, and a sheen of sweat coated his skin, glinting purple in the stage lights.

"We are Toxic Tantrum." He lifted his guitar in salute. "Thank you, and good night."

The gray-haired man with glasses traded places with him as the band shuffled off the stage. "There will be a brief intermission. Please grab a drink and stick around for the Sweet Lillies."

There was another round of applause, then the room lapsed into the ambient din of too many conversations.

Jynx grabbed my wrist. "Come on." She hauled me toward the door through which the musicians had disappeared. Stopping in front of the door, she released her grip so fast I stumbled.

"Watch it!" The woman I'd bumped into spun to face me.

I froze in place, still off-balance, and stared into wide eyes that mirrored my shock.

"Sophie," I breathed. The now familiar cocktail of guilt and anger I experienced whenever I came face to face with my once-upon-a-time friend hit me like a sucker punch.

"What are you doing here?" She crossed her arms and leaned away, nose crinkled as though I smelled bad. With her short green dress and spiked blond hair, Sophie looked like an angry Tinker Bell from the old Disney movies, made before the world learned what faeries really were.

"I came to hear the band."

Maggie leaned around me, squinting like she couldn't see Sophie clearly. "Aren't you the painter who used to show in the bookstore?"

Sophie glanced at Maggie. Then her eyes flicked to Emma, who'd come up on my other side. "Seems you have quite the entourage these days. I hope you warned them."

Maggie frowned. "About what?"

Sophie's lips pulled tight. "Get away while you can. Being Alex's friend is dangerous."

The door to the green room opened and Ava launched into Jynx's arms, squealing.

Oz was the next one out, but he stopped in the doorway, the smile melting off his face. He looked at Sophie, then me, then back to Sophie.

The remaining band members bottle-necked behind Oz, finally pushing him out of the way when he failed to move. That put him right between Sophie and me.

Ava and Jynx were still clinging to each other, but even their exuberance had dampened. Finally, Ava broke the standoff by dragging Jynx toward the bar. "Let's get a drink."

It was like breaking a spell. We all blinked and started breathing again. Feet shuffled, hands shook, congratulations were given. But all the while, I kept an eye on Sophie. She was still stiff, but she no longer stood apart with her arms crossed. She set one hand on Oz's shoulder, pressing close to his side, and the tension around her eyes and mouth eased. When she smiled, she almost looked like the old Sophie.

"Thanks for coming," Oz said to me. "How'd you even know I was playing?"

"Ava."

We both glanced at Jynx and Ava, now entrenched at the bar next to a growing collection of shot glasses.

"You know her from Crossroads?" he asked.

I nodded. Oz had once mentioned that his band played regularly at the fae bar owned by Ava's uncle. Surprising, considering how most werewolves felt about the fae, but Oz had proven particularly accepting. He was like a poster child for One Earth—the flip side of Purity. Or he would have been, if he were human.

He leaned in close, bumping my shoulder, and whispered, "Thanks for helping with my . . . predicament. I'm not sure how much longer I could've lasted."

Mention of Sol's favor soured my stomach, but I smiled as best I could. "I'm glad you're okay."

He turned to Sophie. "This actually works out. I was hoping to get you two together. See if you could bury the hatchet."

"In my back," I muttered.

Sophie glared. "I heard that."

"Good."

"Stop." Oz raised his hands like he was holding back two fighters. Then Sophie shifted her glare to him and he backed down. If he'd been in wolf form, he would have had his tail between his legs.

"Um, Alex?" Maggie tapped me on the shoulder. Her lips were thin and she seemed pale, a neat trick considering her complexion and the purple hue of the lights. "I hate to be a wet blanket, but I need to sit down. Maybe get some fresh air." She swayed on her feet.

Turning my back fully on Sophie and Oz, I gripped Maggie's arms. "Are you all right?"

She nodded. "Just a little light-headed."

I frowned. Maggie was bracing against my hands like she was trying to keep from falling.

"Let's call it a night." I cut my eyes to Emma, who'd stayed silent through the exchange. "Sorry to make you leave early."

She frowned, but shook her head. "It's all right."

"Codswallop," Maggie said. "I won't botch anyone else's night. You should stay."

"What about our talk?" I bit my lip. If Mags was sick, it probably wasn't the best time to drop my bombshell, but I'd promised myself I'd come clean. No more putting it off. "Are you still up for it?"

Her fingers dug into my forearms. "I think I can manage after a bit of a sit down. Maybe a nice cuppa."

Releasing her with one hand, I dug in my pocket and pulled out the keys to the Jeep. I held them out to Emma. "I'll drive home with Maggie. You can use the Jeep." I tipped my chin toward Jynx and Ava. "Keep an eye on those two."

Oz tugged the sleeve of my shirt. "Alex, I—"

I held up a hand to cut him off, pulling free of his grip at the same time. "Not tonight, Oz."

I chanced one last look at Sophie, who seemed to be studying a pattern on the wall beside her. Then I gripped Maggie's elbow and led her to the exit.

Movement on the stage drew my attention as I pushed open the door and ushered Maggie into the crisp, cold night. The announcer was back. He raised his hands for silence. "Now, for the headliners of tonight's concert. The Sweet Lillies."

A cheer went up. Then the door swung closed, cutting off the heat and noise of the concert.

Maggie and I shuffled over frosted gravel toward the back end of the lot, our breath condensing and mingling into a trailing cloud. A few other people passed through the rows of cars, leaving early or arriving late, but for the most part, the night was cold, and still, and silent. It was crazy what could be hidden behind concrete walls.

I spotted Maggie's white Forester. "Give me the keys. I'll drive."

She didn't argue, just reached in her purse and pulled out the jangling mass of rings and fobs that held her keys. Now that we were out of the purple glow of the Caribou Room, Maggie looked downright green.

I unlocked the door on the passenger side and helped her sit down. "Are you going to throw up?"

She shook her head. Then gave me a shove and pulled the door shut.

I chewed my lip, then shrugged. It was Maggie's car. If she wanted to risk throwing up in it, so be it.

The parking attendant was still at the mouth of the lot, puffing breath into his hands. He waved as we passed.

"Would you rather go home?" I asked. "I can crash on your couch and have Emma pick me up in the morning."

She shook her head again. "I'll be okay. It's just nausea." She took a deep breath. "Comes and goes." She turned to me, and I risked taking my eyes off the road to meet her gaze. She smiled. "I'm pregnant."

My breath caught. I opened my mouth to say something, though I had no idea what. Then something slammed into the side of the car.

Chapter 24

THE FRONT OF THE Forester crumpled against a guard rail, then dropped as the rail tore free. The world spun end over end as I bounced between the seat, the door, and the airbag. My forehead collided with the side window, and something crumpled the roof. Light and dark swirled through my vision, and screams filled the air, though whether they were mine or Maggie's, I couldn't tell.

When the car slammed to a stop against a pine tree we were upside down, pinned by crushed metal, straining seat belts, and sagging airbags. It felt like we'd fallen for an eternity, but there had been scarcely time to draw a single breath.

"Maggie?" I croaked. Then I coughed. My mouth was full of blood and the world was fading in and out of focus. I shifted to find Maggie dangling beside me, and pain flared through dozens of points in my body.

Unsnapping my buckle, I dropped into the ceiling of the car with a groan. Moving hurt. Breathing hurt. Living hurt. But I was lucky to be living and breathing and moving after a crash like that, so I held on to the pain.

My mind was still spinning. What had hit us? A deer?

I reached up and pressed my fingertips to the side of Maggie's neck as I'd seen people do in movies, looking for signs of life. A steady throb beat beneath her skin, pumping blood out the many gashes I knew she was sure to have. Maggie wasn't fae, not even a little. She was human. And she was pregnant.

My hand dropped away from her neck as that fact hit me with the same impact as the collision. Could a baby survive a car wreck? But babies were floating, right? Surely it would be protected? My hands started to shake. The shaking spread to my arms. Soon my whole body was vibrating like the old dancer who looked like he'd been electrocuted.

I had to get her out of there.

Light flared above me, silhouetting the hill we'd come down. Headlights. There was someone on the road.

Slinking under Maggie's dangling form, I crawled out the shattered window. Twisted metal scraped my side.

"Help!"

Cold gravel crumbled under my hands as I scrambled free of the wreckage. I cast a glance back at Maggie, guilty at the way I was leaving her, but she needed help. For all I knew, moving her now might kill her, so I stumbled to my feet.

Two figures stepped into the beam of headlights and I raised my arms, waving with all my might. "Help, please, my friend is hurt. We need a doctor."

Then one of the back-lit figures raised a long, thin tube. There was a muffled *thud*, and something hit my chest like an angry wasp. I looked down, too stunned to speak. A shiny metal cylinder with a silly red tuft at the end was sticking out of my chest.

I looked up. The silhouettes were moving down the hill. Then my knees buckled, and the world tipped again.

MY HEAD WAS AN echo chamber, and someone was trying to break in with a jackhammer. Groaning, I rolled onto my side and curled into a ball, digging my fingers into my scalp. Everything ached, inside and out.

There was a grunt from somewhere near my feet, then a string of muttered curses.

Cringing, I forced one eye open and rolled it, searching for the source of the sound. Long, smooth legs came into focus, then a short green dress on narrow hips, and finally a tuft of yellow hair. Sophie had her hands wrapped around a metal bar. She was pushing and pulling to the point that her body jerked back and forth, but the bar held fast.

I managed to coax my other eye open. "Where are we?" I pushed into a sitting position, gasping at the pain in my side and the throbbing pressure in my head that made the world fade in and out like the lights were on the fritz. "What happened?"

"I don't know what happened to you." Sophie kept her back to me, testing each bar in turn. "I got shot."

I stared at the back of her head. "Shot?"

She yanked on the next bar. "With tranquilizer. They ambushed us after the concert. Drove us off the road, then came in with dart guns while we were climbing free of the wreck."

My stomach heaved as flashes of last night came back to me. The red-feathered dart sticking out of my chest, the silhouettes on the hill, the crash. I looked around, turning fast enough to make my brain rattle. Maggie was lying on the ground beside me. Congealed blood caked one side of her face, covering a dark, purple bruise and matting her hair. Her bottom lip was split open, and one of her wrists was swollen to twice its usual size and sported a sickly blue color.

I crawled to her side and pressed my fingers to her neck, just as I had as she dangled upside down in the car. Her pulse was still there, steady and strong.

The three of us were in a large cage, about eight feet square. Just past our bars was a second, smaller cage. This held only one person. Oz sat cross-legged in the middle of his prison, eyes closed. His hands were bound.

Was he remembering his last stay in a cage? The echoes of his screams poured through my memory, filling my senses as they'd filled the caverns of the vampire nest. At least this cage wasn't made of silver, so the smells of burning flesh from that time were blessedly absent.

"Oz?" I crawled to the side of the cage nearest him, still not steady enough to stand. "Are you okay?"

Sophie snorted. "What kind of stupid question is that? Of course he's not okay. None of us are okay."

"Fine, you don't have to be a bitch about it."

"But that's what I am now, thanks to you." She pinned me with an acid glare.

I tried to meet her anger head-on, but guilt swelled alongside it. I looked away. "It wasn't my fault."

"I would never have been there if not for you."

"How could I have known?" I snapped, bringing my gaze back to hers. "Did you know who owned Abandon when you took me there?"

This time, she looked away.

"Stop it, both of you." Oz's eyes were still shut. His posture was stiff. "We're not alone."

"Oh, don't stop on my account," said a voice.

Sophie and I both whirled toward the source of the words, and again my vision seemed to lag behind. My stomach cramped.

Agent O'Connell stepped through the open doorway. "It was just getting good."

I went cold, as though even my blood had withdrawn in the face of the enemy.

"You can't do this," I stammered.

He smiled. "Oh, but I can."

I shook my head. "Mandatory testing is one thing, but this was an attack. You could have killed us."

"The laws are changing, Ms. Blackwood. Soon, paranaturals and their sympathizers won't have any rights at all."

I studied the room around us, beyond the cages. There were machines similar to what Kai had been hooked up to during his PTF test, but also stacks of cardboard boxes, metal cylinders, and a camera set up on a tripod in the middle of the room. Two of the walls were made of brick, and two were unfinished drywall lined with what looked like chicken wire. Exposed beams criss-crossed the ceiling. Most surprising were two tiny, blacked-out windows set high in one wall.

"This isn't the PTF building." I narrowed my eyes at O'Connell. "I've seen your testing facility, and this isn't it. What you're doing here isn't sanctioned."

His smile faltered. "Not by the PTF, perhaps—not yet—but we have the blessing of a higher power."

A sour flavor crept into my mouth. "You're working for Purity."

"It's time to remind the world of the truth." He stepped up to the camera and focused it on Oz. "This generation has forgotten the horrors of the war, the death and destruction that paranaturals bring. They've grown complacent, living side-by-side with monsters."

"The only monster in this room is you."

His lips twitched. "We'll see."

Sophie shook the bars. "You have no right to hold us here."

Maggie groaned, raising a hand to her head. I could only imagine the hangover she must have. Sophie, Oz, and I all had elevated healing thanks to our non-human blood. But Maggie . . . she was going to feel both the crash and the tranquilizer to full effect. Especially—

My mouth dropped open as more details filled in the gaps in my memory. Right before the impact, Maggie told me . . . she was pregnant.

Horror filled me as I darted to her side. I took hold of her questing hand and squeezed it tight. "You're all right, Mags. I've got you."

Her eyelids fluttered. "Where?" Then her second hand moved to cradle her stomach, and the baby I could only hope was still safe inside.

I cut my attention back to O'Connell. "Maggie has nothing to do with any of this."

He continued fiddling with the camera. "She's your friend. That's reason enough."

My heart stuttered. I'd tried so hard to keep Maggie away from this part of my life, thinking she'd be safe so long as she was ignorant, believing I could keep my two worlds from colliding even as they warred within me. I'd been a fool. And now Maggie was paying the price.

I squeezed my eyes shut, damming off the tears. "Please." My voice cracked. "She's injured. She needs a doctor."

He glanced at Maggie, then scanned the rest of us, and there was the faintest flicker of doubt in his eyes. I could almost picture his thought process. Oz and Sophie had already been up and moving when I came to, and neither seemed to be sporting any injuries from their crash. I didn't know if their wreck had been as bad as ours, but they should at least have had some bruises to show for it. I was achy, and bruised, and bloody. I'd taken longer to recover from the tranquilizer, and my wounds weren't healed. I'd recover faster than a regular human, but not crazy fast. Not werewolf fast.

Then there was Maggie. Even compared to me, she was in bad shape. O'Connell had to realize that either her injuries were much more severe than ours, or she was totally human. Either way, I was hoping he wouldn't go so far as murder.

"Keep her prisoner if you need to," I pleaded. "Just get her a doctor."

O'Connell's gaze snapped back to me, and the doubt in his eyes disappeared. "Casualty of war."

"Alex? What's going on?" Maggie's voice slurred a bit as she spoke, and her eyes were rolling, unfocused.

I hugged her, holding my weight off her so as not to cause further injury. "I'm so sorry, Maggie. Just lie still and rest, okay? I'm going to get you out of this."

"You shouldn't make promises you can't keep," Sophie growled. She was standing as far from Maggie and me as she could get, arms crossed, glaring.

"Shut up, Sophie."

Her shoulders arched. If she'd been in wolf form, her hackles would have been up. Her fingers tightened where they held her upper arms, digging in. I stilled, staring at her hands. At the tip of each finger was no longer a rounded, white nail, but the yellowish curve of a claw. Sophie was changing . . .

I met her gaze for a second, then looked away. The last thing I wanted was to have Sophie change while Maggie and I were locked in a cage with her, never mind what O'Connell would do with such knowledge.

When a new werewolf wakes up, it wakes up hungry, and it doesn't think of humans as anything but food. Marc's warning drifted back to me. Sophie had been a werewolf for a few months now. Long enough to change a time or two, get used to it. But she was still pretty new. New enough to lose control if the wolf came out.

"Now, I know you're not average faeries," O'Connell said. "Or you'd have reacted to the iron in these cages. But I'm sure you're not human, so let's see if we can't figure out what you are."

He raised a hand and three people in white lab coats came through the door. I recognized one as the snowy-skinned redhead who'd run Kai's test-slash-torture at PTF headquarters. There was also a stout brunette woman with broad shoulders, and a middle-aged man with frameless glasses. Behind them, two muscular men in camo pants, black t-shirts, and combat boots stepped into the room. They each carried a gun. Not a pistol, like mine, but the type of two-handed rifle you see in Rambo movies. David would have known what model they were. All I knew was that they would kill me. But really, what else mattered?

The room was pretty crowded with the addition of five extra bodies, but the soldiers and scientists were all very careful to stay out of reach of the bars. My stomach twisted. This wasn't their first rodeo. How many people had died in this basement? Were their screams recorded on that camera like the video journal of a serial rapist?

Maggie pulled her hand away from mine and sat up, cupping her belly. She caught my eye and whispered, "What's going on here, Alex?"

"Purity," I whispered back. "Purity and rogue PTF agents kidnapped us."

Her eyes widened. "Why?"

I opened my mouth. I'd never get a better segue. She was waiting for the truth, but we were surrounded by the enemy. How could I out myself when there were men standing at the ready, eager to kill any non-humans?

"We'll start with the male, since he was already suspected."

I snapped my mouth closed and glared at O'Connell. He was watching me when he spoke, waiting for my reaction.

"I told you Solomon couldn't protect you." He smiled. "I'll expose your secrets. Every one of them."

I glanced at Oz. Two of the scientists now held metal poles with loops around the end. They'd slipped the loops around Oz's neck, like animal control workers snagging a rabid dog. Oz reached up, but before his fingers even touched the cords, an electric shock seized his muscles. He collapsed to the cage floor, panting.

A muffled growl resonated in Sophie's throat. Her eyes no longer looked human.

"Don't do this," I begged.

O'Connell crossed his arms. "Then confess."

My mouth opened, but no sound came out. Even if I confessed to being fae, it wouldn't save the wolves. But it might get Maggie out. I glanced over my shoulder. My one remaining human friend was shaking like a leaf, curled up in the corner of a cage in the basement of a fanatical group of bigots.

O'Connell lifted one hand, and another shock ran through Oz, longer than the first. His lips peeled back from gritted teeth, but his scream still found a way out.

Sophie screamed with him and slammed herself against the bars. Fur now coated the backs of her knuckles, and her fingers had shrunk, the claws growing more pronounced. Her breath came is short bursts through flared nostrils, and her lips could no longer cover the points of her teeth.

Sophie slammed into the bars again, making everyone jump.

O'Connell looked between her and Oz. "Maybe I chose the wrong subject." He swiveled the camera so it was focused on the larger cage.

Sophie slammed into the bars again, howling in rage. She wrapped inhuman hands around the metal, and the muscles in her arms flexed. The metal groaned.

Both guards raised their guns.

"Don't." Oz's voice was hoarse and quiet. He rolled to his knees. "Sophie, don't."

Sophie screamed. A sound that was neither human nor animal.

O'Connell was laughing.

"Okay!" I bellowed. "Okay, I'll confess. Whatever you want. Just let us out of here."

"What? Not so comfy snuggling up with the monsters when you can actually see what they are?"

I shook my head. "Maggie's pregnant!" I focused on Sophie when I spoke, praying she still had enough control to hear me. "She's pregnant. Please, let her out. Only her. I'll stay. I'll tell you anything you want to know. Just let her out."

Sophie stumbled back against the bars, the angry fierceness in her eyes softening. She was looking at me, seeing me. She was holding the wolf back. But who knew for how long.

I turned to O'Connell. "Please."

"Very well." He adjusted the camera again, zooming in on me. "Start talking."

"Let her out."

"Confession first."

I glanced back at Maggie and licked my lips. "I'm sorry. This isn't how I wanted you to find out." Then I stared into the lens of the camera. "My name is Alex Blackwood, and I'm a halfer."

Chapter 25

"HOW LONG HAVE you known?" O'Connell prompted.

I swallowed, picturing my world of lies shattering like glass around me. Again, I glanced back at Maggie. She was holding so still I couldn't tell if she was even breathing. Her mouth was parted, her eyes unfocused. "I found out months ago, and kept it secret from the PTF."

O'Connell leaned forward. "How can you handle iron?"

"A genetic anomaly. A one in a million fluke."

"You expect me to believe that?"

"It's the truth."

"No." He shook his head. "You've found some secret. Some potion or spell to counteract the iron. It's our greatest defense against you. Of course the fae would focus all their efforts on finding a way around it." He pointed his finger around the room to include the two werewolves. "Hardly one in a million if I've got three examples in this very room."

"But that's not—"

"Lies won't get you anywhere." He motioned to one of the guards, who moved to stand next to Oz's cage. The barrel of the guard's gun was leveled at Oz's chest.

"Last chance," O'Connell said. "How do you do it."

I gripped the bars, mind racing. "Okay, yes. There's a serum. It doesn't work on full fae, but it can reduce the reaction in a halfer."

"How do you make it?"

"I don't know the formula. Honest. Why would the fae trust a half-breed like me with something so important?"

"Then how did you get it?"

My palms were sweating. I needed a lie I could maintain. Something he couldn't prove. What would he believe?

He raised a hand, two fingers pointing toward the ceiling, and caught the gaze of the man with his gun leveled at Oz.

"Kai!" I shouted. "It was Kai. That's why he came to town. He was inoculating halfers. And now he's moved on to another town to carry on his work."

I closed my eyes. I'd just made Kai public enemy number one. Sure, he was trapped in Enchantment for the next fifty years, but the PTF wouldn't just forget about him. Not when he had a secret weapon against their cause. They'd hunt him forever. Now, he could never come back.

Tears leaked out the corners of my scrunched eyes. I took a shuddering breath.

"Thank you."

I blinked.

O'Connell's expression was radiant with triumph. "That's all I needed to know."

He shifted his camera to focus on Sophie, then dropped his hand with a cutting motion.

A string of gunshots rang out in quick succession, faster than I could believe. In the time it took to shift my eyes to Oz's cage, five red stains had bloomed on his chest. He toppled back with a wet thud.

Sophie shrieked, her voice shifting with her body so the scream grew lower and louder. Her mouth stretched, elongating to fit two-inch teeth. Her pupils dilated, spreading across her irises like ink stains. Bones popped as she arched, snapping and reforming into a new shape. Clawed hands tore at her clothing, ripping it to shreds in a reenactment of the night she'd been turned. Light brown fur erupted from her skin, rolling across her body like a wave. The wolf dropped to all fours, tipped her head back, and howled—a cry of sorrow and rage.

Maggie screamed, adding terror to the mix, and the werewolf swung its head in her direction. Maggie clung to the bars of our cell, sobbing.

The wolf lunged at the shivering prey, so close, so weak . . . but I was closer. Pushing off the bars, I slammed my shoulder into Sophie, knocking her off course. Then I dropped over Maggie, shielding her with my body.

The first swipe tore across my back in four burning lines, and my scream joined Maggie's. I gritted my teeth as warm, wet blood dripped down my sides. O'Connell and the guards faded to the periphery as I focused all my attention on keeping my very human friend from getting a single scratch from the rampaging werewolf in our cage.

Teeth pierced my calf, and I screamed again, sobbing into the wash of numbness that followed close on the heels of the pain.

A sharp tug jerked me across the floor, away from Maggie, and I wrapped my hands around the bars to fight the pull. She was here because of me, I wouldn't leave her unprotected.

But even as I guarded her I saw the truth in her eyes. She knew what I was. She looked between Sophie and me, and her expression didn't change. We were both monsters.

Sophie yanked again, and another jolt of pain raced through my nerves, but the cage was too narrow for her to get a good angle. She couldn't use her full strength. I tightened my grip on the bars.

It didn't matter if Maggie never forgave me. I wouldn't let her die here. But how could I save her?

My fingers were starting to slip, slick with sweat. I clung to the metal, willing my grip to hold, focusing on the unyielding strength of the bars. And then I felt it. The core of the metal. If inanimate objects could have souls, I was looking into the soul of the iron—cold, and hard, and steady.

I wasn't a human anymore. I never was, never would be. Maggie knew the truth. O'Connell knew the truth. There was no more hiding what I was.

Pulling my awareness in to block out Maggie's horror, the pain in my back and leg, and the audience watching with glee, I focused on that part of myself Bael had shown me. The part of me that could change things. I found my magic and called it to me, and it filled me to bursting.

Heat and pressure flooded my body, soothing the wounds in my back and legs and the lesser aches of the car crash. The world faded to a washed-out twilight of gray shadows and phantom images. Maggie seemed frozen—a cardboard cutout bleached from exposure. The pull on my leg was still present, but constant and unchanging, like my leg was suspended in a vise rather than the jaws of a living creature.

Then the demons came. Darkness taking form, coalescing out of the shadows. One pair of glowing eyes locked on to me. Then another. Soon, the room was full of hungry, unblinking orbs that floated in swirls of inky fog.

I swallowed, shifting my brain into gear. This was no time to sightsee. The longer I stared the more solid the demons became.

Latching onto the truth at the heart of the iron bars, I siphoned off a thread of purplish energy from the reservoir inside me and wrapped it around that truth, coaxing it open. It resisted—an eternity of holding certain properties was hard to overwrite—but I'd managed this much in my training with Bael. I could do it again. The question was, could I do it on my first try?

Clawed hands formed in the fog, long fingers emerging like a lava flow. Darker patches yawned, framed in glinting teeth. The demons were nearly solid. Or perhaps I was becoming less solid, shifting over into their plane. A worry for another day.

The metal's heart cracked, and I poured my magic inside. Then I gave it a mental twist.

The resistance under my fingers softened . . . then vanished.

Cutting off the flow of magic, I wrapped my hands around Maggie's arms and prayed.

The werewolf gave another solid tug on my leg as I dropped to the ground, dragging me along the floor even as I gathered Maggie to me. The two of us were pulled to the middle of the cage.

I arched to face Sophie, hoping there was enough of her to hear me, to understand. Her teeth were still buried in my leg. I forced myself to meet her gaze and hold it. "It was O'Connell who killed Oz."

Sophie growled, and the vibration traveled through her teeth into my bones.

I pointed to the bars I'd been gripping, the ones I'd changed. They were still there, but faded, like cylinders of gray fog from that other place where the magic lived. I leaned toward her and whispered, "You can get out now."

The werewolf opened its jaws. Blood and pain rushed into the void left by her teeth, but I didn't move. I didn't dare.

Sophie stared at me, lips peeled back, ears flat.

Then she lunged.

I cringed, pressing back against Maggie, but Sophie sailed right over us and barreled into the altered bars. The metal that was no longer metal bent on impact, warping as Sophie forced her way through.

A startled cry brought my attention back to the world outside the cage, and the guards who now had their guns trained on Sophie as she struggled to slip through the bent bars. O'Connell stood behind his camera. His hand was raised again, two fingers up.

Then someone screamed.

All eyes, and guns, spun toward the sound. The redheaded scientist was scrambling and slipping in her own blood as Oz pulled her leg between the bars of his cage until her thigh wedged. She must have moved closer during my confession, trusting that five bullets to the chest would kill even a fae. That mistake would cost her. Oz's fingers each bore a long, sharp claw buried in the woman's flesh, and his mouth had stretched into a snarling muzzle while the rest of his body remained unchanged.

He pulled again, and the woman's scream rose in pitch. Gunfire rang out as the guards opened fire. Bullets ricocheted off bars and tore through the boxes stacked against the wall. For one moment, the room was filled with noise, and chaos, and the smell of spent fireworks. Then Sophie was free, and all hell broke loose.

The first guard was down before he could even turn. Sophie, as a hundred-fifty-pound wolf, rode down on his back when he dropped, her muzzle latched onto the side of his neck and slick with blood. The second guard spun, still firing, and bullets whizzed above where Maggie and I huddled on the floor. Chunks of brick and mortar erupted from the wall behind us, filling the air with dust, and one of the punctured metal cylinders emitted a steady, high-pitched whistle.

O'Connell tore the camera free from the tripod.

Sophie crouched above the unmoving guard, head lowered, ears back.

The second guard finished his turn, bringing the barrel of his gun in line with Sophie. But she was already moving. She launched herself at O'Connell. Bullets tore into the ground, making the dead guard's body jump and jiggle like he was having a seizure.

O'Connell was already moving toward the exit. I thought Sophie would land on his back as he scurried away, but O'Connell grabbed the arm of the middle-aged man in the white lab coat who'd also been making for the door and yanked. The older man stumbled, spinning into Sophie's path, so it was his throat the wolf's jaws closed on.

Dark blood poured down the man's chest, seeping through the white fabric of his lab coat in a rolling gradient of bright red to deepest crimson. The blood nearest the wound was almost black. He let out one garbled moan and his eyes glazed over. He was dead before he hit the floor.

O'Connell was out of the room before the man he sacrificed stopped breathing. A large, steel door slammed into place, and a light on the black panel above the handle flashed red. We were locked in.

The redheaded woman was still screaming, groping at the pant-leg of the remaining soldier even as he tried to shake her off and train his gun on Sophie. Somehow, Oz was still holding on, though his body resembled pulped meat wrapped in stained rags. The woman seemed to be trying to climb up the soldier's leg, like that would save her. The soldier, unable to steady his aim with the hysterical woman clinging to him, brought the butt of his gun down into her panicked face.

There was a *crack*, and she fell back. Her scream cut off, replaced by wet, choking sobs as blood gushed out her nose and coated her chin.

Sophie turned toward the last threat in the room, but too much space separated them. Fast as I knew a werewolf could be, she couldn't cross the room before the man squeezed his trigger.

The soldier braced his gun against his shoulder, but he hesitated. With the carnage of Sophie's attack laid out between them, he had to be wondering if a bullet or two would be enough to stop her. Maybe a standoff was the safer bet. How long would it take reinforcements to arrive?

I glanced at Maggie. She lay, quivering, on the floor, her eyes wide. Tears streaked her cheeks. She was alive. That was something. I just hoped she'd managed to avoid getting scratched during Sophie's prison break. Bad enough to turn into a werewolf, but what would such a transformation do to a child? Could werewolves even have children?

Gripping her shoulder, I gave her a tight squeeze and what I hoped was a confident smile. Then I crawled through the bent bars that still held their shape despite having the insubstantial quality of smoke. My calf burned. When I settled my weight on it, pain flared through my leg. I gritted my teeth. I could manage.

Sophie and the soldier had their eyes locked on each other, waiting for some signal to engage like gunfighters listening for the stroke of noon. I was between them, easily visible if either cared to look, but neither turned my way. I wasn't the biggest threat in the room. Yay for being underestimated.

I inched toward the soldier.

His eyes flicked toward me, drawn by my motion. In that instant, Sophie sprang. The soldier pulled the trigger.

Using every ounce of speed my fae heritage afforded me, I darted toward the soldier.

Sophie was halfway across the room when the first bullet hit. She stumbled, but her momentum kept her moving.

I launched myself at the gun, knocking the second bullet off course as the shot rang out.

The soldier stumbled, wrestling me for control of his weapon. Then Sophie slammed into his side, taking all three of us down. We landed on the red-haired woman, and the four of us became a tangled mass of flailing limbs, screams, growls, pain, blood, and bullets.

Fur, skin, cloth, and claws pressed against me. Warm metal slammed into my cheek and I tasted blood. Bone crunched somewhere beneath me. The soldier's scream combined with the woman's and fought to drown out the wolf's snarls.

Wriggling, squirming, pushing, and clawing, I managed to shove myself away from the group. My back hit hard against Oz's cage.

Then it was over.

The red-haired woman lay beside me, arms wrapped over her head like a child hiding in the open. Her leg was still wedged between the bars of the cage, but her thigh was bent at an angle that made my stomach cramp. A steady stream of sharp, shallow breaths matched the fast rise and fall of her ribs. From the sound of it, she was gasping through clenched teeth but trying to stay quiet.

The soldier wasn't moving. His head was tipped away from me, for which I was grateful. His hair was matted with blood, and what I could see of the side of his face was ragged lines of shredded muscle and glinting bone.

Sophie stood above them both, blood and saliva dripping from drawn back lips. Her eyes locked with mine. A low rumble rolled out of her chest. She watched me the same way she'd watched the soldier, waiting for her moment to pounce.

I didn't move. I didn't blink. I didn't even breathe.

Chapter 26

"SOPHIE." OZ MOVED inside the cage at my back, but I didn't dare take my eyes off the wolf in front of me.

Her dark eyes flicked to the side, then came back to me. Her lip quivered. A small whine escaped.

"Please," Oz whispered. A blood-covered hand reached through the bars to my left. His nails were ragged, but human once more. "Stop."

Another whimper. Sophie stopped growling, letting her lips seal over her long, gory teeth.

Oz stretched farther, his words coming in breathy gasps. "Alex . . . is a friend."

Sophie snorted. Her eyes darted back and forth between us. Then she unhunched her shoulders and stepped forward.

I sat like a statue as she found body-free footing for each paw until she was inches away. She kept her eyes on me until her fur brushed my leg. Then she slid to the side and brought her nose to Oz's outstretched palm.

"I'm sorry," he whispered.

A longer, higher sound keened from Sophie's throat.

Oz's hand moved, and bloody fingers wrapped around my wrist.

I stiffened.

He dragged my hand up, forcing me to take his place against Sophie's wet fur.

She growled.

I fought the urge to jerk away.

"Forgive each other." His hand fell away. "Please."

For a moment, Sophie and I just stared at each other. My hand lay alongside those terrible teeth, shielded only by a thin veil of skin and fur.

Oz sighed, then went still.

The dark orbs of Sophie's eyes shifted to my left, and I swear I could see her heart break. Then she was racing across the room toward the steel door.

Her shoulder slammed into the metal, again and again, all the while filling the room with a sustained, pain-filled howl.

Struggling to my hands and knees, I reached through the bars to feel Oz's neck. I moved my fingers along both sides, feeling muscles and tendons . . . but no pulse.

Pressure built behind my eyes and a thick knot constricted my throat, choking off my breath.

Sophie slammed into the door again, making me jump. Her impact echoed through the room. She was going to hurt herself. Or her anguish would push her past the point of reason and she'd turn her rage on the people she could reach.

I glanced at Maggie, huddling alone in the cage that would no longer protect her if Sophie went wild.

Now was not the time to grieve.

Licking my lips, I crawled to the fallen guard and groped through his pockets. No keys. Then something moved at the edge of my vision.

The red-haired woman. She was still alive, still clinging to consciousness though her leg bore several deep lacerations.

I wrapped my fists in the front of her lab coat and pulled her up enough to face me. "How do I open the door?"

She gasped, cringing from the pain of being moved, or perhaps the fear of being discovered still breathing.

I gave her a little shake. "How?"

"K . . . k . . . key card," she stammered. "On m . . . my coat."

I released her and she dropped, hard. She didn't even try to arrest her fall. The key card was clipped to her pocket. Red smears streaked the lamination.

Tearing the key off, I hobbled after Sophie. Each limping step sent a wave of pain through my leg.

As I crossed the room, my eyes flicked toward movement off to one side. The last scientist, the brunette woman. She was crouched, half-buried in boxes, on the side of the room. Our gaze met for a moment. Her face blanched. Her eyes were wide and wet. I turned away. There were too many loose ends, too many dangers. My first concern was to get the door open and deal with whatever was on the other side.

O'Connell had a head start. That meant any other guards in the building were probably on their way to put us down. We'd have to get past them to get out. Even then, I couldn't just leave. I had to find O'Connell and the camera holding all our secrets. Otherwise, the danger would follow us no matter where we went.

From the wild rage in Sophie's eyes as she bounced off the now dented door yet again, I knew she'd probably charge head first into the fray despite already being injured, but I wasn't about to stand between an angry werewolf and her revenge. I wasn't suicidal.

I swiped the key card over the black panel on the door. There was a click, and the next time Sophie slammed into the metal, it buckled. Without the lock's reinforcement, the latch snapped and the door swung outward, hanging askew in its warped frame by one set of battered hinges. As soon as the door popped, a storm of bullets filled the hall.

I tackled Sophie before she cleared the cover of the steel door. Okay, so maybe I *was* suicidal . . .

Luckily, the bullets were all flying in the same direction and most clinked into the door like angry wasps. Sophie squirmed under me, twisting to snap at my face as I clung to her bucking body.

"Come on out, Alex." The shouted taunt was muffled by the gunfire, but it was O'Connell's voice, no mistake. No other sound made my stomach twist like that.

A sharp whistle hissed to my left. A few feet away, past a second door, the hallway dead-ended in a collection of tall metal cylinders and a brick wall. A sign dangled around the neck of one of the cylinders bearing a picture of stylized fire. A second whistle joined the first as another hole was punched in the gas tanks.

Eyes widening, I planted my feet and hauled back with my full weight. My calf screamed at the abuse. Sophie's clawed paws scrabbled against the floor as she tipped up on her hind legs. Then we both toppled backward through the doorway. My back hit the floor, and one hundred fifty pounds of werewolf landed on top of me, pressing the air from my lungs. I gasped, my grip loosened, and Sophie rolled to her feet.

She spared me a growl, then threw herself back toward the open doorway. Even if I'd been wrong about the ruptured tanks, she'd be mowed down by the soldiers' bullets.

I reached for her, but I was still gasping for breath. My hand fell short.

Then a sound like tearing metal and rushing waves filled the basement. A cloud of red and orange fire bloomed in the hall. Most of the force and fire was funneled toward O'Connell's men, but the door diverted some of the blast into our room before tearing free of its remaining hinge and bouncing out of sight on a billow of flame.

Sophie yelped and dropped to the ground beside me. I curled onto my side, scrunched my eyes shut against the bright heat, and wrapped my arms around my head. The rushing in my ears disappeared as quickly as it had come, leaving me cowering in dark silence.

I wrinkled my nose at the acrid scent of singed hair. My skin felt tight, like canvas stretched thin over a too-large frame. Blinking, I uncurled and looked around.

The fire had devoured all the gas as it moved through the room, burning itself out as it traveled, but some of the cardboard boxes piled near the door had ignited, along with a few splinters in the exposed joists above. Smoke curled off these secondary fires, collecting against the ceiling.

Sophie lay on her side, panting. Patches of her fur were charred black. Maggie was still in her cage and seemed unharmed. The brunette scientist was using her lab coat to whack at the nearest burning boxes, but the flames quickly spread to the white fabric and she was forced to drop it beside the boxes she'd failed to extinguish. She looked over and met my gaze. Tears stained her cheeks. Her eyes were red and puffy.

Fire didn't care about species. Her fate was now the same as ours.

Grabbing one of the guards' guns, I found a release to detach the clip, then crossed the room and shoved the disarmed weapon into the woman's hands. I pointed to the windows set high in the brick wall. My ears were ringing, hers probably were too, so I raised my voice. "See if you can get those open. Maybe we can climb out. At least we can clear some smoke."

Setting her jaw, she gave a jerky nod and moved to the back of the room, where she began pounding against the blackened glass with the butt of the gun.

I coughed. Only seconds had passed, but my throat was already growing scratchy from the smoke collecting in the room.

Keeping low, where the air was cleaner, I ducked back through the missing bars and crouched in front of Maggie. "Are you hurt?"

Her eyes were scrunched closed, her arms wrapped tight around her stomach.

"Maggie!" I gripped her shoulders. "Are. You. Hurt?"

She shook her head.

"Then we need to go." I grabbed her hand and pulled her through the insubstantial bars, but released her before approaching Sophie.

I covered my nose with my sweater sleeve to block the smell of burnt fur, but it didn't help. She was breathing more regularly and her tongue no longer lolled on the floor. When I came close, her eyes snapped into focus.

"Can you change back?"

Sophie rolled onto her belly, pulled her four legs under her, then pushed unsteadily to her feet.

I waited, but nothing happened. Guess she wasn't calm enough to change. Not that I could blame her. My heart was racing with adrenaline, and panic was clamoring at the edges of my control. My throat burned. It was hard to take a breath without coughing. The fire had been burning for less than a minute, but the temperature had skyrocketed, and the smoke was getting thicker as the flames spread.

"Help me . . ."

I twisted toward the voice. The red-haired woman was on her stomach, dragging herself toward us. A crimson streak trailed behind her.

When she saw me looking, she pointed to a white box attached to one of the not-brick walls. "First aid kit."

A growl vibrated deep in Sophie's chest.

I felt my own lip curl. "Why should we help you?"

"I'll die if you don't."

"You kidnapped, tortured, and killed innocent people." My voice hitched, and my eyes flicked to Oz's lifeless body. "You have no one to blame but yourself."

But even as I shouted my defiance, I knew I couldn't do it. I couldn't leave her there to die. I might not be human anymore, but I wasn't a monster.

Then a thought popped into my head. A wonderful, terrible thought. I glanced at Sophie, then smiled at the maimed woman.

"I hope you like meat." I shuffled to the first aid kit and tore it off the wall with a grunt that turned into a cough. "Sophie was a vegetarian when she was turned, so she had a lot of trouble."

The woman narrowed her eyes. "What are you talking about."

"Sophie and Oz were never fae." My smile widened. "They're werewolves."

Her face went slack as comprehension dawned.

I dropped the first aid kit beside her. "Welcome to the team."

The brunette woman continued to bang against the window, each blow punctuated by a bout of coughing, but the glass just rattled. Coughs and clangs weren't the only noises however. From beyond the charred exit came muffled voices.

I looked at Sophie, who was the only one of us not coughing. Her face was turned toward the sound, ears swiveling like radar dishes to pinpoint the source. Her lip pulled back, exposing teeth. If the soldiers were regrouping . . .

I gritted my teeth. "We have to go."

"I'm trying," The brunette woman panted as she brought the butt of the gun against the window again.

I shook my head. "If it hasn't broken yet, it's not going to."

I glanced down at my wrist and pictured Galen's silky, black ribbon on my dresser back home. A shadow walker could have taken us right through the walls. I gritted my teeth. "We'll have to make our way through the building."

"What about the guards?" Maggie piped up, her eyes wide. "They'll shoot us if we go out there."

"And we'll suffocate or burn alive if we stay here," I countered. The cardboard boxes were nearly gone, their contents reduced to a pile of flaming rubble, but the fire hadn't ended with them. Flames danced in a gap where the twisted door frame exposed a wooden beam in the wall, and the fire kindled by the splinters in the joists above had spread, rolling like water along the ceiling. The bricks of the outer walls wouldn't burn, but they were heating up. Already, my shirt was drenched in sweat and slick tendrils of hair stuck to my forehead.

I looked at the red-haired woman and frowned. She hadn't touched the first aid kit. She just sat, staring at nothing. I pointed to Maggie and the brunette. "You two help her."

Maggie opened the first aid kit and grabbed a roll of gauze, which she tossed to me. "You first." She pointed to my injured leg.

Nodding, I tore off the bottom half of my blood-soaked legging and began wrapping the wound. My skin was green and purple around the puncture holes created by Sophie's teeth, but the damage wasn't as severe as it could have been. Maybe Sophie held back. Or maybe that warmth I felt swirling through me when I called my magic had done more than just soothe the pain. Whatever the case, my leg was usable—so long as I didn't mind the sensation of needles jabbing into my nerves every time I took a step.

"Sophie." Lifting another of the fallen guns, I hobbled to the exit and turned to the wolf.

She was vibrating with a steady growl.

I searched her eyes. Could she understand me? Was the human part of her even present in this form? There wasn't time to test it, not with seconds eating away at our chances for survival. I'd just have to hope for the best. "Don't get caught in the crossfire."

I caught Maggie's eye as she started to bandage the injured woman's leg. "We'll clear a path. Follow as fast as you can. We need to stay ahead of the fire."

Chapter 27

I TOOK A SHALLOW, wheezing breath, then jumped past the flames licking up one side of the bent door frame. Ruptured cylinders littered the floor, mixed with chunks of brick and wallboard. A hole had been punched in the wood paneling that lined the lower half of the hallway, probably by one of the tanks. The pale, paisley wallpaper that ran along the top was scorched brown at this end of the hall. Wisps of smoke curled off it. Once that wallpaper ignited, the fire would spread fast.

Most of the overhead lights had blown out, making the landscape a collection of shifting shadows and highlights cast by the flickering orange glow that filtered in from the other room. At the far end of the hall, a single bulb still burned.

Soldiers lay scattered along the hall. The ones nearest me weren't moving, their exposed skin black and peeling. They'd taken the full impact of the explosion. The scorched and dented door of our cell covered one of the bodies. Three other men were extricating themselves from the corpses. Blood gushed from one man's forehead, bathing his face in a curtain of red. Another clutched what looked like a piece of shrapnel sticking out of his chest. The black fabric of his shirt hid any stain. The last man struggling up wore a brown jacket.

O'Connell. Of course the cockroach had survived.

Smoke leaked from the room where we'd been held, but the dead end by the now ruptured cylinders remained blessedly flame-free. The fire must have moved too fast in that first rush to ignite the walls.

O'Connell struggled to his knees, turned, and saw me. He raised a shaking hand, pointing. "Shoot her!"

I lifted the stolen gun to my shoulder. I'd only ever shot my pistol, but the men were packed tight in the hallway, groggy and disoriented from the explosion. I couldn't miss.

My finger rested on the trigger. The soldiers looked at me with dazed expressions. None were holding their weapons.

O'Connell grabbed something off the ground, the battered

camera, then turned and ran.

I sighted down the barrel of the gun. My vision narrowed to O'Connell's back, bobbing away. I squeezed the trigger.

As I did, Sophie lurched through the doorway. She hit my leg, knocking me sideways. The gun fired, and a chunk of plaster dropped from the ceiling, showering O'Connell's shoulder.

"Damn it!" I straightened the gun, but O'Connell was already climbing the stairs at the end of the hall.

The soldiers were moving now, groping for weapons as Sophie charged them, snarling. If I shot again, I'd hit her as likely as them.

Behind me, something clanged. I jerked to inspect the gas tanks. Surely they'd all gone up in the first explosion?

The clang sounded again, not from directly behind me, but from behind the still closed door on the other side of the hall.

Sophie reached the soldiers. The first man's scream was cut short. The second got two shots off before his throat opened in a shower of blood and bubbles. Sophie staggered, leaned against the wall for a moment, then stumbled towards the stairs. She wasn't moving werewolf fast. She wasn't even moving human fast. She left a bright red streak on the wall. At least some of that blood was hers.

The metallic clang repeated, jerking my attention back to the sealed door. I took two steps and reached for the handle. Hot metal seared my palm. I yelped, cradling my hand.

Maggie and the two scientists stumbled into the hall behind me. Maggie and the brunette were struggling to support the redhead between them. The woman's leg was bandaged, but blood had already soaked through the gauze. Maybe she wouldn't survive to turn into a werewolf after all.

"What's through here?" I indicated the closed door. "Can we get out?"

The brunette tore her attention away from the carnage in the hall to see where I was pointing. Her face was drained of color. She shook her head. "No."

"I heard something."

"There's no way out through there."

The clang repeated, and I pointed at the door. "That, there."

She shook her head again. "We can't." Her voice cracked. Her lip began to quiver. She was barely holding herself together.

A dry lump formed in my throat. "Are there people in there? More prisoners? Like us?"

"I'm just a tech," she sobbed. "Not even that. Just an assistant."

Dropping my borrowed gun, I grabbed the woman by the shoulders, pulling her away from Maggie and the injured woman, and gave her a shake. "What's in there?"

"Fae," she whispered. "Prisoners we were . . . experimenting on."

I inhaled, only to choke on smoke. The fire had made it into the walls, thanks to the exposed beam near our broken door. It wouldn't take long for it to spread through the whole basement, including the room where those people were trapped. "We need to get them out."

She shook her head. "There's no time."

I pushed past her, past Maggie and the redhead, and jumped back through the burning doorway. The heat in the room had grown more intense. My eyes streamed, blurring my vision as I searched the area around the door.

"Alex," Maggie shouted. She lowered her charge to the floor and stood beside the brunette. Their faces were equally ashen, their eyes wide. "What are you doing?"

There, on the floor, was the plastic rectangle I'd used to unlock our door, slightly melted along one edge. *Please, let it still work.*

Pulling down the sleeve of my sweater to protect my hand, I grabbed the key card.

A gunshot rang out, breaking through the crackle of the flames and our punctuating coughs.

Maggie spun and screamed.

I raced back into the hall, looking for the threat I'd missed.

The red-haired woman was motionless on the floor. Her hair now bore darker streaks, slick and shining. Her eyes stared blankly at the ceiling. The gun I'd dropped lay beside her limp hand.

Some people would rather die with as much of their humanity intact as they can. It felt like a long time ago that Marc told me about the choice every werewolf was forced to make.

Maggie was standing in the middle of the hall, both hands over her mouth. The brunette was slumped against the far wall, just to the side of the locked door, a stunned expression on her face.

Gritting my teeth, I stepped over the dead woman. Had she been too weak to face her fate? Or too strong in her faith to let it happen? Was it bravery or cowardice that led her to take her own life? I was betting on cowardice.

I swiped the card, sighing with relief when the lock clicked.

Using my sweater-wrapped hand, I grabbed the doorknob and

twisted. The split second of contact was like pulling a tray of brownies out of the oven with a towel.

Smoke poured into the room with me. Behind me, the flames around the burning doorway surged their glee at finding a new pocket of oxygen. The paisley patterns of the wallpaper lining the hall had all turned black.

The new room was at least as large as the one I'd been locked in, but far more crowded. Cages lined the side walls. Not cages like the one I'd been in, or even Oz's smaller prison. These cages were barely four feet square, stacked two high, and there was a fae crammed into every one.

I glanced toward the doorway. I couldn't see the redhead in the hall, but I remembered the look on her face when I told her she'd become a werewolf. Cowardice. Definitely cowardice. She knew exactly how paranaturals were treated, because she'd done it herself. She couldn't face a life on the other side of those bars, couldn't accept what she'd become.

"Alex!"

I swung my attention back around and found a porcelain-doll face staring at me from one of the cages. Tears streaked her sunken cheeks and her eyes were red and swollen. She knelt, naked, in the center of her cage, as far from the bars as she could get. Her shoulders were draped by the long wings I'd seen once before, but their iridescent color had faded. They hung like rags over her back, dull and tattered.

"Kayla!" I reached her in three long steps and wrapped my fingers around the bars that separated us. The base of her cage was lined with plywood, so she wasn't sitting directly on the iron bars.

Behind me, Maggie gasped.

"Please," Kayla whispered. "Get us out."

I rattled the door of Kayla's cage. "Where's the key?"

Kayla shook her head. "Electronic lock." She pointed to a laptop on a desk against the far wall. A cable connected it to a junction box, from which a number of other cords snaked up over the ceiling or down along the floor. The lines each ended at one of the cell doors.

To one side of the computer was the setup of a science lab—beakers, Bunsen burners, glass tubes, petri dishes, a microscope. Tools lined the counter to the other side of the computer as well, but they looked more like torture devices from a medieval dungeon. My gaze settled on a brass-bristled brush with flecks of glitter caught in its tines. *Pixie dust.*

My stomach cramped.

Pushing down my revulsion, I yanked open the laptop lid. A login screen greeted me. "We need the password."

Maggie ducked out of sight for a second, then pulled the sobbing brunette through the door. She gave the woman a shove. "Unlock the cages."

Around us, fae hissed from their cells, baring their teeth at the stout woman they obviously recognized as one of their captors.

"They'll kill me," she whispered.

"Not if you let them out." I looked into the nearest cages, making eye contact. "Promise not to kill her if she lets you out."

"She deserves to die," said a nixie whose yellowish skin bore cracks like the shell of an egg. He glared, his large golden eyes full of pain and hatred.

Several others murmured agreement.

The lights flickered, and all eyes turned to the long glowing tubes on the ceiling. The lights remained on . . . but for how long? The melting point of copper was about 2,000 degrees. Would the electrical wires get that hot?

I stiffened my voice. "Then we all die together, because I can't open these doors without her help."

The silence stretched. The smoke grew thicker.

"We agree," Kayla cried. "A life for a life. She frees us, we let her live."

"Agreed," growled the nixie.

Each fae gave their word as I looked at them. Self-preservation was a powerful thing.

Gunshots sounded somewhere above us.

I looked up, clenching my fists. "I have to help Sophie."

Maggie nodded. "I'll see this lot gets out."

I looked her in the eye, then dropped my gaze to her stomach. "But—"

"Go," she said, giving me a shove on the shoulder to turn me toward the door. "Help your friend."

I choked back a laugh. Friend, huh? Maybe—once upon a time—before werewolves, and vampires, and blame.

Forgive each other.

I wasn't sure what exactly Sophie was to me anymore. Not a friend. Not an enemy. A regret maybe?

Whatever she was, I couldn't leave her to face O'Connell and his remaining forces alone.

I stumbled out of the room and through the burning hallway as fast as my aching leg would allow, pausing only to grab the gun the redhead had used to end her life. Streaks of flame now raced along the peeling wallpaper highway on one side of the hall as the fire sought out the oxygen-rich upper floors. The air was so hot it was hard to breathe, even down below the smoke that trailed along the ceiling and poured up the stairs.

As my foot came down on the first step, a terrible crash echoed behind me. I couldn't see into the room where I'd been held, but I'd guess one of the burnt joists had given out. I pictured Oz's body, still locked in its steel cage as the flames closed in around him.

I bit hard on my lower lip.

There was nothing more I could do for Oz, but there *were* others I could help. Sophie was above, wounded, fighting alone. And if O'Connell got out with the camera footage, it would mean exposure for all the werewolves—and for me.

I'd thought I was ready to accept my fae heritage, to come out of hiding, but with my lie about an iron-resistant serum, I'd just handed O'Connell all the leverage he needed to start a war against the paranatural community. If that happened, Oz's death would be the first of many.

Every step tightened the knot in my chest as I raced the fire upstairs in search of Sophie, O'Connell, and that stupid camera.

IT WAS A LITTLE easier to breathe on the upper floor, not because there was less smoke, but because I'd entered a larger room.

I couldn't see the vaulted ceiling through the billowing black above, but fire climbed pillars and jumped from pew to pew in what looked like the main room of a church. One corner of the room was fully ablaze—the area directly above the first room I'd been in—and it looked like a section of floor was missing. To one side of that hole, the double doors leading to freedom were already in flames. Where the walls and doors had helped contain the fire below, there were no such obstacles here and the fire roared with glee as it expanded to fill the open space.

The wall nearest me had a window. The glass was broken, and cold air rushed in toward the fire like a lover racing to an embrace. The tightness in my skin eased briefly under the cooling touch of the breeze.

The world outside that window was dark, unbroken by the comfort of streetlights or neighboring buildings. We weren't inside a city. Not somewhere people would notice the fire and call for help right away. Considering what was going on in the basement, this was probably the type of place where help would never come.

Timber groaned and another chunk of floor fell away, disappearing into the lower level in a roar of licking flames and a fresh plume of smoke.

I crouched near the top of the stairs and strained to hear sounds of combat, but only the crackle of the fire and the creak of the building as its supports collapsed reached my ears. Covering my mouth to stifle a cough, I climbed the last few steps, steadying myself on the railing that separated the stairs from the rest of the room.

The banister exploded next to my hand, sending splinters of wood tearing through my skin.

I dove for cover behind the nearest pew.

The gunshot had echoed, filling the whole room. It was impossible to know where the shot originated. But if I had to guess, anyone still in that room would be as close to the exit as possible.

I flexed my fingers to make sure they still worked. Blood leaked down my wrist like an icy lava flow cooling my skin. At least it had been my left hand. I tightened my grip on the stolen gun. I could still shoot.

I scanned the room at ground level, peeking through a forest of furniture legs. Several dark shapes dotted the floor. One row over, a man lay facing me, his eyes open and staring. One pale cheek glowed orange in the light, while the lower half of his face was lost to shadow. The black fabric of his shirt hung in strips around a ragged gash in his chest. He lay in a dark pool so wide I could have touched it without straining my reach.

Sophie had definitely come this way.

A hoarse cough narrowed the position of my attacker. I'd been wrong. He wasn't near the exit. He was at the other end of the building, near the stage where a preacher would speak.

"Is that you, Alex?" the voice called.

My scalp prickled. O'Connell. At least that meant I hadn't lost my chance to recover the camera.

I cleared my throat, trying to work up enough moisture not to choke on my words. "Where's Sophie?"

"Rabid dogs need to be put down."

I scraped my belly along the ground, moving toward O'Connell's voice. A section of plaster crumbled off the nearest wall, exposing the bricks beneath. Sparks jumped off the debris as it fell, igniting a heavy, purple curtain that hung near the pulpit. The cloth went up like kindling, turning to ash and embers that drifted on the hot currents, looking for a new source of fuel. My lungs ached. My head was pounding. I clung to the floor as if the room was spinning, trying to shake me off. I could no longer tell if the shadows dancing in my vision were in the room or in my head.

Choking down a wave of nausea, I crept to the end of the pew and peeked around the corner. A furred shape lay on the ground, unmoving. Beyond Sophie's still form, O'Connell was scooting toward a small door tucked to one side of the stage. He held one arm extended, gun in hand, while he braced with the other and dragged himself backward. His legs left long, dark streaks across the floor. Sophie might not have stopped O'Connell, but she'd slowed him down.

More than that, she'd gotten her revenge. One way or another, O'Connell's life was over.

O'Connell's gun swung from side to side, jerking at every creak of wood and pop of flame. He wasn't sure where I was.

I slipped under the pew, into the next aisle. The dead man's blood seeped into my shirt while the rough wood of the pew scraped my back. There were three more rows between me and O'Connell.

"You're not getting out of here alive," he called to the room. He scooted another foot toward the door. Another foot away from me.

I had to move faster. I pulled myself under the next bench. This one had fire lining its upper edge. Flames chewed down the wood toward me. I hurried, crawling across the last aisle.

Holding my breath, I inched into the shadow of the last pew. O'Connell was six feet away; there was nothing but clear space between us.

I brought the gun around in front of me, bracing it with both hands. The metal was getting hot, but I wrapped my fingers tight around it. This was my chance. I could end O'Connell, end the threat he represented to me and all the people I cared about. Maggie and the fae had to be close by now, on their way up. I needed to clear the path.

My throat constricted in a dry swallow, and I slid my sandpaper tongue over cracked lips.

O'Connell had kidnapped, tortured, and killed people. He wanted humanity at war with paranaturals—a war that would decimate both sides. He had to be stopped.

I set my finger against the trigger . . . and squeezed.

Chapter 28

THE GUN JERKED as it fired, bucking into my shoulder hard enough to bruise. The first bullet tore through the wooden platform an inch to the left of O'Connell's leg. The second never came out.

I squeezed again, but the gun wouldn't fire.

O'Connell jerked away from the impact and swung his gun in my direction. Bullets tore through the pew, splintering the wood, sending burning debris showering around me.

Pain tore through my left shoulder as I wriggled free of my dubious cover.

Then the bullets stopped.

I clapped a hand over the blazing line of pain where a bullet had clipped me. O'Connell was now less than four feet away. Close enough for me to see the fevered hatred in his eyes as he tossed his gun aside and pulled a knife from a sheath on his thigh.

"I won't let you stop me." Jaw clenched, he climbed to his knees with a grimace of pain. Then he lunged at me.

I rolled to the side, crying out when his knife grazed my arm.

My head pounded. My lungs ached. Every movement seemed to blur the world into a series of afterimages streaking around me.

Tucking my legs to my chest, I kicked out. Both feet connected with O'Connell's chest.

Pain rippled through my calf, causing me to gasp. Smoke scorched my throat.

O'Connell fell back against the pulpit, cracking the weakened wood of a railing designed to block direct access. He struggled to disentangle himself from the wood, coughing and flailing.

I grabbed one of the splintered rails. The wood felt flimsy in my hands. Rough and clumsy compared to the steel O'Connell was wielding.

If only I had a blade.

O'Connell swung again, and I batted the knife away with a clumsy parry.

The wood was too light. Too little protection. I gripped it tighter, thinking of the solid bars I'd gripped in the cage below.

O'Connell thrust at my side, and I nearly missed the block as my hazy mind reeled from oxygen-deprivation.

If I could make metal weak, I could make wood strong.

I groped for the magic hiding inside me, and it jumped to greet me like a lonely puppy.

I scanned for demons. If there were any, they were obscured by the dark clouds of smoke already filling the room.

O'Connell swung again.

I dodged, trying to put some distance between us so I could concentrate, but one whole side of the stage was in flames now and the raw heat stopped me from backing up any farther. O'Connell's elbow connected with my shoulder, and I cried out. His bared teeth glinted in the orange light.

Desperately grasping the threads of my focus, I poured my magic into the wood, searching for the truth of its being.

I found it, buried deep. The memory of life, and wind, and rain—before it was shaped and dried.

I peeled back the layers until the wood's heart lay exposed in my hands. Then I started to reform it, to coax it toward a new truth.

O'Connell jabbed, and I was too slow to avoid the blade completely. Pain slid against my ribs, slicing deep. My concentration shattered. The magic skittered away.

He raised the knife again, unrelenting.

An ear-splitting groan tore through the night as one of the ceiling beams ripped loose and came crashing down. A wave of smoke billowed over us when the timber hit the floor. Pews splintered, and another section of floor collapsed in an eruption of sparks and reaching flames.

I blinked, eyes streaming from the burning air.

The beam had fallen across the stairs. The basement—what was left of it—was blocked.

I strained my ears, but there were no screams, no shouts for help. Had Maggie and the others been crushed in the collapse? Had they even been alive when it happened?

My heart raced. My eyes filled with tears caused by more than smoke. Fire was licking up the walls around me, crawling across the floorboards, climbing the vaulted ceiling that now shone with burning light. Sophie still lay unmoving, unaware of the fire creeping closer.

O'Connell knelt, one arm lifted to shield his face from the heat as he took in the sight of the raging inferno now blocking the stairs. Then he grinned, his teeth unnaturally red in the firelight. "And then there was one."

He swung again, and I lifted my flimsy piece of wood to block the blow. Wood met metal. The wood snapped.

I had nothing left. No friends to call for help. No weapons. Not even a lousy piece of wood. Even the air was gone, replaced by acrid smoke that seared my lungs with every ragged breath. Reality blurred around the edges as my oxygen-starved brain struggled to function. I'd failed.

You can shape magic the same way you shape a piece of wood or metal. Bael's voice whispered through my mind. It was the last lesson Bael had given me. The one I'd spent most of a day failing to achieve.

I looked at my empty hand. The skin across my palm was bright red, stretched to the point of tearing. Bael could change the properties of the world to suit him. He was the Lord of Enchantment . . . and the same magic ran through my veins.

"There is no spoon."

O'Connell raised his knife. The blade glinted orange with reflected light.

I closed my eyes, blocking out the encroaching fire, the knife, O'Connell's face, everything. I focused on the magic inside me.

Fae could kill themselves by using up their magic, but I was as good as dead anyway. I had to try. I gathered all the magic within me and focused it into my hand so a pool of glowing energy sat in my palm.

It wasn't enough.

I pulled harder, drawing every available drop of magic. Then I noticed a tingle on my skin that had nothing to do with heat.

Daughter of two worlds.

I'd failed as a human. I'd failed as a fae. But I wasn't either of those. I was both. I reached farther, grasping for magic beyond my body, for the energy that filled the world and connected all living things.

I found it in the air, the fire, the wood. I found it in O'Connell, his knife raised with the promise of death. I found it, grabbed it, and pulled.

The tingle became a flood of ice and fire as the magic answered my call, tearing through me like a river breaking its banks. I channeled the current as best I could, creating mental dams to focus the flow.

Magic poured into my hand, and I fused it into the shape I was creating, long and thin. As more magic was added, I tapered the form, forging it with my will as though hammering the edge of a blade.

But magic wasn't the only thing I'd called. Whispers filled the air, drifting on the currents that spilled into me.

My eyes snapped open.

O'Connell's knife came down with the slow-motion filter of inevitability. I wasn't ready.

I shifted to the side and lifted my left hand, already torn and bloody, to intercept his blade. The point brushed the side of my wrist as it slid past, splitting skin. Then I wrapped my fingers around his arm and gripped with all my strength. There was no way I could stop the fall of his knife, so I did my best to redirect it, pulling O'Connell down as he completed the arc of his attack.

I dropped the last few inches to the floor, my breath coming out in a *whoosh*. The first inch of O'Connell's blade buried itself in the wood beside my cheek, sheering off a clump of my hair.

O'Connell, overbalanced on his injured legs, crashed down on top of me.

My focus wavered, but magic continued to pour into me. The whispers turned into shrieks as the smoke around me filled with faces. Eyes glowed like sparks from the fire. Mouths gaped in yawning grins. The demons weren't screaming. They were laughing.

The half-solid body of the nearest demon flowed into me along with the magic I so desperately needed. I couldn't block one without stopping the other.

Suddenly, my veins were full of acid, and a terrible pounding filled my head, as if the demon was knocking on the door to my mind. I jerked as my body reacted to the pain, muscles seizing. I'd felt this before . . . on the day I died and came back. James had poured part of his demon essence into me. He'd saved my life, but it had burned like a living flame trying to consume me from the inside out.

My body bucked and shuddered, trapped between O'Connell and the floor while I strained to hold the magic, to shape it into what I needed. I felt like I was unraveling, splitting at the seams. The terrible laughter continued all around me, but it was inside me too.

Was this possession? The danger practitioners faced when they tapped into the darker magics reserved for the Sorcerer Troops? But fae and demons were antithetical. A fae couldn't be possessed. Would it just kill me? Or would I become a soulless husk, like the burnout victims from the war?

Terror gripped me as I struggled for control.

O'Connell rolled off me and pulled his knife free of the floorboards.

I pushed against the demon, not with words, but with thoughts. I chased it through the corridors of my own body, hunting it as I'd hunted for the heart of the wooden rail with my magic. The demon pulled away where I advanced, racing ahead, hiding in corners, splitting my focus.

"I can help you." The demon's voice came from everywhere and nowhere, buzzing in my consciousness like a swarm of wasps. "I can make you strong."

I finally found the center of the beast. A cold, dark knot like the one I'd seen in James's soul.

"I'm strong enough." Gritting my teeth until my jaw ached, I tugged loose some of the magic still coursing through me, wrapped it like chains around the demon's heart, and yanked.

It hurt. The demon had invisible barbs fastened in my flesh.

I pulled harder, trying to force the demon out of me.

The demon dug in, gripping tighter. "You belong with us," the voice whispered.

Screaming, I tore at the demon's anchors, ripping them loose.

The demon fell away, freeing my body from its paralysis. It laughed as it left, high-pitched and wild.

I slammed the remaining magic into my right arm, forcing it into place like metal from a crucible poured into a mold. When I glanced down, a shimmering dagger of energy rested in my palm. The magic pulsed, bluish purple, darker at the edges. The blade was done.

O'Connell brought his knife down for another strike, but I was faster.

I plunged my glowing dagger up under his ribs, and his own momentum drove it home.

O'Connell's eyes bulged. For a moment, his face was overlaid by that of a demon, a smoky mask pinned to his features. The demon smiled.

Bloody bubbles dribbled down O'Connell's chin. His eyes found mine. He gurgled, unable to speak. Then he tipped sideways. My blade pulled free as he fell. It was covered in bright, warm blood that coated my fingers and dripped down my arm.

Finding the heart of the knife, a glowing ball of power, I tugged the threads I'd used to weave the magic together. The knife came apart in my hand, splintering back into energy and darting off like fireflies let out of their jar. Then I severed the flow of magic.

The demon's black lips formed one word, whispered on its parting breath. "Welcome." Then it faded into the smoke.

I doubled over beside O'Connell's body, gasping and choking, shaking like a leaf in a hurricane. The demons were gone—the smoke was just smoke—but every inhale made me want to hurl, to purge the contamination I'd felt inside me. "I'm never . . . doing that . . . again."

A chunk of plaster hit the floor a foot away, bursting into a cloud of burning sparks. As much as I hurt, as scared as I was by what I'd seen and what I'd done, there wasn't time to wallow.

I groped in O'Connell's pockets until I found the camera. Its lens was cracked, its casing dented. It wouldn't be recording any more confessions. Gripping the broken camera, I pushed to my hands and knees. The world swayed like it was trying to buck me off. I didn't even try getting to my feet. Instead, I crawled across the burning platform, the camera clanking each time my left hand came down. But I didn't head straight for the door at the far end.

Sophie still lay on her side, unmoving.

"I'm sorry I wasn't faster." I burrowed the fingers of my empty hand into her coarse brown fur, streaking it with O'Connell's blood. "I'm sorry about a lot of things."

The smallest movement twitched under my palm. A pulse? A muscle spasm? A breath? Maybe just my imagination, but I couldn't take that chance. I glanced at the collapsed staircase. I'd lost enough tonight.

Shoving the broken camera into my waistband, I dug my fingers in Sophie's fur and pulled and wriggled until she was draped over my back like a sack on a donkey. Her paws dragged along the floor on either side of me, claws scraping, as I crawled toward the door.

Chapter 29

THE GRASS WAS cold and wet against my cheek. Water soaked through my shirt, chilling my tight, hot skin, sucking the warmth from me as I sank farther into slushy mud. I pulled in great gasps of night air, trading out the poisonous gases in my lungs in a coughing fit that strained my muscles and made my ribs ache.

Sophie lay beside me, still unmoving. I might have used the last of my strength to rescue a corpse.

I pushed my face away from the cool balm of the grass enough to look around. Twenty feet away, the brown grass on which I lay washed up against a wall of trees. Not the wild, rambling pines of the mountains, but sculpted cones all in a row. A wall of growth that ringed the property and blocked the house from casual sight. Other than the column of smoke billowing off the pyre behind me and the first tongues of flame to breach the bricks and lick up the roof, nothing moved.

I scanned the tree line, hoping against hope to see a familiar face. Then I pulled as much air into my ragged lungs as I could bear and bellowed, "Maggie!"

The word scraped against my raw throat, choking off in a sob. Beyond the crackle of the hungry fire and the groan of collapsing timber as the building buckled under its own weight, the night remained silent. She hadn't made it out. None of them made it out.

I screamed and screamed, and pounded my fist into the ground, pulping the grass, and slush, and mud.

Maggie. Human Maggie. Loyal Maggie. Wonderful Maggie. Pregnant Maggie. . . . Dead Maggie.

I'd tried to protect her with secrets and lies, to isolate my mortal life. But I'd made a terrible mistake.

I never had separate lives. That was a lie I told myself because I couldn't handle the truth. There was only ever me. Not human, not fae. Just me. But I'd been too stupid, scared, and stubborn to see it. And now there was nothing left.

I rested my forehead against my fists. My nose hovered just shy of the mud. My breath bounced back to me, stale and warm.

A piece of wood snapped somewhere to my right, debris settling. Except . . . the house was behind me.

I pushed to my knees, blinking blurry eyes.

A dark shape rushed into my field of vision. Maggie's knees hit the mud with a wet squelch. Then she was squeezing me until I couldn't breathe, and I was squeezing her right back, holding on for all I was worth.

I pushed her to arm's length, studying the details of her soot-streaked face, trying to convince myself she was real. "How did—I thought you—"

I shook my head, unable to complete a thought, much less a sentence.

Maggie laughed. Or maybe she was sobbing. It was hard to tell. Either way, there were tears in her eyes and sliding down her cheeks. She released me, and wiped a drip of snot from her nose. "I thought so, too."

I gave her another squeeze.

Kayla stepped up behind Maggie, a small smile on her lips, her pale skin orange in the firelight. She now wore a soot-streaked lab coat that hid her battered wings. The bottom edge of the fabric was ragged, and stained a rusty brown. Farther back, the brunette scientist stood at the edge of the grass, just beyond the glow of the blaze. She shifted from foot to foot and kept glancing behind her as though she suspected something might have followed her.

"So," Maggie's voice brought my attention back. "You're a faerie."

A vise closed around my chest, locking my breath in place. I licked my lips and sucked enough moisture from my cheeks to swallow. "Yup."

She looked at the blazing remains of the building, taking in the wreckage. "And this is what your life is like now?"

The vise squeezed tighter. "Sometimes."

"All those missed shifts . . ." She shook her head. Then her green gaze locked on, boring into me. She crossed her arms. "Why didn't you tell me?"

"I was . . ." I wanted to say I was trying to keep her safe, but the words lodged in my throat. Maggie had been kidnapped because of me. Injured because of me. I swallowed. She might have lost her baby because of me. I looked away. "I was scared."

Her eyes softened. Then she leaned forward and wrapped her arms around me again. "I'm sorry," she whispered.

I made a choking noise. "What do *you* have to be sorry for?"

"I thought you were just being flaky. I was mad, and hormonal, and freaking out about being pregnant." She shook her head and her frizzy curls tickled my cheek. "I abandoned you when you needed me."

"I pushed you away."

"Yeah," She sat back on her heels. "You always have." Then she surprised me with a punch to my arm. The hit was light, but it jostled my wounded shoulder and made me hiss in pain.

"Ow!" I wailed. "What was that for?"

"For being a pain in my backside." She lifted her chin, then cracked a smile.

"Not to interrupt," Kayla said, "but shouldn't we get out of here?"

No one had come out of the trees behind the brunette. "Where are the others?"

"Gone," Maggie said. "Once they were free of the iron, one of the fae opened a sort of . . . hole." She pointed in the direction from which she'd come. "Just past those trees there's a big field. We came out there. Other than Kayla, the fae scattered as soon as they were through."

"Probably didn't want to risk getting captured again if there were still soldiers about." I shifted to glare at the brunette woman. "What were you guys doing to them anyway? That was more than just a prison down there."

The brunette stepped closer, stopping just far enough from our little group to mark her as an outsider. She glanced at Kayla, then away. "We were distilling their magic. Turning it into something humans could use."

"The drugs," Kayla clarified. "The ones that have been making people stronger and faster."

"And crazy," Maggie added.

"So the drugs the PTF said they were trying to track down . . ."

"Were made by us," the woman confirmed.

"But we've shut it down." Flames had sprouted fully from the roof now, dancing over the tiles like joyful children. "The lab is gone."

"This lab." The woman turned her face toward the fire. "There are others."

"Why?" I shook my head. "Why would you do this?"

"Because humans need a way to fight the fae." The firelight reflected in her eyes, turning them red. "That's why I joined the PTF. Then Jen recruited me for a special project. At first, I didn't realize it wasn't sanctioned, that it was funded by Purity."

"And when you did realize?"

"I might not agree with their methods, but they were getting results."

"At the cost of innocent lives."

"And what about the lives *they* took?" She swung a finger to point at Kayla. "What about my sister's life? Doesn't that matter?"

"The war ended years ago," I said. "And we all lost people."

"She didn't die in the war." The woman hugged herself, shivering as though she stood in a blizzard rather than beside an inferno. "An unregistered halfer lost control of his magic. He killed three people, including my sister."

"I'm sorry," I whispered.

"That won't bring her back."

"Neither will hurting people like Kayla." I gestured to the battered pixie, drawing the woman's gaze.

"I know," she said.

Maggie cleared her throat in the silence that followed. "How's Sophie?" She nodded toward the unmoving werewolf, but didn't get any closer. Smart girl.

I crawled to Sophie's side, squelching in the mud, and rested one hand against her neck, the other on her ribs. Her fur twitched. My hand rose and fell the tiniest fraction as her lungs filled and emptied.

"She's alive," I said. "But pretty bad off if she's still unconscious."

"Would Jen really have changed?" The brunette asked.

"The redhead?" I met the woman's gaze and nodded. "Three months ago, Sophie was human."

She paled and looked away, hugging herself tighter. Was she sickened by what had almost happened to her coworker? Or because she now realized Sophie was as much a victim as anyone? A human who'd been in the wrong place at the wrong time. Like her sister.

"We need to get out of here." I set my hand over the bulge of the camera under my sweater. "I don't want to be here when the authorities arrive."

"Where are we, anyway?" Maggie asked.

"A Purity property." The brunette started walking toward the front of the building. "We're about an hour northeast of Denver."

Maggie gasped. "But that's. . . . Are we near the waste?"

The woman pointed past the burning building, where the flaming tendrils of the pyre whipped through the sky, grasping for the stars. "The border's about half a mile that way."

I shuddered. I'd only ever seen pictures of the barren lands seared by magic in the war. "I didn't think anyone lived that close to it."

She frowned. "That's kind of the point. Not a lot of people, and not a lot of fae. Cars are this way."

I patted the side of Sophie's neck. "We'll be back."

No point moving her till I knew where she was going. Besides, even the thought of moving my own body made me want to curl up and cry. It was amazing I'd gotten her this far. I pushed to my feet with a groan, swaying as pain flared through my nervous system and burst behind my eyes.

We walked, or in my case limped, to the corner of the building. Three black vans were parked in front. The first had been crushed by a porch beam that had fallen across its hood. The other two were farther back and seemed intact.

"I don't suppose you've got keys to—"

A howl sounded in the distance. Then another, and another.

The brunette woman froze, fear painted across her face.

The corners of my mouth tugged up. The werewolves were coming.

I turned to Maggie and raised both hands in a calming gesture. "Don't be afraid."

She frowned, her eyes darting side to side. Telling her not to be afraid was like telling a drowning person not to hold their breath, but her fear would only put her in danger. Fear would make her smell like prey.

A dark blur streaked out of the trees, rushing toward us.

My smile faltered. I stumbled back from the shadowy mass, picturing the demon in the smoke. But when the shadow took shape, it wasn't the clawed form of a demon, and the eyes that glowed in its sockets weren't red. They were perfect pools of blue.

James slammed into me like an avalanche, pulling me off my feet and into a tight embrace.

I cried out in surprise and pain, but hugged him back just the same. Cold fingers cupped my singed cheeks and soft lips pressed to my cracked ones, stealing my breath. The world was spinning again when we finally came up for air.

"You're late," I grumbled.

"You're a hard girl to find." His chest rumbled with the words.

I pulled back. "How did you even know I was gone?"

Another shape streaked out of the darkness, then a third. A huge, reddish-brown wolf burst from the trees. He swallowed the distance between us in three great lunges, then bunched his hind legs and leapt. His body morphed mid-air, and Marc hit the ground on human legs. Very naked human legs.

I jerked my eyes up.

Marc glanced at me, jaw stiff, then focused on James, whose arms were still around my waist. "The others are setting up a perimeter. They'll contain any stragglers and warn us before the authorities show up."

"If any do this far out," James said. "We haven't passed an occupied house in miles."

Tires tore up the road and my beautiful blue Jeep slammed to a stop, spitting gravel like a tidal wave. Emma tumbled from the driver's seat. Her gaze locked onto me like a homing missile. She raced across the grass and wrapped her arms around me, catching James as well—which was for the best since I doubted I could've taken the impact on my own.

"Thank God you're all right," she said. "And Maggie!" She abandoned me to pounce on Maggie with an equally enthusiastic hug.

"Emma called," James said, "when she couldn't find you."

I frowned at Emma. "You have James's number?"

Marc snorted. "She called *everyone*."

Emma gave me a lopsided smile that reminded me of Kai. "You weren't where you said you'd be." Her eyes widened. She turned to Maggie and pushed a cell phone into her hands. "You should call Charlie. He's probably freaking out."

Maggie took the phone and moved away from us. Not out of sight, but far enough to give the illusion of privacy.

"It didn't take us long to find where you'd gone through the rail," Marc said. "We found Oz's car too. Driven off the road, just like yours." He looked around our little group, eyes lingering on the brunette. "Are they here?"

"Sophie's around the corner." I pointed. "She's in pretty bad shape."

"On it." Emma took off at a trot.

Marc caught my eye. "And Oz?"

I opened my mouth. My lower lip started to quiver, so I bit down on it. I shook my head.

Marc took a step back, as if I'd slapped him. His eyes were wide and staring. Then he tipped his head up and a ragged howl filled the night.

The gray wolf who'd arrived with him sat down beside his leg and tipped its nose to the sky, joining its voice to his. Far off, a third voice joined. Then a fourth. Then I couldn't distinguish them anymore.

James pulled me closer and closed his eyes. Maggie stopped pacing and looked at us, the phone pressed to her ear. The brunette's face had gone deathly pale. Those of us who weren't part of the pack stood frozen and mute until the last strains of the wolves' song faded. Then Marc lowered his chin, and time found traction again.

Marc shifted his gaze back to the brunette. "Who's this?"

The woman looked to me, eyes wide, pleading.

"She's—" I didn't even know her name. "She helped us escape."

Marc took a deep breath, then let it out slow. "She's seen us."

"Speaking of which." I stepped away from James, swayed, and managed to cross the short distance to Marc. "She's not the only one."

I pulled the camera from my waistband and held it out to him.

He stared at the hunk of melted plastic and cracked glass.

"O'Connell recorded Sophie when she changed."

He snatched the camera. Turned it over. Paled. Looked back at me. Then turned the camera so I could see the little hatch flapping open at the bottom. "The memory card is gone."

I blinked, swallowed, then looked back toward the corner of the house and up at the flames still reaching for the sky. "It could have fallen out anywhere."

"If it's in the fire, it's toast," Marc observed. "If not.... What *exactly* was on it?"

"Oz, Sophie, me." I stared at nothing while my mind replayed the images. I shook my head and whispered, "All our secrets."

Marc set his hand on my shoulder.

I cringed.

Fear and anger were dancing in his eyes, and I thought I could see the wolf there too, straining to get out. "I'll check the surrounding area."

He turned to the gray wolf beside him, who I assumed was Auntie Yu, and gestured to the brunette woman. "Don't let her out of your sight."

Yu narrowed her eyes at the woman and flattened her ears. A small growl rolled out of her throat.

Marc moved off in the direction of Emma and Sophie.

The brunette shifted from foot to foot, wringing her hands. "What happens to me now?" She kept her eyes on her wolf guard, but her question was directed at me.

I didn't have an answer. I didn't even have the energy left to think. Fog was filling my head and it was all I could do to stay standing. "You'll have to take that up with Marc."

She pressed her lips tight together.

I swayed again and thin, cool fingers twined with mine, restoring my balance. I looked down at those fingers, at the hand they were attached to, and realized what had been bothering me since the moment James surprised me coming out of the trees.

"It's gone," I whispered. "I can't feel you anymore."

I'd known it would happen, but that hadn't prepared me for the emptiness I felt at being cut off from him.

He squeezed my hand tighter. "You're wrong."

I frowned. "The bond—the bridge that linked us—it burned when I crossed into Enchantment. I felt it."

His lips curved up. "How do you think I found you out here," he gestured around us, "in the middle of nowhere?"

"The pillar of flame was probably a giveaway."

"Before that, with miles between us. I felt you. Felt the missing piece of my soul tugging like I was tied on a string. And it led me," he poked my chest, "here."

"Then why can't I—"

"Look." He scooped up my other hand to close our circle, close out the rest of the world. "Deep inside. It's there."

I turned my focus inward, searching, surveying, assessing myself and looking for that secret place that lay at the truth of everyone. I found the threads of my being. My humanity. My magic. My past. My fears. My hope. And twisted into it, fine as a strand of hair, was a silver thread. I plucked at the thread, and it thrummed through me. I followed it deeper, past where I thought I ended, and found a voice that wasn't my own.

I'm here.

My eyes snapped open. James's face filled my vision, his forehead pressed to mine.

"But how?" I breathed.

"I don't know." He rolled his forehead side to side against mine, brushing the tips of our noses. "And right now, I don't care. It led me to you."

The link didn't feel the same as before—I couldn't feel it without trying—but now that I knew what to look for, I couldn't miss it. It was a warm, steady weight inside me.

Marc came around the side of the building. Sophie, still in wolf form, dangled limp in his arms.

I took a step toward him. "Is she . . ."

"I've done what I can," Emma said as she ran to open the back of the Jeep. "But she isn't healing as fast as she's dying. We need to get her to Luke."

Marc placed Sophie in the back, then knelt in front of Yu and whispered something in her ear. He turned toward the rest of us. "Time to go."

The brunette took a step toward the Jeep, but Yu growled. The woman froze and looked at Marc.

"Not you," he said. "We'll deal with you later."

"Did you find the memory card?" I asked as he climbed into the back with Sophie.

He shook his head. "Let's hope it burned in the fire."

"And if it didn't?"

He met my gaze. "Best not get too comfortable." He slammed the door.

The rest of us two-legged types piled in. Kayla took shotgun while I settled in the back seat, happily sandwiched between James and Maggie. I could see the brunette woman through the windshield, frozen in the headlights under the watchful gaze of Auntie Yu. I'd never even asked her name. Chances were it didn't matter now. Part of me wanted to ask Marc what the pack would do with her, but the smarter part kept the question to myself. The woman had made her choices. Now she'd have to live with them, just like the rest of us.

Emma put the Jeep in gear and gripped the wheel. "Here we go."

Chapter 30

I SCRAPED THE LAST of Luke's peanut butter out of the bottom of the jar and smeared it onto the last piece of bread from the loaf I'd pilfered from his fridge. Slapping it onto the jellied slice waiting on my plate, I took a bite of the fifth sandwich I'd made since landing in Luke's kitchen. The first four hadn't made much of a dent in my hunger.

James watched me from across the kitchen table, a small smile on his lips.

"What?" I wiped my mouth, wondering if I'd dribbled jelly down my chin in my haste to fill the growling black hole that was my stomach.

He shook his head. "Nothing."

I reached out and set my fingers over his. An electric tingle jolted through me. The ember inside me—the part of me that was also part of James—woke up. The link wasn't a wash of thoughts and emotions anymore, all in my face and overwhelming, but they were still there. Contentment. Concern. And underlying it all, the constant reassurance, *I am here*.

"You're relieved," I said.

"Aren't you?"

I nodded. I was tired, sore, angry, and scared... but I *was* relieved.

Sophie was recovering in Luke's spare room. It had taken longer than I would have liked for Luke to pull her back from the brink of death, but he managed it. Marc had paced the living room while Luke worked—and the rest of us crowded into the kitchen to stay out of his way. He took off as soon as Luke declared Sophie out of the woods.

Then it was Maggie's turn. After Luke had confirmed she was still with child, she and I sobbed into each other's arms until Charlie showed up to collect her. He'd wisely kept his mouth shut about picking his charred and battered wife up from a stranger's house in the middle of the night, but I imagined they'd have an interesting conversation tomorrow.

Kayla was now taking her turn in the back room. It seemed there wouldn't be any more casualties tonight, though that didn't lessen the ache in my chest as images of Oz filled my thoughts.

I squeezed James's hand. "Thanks for staying with me. I imagine Victoria wasn't thrilled you ducked out on her."

"I assist her by choice. I am not sworn to her." He placed his second hand over mine. "Nothing could have pulled me from your side tonight."

I opened my mouth, but Emma chose that moment to pop her head into the kitchen.

"Luke's ready for you now."

I gave James's hand one last squeeze, then released him to follow Emma. Kayla passed us halfway up the hall to the clinic-slash-apothecary shop that was Luke's place of business. Her skin was even paler than usual, and dark circles bruised her eyes. She was wearing an oversized t-shirt that reached nearly to her knees and a pair of loose sweats rolled up at the ankles so she didn't trip.

"How are you feeling?" I asked.

"Alive." She hugged herself. "Which is more than I dared hope for a day ago."

I floundered for words, but could think of nothing to say.

She looked away, her eyes losing focus. "I'm going back to the reservation."

I nodded. She'd grown up on the reservation, or rather, one of the realms the reservation led to. It made sense for her to go home. "When are you leaving?"

"Tonight." She shifted her weight, scuffing the hardwood floor with her bare feet. "The mortal realm is getting more dangerous. . . . Be careful, Alex."

She brushed past me, her gaze fixed on her feet.

I watched until she rounded the corner out of sight, then turned back toward Luke's workroom. I might never see Kayla again. Probably wouldn't. I hadn't known her long, or well, but the loss still hurt.

When I walked into the back room, Luke patted the top of the table in the middle of the room with one wide, dark hand and pushed the bridge of his glasses higher up his nose with the other. Deep crow's feet lined his tired eyes. "Hop on up."

I plopped my butt on the table and waited.

Luke held his hands about three inches from my chest. His deep brown eyes lost their focus.

I looked side to side, scanning the room for signs of demons. If Luke was using magic, as I knew he was, shouldn't I be able to see them? But Emma, Luke, and I remained the room's only occupants.

"Smoke inhalation, dehydration, several lacerations, dozens of burns, and some nasty punctures. Nothing immediately life threatening." He glanced at Emma. "Whip up a batch of tincture number four while I seal the wounds."

He shifted his hands to my shoulder, this time making contact.

I unfocused my gaze, slipping into that strange sight that allowed me to see magic. Luke's hands bore a greenish halo. Still no sign of demons.

I twiddled my fingers in my lap. "Practitioners see demons when they do magic, right?"

"Not always." He slid his hands to my side, over the gash left by O'Connell's knife. After a second, the chronic pinch when I inhaled disappeared.

"Can fae access practitioner magic?"

He shook his head. "Practitioners are always human."

"What about halfers?"

He frowned. "I suppose it's *possible* . . . but I've never heard of it happening. As I understand it, magics don't easily mix."

He moved his hands down to my calf. His frown grew, crinkling the black stubble lining his chin. "Some of this damage has been partly healed by magic. Sloppy and incomplete, but . . ."

He looked at Emma. "Did you—"

"Don't look at me." Emma raised her hands. "I didn't touch her."

Luke swung his gaze back to me, a question in his eyes.

I looked away. Luke already knew, or at least suspected, that I was part fae. That didn't mean I was ready to talk about my powers. Especially when I wasn't sure what had happened. There was no doubt my injuries had been soothed when I called my magic, but was that an aspect of my imbuing . . . or something else?

When I didn't volunteer any information, Luke let the moment pass. His hands traveled from wound to wound until my skin was whole. Then he handed me the concoction Emma made while he worked.

"You know the drill. Drink it all. Take it easy." He sighed. "Not that you'll listen."

I rolled my eyes. "I'll try not to get kidnapped by any psychopaths till I'm all better."

He waved me away, but I could feel his eyes on me as I crossed the room.

Emma opened the door for me. "I'm staying here tonight, to help with Sophie."

"Thanks," I said. "For everything."

She smiled. "Us freaks gotta stick together, right?"

Her smile was bright and wide, but her eyes were sad.

I patted her arm. "Call me when you're ready to be picked up."

James was still seated at the kitchen table, but he rose as soon as he saw me. "Have you received a clean bill of health?"

"Clean enough." I reached out to take his hand and found the underlying thrum—*I am here*. The warmth and comfort of that connection was like being wrapped in a blanket fresh from the dryer.

A little voice inside my head screamed that nothing had changed, a relationship with James would never work, but even my inner cynic couldn't deny the comfort of his presence. I'd lost a lot the past few days, but James was here, now. There were still tangled emotions to unpack, obstacles to overcome, but in that moment I let myself bask in the comfort of not being alone.

It was a feeling worth fighting for.

I shuffled my feet. "About my . . . dating boycott."

He quirked an eyebrow.

"I appreciate you not pushing me."

He smiled. "I've been alive for several hundred years. I know how to be patient."

"I don't."

Dropping his hand, I wrapped my fingers around his coat collar and pulled his lips down to meet mine.

His reaction was immediate—his hands slid around me, pulling me close, tangling in my hair as his mouth explored mine. My freshly closed wounds ached, my skin felt raw, and I was flagging like I hadn't slept in a week, but all those concerns faded to white noise as I leaned into his embrace.

I'd made my decision. I wasn't going to waste another minute. No more keeping him at arm's length. No more dancing between doubt and desire. I wanted him. He wanted me. We could figure the rest out tomorrow, and for as many tomorrows as we had together.

I leaned back just enough to free my lips.

"I'd like you to take me home now." I slipped my arms around his neck, speaking with shared breath. "And I'd like you to stay."

Luke was right . . . I had no intention of taking it easy.

SUNLIGHT CREPT between my lashes and filtered through my eyelids, bursting the illusion that I could stay asleep. I rolled over, and bumped against smooth flesh.

My eyes snapped open. I smiled.

James's face was inches from my own, more relaxed than I'd ever seen it. The tight lines that hovered around his eyes and mouth when he was awake were barely visible. The wrinkles that so often marred his forehead had smoothed out. A long strand of dark hair trickled like a stream in front of his eyelids and over the sharp cliff of his nose. I brushed it aside, tucking the silky threads behind his ear.

I could get used to waking up with a view like this.

My stomach growled, clenching with hunger. Judging by the light, I'd slept the remainder of the night and well into the day. Sunlight streamed through my window, finding the cracks in my curtains. It streaked the covers and lay across James's alabaster skin in bright bars, glinting off the yellow crystal that dangled from his neck and protected him from the sun's burning rays.

I leaned forward and pressed my lips softly to his forehead.

My stomach growled again. Every muscle in my body was limp and achy, but I rolled off the bed anyway. I wouldn't get any more sleep until I fed the beast. Again.

The bedroom door creaked when I opened it, and I glanced over my shoulder. James didn't stir. He looked like an alabaster angel.

I rolled my eyes and gave myself a mental groan. I'd never considered myself much of a romantic, but here I was waxing poetic about a guy in my bed. Shaking my head, I stepped into the hall and pulled the door closed behind me.

Jynx's door at the end of the hall was shut. She might be in there. She might not. I hadn't been paying much attention when James and I finally stumbled through my front door last night.

The door to Kai's room was standing open.

My chest constricted. I guess it was Emma's room now. Her suitcase was tucked in the far corner and piles of clothes lay around the room in a Technicolor explosion. I pulled the door closed, sealing away Emma's mess. Then I headed for the kitchen. My hunger cramps were growing stronger, but my feet dragged slowly along the carpet as my tired legs struggled to move them.

I stopped at the edge of the living room. The afghan was missing from the back of the couch. Not a big deal by itself, but the pair of large, bare feet sticking over the edge of the armrest gave me pause. One set of toes bounced, as though keeping time to some silent rhythm.

I shuffled to the couch, set my hands on the back.

Chase had his eyes closed, but a smile stretched from ear to ear. His arms were folded behind his head. He was humming softly.

His eyes popped open. His smile grew even wider.

"I was going to join you in the bedroom," he said. "But it seems I've been replaced."

His green eyes twinkled.

I smiled. So much had changed in such a short time, again. But not Chase. Chase stayed the same.

"It's good to have you back," I said.

He rolled to his feet, holding the afghan around his waist like a sarong, and gave me an appraising look—a slow scan top to bottom and back to my face. "I think James must be doing it wrong. You look terrible."

I laughed. My stomach gave another grumble, angry at being ignored.

"So." He tipped his head to one side. "What did I miss?"

Sighing, I completed my journey to the kitchen. This was going to be a long conversation. I wasn't about to face it without coffee.

To be continued . . .

Acknowledgements

As always, none of this would have been possible without the support of my amazing family. My husband, who does his best to keep me sane. My daughter, who is my constant cheerleader. And my parents, biological and not, who encourage me every step of the way.

A big thanks to my editor, Debra Dixon, for her astute observations and gentle direction, and to Alexandra Christle from Write Way Editing Services for helping me polish my manuscript. Thanks to David for being my first reader, and Connie for her last minute catches. Thanks to the Rocky Mountain Fiction Writers for providing such a welcoming and supportive community for a new writer. Thanks to my friends in the library industry for helping get my books on their shelves. And finally, my most profound thanks to everyone who has read my books. I couldn't do this without you!

About the Author

Born and raised in Colorado, L. R. BRADEN makes her home in the foothills of the Rocky Mountains with her wonderful husband, precocious daughter, and psychotic cat. With degrees in both English literature and metalsmithing, she splits her time between writing and art. *Fairie Forged* is the third book in The Magicsmith series.

For more information, visit www.lrbraden.com

Milton Keynes UK
Ingram Content Group UK Ltd.
UKHW011829041023
429950UK00004B/344